THE BUILDERS

Books by William Woolfolk

THE BUILDERS
THE BEAUTIFUL COUPLE
OPINION OF THE COURT
MY NAME IS MORGAN

THE BUILDERS

William Woolfolk

Doubleday & Company, Inc., Garden City, New York

1969

FOR JOANNA

who helped so much in the building of this book

DESIGN

On a warm and humid evening in July a black Chrysler Imperial limousine sped north along the Avenue of the Americas in Manhattan.

Alex Johns leaned forward in the rear seat to tap his chauffeur on the shoulder. The limousine obediently slowed. On the square city block bordered north and south by side streets Alex saw an eighteen-story brown-faced hotel and several low rise ocher buildings which housed apartments, a prosperous restaurant, a tavern, a barber shop, an antique store, a print and frame store, shoe repair store, small drugstore, and a dancing school.

This was no longer a fashionable area of Manhattan. The buildings were suffering from the slow decay that was pushing the entire neighborhood toward obsolescence. Alex stared at them from the limousine window. They were like propped-up corpses occupying valuable land he had acquired by months of diligent negotiation, bluster, maneuvering, and threats.

Finally he tapped the chauffeur on the shoulder again and the limousine moved north for three quarters of a mile before turning right to Fifth Avenue. At this hour the fashionable store windows were glassy dark. In their depths smartly dressed mannequins looked out with waxen smiles. The reflection of the limousine passed them in spectral stillness. When the limousine stopped before an office building in the mid-Fifties, Alex got out the rear door.

"I'll be half an hour."

"Yes, Mr. Johns."

He entered a gloomy forecourt that led in turn to a shadowed lobby. Thronging with life by day, the lobby was as deserted now as a marble mausoleum. At intervals the overhead ceiling lights scooped pools of wan illumination out of darkness.

3

A night attendant wearing a white shirt, knitted tie, and dark blue trousers sat on a stool behind a slant table with an open register book.

"Mr. Johns?"

"Yes."

"Thirty-first floor. They're expecting you."

A double bank of elevators confronted each other across the marble lobby. He stepped into an open elevator and pressed a thumb against a transparent cavity marked 31. Heat from his thumb activated the control mechanism. Doors closed him in silently, air conditioning came on with a faint hum and wall panels glowed as soft music began to play. The elevator began to ascend.

On the thirty-first floor he was discharged into immaculate, white walled, blue carpeted, sterile space. Open arches at either end disclosed a picture-frame view of two reception areas with identical curved shell chairs and spotless metal desks.

On the left side area, near a column tinted white, pale yellow and blue on its visible sides, a tall lean graceful man was standing.

"Right on time, Alex."

Alex said, "I always try to be, Vinnie."

Vincent Haleson was an executive vice-president of Zenith Oil Corporation as well as the son-in-law of the president, Peter Druse.

Through the corridors, past empty offices, Alex followed Vincent Haleson to a section of blank wall. Haleson had the slight stoop of the apologetically tall, a certain stork-like delicacy of movement as though he were constantly alert to knee-high hazards. His attitude was at once abstracted and intense. Vinnie touched part of the wall and a sliding panel moved back to disclose a large conference room with a long fifteen-foot white oval table surrounded by pedestal chairs. At the far end of the conference room a portly gray-haired man was seated, incongruously small in the midst of so much space.

"Good evening, Alex."

"Good evening, Peter."

Peter Druse indicated a chair at his right hand. "Well, I see you didn't bring your briefcase today."

Alex sat down and turned his hands inside out to show they were empty. "I've got nothing more to show. You've got all the facts and figures. I've finished making my spiel. It's up to you to give me a simple yes or no."

Druse leaned back in his contoured chair, steepling small hands. Vinnie Haleson had gone around the table to take the chair to Druse's left.

"Nothing ever is simple, Alex," Peter said, with a heavy pontificating air. "Originally we were only interested in leasing space. Then you came along with your proposal for buying this land you assembled."

"My loss is your gain," Alex said. "I put together a midtown site that men with ten times my money couldn't have got together. I'd be putting up a building on it myself if everything hadn't started jackknifing on me."

"You extended yourself too far," Peter said with sad disapproval.

"Okay. That's why I'm here to beg you to buy that precious land I pieced together and put up the building I wanted to build."

"Putting up a building represents a considerable investment even for Zenith Oil."

"All I'm asking is a small profit on my original investment and a deal for my contracting company to put up the building for you."

"We might be willing to go along," Peter Druse said. "But there are a few problems."

"For example?"

Haleson leaned forward. "Whitefield."

"What about him?"

Peter Druse unclasped his hands and put them on the white tabletop. "We don't want to use him."

"Sam Whitefield has put up twenty skyscrapers in New York. He knows his business."

"We're looking for something better than the usual office building," Peter Druse said.

"That's easy to say, but hard to get. The building code practically tells you what you can build."

Peter Druse pushed one of the buzzers on the tabletop before him. "I think my daughter Barbara can explain this particular problem better than we can."

"Your daughter?"

5

"I don't believe you've met her."

"I haven't had the pleasure." Alex's tone did not conceal annoyance. "Is she an architect?"

"She's an artist," Peter said firmly. "She does a lot of sculpture. And she's very interested in architecture."

"The last thing in the world you need in this business is an artist."

"What do you think is needed?" Vinnie Haleson asked, smiling slightly.

"An architect who can give a clear set of instructions to craftsmen who work on the building—so that everyone knows exactly what's expected of him and makes as few mistakes as possible."

Peter held himself stiffly erect. "I happen to have a lot of respect for my daughter's knowledge in this particular field."

Alex shrugged. "As long as you know you're probably asking for trouble."

A few minutes later a woman entered, lanky, tall, about thirty years old, with straight auburn hair and freckled skin and a bony aquiline face. She wore a white twill pants suit with a bright wine-colored sleeveless top under her unbuttoned jacket.

"Barbara, I'd like you to meet Alex Johns," Peter Druse said.

Alex rose to shake hands. He was rather short. She was taller by an inch or so.

"I understand you don't like the architect I want to use for the new office building," he said.

She smiled with strong even white teeth. "He isn't a very distinguished artist."

Alex did not return the smile. There was no reason for this woman to be here except that she was Peter's daughter.

"Tell me what's wrong with his work."

Her clipped voice had a hint of Boston in its speech pattern. "He does the sort of fashion styling that's being done in automobiles and women's clothing. I think Zenith Oil Corporation is entitled to something better than that."

"A good design, Miss Druse, is one that can be built for a price."

"Price is a relative thing. Sometimes the best is the cheapest in the long run."

"There won't be any mistakes made with Sam Whitefield."

6

She sat down in a chair next to Alex's.

"Except the initial one of using his design in the first place," she said. "I know he's your tame architect, but he's been too well domesticated."

Radcliffe, he decided, which accounted for the Boston accent and the assumed intellectual superiority. He had visited Radcliffe while estimating a construction job in Cambridge and he could imagine her as one of those wool stockinged, spectacled, intense, anxious girls.

"Fifty million dollars is what this building will cost, Miss Druse. Personally, I don't like to gamble with that much money."

"Zenith Oil is entitled to a superior building. One that can represent Zenith Oil, be important, symbolize something."

Alex was simmering. "Everybody wants that."

"Then we ought to try to get it."

"Name a building you like."

"The one Falkland built for that detergents manufacturer—what's his name? Pritchett."

"That monstrosity out on the prairie?"

"It's one of Falkland's best."

"I met Pritchett at a Chamber of Commerce meeting not long ago," Alex said, addressing himself more to Peter Druse than to his daughter. "He told me that building cost him thirty percent more than comparable office buildings."

"Money well spent," Barbara murmured.

"And that location! Falkland picked it himself. So far away from everything they can't transport goods efficiently and it's hard to keep employees because they hate traveling so far back and forth to work. During the winter, snow drifts on the highway block the traffic from town. A couple of days last year Pritchett was even forced to shut down."

Peter Druse shivered as though a prairie cold had invaded the windowless conference room. Vinnie Haleson looked down at the white table as though he were studying the grain.

"You're building in midtown Manhattan," Barbara said dryly. "There's hardly any danger of that happening."

"Then something else will. Falkland doesn't care about the practical problems."

7

"At least he wouldn't design something born by a kind of incest with all the other skyscrapers in New York."

"That remark is over my head," Alex said, with a pleasant sense of having won the argument.

Peter Druse cleared his throat. This was a situation which called for a decision and it came out as a show of confidence and force.

"I agree with Alex that we shouldn't use Falkland."

Barbara remained alert and calm. "If Falkland is too strong for you practical men to swallow, there is someone else—a real artist, not a salesman or engineer masquerading as an architect. And he isn't nearly as visionary as Falkland."

"Who's that?" Alex asked suspiciously.

"Karl Schiller."

"Karl who?" Peter Druse asked.

"Schiller. He hasn't built anything in New York. But he's a well-known teacher and he's written books. He's very much admired by other architects."

"Another genius," Alex said.

"Do you insist on an architectural nonentity?" Barbara asked. "Or can you open your mind to a new idea?"

Alex had been watching her with hostility. He was wary of women in business because they always tried to use the fact that they were women. But Barbara Druse seemed to expect no favors in the rough and tumble of debate.

"I'm worrying about the budget, Miss Druse. Fifty million dollars is too much money to risk on an unknown architect."

"Karl Schiller isn't unknown. And he couldn't do anything as tired and cliché as your Mr. Whitefield."

Alex decided the time had come to let others do the dirty work of opposing her.

"I'd like to know what Peter and Vinnie think," he said without rancor.

Vinnie Haleson said, "Frankly, I'd feel a lot safer with what we've got. No matter how we may feel personally, we don't have a right to gamble with our stockholders' money."

Before Peter Druse could reply, Barbara turned to an oil portrait on the wall—of a strong, fierce-eyed, moustached man. "That's how

8

Uncle Elihu built this business. By gambling with the stockholders' money. By never being afraid to take a chance."

Peter's gaze swung slowly to the portrait of his brother and resolutely turned away. He put clasped hands behind his head, increasing his chest girth and his unfortunate resemblance to a pouter pigeon.

"It won't do any harm to see what Karl Schiller can do. I'm in favor of that. But we don't have a lot of time to waste."

Alex's slender body became charged with tension.

"What's the deadline?"

"Three weeks. A good many of our leases around town expire August 1st. We have to know how long to renew them for. That means we have to know something before then."

"And if Schiller doesn't come up with anything you like? Do we go back to Whitefield?"

Peter glanced uncertainly at his daughter. "No."

"What happens to our deal?"

Peter Druse played with a gold watch chain looped across his vest —a duplicate of the one Elihu wore in his portrait. "There's no sense in buying your site, Alex, if we don't have a building to put up on it."

They could dictate terms and there was nothing he could do. He was in no position to bargain because he had taken a chance and lost, trying to become a big-time builder on his own. Why did they call the system free enterprise if everything had become money managers and monopoly and no one was encouraged to take a risk any more?

He tried to keep anger out of his voice. "There isn't a lot of time left to get an acceptable design."

"You did ask for a simple yes or no," Vinnie Haleson reminded him.

He shrugged. "First I'll see what Schiller has built. Then I'll talk to him." He turned to Barbara. "How fast can that be arranged?"

Barbara answered in her crisply decisive tone, "I've already taken the liberty of inviting Professor Schiller to look over the building site and make preliminary sketches."

"You'll have to pay him for it."

"I'm sure Zenith Oil will take care of that. He'll be at my apart-

9

ment a week from Sunday to show what he's done. Can you arrange to be there, Mr. Johns?"

Alex looked at her with astonishment.

*

Alex took a book from the library that Karl Schiller had published. *A New Approach to Modern Architecture* struck him as interesting. A few sketches even seemed possible. There was a tall hillside office building erected in continuous steps and entered on the uphill side by a floor halfway up the building. This entrance floor was open and the building itself was designed as a breezeway with offices extending right through the structure from east to west. Alex also liked an apartment building that Schiller had designed by simply turning on its end a typical street of small houses. At the far end of the "street" where the inhabitants would gather, there was a movie theater, community swimming pool, a school, and a parking area. The "street," put on end, became a high rise building that, as Schiller said in his accompanying note, would "reach to the sky and free the ground below of the many man-made structures incorporated in it."

But even these designs, while interesting, were far from the norm. It was easy to see why only a handful of Schiller's ninety-seven recorded works had been built. Nothing in the world, Frank Lloyd Wright said, is more timid than a million dollars—except two million dollars. Men who controlled the purse strings might not be sure what they wanted but they were damn sure what they didn't want. And they wouldn't put money into a risky experiment with an unknown architect.

The next day Alex drove out to see one of Schiller's completed structures. It was a suburban school. The building was practical—planned to separate noisy activity from quiet activity. In the right wing of the school were the recitation rooms, study hall, and library, and in the left wing were the cafeteria, the gymnasium, and auditorium. At the intersection of the two wings was the administration building. There was no duplication of toilets or service facilities, and there were convenient approaches from the main entrance, from the bus station and from the parking area to the north. An unusual feature was the gymnasium, divided for use by three concurrent classes. The partitions could be opened into a single space for a full-sized basketball court with folding bleachers that could accommodate upward of a thousand persons. Alex's practiced critical eye could not detect a major fault in the design.

Leaving the school, Alex stopped near two teen-aged boys crouching to shoot marbles. When one boy stood up, Alex questioned him.

"What do you think of it?"

"Of what?"

"The school."

"*That* place?"

"Yeah."

"Stinks," the boy said.

*

Ronald Geyer, the structural engineer, was a handsome, pipe-smoking, sandy-haired man whose pink skin was dotted with freckles and whose gray eyes held the quiet certainty attained by men whose principal convictions are founded in mathematics.

"I've got the new reports on soil conditions," he said, indicating the papers he had placed on Alex's desk.

"I'll read it later. Tell me."

"It's safe to assume you've got the forty-ton rock you need down there."

Alex had paid for new reports on the underlying soil conditions because the reports made at the time the other buildings on the site were erected were now more than forty years old. Some information could be gathered from builders who had made excavations and erected new buildings in the vicinity but there were not many of these to consult. So to determine the facts he had hired Geyer to take new borings at several points close to the proposed footings. The new borings went below the level of the footings to test the bearing quality of the rock.

Alex rested his hand on the reports. "May be time and money wasted," he said.

Geyer looked faintly surprised. "Why?"

"There's going to be a new architect. And he may call for new borings to be taken at different locations."

"Aren't you satisfied with Sam Whitefield?"

"Zenith Oil isn't."

"Always mucks things up if you start dealing with a new architect."

"You're telling me," Alex said.

This was only one of his objections to a change in the design. He had also committed himself to the Rand Demolition Company to begin the destruction of buildings presently on the site. He had given Ivor Rand a substantial down payment and work was now underway.

"Well, if there's anything I can do . . ." Geyer said, placidly sucking his pipe.

"Thanks," Alex told him.

*

The Rand Demolition Company had carefully studied in the City Archives the plans of the buildings on the site and based on this and examination by its own experts had estimated the value of salvage. This was subtracted from the estimated cost of demolishing the buildings. By closely figuring the hours of work for men and machines, Ivor Rand arrived at a final figure; he estimated that the job would take five months, and reckoned insurance at a surprising forty-five percent of the total cost, including workmen's compensation, public liability, property damage, insurance against possible collapse of a structure and coverage for the independent trucks-for-hire that might be hired by the company. The cost estimate was boosted by a problem in debris removal. The city of New York had banned any further burning of debris within city limits because of the air pollution. Debris had to be hauled thirty miles to a dump outside the city limits.

One factor enabled Ivor Rand to enter the lowest bid and get the contract. He also owned a company which exported lumber to Europe. There would be a considerable quantity of salvageable lumber, particularly from the hotel—good hard pine scarcely obtainable any more.

*

Abandoned, the doomed buildings were mostly ignored by pass-ersby. The human eye has a remarkable capacity for excluding what it does not wish to see—and therefore rarely observes a building apart from its use or associations. Also, empty buildings gape in a way that remind people uncomfortably of death.

It was time for the wreckers to bring their final gift of obliteration.

*

Tom MacLaren's work gang began removing the fixtures of the tavern. The walls quivered beneath destroying drill and wrecking hammer. The wreckers worked on the insides and the progress they made was hardly noticeable from the street, but the buildings were slowly being eviscerated until only skin stretched over their bare bones.

Tom MacLaren was a tall, soft-looking young man with sloping shoulders and a deep-set neck. He was a "pusher," the foreman of a work gang, who reported directly to the superintendent in charge of the wreckers.

Tom saw Steve Wyatt trying to pry a loosened door off its hinges and went over to help him.

"It's okay. I'm taking it," Steve said.

Tom wrenched the door free with so steady a grip that it stayed level in his hands.

Mike Collyer was passing by. "You'd be more help if you started swinging a pickax," he said sourly.

"We don't hafta wreck buildings," Billy Farrell called out. "We'll just get Tom to push 'em down."

They didn't like him and there wasn't too much he could do to change their opinion. No "pusher" can expect to win the affection of the men in his work gang. It was his job to make sure his gang was productive, and it didn't help that he was also a favorite of the super-intendent, Big Dom, who had promoted him to pusher only three months after he started to work. Big Dom was the villain to all the men in the wrecking gangs, a hulking, hawk-faced man stronger than anyone who worked for him. He promoted Tom because he knew about Tom's Bronze Star. Big Dom never tired of asking Tom to tell

13

about the patrol that had been ambushed, how Tom tried to save a wounded Negro sergeant, staying beside him with a captured VC machine gun and cutting down goons in swathes until the Negro sergeant finally died and he could make his own escape.

Near the lunch hour, Ivor Rand stopped by. Big Dom called Tom out of the tavern to meet him.

Ivor Rand was an older man, in his sixties, with a slightly pushed in face crisscrossed with wrinkles.

"I'm told I ought to keep an eye on you. I hear you want to make something of yourself in this business."

Big Dom, ill at ease, carefully averted his eyes.

"I'd like to, Mr. Rand," Tom said.

"We don't have too many ambitious men who want to get ahead in this business. Too many colored and most of the white men are lazy. They're glad to settle for a day's wages. Do you think you could handle more responsibility?"

"Yes, sir."

"We'll put a few more men under your supervision. Give a smart ambitious young man his head, I say, and see what he can do. Maybe on your next job for us you won't be just a pusher."

"Thank you, Mr. Rand."

When Ivor Rand left a few minutes later, Tom said to Big Dom, "Thanks."

Big Dom seemed embarrassed. "Just make sure you keep those bastards doin' their job."

Tom returned to where his gang was busy removing the roof and joists of the tavern. They worked in the opposite direction from builders—starting at the top and moving down. After the roof was gone they would take out the doors. Other men of the gang used sledges, axes, tin cutters, wrenches to smash walls, fixtures, windows, floors. Steve Wyatt even used the axle of an old automobile that had been beaten in a machine shop to do service as a heavy efficient crowbar.

As they were moving to attack a stairway that now led nowhere, Mike Collyer suddenly stopped.

"Hey, look at this!"

Underneath the protecting arch of stairway a brown dog lay with his head resting on its forepaws. Its large brown eyes were fixed with terror.

"How'd he get in here, I wonder?" Billy Farrell asked.

The dog's fur coat was matted with dust and splinters.

"Must've sneaked in last night," Steve Wyatt said "Poor little fella." Steve squatted on his haunches. "C'mere."

Big Dom looked into the tavern. "What the hell are you doin'?"

"We found a dog," Steve said.

"Get the stupid mutt the hell out of here!"

"He's scared," Steve said defiantly. He was still squatting, trying to persuade the dog to come to him.

"I'll give him something to be scared about," Big Dom said.

Just before his hand closed on the nape of the dog's neck, it swiveled and clamped teeth on his wrist. Big Dom gave a surprised howl, then lashed out with his foot.

The dog yelped, as it was lifted and flung by the force of that kick. Steve Wyatt's voice was shrill. "You bastard!"

"It bit me! I'll call the goddamn ASPCA and have it gassed!"

"Nobody's gassing anybody," Steve Wyatt said. He was a thin little man who looked as though strung out of twisted wire. Bushy hair grew long and straggly down the gully of his slender neck.

Tom examined Big Dom's wrist. "Skin isn't broken. You don't have to worry."

"Get the goddamn mongrel out of my sight or I'll break its neck!"

Steve bent down to pat the dog and it began to tremble so violently its legs did not seem able to support it.

"What the hell are you doin'—buggering it?" Big Dom asked.

Steve Wyatt straightened up suddenly. "Leave me alone, you big dumb guinea, or I'll shove a broom up your ass!"

"You'll do what?"

Steve's green eyes seemed folded in layers of malevolence. "You been riding me ever since I started to work here. Keep it up, and I'll take a hammer to you!"

"Why, you mother! I'll . . ." Big Dom broke off when a pretty young girl, wearing a black and white checked dress, entered the door of the tavern.

"I was passing by," she said. "And look what happened."

15

She showed her dress spattered with dust along one sleeve and across part of the back.

"Who do I see about this?" she asked.

"Why don't you come with me, miss, and fill out a report?" Big Dom said gruffly. "I'll see that your cleaning bill is taken care of."

The girl hesitated, and shrugged. "Well, all right. But you still ought to be more careful."

Big Dom and the girl left together, going toward the trailer office parked on the site.

"Someday that bastard's going to get what's coming to him," Steve Wyatt said with a virulence that surprised Tom.

"Forget it. You know how Big Dom is. He won't remember it happened." Tom reached down to pat the dog's neck. "What'll we do about him?"

"Turn him loose, I guess."

"Why don't you see if you can find a cop?"

"Okay."

As Tom brought the dog out of the tavern, the pretty girl was coming out of the trailer office. Tom smiled at her.

"I'm sorry about your dress. We tape windows in place just to keep dust and stuff from ballooning out into the streets. But sometimes it happens."

"The superintendent was very nice about it." She bent down to the dog, stroking its neck. "Is he yours?"

She was very slender, with narrow child-like shoulders.

"We found him inside."

She looked up at him. "Doesn't he belong to anybody?" Her voice was low pitched and husky.

"Doesn't seem to. We found him under a staircase in there."

"Is he a collie?"

"Part, I think."

She stood up. She had an effortless straight posture.

"I like dogs," she said.

Tom did not seem to know what to do with his hands. They did not belong limply at his side or in the pocket of his work trousers or running through his tangled mop of black hair.

"I like dogs, too." He could not force his huge clumsy body into any sort of graceful posture. "I'm with the demolition gang." For some reason he did not say "wreckers."

Her eyes were light hazel. "I'm a receptionist in an architect's office. Samuel Whitefield Associates. He's building this." She indicated the lot with its half-demolished tavern, gasoline hoists, and clamshell delivering a new load to the dump truck. "The new building will be a big improvement over what's here now."

Through her eyes Tom saw the disreputable buildings, made more disreputable by their abandonment and abuse.

"My name is Tom MacLaren," he said.

She was looking down at the dog but a tiny smile tugged at a corner of her lips. "Sophy Kiron."

"With a K?"

She nodded. "It used to be Kironsky."

Steve Wyatt was coming back down the street with a young blue-coated police officer.

Tom said desperately, "I don't know too many people in New York. I don't even know a good place to have dinner tonight." He gathered up all his courage. "I really want to know if you'd have dinner with me tonight."

"Not tonight," she said.

He was so obviously disappointed that she seemed to feel sorry for him.

"I could make it tomorrow. I get off at five o'clock."

"I get through at three-thirty," Tom said eagerly. "But I wouldn't mind waiting around."

"At my office building? Samuel Whitefield Associates. Four eighty-five Madison."

"I'll be there."

Steve and the law arrived.

"This is the dog, officer," Steve Wyatt said.

Everything became lost in the ensuing mumble jumble. Tom saw Sophy walking away.

"See you tomorrow," he called after her.

The policeman took the dog and Tom and Steve returned to work. The gang was lifting terrazzo off the tavern's kitchen floor. This was a delicate task, requiring exact instructions to a lift truck that was

17

using a blade-like attachment to slide beneath the terrazzo and lift it in salvageable squares.

When Steve Wyatt dropped a three-foot-square piece of terrazzo, Big Dom gave him a five-minute harsh lecture. The sharp cutting edge of his voice could be heard over the sledgehammers and drills.

"Next time you drop a piece of good salvage, I'll take it out of your hide, you mother!"

The lunch whistle blew, and work stopped in the tavern and in adjacent buildings where a work gang was preparing the barber shop for demolition, and another gang was putting up safety scaffolding on the hotel.

Midway through lunch, at the bar and grill, Tom became aware that he was again excluded from the group. He ate his corned beef sandwich on rye and drank beer in silence. The others, seated on stools at the bar, talked freely to each other and Billy Farrell and Steve Wyatt armwrestled to see who would have to pay for a beer.

Sudden silence, as Big Dom swaggered into the bar.

"What do you creeps think ya're doin'?" he asked the two men armwrestling at the bar.

"Never mind," Marty Garfinkel said. "They're not bothering you."

"Strongmen act, huh? Some strongmen! I could take on the both of them."

"You always think you can lick anybody," Mike Collyer said.

"Well, I can. I can lift any two men here on a steel bar. Usin' one hand."

"Why don't you join a circus?" Marty Garfinkel asked.

"Don't be a wise guy," Big Dom said.

The armwrestling contest ended in a victory for Billy Farrell. Steve Wyatt turned silently to the bar.

"How about taking me on?" Big Dom asked.

"No, thanks," Billy Farrell told him.

"I got ten bucks says I can lick anybody in the whole place!"

Steve Wyatt printed a wet circle on the bar with his beer glass. He muttered under his breath.

"Well, what's the matter, you bastards?" Big Dom asked. "Everybody chicken?"

"You couldn't take MacLaren," Mike Collyer said.

18

"Tom? I wouldn't take his money."

Tom smiled. "I don't have any. They cleaned me out at poker last night."

Steve Wyatt said suddenly, "I'll lend you the ten bucks."

Tom didn't want to become involved in a contest with Big Dom, but he saw that his strength was a way to impress these men, a friendship medal he wore in his biceps and in his corded neck muscles, in his deep chest and hidden muscular apparatus.

"I don't know if Big Dom really wants to," he said.

Big Dom gave him a surprised look. "It's your ten bucks."

Tom hesitated. He felt the glances of the other men fix on him. There was no turning back.

"I'll have a go at it," he said.

Arms locked on the polished ebony surface of the bar. Hands gripping, biceps straining. Tom found himself watching the tattooed name on the shoulder of the arm straining close against his. The tattooed name Dominick seemed to stretch out within a heart-shaped outline in which it was intertwined with the name Sue. The flowing indelible ink of the tattoo was visible just below the short sleeve of Big Dom's undershirt.

Tom's pale, slightly protruding blue eyes locked with Big Dom's in a contest to parallel the struggle of arms.

He put more power into his grip. After a minute he felt a small faltering current of electricity transmitted through Big Dom's fingers and the palm of his clasped hand. At this first sign, he turned on additional pressure. Big Dom's hawk-like face remained impassive but his gray eyes shaded slightly. His lips thinned as though he were going to bare his teeth. His power came through intermittently.

Tom steadily increased his thrust. Big Dom's wrist began to tremble. His eyes now evaded Tom's. Inch by inch his arm began a bitter descent.

The men gathered around watched the slow backward movement of Big Dom's arm.

A hopeless snarl shaped itself on Big Dom's lips before he gave a wrenching despairing oath and his arm went shattering down to remain imprisoned on the bar. A crucifix disentangled itself from be-

19

neath Big Dom's sweat-stained undershirt and began to swing slowly to and fro, twisting at the end of its golden chain.

Tom MacLaren slowly stood up from the bar stool.

"You had me off balance," Big Dom said. "It won't happen again."

"We'll try again sometime, if you like."

Big Dom flexed sore fingers and without raising his head slapped a ten-dollar bill on the bar. Tom moved it toward the bartender with two fingers.

"Drinks on me," he said.

Steve Wyatt whooped. While the others crowded to the bar, Big Dom went to the coat hanger for his work shirt, put it on, and left the barroom without a word.

*

North light through the window revealed the blankness of paper, the box of sharpened yellow pencils.

From the window of his apartment, Karl Schiller saw pedestrians hurrying as a looming bus headed directly toward them with ponderous swaying motion. The bus cut in near the corner, discharged its passengers, shouldered out again into the stream of yellow taxis and dark automobiles. Other vehicles seemed to bend and arch around the bus moving out.

New York pulses in a motor rhythm, he thought, to a metronome beat, down one-way avenues, across connecting streets, around the perimeter of the city, teeming over bridges and pouring down ramps like rivers of steel. Some of that rhythm must be caught and held in a building that was to become an integral part of this city. A building in New York must not be a static structure opposed to the main currents of life—like the Pan Am Building that interrupted the once graceful flow of traffic around the Grand Central Building. Movement should flow in and beyond, unimpeded, rising and falling with the very contours of the land.

Ideas too have a flow and change and he was finding it difficult to arrest them.

> Under this stone, Reader survey
> Dear Sir John Vanbrugh's house of clay

Lie heavy on him, earth, for he
Laid many heavy loads on thee

That was always good for a chuckle in the classroom. Students inevitably snickered at the old rhyme, failing to understand the difficulty of sniffing out a usable idea, the palsy of the slow hand that must set it down on paper or the painful wrench of the brain turning in the act of creation.

He had to operate within the limits of what is possible in construction materials, in budgets, in building codes, not to mention what is possible for the architect . . . If only there were some building code to specify the allowable unit stress in the design of a human being. So much might be avoided. Do not ask this of Jones—he will crack. Give that to Smith—he will endure. There are ultimate strengths or factors of safety, and he had once gone beyond the limit, far far beyond . . . He would not think of it. There is always a chance that the thought, the thought only, will tip the precarious structure. The tendency to fail exists in man as in a structural beam.

In the mirror on the wall behind the bed he saw his reflection seated, tall, gaunt-looking, erect as though molten iron had been poured into his backbone. His hair was ruffed out at the sides from having run his fingers through it and his forehead extended almost to the bony shelf of his skull. Unlovely man, he thought.

He examined again the site plan which showed the streets, blocks, and principal nearby buildings with a shaded area that indicated where the new building would be erected. Then he turned to the blank paper before him. Something had to be created, a basic object encompassed in space. But he could not rely on the ability to turn out a superficially pleasing two-dimensional design, a mere heiroglyph of a structure.

More was needed.

From his window, he saw a tall man and a lean athletically trim woman start across the street. The light changed before they could reach the safety of the far sidewalk. An angry taxi driver leaned out of his window to hurl imprecation like a slingshot. Faintly, words drifted up to Karl Schiller.

"Whassamatter with you, mister? Ya blind?"

Everyone might be kinder if the opportunity was afforded them. Those who say there has to be a change in the human heart before there can be progress are simple pessimists. He had ridden the subway yesterday, at the beginning of rush hour, and watched passengers push and claw each other. Would a moral lecture teach them better manners? Would the appearance of Jesus among them protect the Savior Himself from manhandling? The best answer would be more subway cars with enough seats for all. That would uncover a basic kindness in the human heart and reveal brothers under the skin . . .

Any building reflects the attitude of the builder toward his fellow man. The Greek and Roman builders were frugal men who lived simply and were content to make contributions to the common good. That shows in their architecture. Thomas Carlyle remarked that the Chelsea Hospital was obviously the work of a gentleman. More than a gentleman is needed to build a skyscraper in New York. One must return to the idea of function—the purpose for which others wish to use my building.

Ich dien, he thought.

What are the crucial issues? First of all, the population explosion that is changing the nature of man's world. Literally everything. The world of a generation ago is closer to the Pliocene era than to the future encroaching upon us. Man's population will increase more in the next hundred years than in the whole of recorded history. We cannot afford to produce shelter by old-fashioned methods—those methods are as dead as the guilds, the handicrafters. The designer's inspiration must be linked to the mass production system. The job of architecture is to house man. Provide, provide! The swarm of humans is on the way! Technician and artist, die-maker and sculptor, must be linked indissoluble.

Yet we all need more than to be housed and fed. Huddling together in our dry land, surrounded by unknown terrors with the fog closing in, we need something to admire. There is quicksand beyond the edge. Down, down we will all go into the quagmire of time —all the teeming multitudes—but something of what we create will survive from New York and Babylon, Sodom and Gomorrah, Nineveh and Tyre.

Berlin.

Some images the mind must put away forever. There is no price too much to pay for exorcising a demon. Around him he seemed to hear murmurs of voices, Babel accents from past years. His father's ponderous Teuton voice wired through with arrogance, Ernst Maier speaking German soft as Carolina, and Eva's laugh that cut keenly. Memory is such a big country that few can rise above its landscape. He was involved in a Laocoön struggle, riven and crushed by memory, resisting and continually being destroyed.

Back to the problem. A new office building for Zenith Oil Corporation. He had seen their stations along the highways with the identifying sign—a jagged stroke of lightning through pale blue. After a while viewers did not see what they were looking at. Only the sign and symbol that meant: Zenith.

Another skyscraper in New York—a building of exceptional quality. Not the flashy splendor of the General Motors Building rearing above the loveliest plaza in New York. What should it be then? One cannot push a button and order a work of art. And he had never built anything in this city. He had built little enough anywhere. A few private houses, a suburban school, a zoo for a Midwestern city, a small apartment house, an administration building for a college. Most of his designs were imprisoned in books; he was a paper architect.

When he had met Barbara Druse, they had examined the site and the environment in which the building would take place. He had walked with her around the neighborhood and studied certain formations, the congruence of line and mass, trying to discover what sort of building would fit into the scheme of things. It was easier to design a building that would look beautiful to the casual eye than to design one that could be absorbed into its environment. Whatever he created had to be fused into the world. Or there would be nothing but a bland, clever building that lacked the authority of a critical intelligence.

He tried to imagine the city as seen from a plane, a sprawling collection of buildings. It was absurd that people down there were sealed in from light and air, choking in man-made refuse. Along narrow arteries the myriad lights of traffic snarled its way and toward the city's center the close-packed swarm of buildings was threaded

23

through with solid streams of bright lit metal. How many understand the dilemma posed by the automobile in a modern city? Los Angeles is already more than two-thirds covered in its central area by cars parked or in motion.

Back to the problem. Nothing could be done about automobiles or the requirements that modern technology imposed on the construction of a modern steel building. Those who cry: standardization! are looking in the wrong sector for man's enemy. Community life is made endurable because we sleep in standardized bedsheets, eat off standardized tablecloths, use standardized napkins, plates, glasses, forks, spoons. These dimensions are so standardized that their feet and inches can even be expressed in integral numbers. Many kinds of furniture now have standard dimensions to suit the human body. Our chairs are at our best sitting height and the tables we dine upon are at our best eating height. It is time for us to discover the natural dimensions of a new architecture—and proceed to find art in the making. We must accept the message of the machine age. There will be reasons in the design, when it is finished, for the turning of a façade that will not be explainable by logic alone. This cannot be standardized. When all the rules are known, artists must still make people perceive beauty. A lilac sprig, says Leonidoff, must go along with man on his first voyage to the planets because something is needed to please the human heart.

But we have to see the world in the round in order to fully comprehend its essential beauty. Even the ugliest detail of life, even sickness, even poverty, are part of an overwhelming loveliness—the rich blessing that is life. All things experienced are one and indivisible.

He worked a pencil to its blunt end, chose another. The building must belong to its site as naturally as a bird nesting in a tree. Birds nesting are perfect choosers of a site. Always the proper amount of sunlight and the proper amount of shade amid foliage surrounded by the cooling effect of natural air movement. Yet with privacy from intruders, and protected from the sudden storms of spring.

He tore up sheet after sheet and tossed them into a wastebasket. He wanted the sense of the building as a space, not walled in or roofed in, but a great open space. Try again. Here is the cube. The walls must be made less confining, less hindering. What will the people inside the building see? What will those passing by the building see?

His pencil flew. Out of the nature of the plan he pursued a possibility, a design that would give no feeling of enclosure, a building that would share in the movement of the city but would also be part of the sky surrounding and the open space. The idea was melting, changing before his eyes. He began to add a third dimension, alive both within and without the post and beam construction, the superimposition of one thing upon another, the imbecile repetition of slab on slab, of window on window. This new thing would be a way of freeing men from the iron constrictions of walls and roof and even of buildings around them. A simple outward shape is not opposed to the spirit of individual man. A building does not have to be a prison; it can be a building.

Karl Schiller, bending over his table in the north light, thought of that poem by Lucan in which Hermes is showing skeletons of the beautiful women of antiquity.

—But, Hermes, I see nothing but skull and bones. Show me Helen.

—This skull here, this is Helen.

In the bare bones of this new sketch a beauty was waiting to be revealed. He could almost see it. He drove his pencil forward in search of the vision.

*

As an introduction to the living standards of the wealthy classes, nothing could be more disappointing than the building in which Barbara Druse lived. It was a five-story ancient brick edifice that had once been a leather goods factory, located on the fringes of the East Village, surrounded by dingy bar and grills, abandoned stores, and a movie house that played mostly sadism and sex features. On the ground floor of the building there was a men's barber shop.

About noon on a Sunday late in July, following the instructions given him, Alex Johns went into a public telephone booth across the street and called her number.

"Hello," Barbara answered.

"This is Alex Johns."

"Are you in the booth?"

"Yes."

"Wait a minute."

The phone clicked off. Alex left the booth and stood on the sidewalk, looking up uncertainly. On the fifth floor Barbara reappeared, leaning part way out of the window. She extended her hand and a moment later something clinked on the pavement. Alex saw the flash of metal rebound. He went over and picked up a large metal key.

He used the key on the downstairs lock and entered a narrow long areaway with a rickety wooden staircase on the right. He began to climb. On the third landing, he heard Barbara's voice.

"Keep coming. It's the fifth floor."

"Okay."

He climbed steadily and on the fifth floor found Barbara waiting in a doorway. She wore a long, loose, green and white striped hostess dress.

"Thank God," he said. "If I go any higher my nose starts to bleed."

She chuckled. "It's great for keeping in condition. I never have to diet."

The corridor was unfurnished and of dark dusty-looking wood. There was a long oval gold antiqued mirror on the wall at the head of the stairs.

"What's that for? To see yourself having a heart attack?"

"It's for women who like to check their make-up and hair after all that exercise."

He appeared flushed in the dusty mirror depths.

"We've been waiting for you," Barbara said, opening the door wider.

He entered a monstrous, huge open rectangle more than two hundred feet long and thirty feet wide and with many windows intersticed along bare brick walls. The space was partly partitioned to suggest rooms, and at the far end, a hundred feet away, was an open kitchen. A large grand piano was almost lost in the corner of what must have been intended as a living room.

Two people were seated in that immensity of space. The man in the club chair was Vincent Haleson. The woman on the maroon sofa lifted her head as he came in: a young woman with short ash blond hair. She wore large gold hoop earrings, a crisp yellow sleeveless dress, and strapped sandals with high heels. Her expression was bored and slightly hostile.

"You know Vinnie, don't you?" Barbara asked. "This is his wife, Ann. My sister."

"Glad to meet you," Alex said.

Ann Haleson nodded curtly. She seemed impatient with the diversion caused by his entrance.

"I'm not going to wait any longer," she said. "I see no reason to spend a hot Sunday in New York because you want to look at some architect's design."

Vinnie Haleson glanced at his watch. "He'll be here within the hour."

"It's going to take us three hours to get out to Southampton."

"Do we have to go today?"

"Of course. I promised Mrs. Crowley." Ann stood up abruptly. She was not so tall as Barbara but had a riper, more feminine figure.

Vinnie Haleson rose to a slender height.

"I don't suppose that this preliminary sketch will require an immediate decision. And you'll be sure to call me later, won't you?"

"Of course, Vinnie," Barbara said.

Ann offered her cheek to Barbara to kiss. She gave Alex a radiant smile.

"Mr. Johns, Vinnie says you're the most important building contractor in the city. And at your age too."

"Thirty-eight isn't that young, Mrs. Haleson."

"It's when a man starts to get interesting," she contradicted him. She looked at him with twilight hour blue eyes. Then she turned to Haleson behind her. "Why don't we invite Mr. Johns—Alex—to our next party? I'm sure he'd have fun, provided you don't kidnap him for an entire evening to talk business."

"He's a busy man, darling."

"You'll come, won't you?" She put out her hand to Alex. "Promise?"

"I'll certainly try."

"You see?" She took Vinnie Haleson by the hand, reaching slightly behind her to get hold of him and leading him. "Goodbye, all," she said at the doorway. She blew a kiss to Barbara that somehow managed to include Alex. "I do hope you and that German professor come up with something really *gemütlich*."

When she was gone, a faint odor of Arpege lingered on the air.

"That's sister Ann."

"Do you live alone here?" Alex asked.

She nodded. "My parents have a splashy home in Southampton that I visit occasionally for the swimming and tennis. But this is home."

"It's a pretty big layout."

"There's no apartment in the city where I could get this much space so reasonably. I thought I needed it for my sculpture."

A long wall was covered almost from one corner to the other with sculpted stones of every size, mostly abstractions.

"After all," she said wryly, "a room has to be planned according to the ritual to be enacted in it."

"Yeah, sure," Alex said. "Do you still work at it?"

"No. But it was quite important to me once. Something I thought I could do well."

"I'm no judge."

"What I finally learned was the big difference between what I thought I was doing and what I *was* doing. I couldn't believe at first that what was in my head wasn't coming out, even with all that work. It's pretty damn frustrating. I can hardly bear to look at the stuff now."

"Everybody can't be an artist."

"Exactly the truth, Mr. Johns. That makes it even more important to cherish the ones we have." She glanced at a clock on the wall. "Did I tell you what Professor Schiller said when I met him for the first time at the building site?"

"What?"

"He looked at all that space and said it would make a beautiful park."

Alex frowned. "I don't see why anybody would want to put anything but a building there," he said.

28

He could almost trace out the look and texture of the building, the entrance, design of spandrels, shape and tint of tower windows, the particular shade of color on exteriors and interiors, the design of elevator shafts and utility core, of corridors and individual offices. Then he realized he was re-creating one of Sam Whitefield's designs.

"Well, anyhow, you'll see why I call him Professor. He's a darling, but he has such authority." She sipped a cup of black coffee. "Would you like something on the hi-fi?"

She put on a record that he couldn't identify. It was by one of those modern classical composers. He preferred musical comedy. As the sun descended from its noontime zenith, its rays falling directly in the window, she sat in radiant yellow glow with her feet drawn up beneath her on the club chair. One hand was holding her ankles.

When Alex could not bear to look into the sun's glare he looked at Barbara's hand—lean of palm and long of finger, with slightly blunt nails. He was taking inventory of her, mentally touching surfaces.

She looked up at him brightly. "Did you like it?"

"It's okay."

"He's a new discovery of mine. His name is Ernest Parkey."

"I like melody in music."

"There are melodies in Parkey's music. More dissonant, spare and harsh. You have to train your ears."

"My ears will have to get along on their own."

She laughed. "If the world doesn't get hold of him too soon and spoil him, Ernest Parkey may become one of the very, very good ones."

"I'll take your word for it."

"I'd give anything to be able to create something like that. I'd give absolutely anything."

Odd little things about her had begun to interest him. The swift light thrust of her head, her flashing smile, her long shapely limbs and the smell of her, fresh, like after-shower air. It was partly an automatic response to a woman he found attractive but it was also something he did not comprehend and that he knew was uniquely associated with her.

The telephone rang and she sat up quickly.

29

"Do you think it's him? He's early."

Without waiting for an answer she went to the phone.

"Yes, all right. I'll let you in."

At the window she dropped the key out, and returned. Her manner had undergone a slight but noticeable change; her movements were jerky with nervousness.

In a couple of minutes the doorbell rang.

Barbara hurried to open the front door, and returned with a man, about fifty, who was wearing a corduroy jacket and gray slacks. The jacket hung loosely on his tall frame, his shirt was open at the throat and he had no tie. His forehead seemed unusually large because his hair was receding. He was carrying a large sketchbook in his left hand.

"Professor, this is Alex Johns."

"How are you, Professor Schiller?" He couldn't imagine calling this man by his first name. It would be like calling George Washington George.

Karl Schiller put down the sketchbook, unbuttoned and removed the corduroy jacket. His tall erect figure was commanding. "I'm glad to meet you, Mr. Johns."

Barbara took his jacket. "I'll put it away for you. Would you like some coffee?"

"Thank you. I've had coffee this morning. But I am hungry."

"Pancakes and sausages? I love to cook. They can be ready in a jiffy."

They all sat together at the table in the huge kitchen over a delicious serving of pancakes soaked in maple syrup and crisp brown pork sausages.

Finally their conversation, which drifted from one topic (the difficulty of getting taxis in Manhattan) to another (a display of seashells Karl Schiller had seen in a window of a bank, some of them broken open to reveal what he considered to be their amazing structure) was ended when Schiller put down his fork and asked, "May we go into the living room? I will spread out the sketches on the floor, so you can see all the perspectives at once."

In the living room, Schiller removed the pages from the looseleaf binding and spread them carefully on the carpet. Barbara settled beside Alex on the couch. She looked at the sketches silently, her teeth folded over her lower lip in concentration.

Alex was pleased by the workability of the sketches. Schiller hadn't tried to fake it with an easy readable perspective in which all the decorative values were on display. Instead, he confronted them with very sketchy perspectives and plans showing the building in a three-dimensional way. Alex liked the straight forms bare of embellishment and the way the layout showed clearly how he intended to handle the site.

But Karl Schiller had made one terrible mistake. He had placed the structure in the middle of a wide park-like area, with trees and benches and even a waterfall. He hadn't used even half the space that the building code allowed and had tried to compensate for that in the height. The building now rose to sixty stories instead of forty-five.

Schiller said, "There is more to be done, of course. The perspective sketches enclose the building from several points of view. The parts can be fitted together."

Barbara lifted her head. "I think it's magnificent."

Alex said, "There are a few problems that haven't been taken into consideration."

The freckles on Barbara's cheek accented her pale skin. "Will it cost too much?"

"It's way over budget."

"How can you tell? You haven't seen the finished sketches or specifications."

"I don't have to. He's used only a fraction of the site on some of the most valuable real estate in the world."

"How much more will it cost?"

"As much as ten million dollars. To put up an ordinary building costs five or six times the cost of everything else—land, interest, amortization, taxes, fees. To put up this building, with the extra concrete and steel, the extra cost of transporting and erecting, will increase that to seven or eight times. And there's not only the additional cost of design but a loss in rentable area as well."

Barbara looked at him in a distant appraising way. "Every value in the world can't be measured by the dollar."

"It's the best way of keeping score."

"No one's trying to keep score, Mr. Johns."

"Then we're in the wrong ballpark," Alex said mildly.

Barbara seemed to be concentrating on some inward focal point. She turned to Schiller.

"When can you have finished sketches?"

Karl Schiller answered with careful deliberation. "In approximately two weeks."

"Is that satisfactory, Mr. Johns?"

Alex shrugged. "If you want to talk deadlines instead of money."

"We can get a big architectural firm to supply the draftsmen, can't we?"

"I can probably get Sam Whitefield to cooperate."

Barbara turned back to Schiller. "Then I think we're ready to go ahead, Professor."

"Wait a minute," Alex said. "The first step is to get your father and Vinnie to okay that extra money."

"I'll get them to, one way or the other." Standing in the immense high-ceilinged living room, with the shutters drawn against afternoon sun, she added, "I won't let anyone sabotage it. That includes my father. And Vinnie. A building like this is worth fighting for. It isn't going to stay an idea on paper."

She could be relentless in going after what she wanted. That was a quality Alex appreciated in men but in women he feared and mistrusted it. Nevertheless their fortunes were linked. He needed approval for Karl Schiller's design to complete the deal with Zenith Oil.

"You want to try for that extra base, Miss Druse, you go for it."

"How about you, Mr. Johns? Aren't you excited by a chance to help create a work of art?"

"You want the truth?"

"Of course."

"I don't worry about art, Miss Druse. I just put up buildings. Before the excavation starts, I need a complete design and an approved budget. Outside of that, I couldn't care less whose design I build."

"Good. Leave the rest to me," she said.

32

*

He had gone that way. In the steady stream of traffic passing, did anyone know what sort of man he was? There should have been an announcement on loudspeakers.

Alone in her living room, Barbara stood by the window, feeling a little dizzy. An exasperating tormenting familiar emotion was finding a new channel. This unfocused diffuse feeling pre-existed in her as in every woman until some random event directed it toward a specific male. The event had occurred. Now portions of her emotions were being used that had not been since Henry and everything that had happened seemed directed to this instant, when everything about him was as maddeningly provocative as the melody of a song the name of which escaped her.

She glanced back into the living room, to the chair where, briefly, he had sat. Staring at its present emptiness she heard him speak. She became completely still, listening with her face in her hands.

She would have to learn to call him Karl.

*

At dinner in the Russian Tea Room, soft candlelight on the table made a flickering glow on her luminous cheek. Tom MacLaren almost forgot to eat his dinner.

"Don't you like shashlik?" Sophy asked, when she noticed that he had hardly touched his plate.

"I've never had it before."

"I adore Russian food. I wouldn't have suggested this place if I knew you didn't like it."

"Oh, but I do. I love Russian food."

He found himself staring at Sophy in a way that made the blood rise slowly into his cheeks. She was the most attractive girl he had ever dated. She was not merely pretty, she was aglow with fragile beauty. He imagined bare shoulders sensual in lamplight, a clavicle thrusting sharply against pale almost transparent skin.

On their first date he had discovered where she lived, but she had not let him take her home. He was sure that was her way of forestalling the usual amorous overture. She was a few years younger than he—perhaps twenty-two or twenty-three—but she was the kind whose innocence had escaped the hazards of dating.

She said, "I have a favorite candy store near where I live. It serves delicious egg creams. Do you like egg creams?"

"I'm not sure I know what they are."

"You don't? I can't imagine anyone growing up in New York and not . . . But you didn't, did you?"

"No."

"That's why, then. I suppose some people think it's childish. But I don't care. It bores me to be grown up. Grownups always seem so terribly serious."

In the restaurant, amid crimson-shaded lamps, everyone suddenly seemed old. At the very next table an old woman with a patrician air was talking with an overdressed popinjay who was sixty if he was a day.

"Do you ever feel that way?" she asked.

"Sure," he said firmly.

The reply had a suffocating air of untruth. He had never mastered the ritualistic conversation that takes place during the first tentative approaches of man to woman, a time when each is trying to work out a relationship between themselves as possible lovers. He had been falling in love with girls since he was fifteen but Evelyn had been his first real affair, and by then he had been twenty.

A small candle lamp burned within a maroon globe on the table. He signaled the waiter for a check and while waiting, he wondered how Sophy's lovely dark hair, loosened, would look tumbled down beside the white column of her throat. He imagined her with white painted face in a royal court, the kind he saw in movies, where women with indelicate décolletage wore powdered wigs. There were many movie roles that would be suitable to her.

When they left the restaurant they walked crosstown on Fifty-seventh Street. The August evening was stifling. Part of Fifth Avenue was under repair, blocked with yellow wooden barriers and a red warning flag.

He guided her across the torn-up street, holding her by the crook of an elbow. She bumped slightly against his shoulder and the contact was silken. Her face was uptilted and seemed alive in the semi-darkness, a glowing aureole. Once she lifted her hand to her face, to her eyelid—and he felt like a voyeur watching her from a secret hiding place.

She preceded him by a few feet onto the opposite sidewalk. Slender boyish figure. Her legs were too thin. Then she turned to him and smiled and all other impressions vanished: she was beautiful.

"Would you like to see a movie?"

"I'm sorry. I have to be home early tonight."

He sensed a rejection. This was the third time he had dated Sophy in two weeks but he didn't seem to be making any progress. He would have liked to say: I'm really nice, I just never find it easy to talk to girls.

"How about taking a walk? We're only a few blocks from where the new building will be going up."

"I've never seen it at night," she said.

They strolled slowly and when they arrived moonlight was striking the tall brickwalled shell of the hotel standing amid the desolation. They could see through the structure to an eerie ledge projecting from one wall, the remnant of the mezzanine floor. In the cleared area a clamshell, gasoline hoists and a dump truck were motionless in the rubble. There was a fence surrounding the area, attached to the sidewalk bridge that gave overhead protection to pedestrians. They looked through a truck entrance opening secured by a heavy chain.

Tom told her about the demolition work that had gone on during the day. A crane, which operated off the back of a truck on the street, had lifted bulldozers to the top enclosed floors of the hotel, swinging them on a two-hundred-foot boom through panels knocked out in the wall. Inside the hotel the bulldozers had begun work on the interiors.

"Are the floors strong enough to hold them?"

"In old buildings they are. They used to design floors and walls with a lot more strength than they do today. Maybe because they didn't know how much they had to do to make them safe."

He explained how the bulldozers worked to wreck the hotel from the inside, pushing down walls and after useful salvage was stripped

35

out scraping up the debris and pushing it to the open elevator shaft from which the cab had long since been removed. The debris plunged down the open shaft to the bottom where a truck waited to carry it away.

All that roar of activity was quiet now. Sophy looked at a silent landscape over which the moon rode palely. The ungainly shadows of construction equipment were like prehistoric monsters.

"Pretty scary." Her moods had a quickness, an unpredictability. "I've always wanted to work one of those thingamajigs." She indicated the clamshell with its bucket resting idly on the ground.

"Would you like to?"

"Could I? Won't somebody stop us?"

"I'll put you in the cab myself."

He lifted her over the chain barring the way, and then stepped over it. They went across boarded planking into leveled area. As she approached the cab of the dark clamshell, crossing beneath the boom that angled upward, the steel caterpillar treads were almost at her shoulder height.

"It's so big. I can't see the top."

"I'll boost you up. And show you how the gears work."

Sophy stopped to take off her shoe and shake a pebble out.

She giggled. "I don't think we ought to be doing this."

He lifted her up onto the step of the fender. The clamshell loomed above them.

Suddenly a ray of light spotted them.

"What do ya think ya're doin'?"

Sophy turned and blinked in the flashlight glare.

"You've got no right in here. Get a move on before I call a cop."

Tom shielded his eyes against the glare and saw a man wearing a visored cap. He was carrying a short length of pipe in one hand and a flashlight in the other.

"I work on this job," Tom said. "I'm with the demolition crew. My name is MacLaren."

"It's my job to keep people outa here."

"She wanted to see what it's like inside one of the clamshells. We're not bothering anyone."

"Get moving. On your way." He poked Tom in the arm with the foot-long section of pipe.

"Don't do that."

"What?"

Tom felt pressure at the back of his eyes. There were certain ways in which he could not allow himself to be challenged.

"You heard me!"

"What's the matter?" The watchman poked Tom again, less certainly.

"I said don't do that!"

Sophy came down off the fender of the clamshell.

"Oh, a wise guy. Showing off. I've a good mind to call a cop."

"Why don't you?"

"Tom," Sophy said pleadingly.

Finally Tom shuddered. "Okay," he said. "Let's go."

They went slowly back to the truck entrance gate and the watchman followed at a cautious distance. He caught up with them, passed by and unlocked the chain for them to go out. They walked for almost half a block before Tom's anger began to recede.

She smiled a bit uneasily. "I didn't know what was going to happen. You had a funny expression."

He had to avoid situations where he might lose his temper. For a moment back there he had felt like a mountain about to topple in a mighty slide of earth and gravel.

"That dumb watchman annoyed me," he said. "That's all there was to it."

Almost overhead a projecting clock ticked off minutes in dotted white numerals that dissolved to black.

"It's getting late," she said.

"I'll take you home."

She lived in an apartment house in Morningside Heights.

"It's a long ride in the subway. Really, I'm fine. I'd prefer to go home alone if you don't mind."

He was sure she was displeased by what happened at the construction site.

"I enjoyed seeing you again, Sophy."

"I had a wonderful time. Really."

37

What a woman does always makes sense; it is only what she says that is hard to understand. At the subway kiosk he took a chance and kissed her. She offered no resistance.

"I'd like to see you again," he said. "Can I call?"

"Of course."

"How about coming by at lunchtime tomorrow?" he asked.

"I'll try," she said.

His confidence returned. "Even if I can't get you into a clamshell, I may be able to find a stray dog."

She said, laughing, "I've had a lovely evening, Tom. Really. Please call me soon."

"I will."

He watched her descend into the subway. A nice girl.

Above him a skyscraper tower, serene and powerful, reached toward the moon, soaring into a dimension high above the pale shifting lights of electric signs and the babble of neon billboards.

*

Lying on the huge bed in his apartment on Seventy-second Street and Riverside Drive, Alex Johns wore pajama bottoms and his free hand rested on his lower groin. He had a telephone partly cradled against his shoulder.

Louise, his secretary, said, "A messenger just arrived from Zenith Oil with the final sketches by that new architect, Karl Schiller. And there's a note for you from Miss Barbara Druse which I haven't opened."

"Okay."

"Mr. Whitefield called for an appointment. He's very anxious to see you. I put him down for eleven o'clock. Is that okay?"

"Okay."

"It's your mother's birthday. Shall I go ahead with that present?"

Alex had promised to put an additional room onto Mother's two-story mansard-roofed frame house in Concord, New Hampshire. The new room would be an office for his brother Frank, who was a lawyer but worked in the house because he couldn't afford an office of his own.

"Sure. Go ahead. And get her a little something for herself too."

"Like what?"

"Try money. She's sentimental about money."

Swirl and gurgle of water disappearing down the drain from the tub in the bathroom.

"I'll be in soon, Louise."

Alex hung up the telephone as he heard the glass stall partitions slide open. A moment later Ginger appeared in the bathroom door, glistening wet. She lifted sinuous arms.

"Do you want to dry me, honey?"

While he dried her, Ginger tried to snuggle against him.

"Would you like to?"

"Sorry. I have to get down to the office."

She pushed back red hair with one hand, sticking the stray strands behind a pink-colored large ear. "Can't we even have breakfast?"

"Sorry, baby. I'd love to but I'm in a hurry this morning."

"How about coffee?"

"I'll grab a cup at the office."

He came out of the bathroom, shaved and showered, wearing trousers and undershirt. A short while ago he had felt tired, but now his blood was bubbling as if carbonated.

Ginger said, "I hate to see you run off like this."

She didn't understand how important work was to him. At the bar last night, building an intricate crossed matchstick tower, he had collected a small crowd around him to admire the precarious balance of his artistry. Alexander Johns: Creator of the Sulphur Tower. Matchless Building. She couldn't understand that his work was an obsession that had burrowed like a tick under his skin.

On the way downtown in his chauffeured limousine, Alex glanced at the front page of *The New York Times*. Then he turned to the real estate section and saw a familiar face, with a caption beneath showing the man's name and the years of birth and death. There was a column story headed: Wolf Erskine Was an Adventurer in Real Estate.

A tremor passed over him, an alteration in feeling that was like a chemical reaction. Wolf gone? It didn't seem possible.

He had been a welder in a shipyard when he first glimpsed Wolf

Erskine being driven through in a limousine with the top down and a cigar jutting out of his mouth. Alex didn't recognize him; a man working with him on the ship's hull had to tell him who he was. But there was something about the man that caught his attention, and he followed with his eyes the bulky assured figure in the rear of the limousine that slowly circled about in its inspection of the shipyard. He fancied that his eyes met those of the famous man and that some sort of secret message passed between—the kind of subliminal recognition that might pass between a father and his unknown son.

A month later Alex was drafted and sent to Korea, despite frantic attempts to prove he would be more valuable working on the home front. The Army assigned him to be a company clerk because he knew how to type. Instead of welding ships he now typed duty rosters, indicating who had to go on latrine duty or KP, who was scheduled for guard duty or furlough rotation. He took care of the company payroll and spent from six to nine o'clock every evening in the commissary collecting money for the sale of candy, cigarettes, and prophylactic kits and accounting for everything later to the supply officer. That was the routine of Army life until the frantic week when the Chinese broke through the lines and sent our boys reeling backward in retreat. A mortar shell tore through the curved tin galvanized roof of a Nissen hut and Alex got steel splinters in his leg that invalided him home.

When he got out of the Army, he knew exactly what he wanted to do. He went to Wolf Erskine's organization and applied for a job. His future was being shaped for him. His immediate superior enjoyed singing in a male quartet, and although Alex was a natural baritone he sang basso because there was an opening for a basso and no one else would sing it. He liked being in the center of things and was a terrible show-off who knew how to make his superiors think he was amusing. He was always smiling and friendly, and whenever he was given a job to do, however late in the day, it was finished and ready in the morning. Insomnia helped him because he never wanted to go to bed early and sat up late to get any job finished.

Finally he came to the attention of the great man himself. He was called for an interview. He impressed Wolf Erskine immediately. Wolf was a lonely man, ugly, squat, and beetlebrowed, and had come from a small town much like Alex's, a straggly town in the middle of rich farmland, settled not by immigrants from Europe but by families who had lived there for generations. The people were poor, not from lack of social standing, but simply because they lived in a town that progress had passed by. The impulse that started Wolf on the road to fabulous success was much like Alex's—a revolt against the melancholy of closed off towns which offered no outlet into the main stream of the world. Alex was still seeking escape, and Wolf sensed it. They became almost friends. Wolf invited Alex to his home and they would sit up talking until all hours, about building, about people, about plans for the future. Alex was enthusiastic, inflated with youthful ideas, talking off the top of his mind but always precise, accurate, well informed.

With Wolf Erskine's assistance Alex got into the contracting business, first working on some of Wolf's projects and then—after the spectacular bankruptcy in which Wolf came to ruin—on his own. Alex did not intend to repeat Wolf's mistakes, but he did share the man's tendency to the excessive—when Alex worked he overworked, when he smoked he oversmoked (always the same brand of fine Havana that Wolf Erskine smoked), and when he made plans he was willing to take exorbitant risks because the world was a huge ever-expanding bubble that would never burst.

Within a few moments of his arrival at the office he opened the portfolio from Zenith Oil and glanced at the completed sketches. They were in rough crayon and not as finished in detail as Sam Whitefield's sketches. He lifted one after another, placing each behind the others in the sheaf. Schiller's designs looked impressive both from a distance and at close quarters. In perspectives, where the importance of the silhouette was diminished, there were new striking points of interest in the small scale detailing.

Alex did not know much about architecture as art, but he did respond to someone reaching out in a new but practical way.

He opened the enclosed note from Barbara Druse.

I've just come from a meeting with my father and Vinnie Haleson. They're still dubious about increased costs, but I think they'll go along. It was quite a donnybrook. It may help if they hear from you about what a great building this will be.

41

The buzzer interrupted.

"Julius Scobie says he has to see you," Louise said on the intercom.

"Send him in."

A stooped, mournful-looking man with hair carefully trained to lie forward over an almost bald head, came into the office.

"I've just been talking with Henry Tratner," he announced. "He's not going to renew our line of credit."

There were some days when the problems were worse than Alex could have imagined. When tension flooded through him his leg pained from unrecovered pieces of steel shrapnel that were now a part of himself. His leg had never hurt worse than it did now.

"That bastard! He knows we can't pay off that loan in full."

"He also knows how deep we've been getting in, Alex."

Biting down on the gristle of a rubber band, Alex placed a call to Henry Tratner at the Hayden Bank.

While waiting for the call to be completed, he paced the office with a thrusting stride. His belligerence waited to be sparked by an idea. If he had to pay off Hayden Bank, he needed two million dollars. The sum was impressive but figures were only meat and drink for computers. A computer could spell out to the last desperate decimal point his predicament, but no computer could tell how he would get out of it. He would discover some way. He dealt in the plasticity of credit, the infinite variability of deals and maneuvers, the principle of continuous negotiation in which old problems were solved by being submerged into new ones.

The buzzer.

"Hello, Henry? What in the name of Christ's balls are you sons of bitches trying to do?"

"I'm sorry, Alex. If there was anything I could do to help, I would."

"Where else can you bastards get the kind of interest I'm paying?"

"It's the principal we're worrying about."

"If you call in that loan, I'll come up there personally and hang myself from your door. How'll you explain that to your clients?"

"Alex, we're old friends. But it's definite that we're calling in the loan."

Alex stared blankly out the window of his office on the top floor of a penthouse triplex forty-five stories above the street. On the floor below his vice-president, treasurer, secretary all had expensive offices, and there was a honeycombed layout which housed all the other employees of Alexander Johns Enterprises. This organization was as real as the stone panorama of the city spread out majestically beneath the windows—existed in a world independent of bankers, computers, and their calculations.

He flung the rubber band he had been chewing into a wastebasket. "You've got to give me more time. I've got a dozen deals cooking, Henry, and any one can come through any minute."

His glance fell on the sketches by Karl Schiller lying on his desk. Surrounding the building tower there was a huge wide park with ornamental pools and shrubbery, evergreen trees, plots of greenery, even a confounded rock waterfall.

"Alex," Henry said, "we're calling in the loan because if we wait any longer there simply won't be anything to collect. You've mortgaged, remortgaged, sold and leased back until you don't know yourself where you stand. In another month you won't own anything but debts."

An idea began to germinate and suddenly sprouted in Alex's mind in full three-dimensional form.

"Henry, you're making me play my trump card. I know you're still looking for space on the West Side for your new bank. How about your own building on a big midtown site?"

"There isn't any. We've scoured the field."

"How about where Zenith Oil is building? I'm talking about your own annex—right out in front of Zenith Oil's building. On a big new plaza. Practically a whole park."

"Are you having a pipe dream? You don't own any of that property and Zenith Oil would never stand for it."

"I think I can swing a deal for you on favorable terms. A land purchase and a long-term lease. Ninety-nine years."

The telephone fell silent.

"All other things being equal," Henry Tratner said warily, "we'd be interested."

Alex chuckled. "So would ten other banks in this city. In fact, they'd grab it."

"Alex, what do you want?"

"A renewal of my line of credit. You're not actually giving me anything, except time. I still have to pay your bloodsucking interest."

Thought waves pulsated.

"Alex, there's absolutely no chance of extending your line of credit at two million."

"I might pay back a quarter of a million."

"Impossible. Not even for the inside track on that site you're talking about."

"How much, then?"

"Half. If you retire half the loan, we might renew the other half."

"I can't do it."

"What can you pay?"

"I'll stretch it and say four hundred thousand."

"Make it eight. That's the absolute best I can offer."

His brain clicked like an adding machine to register the meaning of the figures. The gap was still wide between his expenses and foreseeable revenue but there might be a few bridges he could throw across. Even the most temporary, the flimsiest. He might borrow more on his stock in Alexander Johns Enterprises although the price had declined sharply in recent weeks. And he could divert some payments Zenith Oil would make to him on their building while at the same time stalling his payments to subcontractors.

Alex leaned back in his swivel chair. Sweat oozed from beneath his arms.

"I'll have to call you back."

"What makes you think you can get us that site? Why would Zenith Oil agree to put up a new building on their land?"

"I can talk them into it. It's in their interest."

Henry Tratner sounded disappointed. "I've seen too many deals like this fall through before."

"This one won't," Alex said. "I'll call you back when I've gone over my figures."

When he hung up the telephone he was soaked through as though he had been in a sauna with the temperature at two hundred degrees. Dry heat worked into his body to root out impurities, root out doubt.

44

*

Vinnie Haleson was fond of quoting the remark that the best part of any family tree is always underground because it pointed up that he had an exceptional family and at the same time did so in a deprecatory unegotistic way.

At a few minutes past five o'clock that afternoon he became annoyed at Alex Johns because the remark occasioned too much laughter.

Alex Johns had been admiring the Haleson home at Queens Point, not admiring structural elements about which he knew something but intangibles of which he knew nothing. When Alex commented on the advantages of living in a house where other generations had "put their roots down," Vinnie countered with his customary remark about the family tree. Alex Johns laughed too loudly, and Vinnie brought the conversation abruptly to the reason for their meeting.

"We're prepared to go over our budget to put up the kind of building Karl Schiller designed. The question is, how much over budget do we have to go?"

"Didn't Barbara Druse discuss that with you?"

Vinnie detected a certain watchfulness behind Alex's eyes.

"Our deal is with you, Alex."

"Look, you're the people who wanted Karl Schiller. If you want a first-class product, you've got to pay first-class prices."

"How much?" Vinnie said impatiently.

"I'm afraid it's going to be a shock."

"Well?"

"Ten million dollars over."

Vinnie touched his gray thinning hair. "Ten million? Doesn't that seem a bit high?"

"I'll guarantee it won't be a dime less."

Vinnie thought about the difficulty of persuading Peter Druse to spend ten million dollars more on Karl Schiller's design. That would require an all-out effort and he would have to bear all the risks if later events proved the additional expenditure unwise.

"Is there anything we can do to cut corners?"

Alex appeared to ponder the suggestion. "There is one way to bring the cost of the whole package way down."

"How?"

"Use part of that big plaza for another connected building. A small one with a separate entrance."

"What good would that do? We don't need another building."

"You can build it for an investment. I know banks who'd jump at the chance to pay a lot more for the land than you paid, and you can make an additional profit on the building either through direct sale or a ninety-nine-year lease."

After a moment Vinnie asked, "Are you sure?"

"It's a natural. Space is at a premium in midtown and any bank would know it's going into a prestige location with a top company like Zenith Oil right on the premises."

It was a tempting proposal. Peter Druse would not care if the intrusion of a separate building on that plaza was indefensible on artistic grounds. Peter was a businessman, not an artist, and had not particularly liked Karl Schiller's design in the first place.

"Of course, money isn't the only consideration," Vinnie said. "A change like that could ruin the whole design."

"All you need is a new approach. And you've got an architect working for you who specializes in new approaches."

"I suppose we could throw it back in Karl Schiller's lap," Vinnie said, musing aloud. "Are you absolutely sure of that ten-million-dollar figure?"

"Nobody estimates costs better than I do. Once I complete my takeoff, I can practically weigh the specifications to find out what percentage to add for overhead."

Vinnie glanced at the rows of bookshelves that lined the study, fine leatherbound old volumes in shelves from floor to ceiling. The gilt-edged pages of these books had been turned lovingly by men who had been proud to call themselves Halesons. They enjoyed gracious living and possessed the means to indulge their pleasure in it. Generations of profligacy, of punitive tax laws and unfortunate investments had withered away the Haleson fortune until even the house at Queens Point had been in danger of the auctioneer's hammer. Peter Druse saved it by taking a first mortgage for more than the house's actual value, enabling Vinnie to meet the estate taxes and keep Queens Point in the Haleson family where it had been for two centuries.

Alex Johns was looking past him.

Vinnie turned to see Ann standing at the entrance to the study. She wore a pink linen tunic with matching slacks and a wildly colorful print scarf tied loosely around her neck.

"Darling, I don't like to interrupt business but it is time we got ready for the party tonight."

"Didn't you get my note?"

"I've been out all afternoon. At Mrs. Crowley's."

He had forgotten, partly because she was not dressed suitably for such a visit. Mrs. Crowley's was the home where their son Richard lived in a world of his own, not communicating with anyone, unaware of either his identity or his inheritance.

"I left it on your . . . on the bed. Your father told me this morning at church that he's coming over tonight. About nine."

"He can't. We're going to the Garsons'."

"I'm afraid we'll have to cancel."

Ann entered the study and draped herself carelessly across the arm of an emperor chair.

"Why, it's that nice Mr. Johns. I didn't know you were coming over today."

"I'm sorry to intrude on a Sunday, Mrs. Haleson. But your husband and I had important business."

"Well, now that you're here why don't we all get cozy? I'll let you mix—provided you can make a good scotch sour."

Alex went behind the bar. "I make the best, Mrs. Haleson."

Vinnie moved Ann to where a close whispered exchange would not be overheard. "We can't go out when your father is coming over."

"We're going to the Garsons'."

Tony Garson had become Ann's latest interest—a pretentious fellow who professed to be an expert on wines and chamber music. Garson's wife was a ferocious vixen who seized upon Vinnie as her prize social trophy.

"I can't," Vinnie said. "Your father wants to discuss business."

Ann gave a tight tiny smile. "Then you won't miss me if I go."

47

She beamed as Alex Johns appeared with her drink. "Ah, here's the man who gets things done." She took the glass and sipped it. "Magnifico. Come over and make scotch sours for me anytime, Mr. Johns."

"It's not my specialty. I do other things."

"I'm sure you're competent in any number of ways," Ann said, smiling over the rim of her glass.

Vinnie was thinking of the telephone call he would have to make to Peter, the new excuse he would have to invent. This might be the very occasion on which Peter would begin to suspect the worst about his daughter's marriage. He would never blame Ann: not darling Ann, the pretty one with the sunny disposition. Peter would blame him.

Ann said, "I'm sorry to have to break this up. I'd love to stay longer and talk to you, Mr. Johns. But I have to go up and dress."

"I'm sorry too, Mrs. Haleson."

"Come back some other time, won't you, when we can get to know each other better?"

"I'll certainly try."

She finished her scotch sour on the way to the bar and left the glass on the counter. Vinnie decided to make one last attempt to reason with her.

"Ann . . ."

He caught up with her in the doorway.

"How can I tell your father you've gone to a party tonight?"

"You didn't consult me when you invited him, darling."

"He's your father!"

Ann touched him on the cheek. "You do worry about him, don't you? Frankly, darling, I don't care what you tell him. I'm still going to the Garsons'."

To suffer her cruelty was another side of gallantry, and he considered it the mark of a gentleman to repress anger, however justified.

Ann started for the stairs. Vinnie said suddenly, as though he had just reached the decision, "Then I'll go with you!"

She turned at the banister, shrugged, and continued up the stairs. When Vinnie returned to the study he was somber.

"Your wife's a pretty woman," Alex said.

"Yes."

"Well, I'll be going," Alex said. "Sorry to take up your time on a Sunday. But I knew you'd want the straight story as soon as I could give it to you."

"I appreciate your coming over, Alex."

At the front door, Vinnie paused a moment.

"Can you make preliminary inquiries as to tenants for the new building?"

"Of course."

"See what you can do."

"If you want the deal, I can practically guarantee it."

"Work up the exact figures on how much more Schiller's present design will cost and why. When I have everything in front of me, Peter and I will decide whether to make the change you suggest."

"Ten million dollars is a lot of money," Alex said. "All you need to do is make one change in the design."

"Do you think Karl Schiller would agree to do it?"

"Just tell him it has to be done. And sweeten the pot."

"We'll do it diplomatically, of course. Peter will invite him to Parkgate. It might be useful if you came along too, Alex."

"Be glad to," Alex said. "If there's one thing I know how to handle it's an architect. You've got to keep their art from going to their heads."

When Alex left, Vinnie started up the stairs. The carpeting was worn thin over the first two steps but he was reluctant to have the material replaced. This was the original material brought over by Junius Haleson three quarters of a century ago, and quite irreplaceable.

*

Ladders leaned aginst the sidewalk bridge on the sixth floor of the hotel and men climbed holding to the rungs with one hand and carrying tin cans of tools with the other. Long staccato bursts of noise. Dust rising. Bricks raining down. Burner's acetylene torch slicing through a steel brace with steady orange flaring into molten shower of white and yellow sparks.

Big Dom paced rapidly across the sidewalk bridge, stepping around old lumber lying in piles wet from overnight showers.

"Hey, Tom!"

His loud voice carried over the constant din of debris falling into dozens of old doors that were slanted together to form a chute that carried debris into the hollowed-out central area of the hotel.

Tom MacLaren went over to him.

"This floor was supposed to be down today," Big Dom said.

"I know that. But we've had problems."

"Everybody's got problems."

"Steve Wyatt was out yesterday—and hasn't shown up today. I'm a man short."

"Get more work out of the men you got."

"Where do you get all those good ideas?"

"None of your lip. You're supposed to keep a schedule."

"It rained yesterday. Today everything is still a little slippery."

"Don't keep giving me problems. Find answers."

"You're just in a lousy mood, Big Dom."

"Don't let the sons of bitches take advantage! If you can't get them to work, I'll get somebody who can."

Since the episode at the bar in which Tom defeated him at arm-wrestling, Big Dom had shown him no favors.

"You go get anybody you want."

Big Dom said, "What's the matter? Touchy?"

"Everybody'll work better if you just get off their backs."

"I'll bet! Hey, you goof-off bastard!"

Mike Collyer had lowered his drill, holding it negligently in one hand.

"What d'ya think that thing is—your dingus?"

Mike shook his head and lifted his drill back into position. With an eardrum-rattling roar, in a thin haze of mortar and concrete, he cracked through another block of stone.

"Mike's a good man," Tom said. "He's doing his job."

"The hell he is! Nobody works if you don't keep after him. That's what you're supposed to be doing."

"The rest of the floor will be down today. But if Steve Wyatt doesn't show up tomorrow, you give me somebody else. I can't keep a schedule with a man short."

"You'll get somebody." Big Dom's hard hat glinted in the sun. "Meanwhile, Mr. Rand wants you to sit in on a meeting."

"A meeting?"

"You just keep your mouth shut and listen. You might even learn something."

Tom followed Big Dom along the scaffolding. A torch blazed as a worker cut into a beam. The hotel had dwindled to ten stories and the insides were hollowed out like a pot with the lid removed. Steel girders were exposed, partly sheathed in rough concrete. Some beams were being cleaned with air hammers to get the brick fill out of them. Along the scaffolding below the top of a wall men of the work gang were line drilling and wedging, swinging piledrivers and loosening the wall with crowbars and picks. From time to time several men joined to push a section of wall down into the hollow interior where a clamshell picked up debris and dumped it into a truck for removal.

He followed Big Dom into an office in the basement of the building across the street, where Ivor Rand and two men were poring over plans and surveys.

There was an old wooden desk in the room on which the plans were spread out, and two wooden chairs. Near the basement window was a washbasin with a paper towel dispenser and on the sill stood an electric coffeepot of a chipped and faded red. Outside of this, and a drafting board with a high stool against a side wall, there was no furniture.

Ivor Rand said, "You know Big Dom. And this is Tom MacLaren. These men are from the utility companies."

Tom shook hands with each of the men in turn, and stood near Big Dom as they went on studying the plans and surveys. The site they were cleaning was in a congested area of midtown where utilities were already in existence.

"Some of these connections will have to be terminated and re-routed to avoid incidents," a man said.

"Incidents?" Tom asked.

"That's a polite word," Ivor Rand growled. "I had one only a

51

couple of months ago on a job. A crane operator dug a little too deep in the wrong place."

"What happened?"

"His shovel hit an underground electric line. A charge of juice shot right up the shovel, across the boom and into the cab. Shriveled him. When I saw him he looked like a piece of black coal."

"We had a beauty last year," the other utilities man volunteered. "Cut through a gas line. Explosion turned the whole area into a blazing hunk of hell. Shook buildings for blocks. Three men blown to bits."

It was the responsibility of the demolition contractor to shut off the old utilities that had serviced buildings previously on the site. That meant all existing utilities had to be located and charted, shored up, braced or somehow protected from damage to the construction equipment. There was no amount of precaution that could prevent all "incidents," but it was the job of these men to try.

As the session neared an end, Ivor Rand folded up some plans that had been on the desk. The utilities men gravely shook hands and left.

"How about the signs the Buildings Department wanted for the sidewalk crossing?" Ivor Rand asked Big Dom.

"They'll be up at eight in the morning, Mr. Rand."

"All permits in order? We're going to need invert elevations on all pipes below grade from the architect."

"That's taking time."

"They'd better get cracking. The Department of Water Supply and the Telephone Company want to know what the building requirements are going to be. Con Edison wants an estimate of how many kilowatts will be needed. That has to be worked out with the architect."

"Somebody told me they haven't got a final design for the building."

"We're taking buildings down, not putting them up. That's their worry. We got plenty of our own." Ivor Rand took his brown coat from the back of a chair and turned to Tom MacLaren. "I understand you were in Vietnam."

"Yes, sir," Tom said.

"Saw some action. Got a Bronze Star."

"That's right."

"I lost a son there," Rand said gruffly. "A damn nasty business."

"Yes, sir."

"Someday I want to hear how you tried to save that sergeant. A Negro, wasn't he?"

"Yes, sir."

Ivor Rand shook his head. "Well, I'll see you around."

As they returned to the job, Big Dom was scowling.

"I thought I told you to keep your ears open and your mouth shut."

"What's the complaint now?"

"You were asking too many damn questions."

"I didn't think Mr. Rand wanted me to stand there like a dummy."

"I'm your boss and I give the orders. Don't forget it."

"Knock off."

"What are you doing—bucking for my job? You won't get it."

"You can shove it for all I care."

At the site of the hotel they parted without a word. He knew why Big Dom had turned against him. But he wasn't sorry for having proved he was a better man. Maybe it was time for him to move on somewhere else.

Except for the hotel the demolition was virtually complete. The site resembled a battlefield strewn with broken pieces of brick, rusting cans, soda bottles and bottle caps, discarded cigarette packs, handbills and a ton of unidentifiable scraps of metal scattered over an area marked with deep holes. When all the demolition was finished, the cleanup squad would come to clear the lot to curb level.

Mike Collyer came toward him, his head tilted to one side and a grin on his lips. Tom liked Mike best in the work gang. He had a basic good humor and gentleness that had earned him the name Sweetpea among others in the gang.

"Listen, I've got a date tonight. She works in a go-go joint over on Seventh Avenue. I can ask her to bring a friend."

"No, thanks," Tom said.

"You won't be sorry. They're willing. Buy a couple of drinks and you're in."

53

"Well . . ." A woman crossed the street at an angle and for an instant, as sunlight glinted off her narrow body, throwing a crooked sliver of shadow onto the street, he thought she was Sophy. "Not interested. Maybe some other time."

Marty Garfinkel steered a bulldozer through the debris and past the square holes that were the excavations for new footings. In the bowels of the hollowed out hotel, lit by an acetylene torch hanging from a beam, the bulldozer resembled a monster emerging from the glare of inferno.

"Hey, Tom," Marty called. "I found out why Steve Wyatt hasn't come in."

"Is he sick?"

"Naw. This is why."

Marty tossed a paper wrapped in a stone and secured with a rubber band. The tattered piece of newspaper, thumbed and grimy, was a newspaper column with a short headline: MAN ARRESTED. The few lines of the story said that Steve Wyatt, construction worker, had been arrested for indecent exposure in the subway. It gave Steve Wyatt's age and address.

"Always knew he was peculiar," Marty said. "I never figured him for anything like that."

He expertly turned the wheel of the bulldozer and it grumped away over the uneven littered ground.

An hour later, when Steve Wyatt reported for work, Tom was supervising the putting up of a netting on the catwalk.

There was a sallow tenseness in Steve's face. Tom decided to treat him as though nothing had happened.

"About time," he said gruffly. "We were shorthanded all day yesterday. And you missed a couple of hours today."

"I had a little trouble."

"Well, get to work."

The gang worked steadily until the noon lunch whistle blew. Tom took out his lunch pail and then noticed Steve Wyatt standing nearby, uncertainly. Tom drifted over to ask, "Where are you having lunch?"

"I thought I'd grab a sandwich."

54

"I packed a couple today. Tunafish, ham and cheese. You can have one."

"You sure?"

"I thought I'd be hungry but I'm not."

Steve looked pathetically grateful. "Okay, then. I'm kinda sick of that bar and grill."

He and Steve sat on the crawler treads of a crane with their legs dangling and Tom passed the tunafish sandwich to Steve.

"Did you hear about me?" Steve asked.

"I saw something in the paper."

"I nearly didn't come in today. But I decided I had to." Steve chewed reflectively. "It never happened the way it says. It's just a mistake."

"You don't have to talk about it."

"You should've seen how Big Dom looked at me when I showed up. I could've folded, but I didn't. It's because I know I'm not guilty, see? That gives a guy courage."

"I suppose so."

Steve Wyatt took a long swallow out of the mouth of a Coke bottle, then held it in his hand, staring off into space.

"It happened the night before last. I was in the subway, going back to my place. I'd just been to a movie on Forty-second Street. I got down in the subway and stood near the end of the platform. I like to catch the first car 'cause that lets me out nearer where I live. I've got a place on Charles Street. Nothing much. Just a room. The train came in, and I was going to get on. All of a sudden this guy nabs me. Says he's a plainclothesman, 'dick to you.' Kidding me along, see? I kidded back at first. Then I see he's serious. You know what it was about? I had my fly open. I went to the men's room in that moviehouse and forgot to zip up. That's the whole story."

It had the ring of a story carefully rehearsed and being tested for the first time. Steve Wyatt looked at Tom, questioning.

"That kind of a mistake can happen," Tom said.

"Christ, you've been working with me. You know I'm not a queer."

The whistle blew. End of the lunch break.

"Stop worrying about it."

55

"A hell of a thing, to put a tag like that on a guy. He just better leave me alone."

"Who?"

Big Dom's raucous jeering voice drifted down, "You canaries gonna sit on that perch all day?"

"Him," Steve said, with venom.

"Maybe I'm wrong. Maybe you ain't canaries. Maybe you're a couple of lovebirds." There followed loud unmusical whistling, amid shouts of laughter from men on the ground.

Steve uttered a swift low stream of profanity. "I've had just about all I can stand from that lousy wop."

"He doesn't mean anything by it," Tom said. But he couldn't help feeling annoyed with Big Dom.

At the first opportunity Tom went to the high floor scaffolding where Big Dom was standing to survey the job—a commanding general looking down at his troops deployed in the field.

"Lay off Steve Wyatt today," Tom said. "He's all wound up. After a day like he's had . . ."

"I don't hafta treat him different because he got his name in the papers."

"It took guts to show up for work today. Look at it from his angle."

Big Dom, with a sly leer that lifted a corner of his thick mouth, answered: "How can I? I'm no queer."

Tom said quietly, "It could've been a mistake. Anyway, as long as he's doing his job, that's all you can ask."

"You feeling sorry for him? The way I look at it anybody who feels sorry for a queer is a little that way himself."

Tom fought down an impulse to put a fist into Big Dom's face.

"I'm just trying to tell you something for your own good."

"You're wastin' my time. Get back to work."

Without a word Tom walked to the end of the scaffolding and started down the ladder. From the floor below he looked up at Big Dom leaning on a supporting rope and roving his eyes over the various enclaves of wrecking activity going on below. From this angle Big Dom's body bulked large, his chest seemed to protrude widely and deeply at an unnatural angle and his neck and torso seemed dense, almost too dense. His face was malicious and dark.

56

Tom descended the ladder toward rutted and torn and craggy ground that was beginning to look like the surface of the moon.

Somewhat to his surprise, Steve Wyatt was more relaxed when he returned. Possibly he had guessed the purpose for Tom's visit to Big Dom. The work gang was drilling and wedging out an inside wall on the third floor. Steve worked as hard or harder than any of the others.

Later in the afternoon a big truck crane arrived. The tall machine held the enraptured attention of sidewalk gawkers, and the workers were almost as bad when the crane began to do its job. Most of them slowed their own work to watch the stately swiveling efficiency of the machine. Steve Wyatt was the only man who worked on without interruption, anxious to please, to show he could be depended on.

Big Dom noted the suspension of activity from his high vantage point. He came down to issue burly threats to the work gang bosses. When he got around to Tom's gang, he singled out Steve Wyatt for a particular target. Air compressors and hammers buffeted the sound away but Tom could imagine what was being said from the hatred bared in Steve's narrow face.

Tom did not want to get involved in the argument but as soon as Big Dom left, he strolled casually over to where Steve had resumed working on an irregular patch of brick wall. The wall had iron bolts sticking out of it.

"Did he give you a hard time?"

Steve's eyes had a wildly dangerous glint. "He gave me my walking papers."

"Fired you? What for?"

"Didn't like the way I was talking back, I guess. I wouldn't let anybody talk like that to me. Especially a dumb dago."

"Take it easy, Steve."

Big Dom was now standing in the clearing below, arguing with the operator of the clamshell. Steve looked down.

"See what he's doing. He's talking about me!"

"You?"

"Making cracks about what happened. I've heard him laughing about it. The dirty dago bastard!"

"You're wrong, Steve. He's forgotten about that."

"He brought it up when he told me to clear out. Said he didn't need any man working for him who spent all his time in toilets in the subway."

"You shouldn't take him seriously." But Tom was shocked. Big Dom should have known better.

"Telling everybody! I know what's going on." Steve's mouth worked convulsively. "Doesn't he think I've been through enough? What kind of a louse would do what he's doing?"

"When he said you were through, he was in a bad temper. You know how Big Dom is."

"That goddamn Eyetie moron. Somebody ought to fix him so he won't talk about anybody again."

Steve's sunken cheeks were shining with collected pockets of sweat. It was clear that he was working himself into a desperate state.

"Steve, you're in no condition to work. It's only an hour to quitting time. Why don't you go home?"

"I'll give him his last fucking hour. He won't say I goofed off."

"You'll get paid for the hour. Go home."

"What are you, on *his* side?"

Tom walked away. There was no use talking to Steve in his present mood.

Ten minutes later, as Mike Collyer was lifting his sledge to knock over a small remaining fragment of wall, Tom heard him give a startled howl.

"Jeesus Keerist!"

"LOOK OUT!" someone else yelled.

Something guided his glance to a dark object hurtling down through the air. In the clearing below Big Dom looked up just as a six-inch bolt struck him in the forehead. A fine red mist seemed to spray into the air and he fell without a sound.

Suddenly everyone was running, down ladders and across the clearing. Big Dom lay without moving.

"Somebody get an ambulance!" a man yelled below.

"Is he hurt bad?"

"I'll say!"

The bolt had gone partly through bone and partly through flesh, knocked out an eye, and emerged below the cheekbone.

58

"Why'd he look up? He could've took it on his hard hat."

Someone called up in choked anger, "Who's the guy dropped that bolt?"

At the far end of the catwalk, Steve Wyatt was standing, holding one hand out, fingers splayed, palm downward. His narrow face was avid with curiosity, shock, and triumph. He pulled back as Tom approached him.

"My God—what a mess," Steve said. His mouth twitched.

"I *saw you!*"

Steve's wiry neck straightened. "It dropped out of my hand."

A haze drifted before Tom's eyes. He saw Steve Wyatt as though through bloody fingers.

"You crazy bastard!"

"Anybody who says it wasn't an accident is a liar!"

"I say so!"

Tom seized him and jammed him back against the railing. Steve's face changed color and his voice squeezed through a fear-strangled windpipe.

"Don't!"

Tom's grip tightened. Wooden planks of the catwalk trembled as someone hurried over, and strong hands gripped his shoulders.

"What are you doing, Tom?"

It was Mike Collyer. With a groan Tom released his grip.

"He dropped the bolt, Mike. It was deliberate. I saw him."

Mike turned to Steve. "Clear out! Quick. While you're still in one piece."

Sudden anger overcame Tom. He shoved Mike aside and gave Steve Wyatt a blow that sent him reeling along the catwalk, grasping for support.

"Get going—*you damn pervert!*"

*

At University Hospital a surgeon performed a two-hour operation to remove the steel bolt from Big Dom's face. He stopped the bleeding and cleared up the area where the eye had been, pulled all the

59

loosened teeth and did what he could to align crushed bones. Then he stitched up the side of Big Dom's face.

At the office of the Rand Demolition Company Tom filled out an accident report for the insurance company. A man from the insurance company went with him to the police station where Tom gave an eyewitness report of what happened and of what Steve Wyatt said just before the accident occurred. The police promised to pick up Steve for further questioning.

Tom's next stop was the hospital where he waited with the others until the surgeon came out of the operating room. The surgeon was a young man, dark and intense and wearing a white smock.

"He'll live. You can see him later tonight when he's out of the recovery room. Might cheer him up. You'll have to check with the night nurse, though."

They were allowed into the room just after Big Dom was given a morphine injection.

"He's very lucky," the night nurse said. She was a small dark woman in a stiff-white uniform. "If that bolt had hit him a couple of inches higher he'd be dead." She bent over Big Dom in the bed. "Would you like to be alone with your friends now?"

Big Dom nodded his bandaged head. The nurse left, smiling at Tom and Mike Collyer and Billy Farrell.

"All them bandages, they got you looking like a mummy," Billy Farrell said. His voice shook.

Big Dom barely nodded.

"Hurt much?" Mike Collyer asked.

"Yeah," Big Dom managed from beneath the gauze.

"Anything we can do?" Tom asked.

Big Dom lifted his hand from under the sheet in a slight gesture, and Tom moved closer and bent down.

"I ain't gonna be able to work no more," Big Dom whispered.

"Let's not worry about that. Just get better."

"You take over," Big Dom said. "You'll be okay."

"They give you stuff for the pain?" Billy Farrell asked.

Big Dom nodded and his head sank back onto the pillow . . .

When Tom MacLaren arrived back in his furnished room that

evening, he sat on the bed and dialed OLympia 7-7577. He felt he had to talk to Sophy. He was still in a state of shock.

The telephone returned a busy signal. He was being denied by a nerveless robot at the telephone exchange.

He dialed again.

The telephone rang.

"Hello."

"Hello, Sophy. This is Tom. I tried a few minutes ago and you were busy. I wanted to get you early before you made other arrangements. I was hoping we could have dinner tonight."

"Well," she said doubtfully.

"Something happened today. First serious accident I ever saw on a job. I need somebody to talk to."

"Well, in that case," she said. "All right. I think I can make it."

*

At Parkgate, a few miles outside Southampton on Long Island, the tall elm trees were stately green and the grass was emerald on the long sloping lawns. A warm September breeze blew through the wire netting of the screen fence that surrounded the tennis court.

A black Lincoln Continental slowly circled the driveway, past the winding path that led off under the elm trees and around the oval garden with the statue of Cupid shooting his bow over a fountain. Dappled shadows fell across the car. A green leaf fluttered slowly down to rest on the hood.

"Karl Schiller is here," Vinnie Haleson said.

Alex Johns was seated in the middle of the drawing room, almost in the shadow of the grand piano. Vinnie Haleson was standing at the large double doors that opened on to the terrace with a view of the driveway and the approaching car. Slightly to the rear of Vinnie, Peter Druse stood with his hands clasped behind his back. His daughter Barbara was at a side table nearby, turning the pages of *Yachting* magazine.

Barbara looked up and said, "You're going to ruin one of the most beautiful things anyone has ever made. You'll end up with something that'll probably become known as Druse's folly."

"That's enough," Peter Druse said, quite sharply.

"You can read in history books how a part of the Parthenon was smashed by an explosion of gunpowder. Gunpowder that the Turks had stored there. You business-suited Turks are no better."

When Karl Schiller came in, Alex noted that his shoes were crusted with dirt and his trousers were slightly baggy. He wore a tweed jacket and was carrying an easel.

"I hope you'll pardon the way I'm dressed," he said. "I came directly from the building site. I was looking it over to see if there was any way to make the changes you want."

"Did you arrive at any conclusion?" Vinnie Haleson asked.

A servant came in to set up the easel in the room.

"Let me show you," Karl said, "why it is impossible to do what you suggest."

Using a small pointer to indicate the sketches he mounted on the easel, Karl pointed out the purpose and advantage of the myriad details of the tower as presently designed. There was an intense vitality about Karl Schiller when he was concentrating on his work. He had a singleness of mind that almost became something apart from him, a quality that existed independently in the world.

Alex sensed that it was time for him to interrupt before Karl Schiller made too much of an impression.

"Professor, nobody ever said this wasn't a fine design. But it isn't going to be put into a museum. It has to make sense as an office building. And that means it has to make sense in terms of the cost per square foot."

Peter Druse nodded approval. "We can't afford to go millions of dollars over our budget."

"If you wish to economize, there are better ways." The wood pointer creaked from the pressure of Karl Schiller's fingers as he tried to show other solutions. He was a master of the technique of his art, flexible, resourceful, capable of transforming an idea into something entirely different yet always essentially the same—each new idea forging to the left when blocked on the right, breaking through, impossible to stem, always arriving where he meant it to arrive. He put together the different parts of the building as though they were different instruments in an orchestra, each change accommodating to the other but making distinct and individual contributions to the whole. The most interesting proposal called for steel braces to combat wind forces and thereby reduce the amount of steel needed by almost a third. The braces would be set in each exterior wall, rising in a series of inverted V's and, besides providing lateral support, would be load bearing.

Alex quickly began to make notes. He calculated that the braces would cut the amount of steel needed from twenty thousand tons to fifteen thousand, a weight reduction that would mean a saving of approximately a million and a half dollars. When he had finished his calculation, he tore the pages out of his small red notebook and passed them to Haleson.

"I have some figures, Professor," Vinnie Haleson said. "Unfortunately the saving on the changes you've suggested would not be nearly enough."

"There are other savings I can suggest. Things that will mean only an alteration of the façade. Different, less expensive materials."

"We don't want to alter your design for the tower," Haleson told him. "We like it. All we want is a design for a new building on the plaza."

"The only important thing is that the plaza be kept open."

"I understand how you feel," Haleson said in a tone that held impatience in a smoothness like a fly trapped in amber. "But the important thing to us is a saving of ten million dollars."

Karl Schiller said, "Perhaps . . . if you will let me show you what I mean . . ."

His voice was calm and moved evenly but tendons were straining in his wrist as he made a rapid sketch of a new suggestion.

Peter Druse said suddenly, "I'm sorry, Professor. I'm afraid the question is no longer open for debate."

Perspiration appeared on Karl Schiller's forehead. "You insist on adding this new building?"

Peter nodded. "We are prepared to offer you a handsome fee to design it. A flat sum of one hundred thousand dollars."

Karl Schiller touched the edges of his easel. "I will not design something I know is wrong."

Alex was rolling a slender silver automatic pencil between his fingers. "Don't be stubborn, Professor. This is a great opportunity. If you don't take it a hundred other architects will jump at the chance."

"There would be nothing left," Karl Schiller said, desperately. "Less than nothing. You can't dump a pile of cement into the heart of my design."

"You're making a big mistake. Don't you want credit for building the Zenith Oil tower? Do you want to share it with someone else?"

"We are damned for one thing or another in this world," Karl said slowly. "And I would rather be damned for doing what I believe than for what I don't."

After a moment Haleson said quietly, "I hope you will reconsider that decision."

Schiller started to remove his sketches from the easel. "It would be quite useless."

Peter Druse said, "We'll get someone else to do it, then." He turned to Alex. "But we'll have to move quickly if we want to keep our original schedule."

Barbara jumped to her feet. "What a pack of damn fools you are!"

Peter Druse's expression turned lumpy with resentment.

"Barbara, we're quite capable of handling this matter without you."

"You don't even realize what you're doing. You're throwing away a chance to create something beautiful."

Her whole body seemed arched with anger. "It's criminal! If you just want to juggle things around, why not get a kaleidoscope? That's the most successful of all inventions for imitating creativity."

"That's enough, Barbara. That isn't the problem," Peter said with forced patience. "The problem is money."

"You agreed to spend more for this building. Now you're suddenly against it. What changed your mind?"

"Approximately ten million dollars," Vinnie Haleson observed. "A considerable sum even for Zenith Oil."

"You'll get it back. This building won't go out of style in thirty or forty years."

"We can't gamble on that," Peter Druse said sternly.

"If all you're interested in is saving money, why not throw up a plant like Con Edison did on the East River? Make it out of the world's ugliest cheapest material. Let the whole tower be corrugated asbestos—a public monument to your bad taste!"

Alex drifted out of the target area. He pretended to glance through a copy of *Newsweek* on the side table.

"We're not in the business of manufacturing art, Barbara," Peter said. "This is a simple question of dollars and cents."

"Does everything have to be fed into your ledgers of profit and loss?"

"You don't understand business."

"You don't understand anything else! You'd sell yourself short if you found out you didn't yield a sufficient return on the space you inhabit."

Alex chuckled; he couldn't help it.

Barbara swung round to him. Under her scathing appraisal Alex felt the air around him turn hostile.

Her voice was absolutely stinging. "What a calamity that men like you help decide what kind of a world we live in."

Peter said, "Barbara, I demand that you apologize."

"You demand it?"

"Yes."

Her eyes sparkled with malevolence. She was poised as lightly as a stabile, almost weightless in the carefully balanced tension of her inner springs.

Surprisingly, she answered, "All right, then, I will."

She took a deep breath and crossed the room to Karl Schiller. "I apologize to you for the mistake they're making."

He blinked in surprise.

Peter's slight stutter was more pronounced when he said, "You'd better leave the room, Barbara."

No response indicated that Barbara heard. She continued looking directly at Karl Schiller.

"When you leave, I'll drive you to the train."

"Thank you, Miss Druse. That would be very nice."

Half an hour later Barbara pulled the black Lincoln Continental into the cinder parking lot of the railroad station. She turned to Karl Schiller beside her in the front seat.

"I'm sorry that I ever dragged you into this miserable affair," she said. "I'll keep trying to make them change their minds."

"I appreciate how you stood up to them. You're a woman of strong convictions."

"If I have any news to report, I'll let you know."

"Thank you. But I'm quite sure they'll add their new building."

The train, snorting, entered the Southampton station. She wanted to keep him longer but couldn't think how to do it.

"Well, I must be going," he said finally.

There was so much more she wanted to say. The momentum of a single spoken sentence can often set in motion a whole juggernaut of events. Other women might have known what to do in a situation like this but she could think of nothing that wouldn't be humiliating or foolish.

The train hooted. He would be gone in a moment. He was already opening the car door. Could she let him go without saying anything?

She said pleasantly, "Have a good trip. Perhaps we'll meet again."

"I hope so."

The car door closed. She watched him cross the cinder parking lot to a narrow walk bordering a hedge along the spur of ground beyond the station. She sat still, gripping the wheel hard to fight down a crazy impulse to jump out of the car and run after him. He was leaving, down one of those nameless avenues that lead away forever.

The fumes of too many trains had withered the hedgetops and she could see over their tops to Karl walking near the train. He swung up onto the platform and entered without looking back.

She turned the key in the ignition and put the gear into drive and drove the Lincoln Continental slowly out of the parking lot.

*

Seated in the church, beside Sophy on the long polished wooden bench, Tom MacLaren heard the minister announce the topic of this Sunday's sermon: Mammon or Christ.

As the cadenced exhortation echoed within the nave, Tom's

thoughts turned to a more meaningful topic: love and marriage. He was in love with Sophy. It had gotten to the point that if they even saw a movie with one of her favorite leading men he was stirred by a jealousy he knew to be irrational.

How did she feel about him? He sensed something lacking but he was not sure what. He worried about the flirtatiousness she displayed toward other men. When he waited for her at the offices of Samuel Whitefield Associates, she greeted each new male arrival with the same smile. There was nothing mechanical about Sophy's smile; the men invariably stopped to banter, as though they had received some sort of covert message.

The minister was now pointing out that those who sell their birthright do so for a mess of pottage. In marriage a man sells his freedom but what did that matter if he got Sophy in return?

He had hoped by going to church with her to create the proper mood for the question he intended to ask later. If she said yes, they could be married here, perhaps by the very minister who was now discussing Mammon and the moral order. Sophy was a lapsed Catholic so an Episcopalian wedding would be a good compromise. Tom began to feel conspiratorial in his relationship with the minister —and when the collection plate was passed he put a five-dollar bill into it without Sophy noticing, as though this were a transaction in which agreement would be faciliated by a payment under the table.

As they were leaving the church, Tom stopped to shake hands with the minister who returned a quick damp wring. Then he accompanied Sophy along the brick walk, near the curving iron rail that bordered off the old cemetery.

"I liked the sermon," she said. "I haven't been in a church in a long, long time." Sophy picked a leaf off the hedge bordering the walk.

"I used to go all the time when I was a kid. My mother was very religious."

"I miss it. It makes me feel . . ." her shoulders shivered with a meaning inexpressible in words, ". . . all clean and good. You know what I mean."

"Sure I do." He was glad that she was not against religion; so many girls were these days. "Why did you decide not to be a Catholic any more?"

She ground the leaf into a pulpy tissue with her fingers. "Oh, it was one of those things. My father is, my mother wasn't, and I didn't want to get into trouble with either one of them. Besides I grew up in a neighborhood where there were a lot of kids from other religions. I couldn't believe everyone else was going to Hell. I don't really believe in Hell."

"It's in the Bible."

"I guess so. But I never met anyone I thought ought to go there."

They walked toward Broadway. He remembered something she had told him during one of their first dates.

"Isn't there a place around here where you like egg cream?"

"Can I have one?"

In the candy store, on the stool at the soda fountain, she sat up straight sipping an egg cream through a straw. He saw the delicate bones of her rib cage beneath small breasts.

He watched her suck up the last few drops with a squishing sound through the straw.

"Have you ever thought of settling down, Sophy?"

"Every girl thinks about it."

They strolled out of the candy store together. Tom took her hand in his as they walked along.

"We can get married anytime," he said.

He did not look at her, and when he did she was staring.

"You shouldn't say a thing like that all of a sudden."

"It's the right thing. It's how I feel about you."

"I don't know if I'm ready for that."

Her hand was trembling, aflutter—it reminded him of a butterfly he had caught as a boy and held in his cupped hand very lightly because its gossamer wings were too easily bruised or broken.

His grip tightened. "I love you, Sophy."

"You're nice, Tom. Really, I like you a lot. But marriage."

She knew what marriage meant. She had seen her mother, old before her time, dragged down into ugliness by a heap of unwashed

68

dishes and soiled clothes, never having anything nice to wear, always worried about paying the rent and keeping a roof over her head. She had seen several of her friends, swollen and uncomfortable with pregnancy and then surrounded by all the sour odors of infants with their diapers and regurgitated milk. And bored. Bored all the time. Nobody around by day, and ignored by their man at night.

"It isn't anything to be scared of, Sophy."

"A lot of times it doesn't work out."

"It will for us."

"I don't know, Tom."

Disappointment left him feeling hollowed out.

"You don't have to give an answer right away."

"I'd like to go on seeing you. I enjoy being with you."

"There isn't anybody else you like better, is there?"

"No," she said without hesitation.

There was Walter. Walter could afford to give her nearly everything she wanted, and he was smart and exciting to be with. But Walter was married.

"Well, then," he said.

"Do you really mean it? You really want to?"

"Of course I mean it."

She caught his unprepared glance. All his feeling was right there in his eyes. She knew how he felt without ever having to say it to herself, and if he only wanted to make love to her she would understand. But marriage?

"I'm really very flattered, Tom."

"You won't be making a mistake."

She tried to draw her hand away because she hadn't meant to give the impression that she was starting to accept anything. He was holding her hand too tightly.

"I'll think about it," she said. "I'm not sure I want to be married."

It would be easier to decide if he was more aggressive. It was hard to tell how you really felt about a man unless you went to bed with him. You could find out more in one night than in six months of dating. All he ever tried was a good-night kiss.

Well, maybe things would move along a little faster from now on.

69

She would encourage him a little. It was the least she could do if he was offering marriage.

His palm was close against hers, and tiny drops of perspiration mingled.

*

In the center of the huge site the hotel was a hollow shell containing within its walls a one-story mountain of dirt and debris. Part of the lobby was intact and a few decorations, the last remnant of elegance, were lit by a hanging torch in the dimness. A girder and columns crossing in an arch marked the height of the original masonry.

Harry Berglun, a stocky graying man who was one of the best building superintendents in the business, visited the site to plan the layout of facilities and how the construction work would be organized. The most impressive thing for most people watching the construction of a skyscraper is the speed with which it goes up but that is the result of careful planning of a multitude of details in advance. Harry Berglun began blocking out the first moves. The earth ramp would be graded to take out fill from the excavation and that same ramp would be used to get in materials for the subgrade work. Then work would begin on temporary structures to handle the deliveries.

Harry Berglun picked a spot to put the sidewalk hoists and the apparatus from which all material would flow to the superstructure. Everything had to be lifted into place the minute it arrived on the site. He decided to use the plaza area for delivery to the hoists. The same route would be used for spoil removal. Nothing duplicated. Nothing wasted. The shanties and tool sheds would be located where they would not interfere with the construction and would give plenty of access to the site.

Harry Berglun entered a small gray office shack on the corner of the site to write his report. Sparks from acetylene torches were raining out from the scaffolding on the hotel down onto the shack roof.

On the seventh floor of the hotel where a corner room was being demolished, Mike Collyer found a blue wallet-size folder wedged behind a top shelf in a closet where it had fallen and been overlooked when the occupant moved. Opening it he found a lock of brown hair and an oval picture of a naked baby lying on her stomach and laughing at the camera. In faded blue ink was written *Editha—age eleven months.*

In *The New York Times* that same morning appeared this notice:

> *Blaney, Editha, on September 30th, beloved wife of the late Charles, devoted mother of Andrew, dear sister of the late Lee Sloan and Mrs. Alfred Hackman, loving grandmother of Hilary Blaney. Services Wednesday, October 2nd, at 11:30 A.M. at the Universal Chapel. In lieu of flowers please make a contribution to your favorite charity.*

When the hotel was condemned Editha Blaney was the last tenant to be moved. The relocation agent found her an apartment nearby and she left the hotel on a stretcher, suffering from the cancer that would soon take her life.

*

In the cleared area of the site, making the rounds with Harry Berglun, Alex Johns listened with only part of his attention to the problems of access from the side street and of truck deliveries that would have to make their way through heavy midtown traffic. None of his present anxiety could be blamed on the logistics of the construction. There were people in his office who would spend all their time checking to be sure that everything shown on the plans and all the needed materials were ordered, shipped on time and arrived just when needed because there was no room for storage. Thousands upon thousands of different items would be ordered, scheduled, traced during shipment so their whereabouts were known at every moment. Railway cars would be scheduled to arrive on time to deliver to the trucks. And experts would carefully chart the journey of the trucks through midtown traffic.

But the whole intricate operation, with its infinite possibilities for mischance or delay, could not really get started until there was an approved design. There was none. A shelf in his office was littered with sketches that were venturesome, dazzling, beautifully rendered. All failures.

So Alex listened impatiently as Harry Berglun proved that he had foreseen most of the possible pitfalls.

"Have you heard about the new borings Geyer took?" Alex asked him.

"What about them?"

"They showed some soft pan. We'll probably have to sink pilings."

"I thought we had a mica schist bed."

"That was for the other footings."

Ronald Geyer, the structural engineer, had supervised the new borings. They had gone down once again from the suface through the fill, through the foundations of old buildings, the soft rock with a bearing capacity of only eight tons to the square foot, had reached water level, hit medium rock with a bearing capacity of twenty tons per square foot, but the searching drills never found the forty ton rock they needed. They would have to pour concrete onto the rock to establish the proper kind of footing.

"Sounds like you've got problems," Harry Berglun said.

"You don't know the half."

"There've been too many delays. I haven't even got foundation specs yet."

"I know."

"At this rate you might have one hell of a big empty lot and nothing to build."

"Don't remind me, Harry."

"I can't keep a schedule the way everything is being held up."

"Just the same this job has got to be finished on time. I'm relying on you, Harry."

"I can't do anything without complete specs."

"You'll get them. Then I expect you to make up for the lost time. There's a big bonus in it for you."

"A crash schedule?"

"Right."

"You know the definition of a crash schedule."

"Sure. It's the theory that if you get nine women pregnant you'll get a baby in a month."

Harry Berglun laughed, broke off in a snuffle and wiped his nose.

"If you're really in a jam, I can make one suggestion."

"What?"

"Get Crispin started with the excavation. He can start digging a hole under where we know the main building will be."

"That's too near the hotel. Demolition isn't finished yet."

"It's a way to get back lost time. Maybe a few weeks."

"It could be dangerous."

"I'm keeping an eye on things, Alex."

Alex grumbled. "Okay. Your responsibility."

Harry Berglun was looking off. "I'm going to have to put up barricade gates right quick."

Alex saw a woman in a short belted trenchcoat, standing on the sidewalk with feet apart, carrying a handbag over one shoulder.

"Excuse me, Harry."

Barbara Druse watched his approach with somber antagonism.

"Miss Druse, what are you doing here?"

"I wanted to visit the scene of the crime." She wore no earrings or jewelry, only a little lipstick. "How's the new design coming?"

He picked up a few pebbles. "It isn't." He tossed the pebbles into the lot. "You're entitled to gloat a little."

"What are you going to do?"

"Keep trying. I've been trying for weeks. I've got plenty of waste-baskets."

"Have you thought of asking Karl Schiller again?"

"He said no. I got his message loud and clear."

"He might have had time to reconsider."

"Why would he?"

Her voice had a cutting edge. "Because it's still his tower. He might like a chance to decide what goes up alongside it."

"Doesn't seem likely. Anyhow, I don't know how to talk to that man."

"It won't cost anything to try."

He glanced at her. "He probably wouldn't listen to me. But he's got nothing against you. How about coming along to try to persuade him?"

"All right. If you think I can help."

"You mean it?"

"Why not?"

He had not thought there was a possibility she would accept.

"I have to stop by my office to pick up the designs that have already been tried. Schiller would probably like to see them."

"You mean—go now?"

Holding her arm, he led her past the sidewalk barricade. "Have you got something else to do?"

"No."

"Then the sooner we find out the better." Before she could protest, he stepped into the street to hail a taxi . . .

He settled back comfortably into the seat beside her.

"You know, I might change my opinion about women."

"In what way?"

"You're trying to help. The women I've known only wanted to get me by the throat—and then put a dog collar around it."

"You met the wrong kind."

"I've met all kinds. I even married one."

"Was that a mistake?"

"Laura? She squeezed me like a lemon and when there was no more juice she threw me out. But she's no better or worse."

"The universal fairy tale, Mr. Johns, is the one that deals with the wicked Them and the good Me."

"You've got a man's way of looking at things."

"That's very sweet of you."

Alex chuckled. "Sometimes it happens that people don't hit it off right away—a deep freeze. Then they get to know each other and it's like breaking ice in a river. Right?"

74

She smiled. "Do you know what they call the breaking of ice in a river?"

"What?"

"A debacle."

*

Karl Schiller lived in tiny unpretentious quarters in an apartment house across the street from the Institute where he taught Advanced Architectural Design. There was a cluttered kitchen, a small bedroom and a cramped living room with a drafting table near the window.

Karl met them at the door. He wore a dark brown workshirt open at the collar and unpressed nondescript gray trousers. His face, frowning slightly, had a flat almost monumental cast and his eyes, piercing blue below the impossibly high forehead, were narrowed and squinting behind black-rimmed eyeglasses. He had been working and obviously was not particularly pleased to see them.

He said, "I have only a little Alsatian wine to offer you."

Alex said, "Professor, I didn't come to pay a social call. I'll level with you." He chose a cigar from a silver case and offered the case to Schiller. "I can use your cooperation."

Schiller refused the cigar. "In what way?"

Barbara indicated the portfolio by the overstuffed chair. "He can't find anyone to design a building that belongs alongside your tower."

"I see." Schiller rubbed his hand over the rough coarse material of his workshirt.

"I'd like you to look over what's been done and give me your opinion, Professor," Alex said.

Karl Schiller hesitated. "I'm not sure if I want to."

"Please," Barbara said quickly. "As a favor to me."

Karl took the portfolio and went to his drafting table to switch on the fluorescent light. He bent over the table and examined what other men had envisioned.

At last he turned off the fluorescent light.

"Well," Alex said. "What do you think?"

"They are all pleasing designs." Karl Schiller returned the sketches one by one to the portfolio and dutifully scanned each of them again.

"There's something wrong with them," Alex said. "What is it?"

"They all use the same approach. In each case there is a low building joined to a tower."

"What else could they do?"

"You can't get another building on the site without radically changing the original design. That design *must* be changed."

Alex felt a twinge of annoyance. "How?"

Karl Schiller did not quite smile, but his rather wide mouth curled deeper at one corner. "All I can say is that these sketches do not exhaust all the possibilities."

Barbara said quietly, "The only way you can be sure of that, Professor, is if you've thought of how to do it."

"I've been thinking about it a good deal."

Alex exchanged a glance with Barbara without their eyes actually meeting.

"And have you come up with anything?" Alex asked.

Schiller answered slowly, "I have an idea, yes."

Barbara could not keep excitement from her voice. "Would you show us?"

Alex tried to school his face to reveal nothing. Schiller moved slowly to the drafting board and fiddled with his pencil, turning it thoughtfully in his fingers. Barbara moved close beside him and Alex moved to a position slightly behind him.

At last Schiller sat down and his pencil began to flash across paper like a teletypist taking down code, only he was translating thought into picture symbols. He accompanied his rapid drawing with a discontinuous halting summary of what he was doing. "We begin again with the *idée fixe* . . . nothing must intrude on the plaza . . . ground taken away by the building must be given back with trees and foliage, sun and air. This is the only essential. . . ." As he spoke, his pencil was drawing a broad outline. He had been talking slowly, weighing

76

the value of words as though they were some kind of building material, but now, seized upon by his subject, he began to speak more rapidly. "Therefore go for the answer to the tower itself. Make it meet new conditions . . . the problem of how to include another building and at the same time repress the individuality of the new building, integrate it . . . Difficult, but there has to be an answer."

The tower rose again in the familiar sixty-story block with its huge plaza laid out with trees and shrubs. Then the pencil halted, holding an instant above the paper before it moved decisively, not to the front of the tower, but to the rear. He drew in staircases, lifts, and sanitary accommodations within a utility core of a very compact design that would service not only the tower but an attached lower block that spread to the full width of the site. This additional building was dissociated while remaining a part of the design and a continuing line led the eye upward to the tower. Space flowed into the ground floor and eddied around the thick lift shafts and into the bilateral symmetry of the new building, a symmetry which repeated the design of the huge plaza in the forecourt. A new over-all effect was given to the entire design, a skyscraper conceived so that it maintained distinctly different front, back, and sides. No matter from which side the building was viewed, the emphasis fell quite clearly one way. Yet now there were two buildings where there had been only one. A dark tower with attached spine held in a unifying net of vertically rising mullions.

When Schiller's pencil stopped, his hand was trembling slightly.

Barbara looked at him in a curious way. "Yes, I can see that you have been thinking about the problem."

"I'm afraid I have an apology to make."

"An apology?"

"I was thinking too much of what I wished to see erected on that site. That's why, when I was told the requirements had changed, I refused to cooperate."

"You wanted a chance to do something really worthwhile, to set a standard. What's wrong with that?"

Karl Schiller shook his head and his blue eyes were sober, serious. "It is the highest test of art to create under the strictest conditions."

77

Alex thought there were times when Karl Schiller sounded too much like a college professor.

"What are you going to do with this now?" he asked, indicating the sketch on the drafting table.

"It will have to be worked out in perspectives, with details, plans, elevations."

"Would you be willing to?" Barbara asked.

"That depends."

"What on?"

Schiller's gaunt face turned to Alex. "For one thing, whether you want me to do it."

"Well," Barbara said, "what do you think, Mr. Johns?"

As the sketch had neared completion, revealing the curious delicacy and power that was Schiller's trademark, Alex had recalled with bitter regret his weeks of futile searching.

"I don't know why he didn't do this in the first place." He caught Barbara's reproving glance and added, "It's exactly what we've been looking for, Professor."

*

On October 11th a carefully finished copy of Karl Schiller's original sketch, together with plans and elevations and accurate and neat perspectives arrived by special messenger at Alexander Johns Enterprises. At the lower right hand corner of the sketch Karl Schiller had signed his name.

*

On the mezzanine balcony a section split off with a wrenching grumble and toppled far down into the hollow interior of the hotel. Long parallel strips of netting hung down to catch the falling debris. A welder on the fifth floor of the hotel got up and walked across a connecting girder to the joint. He bent, a slender man with a huge metal head, and sparks streamed outward from his torch until with a groaning wrenching noise a beam parted and clattered down within the hollowed-out shell of the structure.

"Something's got to be done," Tom MacLaren said. "That rain the past week made the ground too soft."

Not far from where he stood a steamshovel was widening and deepening the excavation.

"I already got a complaint," Harry Berglun said, "from the business manager of the wrecker's union. I told him I'll get the structural engineer in to take readings."

"You don't need readings. That steamshovel is working too close to the hotel foundation. It's causing vibrations you can feel when you're on top."

"What do you want me to do? We underpinned it."

In accordance with the Buildings Department's requirements, they had cut four-foot wide sections beneath the hotel, gone down to the hard pan and poured concrete straight up to a point only three inches below the foundation where they drove in steel wedges to help support it.

"One of my men already refused to work on top," Tom persisted. "You've got to hold off doing any more excavating until the hotel is down."

"One of your men gets scared so I have to delay the whole job. Is that it?"

Tom MacLaren measured the man standing opposite him. Harry Berglun seemed to solidly, permanently occupy the space he was standing in.

"Would you rather somebody got hurt?" Tom asked.

"If I want to complain, I got complaints too. Some of your burners have been pretty careless with their watering down. They put water on lime and mortar and it flew all over. Stuck on some parked cars and hardened. Now we got to pay for their new paint jobs."

"Don't put me off. I'm discussing a dangerous situation."

"Who's the one refused to work? One of them colored boys?"

"One of my best workers."

"See? I knew it. I remember once on a job a lumber pile shifted

79

and one of them colored got trapped. All his pals ran. I had to get down in there myself to get the poor bastard out."

"I'm not going to argue. You've had experience. You know there's risk in doing demolition and excavating at the same time. And with the weather we've had . . ."

"If you want to, file a complaint," Harry Berglun said.

"I will."

"You'll look like a damn fool when those engineers get here tomorrow and say there never was any danger."

"Until they come, at least move the powershovel."

"Move it where?"

"Somewhere it won't cause so much vibration in the foundation. You're excavating too close to the footings."

"I can't go shoving equipment all over the place. Not until those engineers get here tomorrow and tell us where we're at."

"Who the hell ordered excavation and demolition at the same time? That's making this whole dangerous situation."

"It's the way this job is scheduled."

"Didn't you schedule it?"

"I get my orders."

"Who from?"

"Alex Johns. Not that it's any of your business."

For a moment Tom MacLaren was silenced.

"All I know," he said, shaking his head, "is that someone's got to take the responsibility."

"Do your job and I'll do mine." Harry Berglun suddenly cupped his hands to his mouth and shouted. "Hey, you! You with all that hair on your head. How stupid can you get?"

Harry Berglun hurried off without allowing Tom the extra moment or two he needed to continue their quarrel. Harry was twenty feet away, half-running, and it was too late to go after him now.

Al Webb was standing near an orange peel bucket that was clawing up debris from the ground. Al kept giving hand signals to the operator until the bucket was in position over a dump truck and unloaded with a rattling roar.

Tom strolled slowly over to him. Al was the first man who had refused to work near the hotel where the excavator's powershovel was operating.

Al took off his helmet and wiped his balding head. "What'd he say?"

"He's bringing structural engineers in tomorrow to check on the vibrations. If their gauges show there's too much, they'll stop using the shovel."

"I know those guys. They'll prove the buses give more vibration from the street." A small wick of fuzzy hair grew in the center of Al's head damp with his sweat. "They've got gauges can prove anything."

"They're pretty accurate, Al."

"I don't care. I'm not going to work anywhere near that damned shovel."

"Why don't you just work today?" Tom suggested. "Tomorrow we'll get it all straightened out."

"Anybody's crazy who works near that shovel. I tell you, it's disturbing the soil under that foundation."

"All I'm asking is that you don't talk up trouble. Work anywhere you like today."

Al Webb's dark face puckered. "Okay. Those other jerks want to kill themselves, it's none of my business."

"Leave it at that, then."

Tom moved from one working gang to another, checking the progress of the wrecking, ironing out trouble spots. Mike Collyer asked him about something but a second later he could not have said what the question or his answer was. He moved along a scaffolding that resounded with clanking crowbars and picks, and when his feet touched ground again he was aware, with surprise, that he had been aloft. His shoulders sloped under the weight of a personal anxiety that had nothing to do with the powershovel thundering away in the pit near the hotel's foundation nor with the rain that had made the ground dangerous and soft.

At lunchtime he sat with Mike Collyer and munched sandwiches around an improvised fire. They watched a curious bystander trying to move past the barricade for a better view of the excavation.

"Damn fool could be hurt," Mike said. "Always something coming down around here."

"Yeah. Those warning signs are for a reason."

Harry Berglun climbed the slope to order the man away. They could hear Harry's harsh voice lecturing above the air compression trucks thrumming and pounding on the street.

"How're you doin' with that girl of yours?" Mike Collyer asked.

Tom tossed his sandwich wrapping into the fire where it curled, browned, darkened into flame and vanished instantly.

"I asked her to marry me."

"No kidding!"

"I'm not sure if she'll say yes."

He imagined her saying yes, and everything around him turned suddenly bright. But he also thought of how it would be if she said no. He saw her too vividly, beautiful, pixyish face, bones carefully molded under skin like porcelain, the small perfect mouth saying no.

"Why shouldn't she?" Mike asked.

"She's different, Mike. She isn't like other girls—just looking to get married."

"All girls are looking to get married," Mike said.

The lunch whistle blew, ending the half-hour break. A light rain had begun to fall again. Tom took out a handkerchief and blew his nose. The linen turned sodden even before he returned the handkerchief to his pocket.

"This is no weather to work in," Mike said.

"We'll probably quit soon."

*

The roar of the powershovel.

Al Webb guided the orange peel bucket a hundred yards away. Clutching its heavy load, the bucket veered to a dump truck, found a position above the empty bin and on signal released metal fingers to drop a new load thudding to the bottom.

A glassed-up telephone booth beneath the sidewalk bridge. A woman stopped to make a telephone call. She dialed a number, stopped, started again, shook her head at the noise around her and left the booth with her number uncalled.

POST NO BILLS UNDER PENALTY OF LAW.

*

The steamshovel bit heavily into soggy earth. Tom MacLaren felt the earth shiver.

Marty Garfinkel called down, "Jesus, Tom, will you tell that guy to back up? What's he trying to do, kill somebody?"

*

Half an hour to quitting time. Up flashed an acetylene torch. Blue haze rose. Steady drilling, drilling gouging hunks of stone. Two men in yellow hard hats. What projectile can pierce a metal hat, quarter inch thick plus the inch of bone where the skull is implanted above the delicate brain?

In the sunlight, in the blue haze, the men's faces had an almost spiritual air.

*

The ground lurched slightly. A sharp tiny crack, thin as a pistol shot in frosty air.

The welder on the fifth floor of the hotel stopped, with his helmet yawning above him like an open mouth waiting to swallow his head.

Another crack, louder, than another.

"My God," Tom whispered.

The welder dropped his iron or something pulled it from his hand. He reached for a supporting girder, missed it, sprawled flat.

Tom began to run.

Harry Berglun running ahead of him, cried: "No! No!"

The hotel began to come apart. Steel girders snapped like bones being crunched. A section of steel beam flew high.

Harry Berglun stopped, stricken, as a wall of the building seemed to be lifting but was really starting to flow outward in a slow motion silent torrent of splintering concrete and steel.

A cloud of dense light formed around the cab of the powershovel digging near the foundation. The operator within the cab lifted his arms as pulverized debris rained and bellowed over him. The roof of the cab sank beneath a cloud that rolled over it with a thunderclap.

There came a heavy boom like the noise of blasting. The hotel sliced in half and the right side poured onto the ground in a sullen gray mass of twisted steel and broken stone. The left side appeared to form a curve, to hover like a breaking wave, while crackling mounted in a prolonged cannonading.

An immense pile of rubble began forming where a building had been a few moments before. A deafening shattering overwhelming crash reverberated. In the center, hanging between floors of girders, one flat wide plain surface of brick survived above a jumble wreckage of girders, planks, stones, jagged knife edges of projecting walls, mangled carcasses and broken helmets and heads.

A car was demolished in the rubble, and a shattered booth with a black telephone dangling inside it was incoherently muttering buzz buzz buzz. In wounds and the crumple death, with bare bloodied heads men looked out as from a transparent bubble shielding them in a new dimension.

*

Sophy was working at the switchboard in her cubicle when Gloria hurried in to her.

"Didn't you tell me your boyfriend works on that new building going up on the Avenue of Americas?"

There was an air of suppressed excitement about Gloria that caused Sophy to ignore a persistent flashing light on the board in front of her.

"He's in charge of the wrecking," she said.

"Well, you mustn't get excited, honey. But I think there's been an accident. I just heard it over the radio."

Gloria covered the switchboard while Sophy went in to listen for further news flashes. In a few minutes she heard a bulletin, this time mentioning the exact location of the accident. The announcer said a building had caved in, and it was feared that many people were buried in the debris.

Sophy's hand flew to her throat. It isn't possible. Nothing could have happened to Tom. She flung on her coat and ran out to the corridor. Impatiently pushing the elevator button, it seemed an endless wait.

She ran into the street to signal a cab. At the curb a wave of dizziness caught her. Oh, God, why does it have to be him? Her heart was beating at a rate it did not seem she could survive. She had never known such alarm.

Rain drizzled down and her shoes were soaked. I never realized, she thought, how much he meant to me.

If she could see him, alive and well, if he would come to see her tonight—bulking so large that he filled the doorway—she would rush into his arms.

Without realizing it, she had begun to think of Tom in permanent terms. When she thought of a future, Tom was somewhere near. Now it might be too late.

A cab swung sharply over in response to her signal. She pulled at the door.

"Just a minute, miss," the driver said with patient rebuke, and reached over and pulled up the locked door button.

She got in and stammered out her destination.

"We can't go down there. Police have got the area blocked off. There's been a big accident."

"I know. That's why I have to go. Someone I know . . ." and she began to cry.

The driver looked back, a rather good-looking man with thinning hair and kindly brown eyes.

"Okay, miss. Okay."

On the way she kept urging the driver on through the streets filled with traffic. Why couldn't he hurry? She knew Tom was trapped inside that building and alive while she was trying to get to him. If she could get there, she would somehow manage to save him. He would open his eyes and see her there and realize how much she cared. She kept wiping away unavailing tears. There was dryness in her mouth.

Green and white roofed police cars were parked to block off access to the site. Policemen in black slicker raincoats were patrolling. One signaled the cab to a halt two blocks away. While the driver leaned out the window to explain, Sophy flung a dollar bill down on the seat and got out.

If he is alive, let him hear me. If you are alive, Tom, listen. Anything—anything you want.

Stay with me. I need you.

You can't be cruel enough to die.

She began to run.

*

Two men from the police emergency crew scrambled up the side of the mound carrying crowbars. From a small hole in the mound came a scared voice.

"Oh, Lord. Oh, Lord."

A policeman lay down on the ground. "Don't worry. We'll get you out."

Other men scrambled quickly up the mound and began to work with crowbars, axes, sledgehammers, and gasoline-operated buzz-saws. They threw bits of concrete, wood, brick, anything back over their heads to the bottom of the mound.

Finally they pulled out a workman—John Galgano, an air compressor operator. John was quickly carried to an ambulance parked on the site and the ambulance raced off with its siren screaming.

A pigeon circled the spot where the powershovel was half buried in broken concrete, lathing, steel sections, and shredded planking. The operator lay head downward out of the cab, one arm beneath him and the other dangling. Rubble tumbled down the sides of the newly dug excavation.

The pigeon fluttered down slowly to settle down on the caterpillar tread that had been torn away. It began to peck at the ruin of bent pipe and shattered brick.

"Over here!"

A man lowered himself into the excavation, carrying blankets. Two other men gently tried to extricate the operator from the cab of his steamshovel. A priest came to bend over him. Then they put him on a stretcher with a blanket over him, only his feet protruding beneath the blanket . . .

Nearby, Tom MacLaren watched through grit-packed eyes as Harry Berglun was lifted into a litter. Tom kept one foot to brace himself down the slope, his shoe sinking into the ground. His face had deep lines of fatigue.

"I want to go back," Harry said. He was crying. "It's my job. I'm the super."

"It's all right, buddy. Relax," a policeman told him. "If they're in there we'll get 'em out."

"How do you feel, Harry?" Tom asked.

"How the hell do you think I feel? My leg's busted."

He was carried off.

"How do you like that?" the policeman asked. "Worried about his leg when most of his scalp's tore off."

On the far side a fragment of hotel wall remained standing. A yellow tractor moved into position to support it with its scoop.

"Watch out," Tom yelled. "That wall could go any minute!"

Brick by brick, scraped and bruised hands were clawing a tunnel into the heart of the debris that seemed to flow out everywhere like black water suddenly frozen into ice.

A policeman, equipped with earphones and a microphone, was gingerly poking into holes in the high mound near the wall. Suddenly he looked up and waved his arms.

"Medic! This way!"

Tom joined a group of rescuers at the top of the pile. A white-coated intern watched as they opened a small hole to reveal a sort of natural cave supported by the overhang of a twisted steel girder.

The intern leaned into the hole to administer a hypodermic injection.

"Oh, Jesus, Mary, and Joseph!"

Tom knew the voice. Al Webb's.

"Is he going to be all right?" he asked the intern emerging from the hole.

"He's pinned. Got to take his arm off."

Tom munched on his lower lip, eyes staring . . .

Deeper into the mound the tunnel pierced. Chunks of rotten lumber and bloodstained concrete came out and moved along a human chain.

Marty Garfinkel was lying on a stretcher near the ambulance, and blood plasma was flowing into his arm.

"I felt the whole floor tilt up," he told Tom, "and then it started to slide and I knew I was falling. This is it, I said. This has got to be it. Oh, God, I said, somebody come and help me. I was covered in about five feet. It was awful quiet in there. I hollered and hollered and nobody seemed to hear. I'm going to live, ain't I?"

"Sure," Tom said.

An intern looked up, met Tom's eyes and looked sharply away to where the precious plasma was flowing . . .

*

On the sidewalks surrounding the site a crowd had gathered. When Sophy arrived she couldn't see over the heads of men in dark overcoats, women in short coats wearing miniskirts, teen-age boys in stormcoats and heavy madras shirts, messengers still carrying their bundles. They stood behind the gray sawhorses that the police had put up as additional barricades.

Over all brooded the immense silence of a crowd waiting, a silence deeper than ordinary silence because imposed on so many. From the sidewalks they stared at the mountain of sharded wood and broken steel where men were entombed. A plank reached up out of the debris like an outstretched arm.

"What a nice bunch of guys. Five or six of them bought frankfurters at my stand just a little while before. Now, some of them are hurt, maybe dead. I hope they get them all out."

"How many are in there?"

"Are they dead?"

Sophy found a policeman and tugged at his black oilskin arm.

"Officer, I know somebody who works here. Can I get in to see if he's all right?"

"Sorry, miss."

"Please."

"Sorry."

Ticking in her mind was the possibility of a sudden explosive darting run past the policeman. He was standing in front of her, blocking the way, but she had to find Tom. As she stood, her small frame resilient with urgency, she looked past the policeman to the huge mound of earth and brick and stone and plaster. What she saw there was such an ecstatic surprise that at first she could do nothing but nod stupidly.

"Tom!"

The cry strangled in her throat. The policeman heard it and turned involuntarily. In that instance Sophy was past him.

"Hey!"

He took a step to intercept her, saw then that she was already past the barricade and scrambling down the slope. He turned back to hold the crowd in place.

"*Tom!*"

Scrambling up the far side of the slope now, her dress smudged, shoes filling with the loose packed earth. Tom was standing at the height of the mound helping an intern put a beige wool blanket over a dimly seen figure that seemed to be all caked with dust except for a face that was a blur of red. He heard her call and turned and in an instant was running down to her. She fell on all fours, her hands sinking into the ground. She was laughing and crying at the same time . . .

A red-faced man went up angrily to the policeman at the barricade.

"I'd like to talk to somebody about my car."

"Your what?"

"My car. The whole building fell on top of it."

"What do you want me to do?"

"There it is—over there." He pointed to a caved-in Oldsmobile Toronado, with a windshield crazily splintered by a million fractures, and the hood dented as though a giant fist had struck a blow at it.

"Who's going to pay for the damage?"

"How would I know?"

"I mean, can I collect insurance on a thing like that?"

89

"I guess so. You better ask somebody else."

The red-faced man looked at his car, which seemed with its badly caved-in hood to be in a kneeling posture at the curb. He wiped the back of his neck with a handkerchief.

"The thing is, I was parked illegally."

In a jammed luncheonette nearby, people sat on stools and munched hamburgers as they watched the ambulances parked and waiting. Three cars were now parked directly on the site—two police sedans and a Volkswagen with a green four leaf clover painted on the door.

FRAMEWORK

WATCHING rain cascade down the windows of his office, Alex Johns felt like someone Noah had abandoned in a world where hope was being washed away. On a day as miserable as this a short week ago five men had been killed and many others injured in the collapse of the building on the Zenith Oil site.

He tossed a newspaper angrily onto his desk just as Louise entered the office.

"When are they going to forget it?" he demanded.

"I don't know," Louise said sadly. "I passed by on my way to work this morning. There were still crowds all around the place."

"Nobody feels sicker about those men than I do. But it was an accident! Accidents happen. It isn't a capital crime. The newspapers make it look like I'm the man who invented Hitler."

"Did you read what happened today? The governor appointed a committee."

"I read it. What good will that do?"

Louise picked up the newspaper. "It says the committee will recommend legislative remedies to prevent future calamities."

"It's all a lot of nonsense." Alex was becoming angrier. "How can you pass a law against an accident? If you could figure out what was going to happen you'd stop it from happening and nobody would need a law. Right?"

"It's just . . . you know . . . when people are killed . . ."

"Look at the obituary columns. People are getting killed every day in the craziest ways. Does anybody care? People are dying in bushels up in Harlem. Do you even read about it? Something like this happens and what do you get? A whole uproar!"

Louise folded the newspaper and put it with the mail to be removed from the outbasket. "I guess you're right, Mr. Johns."

She had the sort of mind utterly without juice of its own—it could be plugged in and plugged out.

"I'm thinking of suing some newspapers. They're just looking for a scapegoat and politicians go along because they're hungry to see their names in print."

Louise said, "Why don't you sue?"

"Because you never bite the hand of a man who can cut your throat. Get them for publishing one bad story and they'll come back at you with a hundred worse ones."

What worried Alex was that irresponsible reporting kept the public furor alive until logic was lost in the general excitement. On the day of the accident Alex had felt as though he were one of the victims: he had stayed at the site until late in the evening when the last man was removed from the rubble. The next morning, when he saw news items hinting at the possibility of culpable negligence, he moved quickly to get depositions from Harry Berglun in the hospital, from Ivor Rand, from Ronald Geyer, the structural engineer, and from the company that had taken core samples of the foundation bed. If an investigation tried to blame him he was going to be prepared. But he couldn't do anything about the effects in the financial community with all its myriad connecting lines into the dollars and cents meaning of tragedy. His usual financial sources were treating him like a leper in prison stripes.

Louise placed a letter on top of his desk.

"This came special delivery."

He opened the letter and read it. One more rejection, this time for a million dollar loan at fourteen percent interest. He wadded the letter in his hand, sighed heavily, then slowly uncrumpled the letter, laid it on his desk and ironed it with the side of his hand.

"I swear to God, Louise, sometimes I don't know what to do."

"Mr. MacLaren is here to see you."

"MacLaren? Oh, the one who gave that story to the newspapers. Wait a minute, then send him in."

He took a news clipping out of his desk drawer and read it over. Tom MacLaren, in charge of the wrecking gang, was quoted as saying that he didn't believe that the building collapse had been an accident. He told a reporter that the tragedy had been caused by a speedup in which demolition and excavation work were allowed to proceed side by side, and his repeated warnings about a dangerous powershovel had been ignored.

Alex Johns put the clipping back in the drawer and slammed it. A young giant in a checkered workcoat, neatly pressed slacks and brown-laced boots entered.

"Mr. MacLaren?"

"Yes."

Alex stood up and shook hands. The young man had a powerful grip.

"I've been wanting to talk to you," Alex said. "Have a seat."

Tom MacLaren sat down near a corner of the desk. A flash reflection in the polished mahogany showed his expression. Glacial.

"Have a cigar?"

"No, thanks."

Alex was aglow with amiability, positively rippling with movements of good will. "Don't you smoke?"

"No."

"All those statistics getting through to you, eh?"

Alex chose a cigar, puffed the tip cherry red and exhaled bluely. Through the concealing haze he measured the big man opposite, who sat with a slight hunch, his stomach slightly folded over. Tom Mac-Laren would go to fat in a few years.

"Why did you want to see me, Mr. Johns?"

"I read a newspaper story that bothered me. Nobody has to tell me how newspapers can get things screwed up. But I thought we ought to have a talk."

"What was the story?"

"Just a few lines. Something you said about that accident over at the site of the new Zenith Oil building."

"Accident?"

Appraising Tom MacLaren through smoke, Alex saw an unbroken façade of hostility.

"Don't you think it was?"

"It wasn't."

"You can't mean it was deliberate!"

"I warned your man."

95

"Harry Berglun?"

Tom MacLaren nodded. "I told him what would happen if that powershovel kept working so close."

"What did he say?"

"He said he couldn't move the shovel because he was under orders from you."

Alex was startled. "From me? What kind of orders?"

"Demolition and excavation were to go on at the same time because you had to meet a crash schedule."

"I never gave orders like that."

"That's what Harry Berglun told me."

Alex pondered this. "Exactly when did he tell you?"

"It was just before the building collapsed. I had a complaint from one of my men, who said the vibrations from the shovel were shaking the building . . ."

With eyes half-closed, listening, Alex felt his uneasiness growing. He had clung to a hope that the newspaper account was distorted, but it was becoming clear that this young man felt that the speedup had been the sole cause of the accident. His story would be repeated to the governor's investigating committee.

In all truth, of course, Harry Berglun's recklessness existed only in hindsight. Harry was a cautious man with a good safety record and could have made exactly the same decision about that powershovel a hundred times, a thousand, and nothing would have happened. There were contributing factors, the terrible intrusion of the unpredictable.

When Tom MacLaren finished with his account, Alex sighed, removed his cigar and placed it on the copper ashtray with the flowing scroll *AJ*. "I want to personally assure you that I never gave orders of any kind for Harry Berglun to take unnecessary risks. I hope you believe that."

"I don't know what to believe."

Alex felt that he needed to establish confidence.

"Let me tell you this," he went on, with deliberate assumption of superiority, "I've never in the years I've been in business given my word about anything and not meant it. I've shook hands on deals and gone through with them even when it meant losing hundreds of thousands of dollars because I believe a handshake between people is as good as a contract. In the final analysis everything begins with faith in the human factor—that's what counts in business. And the bigger the business the more it counts. You know what I mean?"

Alex sensed a subtle shift in attitude emanating from Tom MacLaren like a physical odor.

"Let's say I take your word for it, Mr. Johns, that you didn't personally give the orders. But that's still how the accident happened."

Alex opened a drawer of his desk to remove a typewritten sheet which he placed on the desk. "I have here Harry Berglun's statement saying the collapse was caused by treacherous subsurface conditions."

"Naturally, he'd say that."

"I want the truth, no matter where it leads and no matter who it hurts. I'll see the blame is put where it belongs, even if it means putting my own neck on the block. This is where the buck stops. I can't evade the responsibility and I won't try to—if it's mine. But there are some problems you don't know about, Tom. Things that back up Harry Berglun."

"What things?"

Reassured by the fact that the young man was at least asking questions, Alex warmed to his task of explanation.

"When we first tested the subsurface—before we even started to do any excavating—we found patches of soft rock in the foundation bed. The Buildings Department made us pour concrete to improve the footing. I can show you the records."

"Mr. Johns, I saw what caused the accident. I was there."

"Doesn't it stand to reason that if there were patches of soft rock in some places, there might have been one under the building that collapsed?"

In this intricate game, in which so much of another man's character had to be deciphered, Alex saw that he had made the right move. MacLaren, basing his convictions on what he had observed, could not be shaken by a frontal assault but could be outflanked.

"I don't know anything about that," MacLaren said dubiously.

"One other thing. We were pumping out water. You know that overpumping can lower the water level."

"Sure it can."

"And lowering the water level could easily undermine a foundation."

"Anything *could* have happened."

"That's all I'm saying. I'm pointing out some other possibilities."

"I suppose the people investigating for the city and the insurance company will figure in all those things, Mr. Johns."

"Of course they will."

"All I can do is tell them what I think."

Over many years of dealing with people Alex had learned to weigh the delicate choice of words that, even with inarticulate men, reveals the trend of their thinking. Tom MacLaren was not as sure of himself now as he tried to sound.

"I just ask you to remember that accidents can happen even when you've tried to take all precautions. And, believe me, we did. We put in more temporary underpinning than the Buildings Department asked for. Nobody wanted this tragedy to happen."

"I didn't say anybody did."

Alex put his cigar down in the copper ashtray. The long corona of white glowed dully. "This hearing can lead to a charge of culpable negligence. That's unfair. Until this happened Harry Berglun had a fine safety record. Suppose he made a mistake. Was it the kind that rates a prison term? Because that's what a conviction on culpable negligence can lead to."

"I have nothing to do with that."

"I'm not defending him. But I can't help feeling a little sorry for him. Did you know the poor bastard turned out to have a fractured skull? For a while it didn't look as if he was going to make it. It was all he could do to even sign that statement."

Tom MacLaren's face softened. A match flame was glowing behind the ice.

"I'm sorry to hear that."

"And no matter what happens at the hearing, Harry is through in this business. He'll never work another day. Of course," Alex added, "we ought to save our pity for the men who died in that accident and for their families. That's why I've set up a trust fund. Enough to send their kids through college. That's in addition to the pension and the insurance they'll get from the union."

"Very generous of you, Mr. Johns."

Alex had not thought of his gesture as generous when he made it. It had been a genuinely impulsive act motivated by shock and empathy for the victims of the tragedy. But he saw no reason not to use it for his benefit now.

"It was the least I could do. I only wish I could have done more." Alex sat back and steepled his fingers.

"Is that all you wanted to talk to me about, Mr. Johns?"

"Not quite. Where are you working now, Tom?"

"I'm still with Ivor Rand. I'm at the Broad Street site. Clearing space for the new Exchange Building."

"Ivor's an old friend—and a lucky bastard. He's the only one who gained by that accident."

"I don't see how. He lost some good men."

"That's true—but he also got the demolition over with a hell of a lot sooner. That's the wrecking business for you. Everything works ass end up. You don't want to spend the rest of your life in a business like that, Tom."

"Mr. Rand says I've got a good future."

"Not in wrecking. That's the wrong end of the business. You're a young man and you've got to look for the best way to get ahead."

Something clicked liked a shutter in the room. "Have you got any ideas, Mr. Johns?"

Alex thought: no completely honest man ever negotiates a principle; that's why the work of the world is done by slightly dishonest men.

"I might have."

Tom said politely, "I'd be interested to hear them."

"Well, do you think you could handle a building super's job?"

"I might be able to."

"It isn't easy. It takes a real man to handle everything connected with a big new building under construction. You've got to be able to give orders and make them stick."

"That part's okay."

"There are no excuses in a job like that. If you don't measure up, out you go. That's the way it is. Does that worry you?"

"Nobody's offered me the job."

Alex grinned. "How'd you like to work for me? I need a replacement for Harry Berglun."

Tom stared at him without surprise. "How much does it pay?"

"You start at three hundred. And there's a big bonus if you bring the building in on schedule. After that, who knows? The sky's the limit."

Sunlight suddenly came through the windows and coated everything in the room with golden shellac.

"I like the money," he said. "But I don't have a lot of experience. All I know is the wrecker's trade."

Alex leaned back in his chair and stared thoughtfully beyond Tom. "I'd be willing to overlook inexperience to get the right man. And there's somebody I could put there with you—as your assistant—who knows all the ropes."

"Who's that?"

"His name is Otis—Jim Otis. A college graduate and a qualified engineer. I could give him the job—but there's one thing against him."

"What's that?"

"He's colored. I've got enough trouble with the unions without trying to put a Negro super in on the building. Those mechanics won't take orders from a black man."

"I guess some would resent it," Tom said.

"You'll learn everything you need to know working with Otis. I can tell you're a bright man. Where are you from, Tom?"

"Virginia."

"Fine state. I'm from New Hampshire myself. You might have a little trouble with Otis at first but you can figure out how to put him in his place."

"I'm not worried about that."

"Good. I like a man with confidence. I like your style, Tom. Now, this doesn't have anything to do with what you say to the commission about that accident."

The soft cheeks that rounded Tom MacLaren's face flushed vivid.

"I didn't think it would, Mr. Johns."

"Call me Alex. You go ahead and tell the commission whatever you want. There won't be any pressure from me."

Tom MacLaren nodded soberly.

"How about letting me know the end of the week?" Alex asked. "There's nobody in charge now at the Zenith Oil site."

"Okay. I'll do that . . . Alex."

Intuitively probing for secret springs Alex had found what he was looking for.

He stood up to shake hands with Tom MacLaren. A handshake between two people who understand each other is as good as a contract.

*

On October 23rd, when the site had been cleared to curb level, and there was no longer any sign of the mound in which five men had been prematurely buried, a group of people gathered at nine o'clock in the morning to witness ground being broken for the foundation of the new Zenith Oil building.

Present at the ceremony were Peter Druse, Vincent Haleson, three members of the Board of Directors, Alexander Johns, Karl Schiller, and Ronald Geyer, the structural engineer. Among the women present were Mrs. Peter Druse, her daughters Barbara and Ann (Mrs. Vincent Haleson), two wives of the three members of the Board (a third wife was enroute to Juarez, Mexico, to obtain a divorce), and Mrs. Ronald Geyer.

They stood at almost the center of the place where, two weeks before, the hotel had been. On the sidewalk at the west border of the site, photographers got out their cameras and sound equipment from TV newsreel trucks. In two other cars adorned with Press stickers on the windshields, reporters and photographers arrived from the *Daily News* and the *Times*. The *Post*, although invited, did not assign anyone to cover the event.

The Mayor and the President of the Borough of Manhattan arrived in separate limousines. Shortly afterward, for the benefit of newsreel cameras, both men said that the new Zenith Oil building would indeed be a credit to the great and glorious city of New York.

Peter Druse made a short speech on behalf of Zenith Oil Corporation, reading from a typewritten sheet. He reached the end of his speech, removed his spectacles and stuffed the typewritten sheet into his pocket. The Mayor shook hands with Peter, congratulated him, then shook hands with Alex and with anyone else near enough to him, returned to his limousine and sped off to keep another appointment.

The President of the Borough of Manhattan handed a gold-plated shovel to Peter Druse.

"It's your privilege, as president of a great corporation, to break ground for a great new building."

"Thank you."

Newspaper photographers began clicking away. Peter Druse kept a dignified expression as they snapped him from every angle.

"Shake loose," one photographer demanded.

Peter drew himself up to his full height.

"At least take off your topcoat," said a photographer resignedly.

Peter dutifully removed his topcoat and gave it to his wife. It was a comparatively mild day. A small crowd had gathered on the nearest sidewalk to observe the ceremony but was prevented from entering the site by two policemen on duty at the barricades.

Peter held the gold-plated shovel in one hand, letting its edge touch the ground.

From the sidewalk a lumberjacketed youth yelled, "Use the shovel, grandpa! It won't bite you!"

Peter smiled self-consciously and turned to Alex Johns.

"Where shall I dig?"

"Anywhere."

Peter took the shovel firmly in his hand and dug into the earth. He brought up half a spadeful of earth.

"Boy, that guy's a real Tarzan!" the lumberjacketed youth yelled.

Everyone else applauded.

*

On the site the pumps were draining the water out of the excavation. The excavation went down far enough to uncover foundations of previous buildings. A hoe ram—a crawler mounted air hammer—moved into position and delivered three hundred blows a minute to the old concrete walls, banging away without stop until resistance ended or the operator raised the hammer for a respite. As each slab of concrete broke loose, the operator manipulated the moil point to nudge and maneuver the broken piece back and away.

These pieces were lifted by a clamshell and carted away in a tough heat-treated steel frame fifty-ton truck.

*

Tom left his rooming house at seven o'clock and walked three blocks to the subway. Trains were crowded at this hour and there were many men in checkered red coats who had almost the same broad powerful physiques, their shoulders arms and hands forming a perfect parenthesis. He got out at Times Square and walked crosstown toward the site. Other steelworkers and construction men turned south to where an almost completed red steel tower loomed. He turned north.

A board fence surrounded the huge excavation. There were open viewing areas cut into the fence at regular intervals that most people thought were put there for the sidewalk superintendents, the idly curious passersby who always gather to watch work going on. Actually these viewing holes were placed in the fence at regular intervals, usually every fifty feet or so, for the benefit of surveyors who needed them to establish levels and lines. These access lines to the site could not be placed in the lot itself because they would be destroyed by the excavation, so the city surveyors put marks on the curb for the general contractor's surveyors to pick up and transfer through the fence to use in their work. The fence portholes were the locations the surveyors looked through. On some construction jobs where portholes were not furnished a few planks were knocked out of the board fence and then put up again.

A large sign had been erected over the board fence:

DANGER! BLASTING!
No Radio Transmitting In This Area

The blasting crew arrived at seven-thirty and set up their equipment. They would begin promptly at eight o'clock, the earliest that Fire Department regulations allowed. Their job was to clear an obstinate shelf of rock from the deep and steadily widening pit.

The excavation was proceeding on schedule. Yesterday Tom and Otis had conferred with a Fire Department inspector and with the foundation contractor in charge of the blasting operation. The inspector wanted to know how much dynamite would be stored on the site and how far it would be kept from adjacent buildings. Otis showed the inspector the sturdy four by four by five foot metal shed in which the sticks would be kept and outlined the safety procedures that would be used in handling the dynamite. The inspector agreed to a compromise on how much dynamite could be stored on the site. Later there was another conference with representatives of the Transit Authority and the New York Telephone Company. The Transit Authority representative was worried about possible damage to the walls of a subway line that passed beneath the avenue not far from where blasting would occur. The subway tunnels in some places ran within five feet of the surface. The New York Telephone man was concerned about the underground cables for television stations, the Fire and Police Departments and Western Union. Otis finally satisfied both men by agreeing to a reduced amount of charge in blasts that would occur near the subway and the underground cables. Within the hour they were back again in conference with a Buildings Department inspector and the owner of the nearest building to their site, both of whom were worried about injury to the footing that might be caused by shock waves from the blasting traveling through rock. The building was across the street from the site but had a history of settlement problems. An inspection had recently discovered some new cracks in the basement and this was duly entered in the city record, and the Buildings Department inspector was on hand to be sure every precaution In was taken. Otis asked the foundation contractor to sit in on this problem because any real underground damage would cost a fortune to repair. With the help of the foundation contractor Otis worked out a line in the adjacent rock along which they would drill small holes an inch or so apart. These holes would break the impact of the shock waves and force them to run along the path of least resistance away from the footing of the other building. Everyone was satisfied.

Tom was learning from Otis the essentials of his job as a building superintendent. He would be a machine watcher constantly alert that all the intricate pieces of a great apparatus meshed and kept turning. Luckily, so far, the job was in its early stages and there were not many trades at work so he was able to learn before pressures mounted. But, basically, the requirements of the job would not change; they would merely become more complex. He would still be a machine watcher.

Tom wanted to make good on this job more than he had ever wanted anything except Sophy, and it was because of her that the job was so important. The turning point had come the day of the accident when she came running into his arms, sobbing. Ever since then he had known how much she cared and when they met now he always sensed her gladness to see him—as though a worry was taken from her. She told him once that when she was away from him she felt as though she were floating in space. Nevertheless, when he proposed to her again he didn't know if she would accept until suddenly she lifted her arms and embraced him, squeezing his neck and pressing against him so fiercely that he almost asked, "Is something wrong?" She did not speak a word until she said, "I was afraid you weren't going to ask me."

In that moment he had everything, all he wanted, more than he could find if he traveled the whole world over.

The time since had passed so slowly he sometimes wondered if days had forgotten how to follow each other. It seemed too long to wait. He had picked the place to spend a brief honeymoon, the White Antler Inn. Those three days would be as close to heaven as he was likely to get.

He forced his attention back to watching the machine. The blasters had finished with their preparations and were waiting for eight o'clock.

Promptly on the hour the drilling began. Two men wheeled their portable drills into the chosen area of rock. There was an art to drilling exactly where explosives would do the most good. Rock has grain like wood has and must be treated with respect. The drillers had to find the crevices and faults in which to sink their shafts and place the dynamite so the explosion would clear as large an area as possible. A bad blasting would simply pulverize rock without accomplishing a good deal.

Tom watched the drill, powered by air compressors, cut three to five foot narrow shafts in the rock, then the men inserted dynamite into the holes and wired the different sticks together. They led thin wires from the dynamite to larger connecting wires, stringing those back and almost running until they reached a safe distance. Then blasting mats, heavy steel mesh covers, were placed into position by a crane over the area of the impending explosion. The blasting mats were to prevent debris from flying out of the holes.

A whistle was blown, a warning to clear the area. Tom moved everyone back out of danger. The blasting foreman unlocked a padlock on an electric box.

"Blast!"

Everyone put thumbs on their ears and fingertips on their metal helmets. The foreman pushed a button in the electric box. A series of quick dull thuds merged into a deep roar, the ground shook, and heavy steel mats jumped like live things. Smoke and dust curled up thickly, mingling and rising in a wide ragged plume. For a minute Tom saw no color except shades of gray and brown, then the air began to clear and color returned—the orange and red of plaid flannel shirts, the black of leather jackets, the silver and blue and green of helmets.

Where the shelf of rock had been there was only shattered bits and pieces of fragmented stone.

The crane swung over to pick up the displaced heavy steel mats, and a powershovel moved in to remove the loosened debris.

Watching the shovel at work, Tom was reminded of the accident in which five men of the wrecking crew had died. Now the wreckers had moved on to a wholly different project downtown. One evening last week he had gone out with his former co-workers, Mike Collyer and Billy Farrell. They had met other men from the wrecking gangs in a bar and later they all went bowling. There had been sixteen men in all, and he noticed a difference in their attitude toward him. They accepted his new status. He had gained their respect. A sense of power excited him. He wanted not only respect but deference—the sort of stepping aside that acknowledged the solidity of his presence in the world. That was an attitude he would demand from men who worked with him. He could remain easy in his relations with them without losing the discipline that it was his first duty to enforce.

He unrolled a copy of the construction schedule he carried in his hand, and tried to figure out what would happen on this site for days and weeks to come. It occurred to him that he could forecast his life in the same way. On a building, when the excavation was complete, and the side banks sheeted, the foundation was laid in and the steel skeleton began to rise at an average rate of ten inches per hour, five days a week. Similarly, when a man married he laid in the foundations of his future. Life with Sophy would rise tier after tier through all time to come. The construction of a life could be as closely supervised as the construction of a building. All that was necessary was to coordinate the various strands as carefully as the work of different trades on a construction, leaving nothing to chance within the daily labyrinth of activity.

A big dump truck was making a tight forty-degree turn from the ramp into the street amid honking indignant traffic. Tom Mac-Laren entered the basement office in a building opposite the site.

At a long wooden table in the front room James Otis was seated. He was a slim light-skinned good-looking Negro wearing a brown sweater, blue workshirt, and corduroy trousers. He was busily writing.

"What are you working on?"

"The Police Department called the office. Something to do with traffic jams caused by all our trucks. The project manager asked me to check on it and give him a report."

Tom nodded and entered the private office. A few minutes later, Otis came in to say a police lieutenant was waiting outside.

As Tom emerged, he saw the lieutenant looking through a copy of *Playboy*. The lieutenant was a husky man wearing a uniform and visored cap. He put *Playboy* down.

"You in charge here?"

"I'm the field superintendent."

"We called your office."

"What's the problem, Lieutenant?"

"We're getting complaints. The way you're tying up traffic on the side streets around here. We had a jam here the other day that didn't break up for an hour."

"We're doing our best to space out our truckloads. But there's been a lot of excavation going on. Thirty truckloads a day."

"You can't put thirty trucks a day into one of the busiest streets in Manhattan. You've got to find some other way."

"We'll be finished with the excavation in the next couple of weeks, Lieutenant."

"No more trucks at heavy traffic hours. You won't start any trucks until ten A.M. and you'll finish at two-thirty."

"We've got a permit, Lieutenant."

"All you got is permission to remove. It's up to us to decide how. And I may want a trestle put over the whole site and a rig on top to remove the spoil from beneath."

"It's a little late for that now, Lieutenant," Tom said mildly.

"You want me to get tough about it?"

"Lieutenant, I didn't mean that. But I do have a couple of ideas. I think I can show you how we can handle the spoil removal so it won't bother anybody too much. Why don't you step into my office?"

As the lieutenant crossed in front of him to enter the small private room, Tom MacLaren saw Otis watching with a cynical smile. Otis was aware of the deal that would take place in the office, and it was nothing that would show up in the signed weekly report. Well, it would be no different if Otis was in charge; he'd have to find some way of greasing the wheels.

Black and white, Tom MacLaren thought, closing the door behind him, we're all hypocritical bastards.

*

Shortly after four o'clock in the afternoon only occasional calls lit the switchboard, and it was then that Sophy made and received her personal calls.

While watching the glassy entranceway to see if any visitor entered during her conversation, she said, "Really, Walter, you have to understand. I'm going to be married."

"That doesn't have to change anything."

"Of course it does. We're getting our license this week. I can't keep on seeing you."

"Why not?"

"It wouldn't be fair."

"What counts is how we feel about each other. I know how I feel about you, Sophy, and you can't pretend you don't feel the same way."

It had been almost two weeks since she had met Walter on an evening when Tom had gone bowling with some men at his job. Walter took her to dinner, but if she hadn't had too much to drink she never would have gone with him to a room at the Sheraton Motel.

"We can't see each other any more."

"I won't let it stay that way. How about tonight?"

"Walter, *please*."

"You know as well as I do it isn't over between us."

"I really can't talk."

"Sophy . . ."

"I have to hang up. Someone's coming." She pulled the plug from the switchboard, effectively ending the conversation.

Footsteps clicked up to her booth. It was her friend Gloria.

"Hi, Sophy. I'm having some people over tonight. How would you like to come?"

"I don't know. I'll have to ask my boyfriend."

"This'll be fun. Super people. Besides, I need you. I always hang out a BYO sign but in the end some moochers never bring their own liquor. Bring gin or vodka."

"I'll ask Tom."

"Oh, he'll say no. You told me he doesn't enjoy parties."

"What can I do about it?"

Gloria shrugged. "I'd put my foot down. Nothing a man likes better than to act as if he owns you."

Gloria didn't think much of Tom. Sophy had introduced them once when Tom came to pick her up at the office and Tom had been shy and stood around shuffling his feet. The next day Gloria said that Tom was nice, but he certainly wasn't at all like Walter. Gloria had met Walter and thought he was very smooth and sexy.

Sophy said, "Well, I guess it isn't going to be too much longer before he does own me."

"That's what you have to make clear *before* the marriage. No one owns anybody. I wouldn't let any man tell me what to do."

"I guess I could make him come to the party if I wanted to."

"It isn't as if you're getting such a bargain that you have to do everything he says. He's lucky to get anybody as pretty as you."

"He isn't so bad. You don't know him."

After Gloria left, everything seemed as blank and dark as the monitor board she was facing. She hated to be defensive about Tom. Gloria had no right to act superior. Everyone in the office knew what Gloria was doing with her boss, Bob Munro, and wouldn't believe he was just stringing her along. If Gloria could find a man willing to marry her, she ought to settle down herself.

The trouble was that the kind of man a girl wanted for a husband was either already spoken for like Walter or wasn't the marrying kind. Sooner or later a girl had to make some sort of decision. It couldn't always be fun and games. She was twenty-three and most of her friends were already married. There had been only five girls left of the group and they called themselves the Spinster Club, just joking, of course, but now even one of those girls was married and another was probably going to be engaged any day. That left three, and she certainly didn't intend to be the old maid. The other two weren't even good looking. In fact, they were homely.

She would have married Walter in a minute, but Tom was something different. She didn't know too much about him. They had never become lovers and it was clear now that he was going to wait for the wedding. By then everything might be too late.

She might never have said yes if it hadn't been for that accident. When she thought Tom might be dead that changed everything and put her into a real panic. But there was a big difference between worrying about somebody and wanting to live with him the rest of your life.

It was quite surprising in a way how she had become so deeply involved. It was probably a combination of things. Tom wanted to so much, and she wasn't getting any younger, and he seemed nice, and he was always around. He was more fun than staying home evenings with old movies on televison and getting a phone call around midnight from Walter after his family had all gone to bed.

A girl had to think about the future.

A summoning light appeared on the board and discontentedly she plugged in.

It was Tom. "How are you, darling?"

"I'm all right, I guess."

"You sound a little upset."

"I was just talking with my friend Gloria. She's going to give a little party tonight."

"You didn't say we'd come, did you?"

Gloria was right. He would say no. He just never wanted to have any *fun.*

Sudden inspiration: "I couldn't. She wants to make it a kind of celebration for the wedding. She's invited only the girls from the office."

"Are you going?"

He sounded disappointed but she couldn't help that. He probably wouldn't fit in anyhow. Gloria and her friends were lively and talkative and there was dancing. Tom wasn't a very good dancer.

"What can I say? She's gone to all that trouble."

"It seems awfully sudden. The same night."

"I know. But she went ahead and did it. I can't ask her not to, now."

"You want me to pick you up afterward?"

"No," hastily. "These things sometimes go on until all hours. I don't want to go but I can't think of any good excuse."

"You could say you weren't feeling well."

"She'd know I was making it up. I don't want to hurt her feelings."

His voice took on that patient tone of trying to be reasonable: "Do what you want to, dear."

"What will you do?"

"Oh, I'll manage. I'll have a drink with some of the boys. Maybe I'll give Mike Collyer a ring and see what he's doing."

"Why don't you? You'll enjoy it."

"All right, then. Have a good time."

"Thank you, darling."

She made the faint smacking sound of a kiss.

For a moment after she unplugged the call, she sat staring at the board, utterly motionless. Finally she nodded her head and with quick finger movements began to dial Walter's number.

*

On the fourth day of the blasting operation, a dynamite charge "got away." Thirty sticks of dynamite had been placed in six holes and the explosion went off with unexpected force. Some cars parked on the street suffered broken windshields and other damage from falling stones. Steel mats weighing over two tons each were blown fifty feet into the air. Air conditioners on a nearby building were shaken loose and fell to the ground. No one was injured, but a cardiac patient in a nearby building suffered an attack and was taken to the hospital. The police came down to check all the permits and the Fire Department temporarily revoked the certificate of fitness of the foundation contractor to prevent him from carrying on further blasting operations until the investigation was completed.

Most of the damage claims were justified and settled by the insurance company but there was difficulty with the Wearwell Carpet Company whose headquarters were in a building two blocks away from the construction. They complained about serious structural damage to their offices and threatened a lawsuit.

Alex Johns called Vinnie Haleson and arranged a convenient time for them to drop in at the Wearwell Carpet Company headquarters and see for themselves what it was all about.

The Wearwell Carpet Company occupied ground floor space in a skyscraper. The windows were all double-thick plate glass and carpets were on display in the windows.

Vinnie Haleson entered the showroom with Alex. A smiling salesmen came toward them.

"Is Mr. McGrady here?" Alex asked.

"Is he expecting you?"

"Tell him that the people from the Zenith Oil Corporation are here to see him."

The salesman retreated toward the rear and down a short corridor that apparently led to offices. In a moment he returned with a solid-looking athletic young man, who had a square good-looking face, and close-cut brown hair.

"Mr. McGrady?" Alex asked.

McGrady nodded.

"I'm Alex Johns. I'm putting up the Zenith Oil building. This is Mr. Haleson. He's vice-president of the Zenith Oil Corporation—and in charge of the construction."

McGrady smiled and shook hands. He had a boyish engaging smile.

"I'm glad to see that our lawyer's letter got prompt results."

"We don't like to be bad neighbors," Alex said.

"Let me show you something," McGrady said.

He led the way through aisles of carpets spread out on rollers. In a corner of the large showroom he stopped, and pointed to the ceiling.

Above their heads a portion of plaster had dropped out and a large central crack sent radiating lines like a spider's web a distance of five or six feet in every direction.

"Is this the only one?" Alex inquired.

"There are a couple of smaller ones."

Vinnie Haleson asked, "Are you sure that this was caused by the blasting at our construction site?"

"It wasn't there until after the blasting."

"I imagine it would be hard to prove cause and effect."

McGrady's smile vanished. "We wouldn't like to go to court about this. But we will if we have to, Mr. Haleson."

113

"It doesn't seem important enough for that. If you will send us a bill for replastering your ceiling . . ."

"That won't do."

"Why not?"

"It isn't just the replastering. There's also the time and trouble it will cost. This is our busy season. We can't have plasterers and painters in here without affecting our business. And that's another important point I haven't brought up, Mr. Haleson. All the noise from that blasting this past week has already affected our business. We estimate our trade is off twenty percent. And those customers aren't coming back. They've gone elsewhere to get their carpets and won't be in the market again for years. I might add that when the blasting is going on the salesmen aren't even able to communicate with customers who do drop in."

"You hardly expect us to compensate you for the fact that you may be losing customers."

"We've already informed our lawyer to start legal action. But I hoped that your coming here today would lead to some sort of compromise that would help us avoid unpleasantness."

Alex gave a slight touch to Vinnie's elbow.

Vinnie said promptly, "I'd like to talk to Mr. Johns a minute, if you don't mind."

McGrady nodded curtly, "Of course," and moved a few feet away.

"Does he have a case?" Vinnie asked.

"A good one, I'm afraid."

"Then you think I ought to settle."

"Feel him out a little first. See what he wants."

They returned to where McGrady was standing.

"I've talked it over with Mr. Johns and we would like to do the fair thing, Mr. McGrady. Do you have any approximate amount in mind?"

"I hadn't thought in terms of any specific sum. In fact, I'm only one of the owners of this company, Mr. Haleson, and I haven't even talked it over with my partners. However, in view of your reasonable attitude, we might be able to work out an arrangement that wouldn't cost you anything."

"What's that?"

McGrady indicated the large showroom with its hundreds of carpets on display.

"We've been in business almost forty years. I'm second generation ownership. If you'll check our credentials you'll find that we have a reputation that's second to none in our trade."

"I have no reason to doubt that, Mr. McGrady."

"Fine." McGrady's boyish smile returned. "Our prices are also fully competitive. If we got the carpeting contract for the new Zenith Oil building, Mr. Haleson, I'm sure I could persuade my partners to forget our complaints. Doesn't that make sense to you?"

*

On an early December morning, Tom MacLaren, riding in a taxi to Sophy's apartment house, thought about the wedding that would take place today. Beneath his bulky black overcoat, he wore a blue suit, a pale blue shirt, and a dark blue figured Countess Mara tie that Sophy had bought for him. A leather suitcase, borrowed from Mike Collyer, was waiting in his room packed with other clothing he would need for the three-day honeymoon. They were taking the train to upper New York State and the White Antler Inn.

He had bought a camera, a good one, and this would be the beginning of the family scrapbook. The first page would be their wedding, and not too many years from now there would be photographs of a house, one of those modern slant-roofed ranch homes with plenty of room for everyone and a finished basement. Someday their own children would look at the photographs. It was all beginning today, and the future looked bright. There would always be plenty of opportunity in the construction field for a man who could do an honest sturdy job and knew how to build. The city needed good workable buildings, plenty of them. Jim Otis said that if a building was good it helped to make the sum of a city somewhat different the way a single drop of water changed the temperature in a glass it's poured into. More like pouring a drop of water into an ocean; it's a big city.

Thinking about Otis caused Tom uneasiness. He did not get along with his assistant and the chief reason was that Otis had been trained to be an engineer and had a college degree. It wasn't a good idea to educate a man beyond his proper position in life because he kept trying to prove how superior he was. Otis would pretend to get excited over the architect's design—a few scribbles on paper. He said that they were putting up one of the best office buildings he had ever seen, one that would become an architectural landmark. Otis was only showing off because how would he know about things like that?

Besides, the architect wasn't really important in the building process. When that design was finished the architect would forget all about the building and just do the kind of inspection he had to by contract. That was when the real work started. Somehow Otis did not see the drama, the real excitement, in watching a mechanized steamshovel move forward on its crawler chassis while its great steel jaws tore chunks out of the earth. Tom always watched the earth-moving machines at work because he had a real feeling for the day-to-day adventure of building.

He put Otis down every once in a while, just to show him. Wednesday morning, for example, he and Otis had made a tour of the deep pit. It was freezing cold. Workers had to stamp their feet to keep blood circulating, and ducked frequently into a windowless van on the northwest corner where they could huddle around a propane gas stove.

Otis said, "The compression lines are freezing and the jackhammers don't work. Only twelve out of forty even showed up."

"We can't pay them for sitting around a stove. We've got a schedule," Tom reminded him.

Otis wiped a frozen tear from his eyelash. "They're earning their money just by being here. You can't expect them to get much work done on a day like this."

At a corner workmen wearing babushkas beneath their hard hats were trying to keep warm beside a tin drum filled with blazing wood. Otis dropped a two by four into the blaze.

"We ought to send everyone home," he said.

"We've lost enough days. And the winter's just getting started."

Tom looked away from the warmth. The shivering men gathered near the small solace of the fire had pinched blue faces.

"Let them take a vote on whether they want to knock off for the day," Jim Otis suggested. "That's what they did on that building over on Eighth Avenue. The welders knocked off first because they can't weld in temperature under twenty degrees. Then they tried bolting the frame together so the welders would catch up in warmer weather, but it was too cold for the bolters too. Everyone packed in."

"It may get better in the afternoon," Tom said. "As long as they showed up, let them work."

"Yes, Mr. MacLaren." Otis's voice sounded dry and shriveled in the cold air.

As the taxi drew up now before Sophy's apartment house Tom was thinking of how well he had handled that situation.

He took from the taxi's rear seat a long box of white roses. He had waited all his life for this day. If Mother was alive she would have approved because in many ways Sophy was like her. Much prettier, of course, but the same virginal quality, the same purity, that once made his father exclaim, "Your mother Tom, is a living angel. The best woman who ever lived." Mother, sitting on a slant-backed wooden chair on the lawn of the clapboard frame house near Richmond. Plain woman with short hair curled at both sides and parted at the left. Downcast eyes in a sad brave face. Very religious. Fate had outwitted her faith, left her prey to invincible terrors. After Father died on a mountain highway while returning an empty bus to the terminal and swerving to avoid a car on the wrong side of the road, Mother lost the rudder that had steered her through invisible storms. Dark days led down and down to the sanitarium from which she never emerged.

As the elevator started up, he refused to let his mind dwell on painful memories. Sophy was waiting.

She was wearing a white dress with a collar of ruffled white lace. The quick spill of dark hair down the left was caught back and controlled by a camellia.

"Approve?" she asked with small coquetry.

Her lips seemed to glow with an almost golden color. He could have sworn her hazel eyes were shimmering with light.

"You're gorgeous."

He couldn't believe anyone as pretty as Sophy was really going to marry him. Her beauty moved him in ways that he did not under-

117

stand. Sophy would never have to worry about him. He welcomed marriage with its iron fidelity.

"These are for you," he said, giving her the roses.

"Oh, Tom, you darling!"

She got a vase and filled it with water and arranged the roses in it.

"Where's Jasmine?" he asked.

Jasmine was her Siamese, a slinky unfriendly cat with whom Tom's relations remained distant and strained.

"Somewhere under the bed. She doesn't like the whole idea of our getting married."

"We can always put her out for adoption."

Her expression grew petulant. "I could never give up Jasmine."

"Well, then, she'd better start acting friendlier."

"You wouldn't make me, would you?"

"I'd never make you do anything." He bent over and kissed her lightly on the forehead. "It's all right. Jasmine can live with us."

Her mood was changing into the sadness of self-reproach. "I know I'm a child. I don't really want to be anything else."

"I like you just the way you are."

"Are you still sure you want to marry me?"

"A fine time to ask."

She replied, with surprising intensity: "It isn't necessary. We don't *have* to get married."

"What kind of a thing is that to say?"

She did not meet his gaze. "I may not be the kind of girl you want for a wife."

"You're exactly the kind of girl."

"I can't cook or keep house . . . and I'm afraid to have children. I don't want children. Not for a long time anyway."

Suddenly he understood her fears were not specifically connected with him. All brides are upset on their wedding day.

"There'll be plenty of time to talk about that."

"Oh, Tom," she said, looking up at him with her eyes brimming. "I wouldn't want to hurt you."

"We're going to be very happy," he said, putting his arm about her. "Wait and see."

118

She was rigid for a moment before resistance went out of her and her head came softly against his chest. He saw her white camellia.

*

Entering the church she was sure she saw him. She looked over the heads of the crowd. Yes, there, with well-formed head, graying close-cut hair, motionless, yet seeming to bob because of the crowd's movement on the sidewalk. Walter always stood out from a crowd. They entered through a grilled gate that led down a path to the chapel and the small crowd of the curious on the sidewalk gave a ragged cheer that caused their breaths to steam in the cold air.

Why was he here? It was foolish. Her heart was beating fast. Oh, he should not have followed her to the door of the chapel. They started down the path and when she looked back people blocked her view.

She really should be angry with Walter. He was taking a terrible risk. He simply would not accept that she was free to marry. Her face was flushing. He had no real claim on her. He was married and had children and a home and a separate life from her.

Tom and Walter were going to meet. She had a sense of doom about it. She had always been a mystic. She still remembered that horrible night when her mother wakened and heard a bell tolling. It wasn't long after when Mother died. One has to believe that there is a world unknown and be afraid of it. She was afraid of darkness and afraid to sleep alone. Walter never understood. Once there had been a prowler in her apartment building. They caught him trying to force the door of an apartment on her floor and she could hear from inside her apartment the terrible cries and sounds of the beating the police gave him. After that she put bars on the kitchen window that opened into the courtyard and a combination lock on the door. But these did not offer the same protection as a man. She needed a man around most of the time. That was why she was marrying Tom.

"Do you take this woman . . . ?"

Tom's answer was clear and loud and confident in the small chapel. She was aware of Gloria, her maid of honor, and Mike Collyer,

119

Tom's best man. She was aware of everyone including herself, angelic in her white dress.

She thought of Walter, stocky and well built and with a way about him that was very attractive and young even if he was forty-two years old. She was proud of Walter. Even his eyeglasses seemed to fit his face and there weren't too many men you could say that about. Her heart kept beating faster. She had been very much in love with Walter at one time. But she was too young to spend the rest of her life with a married man.

"Do you take this man . . . ?"

She heard the question clearly and half-turned to Tom. A small smile touched her lips. "I do," she said.

As she was leaving the chapel, with Mike and Gloria throwing rice and laughing, a few people were still waiting at the gate. She looked for Walter but saw only a rather stocky young man standing behind a woman in a green coat.

That isn't him, that isn't him.

Her stab of disappointment was like a betrayal.

"Ready?" Tom asked.

They were at the curb. The taxi was waiting. She was married.

"Ready," she said, and took his arm to get into the waiting taxi.

*

Sophy was asleep, her head resting on his arm, the sheet drawn up beneath her armpits and her bare shoulders showing.

He crossed his other arm over his body to turn on the bedside lamp. Last night was the sort of shattering experience he had approached only once before, and that experience had nothing in common with this.

Sophy's small hand flung out on the pillow was reaching toward him. Her hand was in shadow, the fingers stained with light . . .

The mission will start out at midnight—the first platoon starting fifteen minutes earlier than the second.

Snaking through the dark rows of trees that grew so densely one could not see the stars, the radio man with his PRC-10 strapped to his back was ahead and so was the point man who kept looking at the illuminated dial of his compass. They were to come out on the western edge of the rubber plantation and move across the east-west road to the objective village. From the flanks came the crackling of rifle fire.

They're getting it, Sergeant Jonas called, waving to the platoon to follow him.

He followed closely though it was hard to see Sergeant Jonas with his black face and jungle camouflage fatigues. They came out onto the road where the flank security had been ambushed. Flares from M-79 grenade launchers illuminated the area. Men were dying and dead on the road in broken bloody messes. The yellow light of flares gave the whole scene a ghastly look. Some men who tried to flee the ambush had triggered mines on the sides of the trail. They were hard to identify as men. Others had fallen on pungi stakes planted beside the road.

There was no time to think. His carbine had sixty rounds belted to the folding stock and two banana clips taped butt to butt in the lock. He fired off his whole basic load at scampering black pajamaed VC's in semidarkness. BAR men were pumping heavy slugs back at the ambushers. He smelled acrid cordite from rifles and machine guns. Then the scrub jungle on the right erupted in blazing fire, and the BAR guns fell silent.

Fall back! Sergeant Jonas yelled.

Constant grinding and rattling small arms fire as they retreated toward the plantation. Men crumpled and fell.

Incoming! someone yelled.

Crump, crump, crump of 60 mm. mortar rounds blasted trees behind them in a shattering series of explosions. Two men tried to set up an elephant gun—M-79 grenade launcher—to cover their retreat. A mortar landed near and they disappeared with their weapon.

The survivors fell back, hurling grenades at the enemy's automatic fire positions. Sharp ringing notes of a bugle signaled a fresh attack and black pajama-clad figures swarmed. He jerked a grenade off his combat harness and lobbed it. Then he ran. Everyone alive was running.

Sergeant Jonas rallied Lewes and Turner and himself in a small clearing. Tom had lost his soft cap. Lewes was coughing with racking noises. Sergeant Jonas gave him a slug of GI gin—80 proof terpin hydrate—guaranteed to give an hour's relief from coughing. He warned them to observe strict noise discipline.

Soon they heard a voice on a bullhorn in heavily accented English. *Surrender—or you die.*

The voice went on at regular intervals for hours.

In the morning a VC patrol found them. In the sharp firefight Lewes got it and Turner was shot through the lung. He burbled blood as they carried him. Sergeant Jonas insisted on trying to save him. Although Tom knew it was useless he did not argue with Jonas because Jonas was his hope of survival.

In their combat packs were three days of rations and two canteens. They took salt pills every three hours and carried their rifles at ready —a tiring way to carry a weapon on a long march—but they had to be ready to react to a new ambush. Turner died the first night.

Other VC patrols were looking for them so they could not circle back toward the camp. They stayed in the shelter of the rubber plantation. The radio man had been killed and there was no way to alert air rescue. At five o'clock in the morning of the second day Jonas was cut down by submachine-gun fire through both his legs. But he got the VC gunner with a grenade. Tom helped Jonas set up the machine gun and Jonas sat back against a tree.

They'll be along soon, he said. *I'll hold them off as long as I can.*

Tom said goodbye and shook hands. In the light of a false dawn filtering down he saw blood on Jonas's hand . . .

Sophy slept peacefully while he stared at the dim ceiling of the bedroom. A metallic clangor startled him. He sat up in shuttered darkness, quietly moved his arm away from Sophy, and slipped out of bed. As he turned the window blind he saw two kitchen workers loading trash cans onto the rear of a truck. That meant breakfast was over. They had slept late.

He put the window blind back into position and went into the bathroom and turned on the shower and splashed in the cold water. There was a tightness between his ears and a staring feeling in his eyes almost as if he had drunk too much the evening before. He wondered if going without sleep had affected him. As he dried himself with the big rough bath towel (*Property of White Antler Inn* was printed on it like an accusation before the crime) he saw on the bathroom door behind him, hanging from a hook, a pink lace chemise. He must have surprised her. Each time he had held her in his arms he desired her again.

He stepped back from the bathroom mirror and put both hands on his hips. Beneath slightly lifted shoulders, his chest muscles protruded. One-two. Retracted stomach retreating to the navel and the flat abdomen. All man. One-two. This is my body. This is where I live. He squatted and rose on sturdy thighs.

When he emerged from the bathroom Sophy turned her head, the rest of her slim body remaining in the same position.

"What time is it?"

"Eleven o'clock."

She gave a small moan.

"Are you all right?" he asked.

She stuffed a pillow behind her head against the bedframe and sat up. The sheet slid down around her navel.

"Tom?"

"Yes, darling?"

"I'm hungry."

"We're too late for the dining room. I'll have to order it up."

"I like room service better anyway."

He thought how wonderful it would be to have Sophy making breakfast for him. This would be life from now on, the two of them.

"What are you thinking about?" he asked.

"Nothing."

"Nothing?"

"I can't think about things in the morning. I mean, I can't ever think what to think about . . . I'd like a cigarette."

The waiter brought up breakfast on a wheeled table. They sat facing each other across the small table.

"Is everything all right?" he asked.

"Everything is fine." She was having thick munchy Canadian bacon and scrambled eggs. He had ordered two boiled eggs in their shells.

"You slept pretty late this morning."

"I always sleep late when I can. I'm half-awake when I get up early."

"Are you tired?"

"No."

"Not a bit?"

"Are you?"

"Me? Never felt better."

"It looks like a nice morning. What do they have to do here?"

"Well, there's skiing."

"Aren't people always getting hurt?"

"Usually only good skiers. The beginners don't take any chances."

"Did you ever see anyone get hurt?"

"Sure. At Big Stowe a guy really got racked up. Took off from a hill going just like a bird before a ski fell off and there he was trying to make a landing at eighty miles an hour on one lousy ski."

"What happened?"

"Two busted kneecaps and all sorts of special surgery. I saw him a few days later with both legs in plaster casts."

Sophy shuddered. "I don't think I want to go skiing."

"It'd be the wrong sort of accident for me. I'd rather put my hand in boiling oil or have all my teeth drilled." He rather liked the violent proud images of himself manfully combating pain. "Anything just to get it over quickly."

"Well, if we don't go skiing, what else can we do?"

"We'll think of something." He hoped that she would mention last night. The sound of her voice talking about it would have been indescribably thrilling. He would never forget this room, the orange light and velvet darkness of last night, and the amazing thing that had happened.

"That's the trouble with these out-of-the-way places," Sophy said. "There isn't much to do."

*

Alex lay stupefied on his back, Ginger prone beside him with her forearm skin flattened against the hair mat of his chest.

The telephone rang.

"Don't answer," Ginger said laxly.

He was already disentangling himself.

"Hello."

"This is Jim Otis, Mr. Johns. I hate to bother you on a Sunday morning."

"What do you want?"

"Ed Fregoni, the watchman, called me this morning. Something's wrong with the foundation."

Alex's head lifted as sharply as though he smelled smoke. "*What?*"

"It seems to have moved, Mr. Johns. We don't know yet what caused it."

"Moved! It *can't* move!" Anger rose simmering to the top and boiled over. "Where the hell is Tom MacLaren?"

"He got married this weekend, Mr. Johns."

"Oh, Christ! You don't even know what you're looking at. How can a foundation move? . . . Listen! Find out what . . . No, never mind! I'll come as soon as I can."

He showered and dressed in ten minutes. Through a short foyer he entered a living room with artful arrangements of paintings from the English school of the eighteenth century. There was a life-size sculpture in a foyer niche. His apartment had been created for him by an interior decorator but he felt like a transient in it. His real home was his office.

As the taxi sped onto the West Side Highway, Alex re-created in his mind's eye the site of the Zenith Oil building. On the site were foundation walls and soon there would be grillages deep in the excavation and husky anchor bolts sticking up out of the bottom ready to position the bottom columns and hold them in place when the construction began. That steel was almost ready to be delivered. His contract with Zenith Oil specified that a crucial payment would be made when the actual erection of the tower began. He needed that money. In order to stall until he got it he had done something he vowed never to do. When his regular sources were tapped out, even at ruinous fifteen and sixteen percent interest rates, he broke a long-standing rule and did what many other men in the general contracting business did: took a loan from the Mafia. The Mafia bankrolled half the contractors in the construction industry, but he knew too many stories about the way they did business. Nevertheless, he borrowed two hundred thousand dollars to see him through until that payment came in from Zenith Oil.

It would be disaster if anything went wrong now.

The taxi turned off at the Forty-sixth Street exit from the Highway and began making its way crosstown. Jim Otis said the foundation had moved, and what did he mean if he wasn't being hysterical? Could an error have been made? If so, by whom? It wasn't credible that either the architect or the structural engineer had made a serious miscalculation. Their judgments were based on mathematics. A column or exterior masonry wall brings a certain calculable load to bear on the ground on which it rests. Figuring the support necessary for it is a matter of simple arithmetic. Assume the column or wall brings a load of thirty tons to bear on a soil that will only carry one ton per square foot. All that is necessary is to place the column or wall on a spread footing of the size required to obtain thirty square feet of support. The same principle is used by a housewife who places a piano on her living-room floor. If the load will be too great, causing the piano legs to make dents in the floor, she puts a glass or wooden cup under each leg to distribute the load.

Nevertheless, Jim Otis said the foundation had moved.

How could it? The foundation walls were reinforced concrete. Inside the portland cement there were deformed steel bars having lugs or projections on their surfaces to develop a greater bond between the concrete and the steel. The grade of steel on this job had a tensile strength of 20,000 pounds to the square inch.

Move walls like that? Ridiculous! Jim Otis was having a nightmare.

He leaned forward in the back seat of the taxi, urging the vehicle on with the muscles of his thighs.

*

Sunday quiet reigned over the excavation. The hole was wide and deep. The foundation walls rose at a sheer angle above an immense cavity partly filled with two derricks that were being assembled, piles of cable and timber, jackhammers, a 600 CPM compression machine, two paving breakers, and an endless intertwining of pipes.

126

It was a disaster.

At a barricade gate Alex Johns stood sorrowfully beside Ronald Geyer, the structural engineer. A few feet away, like a mourner not a member of the immediate family, Jim Otis was watching them.

"I can't believe it," Alex said in a voice that carefully screened out emotion.

Ronald Geyer said, "You went ahead with backfilling too early. My drawings clearly stated there should be no backfilling until the first floor steel framing was installed."

"Nobody's blaming you," Alex said.

Alex could not deny that he had proceeded to backfill behind the foundation walls before steel framing was in to support and keep the walls in place. The procedure saved time, and nothing would have gone wrong if there hadn't been a break in a city water main close by. The Department of Water Supply had sent in emergency crews and fixed the leak but the pressure of the water had taken subsoil beneath the street and sidewalk and pushed it up solidly against the wall.

That pressure had moved the wall ever so slightly into the lot.

"How far in is it?" Alex asked.

"I went down into the pit and measured. A couple of inches."

"Enough to throw everything out," Alex muttered.

Ronald Geyer shrugged. "It doesn't take much."

Anchor bolts in those concrete piers had to be positioned with absolute accuracy to the steel columns. The billet plates with their two holes in the bottom for the anchor bolts had a lateral tolerance of only one quarter of an inch.

"Just the other day the surveyors finished checking the foundation," Alex said. "They okayed it for steel to be put in place."

Those surveys were meaningless now. A couple of inches made all the difference.

"Well, the sooner you get to work on it the better," Geyer said.

"What can we do?"

"There isn't anything to do but take the north wall down."

"We can't."

"I'm afraid you'll have to."

"You're the big expert," Alex said. "Think of something."

"I'm an engineer. Not a magician."

"We can't take the wall down," Alex said.

Ronald Geyer said, "It's just too bad you didn't pay attention to the instruction in my drawings. You never would have started with that backfill when you did."

"Why don't you go home and shore up your head?" Alex said.

After Ronald Geyer left, Alex walked the length of the accursed north wall. How could anybody beat timing like this? He had performed prodigies to get through to this moment. If he had to postpone delivery of steel he would not only fail to collect vital money from Zenith Oil but penalties would mount up from the steel fabricators. His whole financial situation would tailspin down to ruin.

As he returned to his vantage point, Jim Otis was waiting for him.

"A rotten break, Mr. Johns."

"We've got to figure out some way to keep from tearing down that north wall."

"It's out of whack, Mr. Johns. As an engineer, I can't help agreeing with Mr. Geyer that . . ."

"Will you shut up a minute? *I'm thinking.*"

He studied the thirty-foot-high, two-hundred-foot-long north wall with measured belligerence. Pressure from the broken main had pushed it into the lot. There must be some way to push it back.

Alex turned to Jim Otis. "Can you start rounding up a crew to start first thing tomorrow? We don't have an hour to lose."

"I suppose so, but . . ."

"Tell them to get heavy timbers. Place the timbers every twenty feet along the wall. Drive steel wedges between the top of the timber and the wall."

"What for, Mr. Johns?"

"We're going to push that wall back into position."

Otis said incredulously, "Push it back?"

"That's what I said."

"It won't work, Mr. Johns. All the subsoil is in there from the street and sidewalk. It's packed solid against the wall, creating pressure."

"Then it has to be taken out."

"I suppose we could do that," Otis said doubtfully, "with a bulldozer and a clamshell. But the wall would still be out of whack," he said, with the patient tone of someone pointing out an elementary fact.

"When the pressure of that stuff behind the wall is moved out," Alex said, "the timbers and steel wedges will push the wall back into place."

"Mr. Johns, concrete doesn't have the resiliency. It won't stand up to that kind of treatment."

"We've got to take the chance. The concrete may crack, but nobody *knows* what will happen."

Otis shook his head slowly. "It's a waste of time. You can't push a wall that big."

Alex took him by the arm and walked him up the ramp. "Don't think you're such a hell of an engineer. I'd rather have men working for me who are willing to take a chance."

"It's such a long chance, Mr. Johns."

"This whole job has been a Jonah from the beginning. I can't put off steel, understand? I simply can't."

Otis shrugged. "I'll do my best."

Alex patted him on the shoulder. His voice rasped like a saw against an unyielding surface. "Get a crew together and push that goddamn wall back where it belongs."

They paused on the edge of the massive pit with its great enclosing foundation walls. In the depths a huge derrick was tied by a cable to a metal hook. The hook was set in a large block of concrete that acted as a counterweight to keep the derrick from toppling over when lifting a weight. Alex knew the name for that concrete block with its hairpin anchor. It was called a dead man.

*

In the early hours of Monday morning the whistle cried up men to their work. Compression engines began to snort and steel drills to clatter and concrete workers labored on their white lava amid swirling dust.

On the north side of the excavation, at the shifted wall, ladders were propped against the scaffolding below the street level.

Tom MacLaren watched men climb the ladders to fix timbered supports into position against steel wedges.

Jim Otis said, beside him, "Alex Johns has got to be desperate to try a thing like this."

"He's been in this business a long time. I guess he knows as much as you do about it."

"I'm an engineer and I can tell you . . ."

"You can't tell me anything," Tom MacLaren said shortly. "Just do your job."

He had no patience with complainers. He had returned from an all-too-brief honeymoon to this bad news.

The clamshell bucket moved toward the packed-in earth behind the wall. The bucket dipped and swung up with a load of muck. The bony crane swiveled the load high above a dump truck.

"It's not going to work," Otis said gloomily. "Certain laws you can't break. Laws having to do with forces at rest and forces in motion."

"They teach you that in college?"

Below the scaffolding a timber joggled up and down without settling firmly into place.

"Over here," Tom yelled suddenly. "More left! More left, you lunkhead!"

The pared edge of timber, like a roughly sharpened pencil edge, slid into position against the steel wedge.

Tom indicated to Otis other men struggling with a timbered support.

"Get on down there. Make the bastards push it up. Get their backs in it!"

Otis hesitated and then went down to work with the men who heaved until the dead tree rose in all its stripped and branchless power. They maneuvered the timber until a sudden push locked it into position and it held. Offended timber groaned and creaked as it held the steel wedge in place to fight the concrete. It reminded Tom of armwrestling. Now we'll see which is the stronger, the powerful braced timber and steel wedges or the heavy resisting weight of the wall.

Otis came up the ramp to him, perspiring under the underarms of his heavy leather jacket. His blue workshirt was wet at the armpits.

"We'll have all the timber in place before we quit tonight," Tom said.

"And we'll be taking it down in a day or so. Even if we do move that wall, the concrete will break up like a lot of dropped crockery."

"Nobody asked your opinion," Tom said.

He ranged over the site. The laborers paid no attention to his shouts and curses. They had been goaded and pushed for too many years. They did not lower their eyes or submit. They struggled against massive unmoving power, the sweat of their bodies mingling with the smell of timber and mortar and brick and their breath joining in the haze. Above them a square red sign on the sidewalk announced in white letters:

ALEXANDER JOHNS ENTERPRISES
To Be Built on This Entire Block a Sixty Story Air
Conditioned Building. For Information Call 444-1234.
Owner: Zenith Oil Corporation.
Architect: Karl Schiller.
Consulting Architect: Samuel Whitefield Associates.
Structural Engineer: Ronald Geyer.
General Contractor: Alexander Johns.

*

Tonight Barbara was at a Christmas party being given by the Paul Cornells. She was there because Alex Johns had called to ask her out. Alex had been a persistent caller, and this time Barbara went out with him because there was no male alternative at hand and she did need an escort.

The Paul Cornells lived in a home that was a relic of the days when rich people spent with more flamboyance and less guilt. A Scottish castle large enough to hold the commuting rush in Grand Central Station had been imported by Ebenezer Cornell stone by stone. There was a twelve-acre pond on the estate, crossed by a bridge imported from Devon where it had struck the fancy of Ebenezer's son, Joseph. Paul Cornell did not share the exuberance of either his grandfather or father; he managed to indulge his taste for luxury more discreetly, well screened from the public gaze. As he explained to Barbara once, there was no longer a credulous peasantry to gape through iron gates

131

or over the spike-topped stone fences. The envy of the masses had turned sour; there was something almost pre-revolutionary about it.

"You having a good time?" Alex asked.

"No," Barbara said.

"How about champagne?" Without waiting for a reply he vanished into the throng at the long table where bartenders were serving. He moved as though in his natural element, gracious, smiling, but with a bright acquisitive expression. Barbara knew what he was up to.

At the bar Alex got into conversation with Robert Percival Stern, former Ambassador to Israel and scion of the Stern fortunes, and he began talking rapidly, not blatant or offensive, but with a little too much insistence. He really should be warned not to use the same money-raising techniques he had learned in dealing with bankers or rich people of the second rank.

As Barbara approached the bar, she heard Alex saying, "Yes, Mr. Stern, Israel has a wonderful potential. But I don't believe in building just for the sake of building. It has to be profitable. And with the situation in the Middle East the way it is . . ."

"Yes, yes," Stern said absently. "Ah, Barbara. It's good to see you. You having a good time?"

"No," Barbara said. "Mr. Johns promised to bring me champagne."

"I'm sorry," Alex said, contrite. "I got talking business, but I know that's no excuse."

Alex submerged himself into the bar crowd and surfaced directly with the champagne goblet. Robert Percival Stern chose the interim to make an unobtrusive retreat.

"Forgive me?" Alex asked. "I can't help it. When I sniff money around, I get acting like a bird dog."

What she liked about Alex was a genuineness particularly noticeable in a crowd like this—he was not pure gold, but he was certainly not an alloy. An honest coal among flawed diamonds.

"You shouldn't make it so obvious."

"Frankly, I'm in a spot where I could use more capital in my business. There was a delay on the construction. A problem with the foundation that nearly finished me completely."

"Is it all right now?"

"I took a long chance and got away with it. But it was such a close squeak that I wouldn't want to go through anything like that again. The only way I can be sure I won't have to is to have plenty of money around when I need it."

"The best way to get these people to part with money is to set a snare, turn your back on it and pay no attention. Let them become curious enough to want to do it themselves and not turn it over to financial advisers."

"I'll remember that."

She felt sorry for him, really. He would fit quite easily into the life of the very very rich. Houses in New York, London, Palm Beach, and the Riviera, a sizable staff of servants in each house so he wouldn't have to tote luggage or waste time at customs. Expensive art, authentic period furniture and closets bulging with Huntsman suits, Sulka shirts, and Lock hats. That was Alex's idea of gracious living.

She sipped champagne, keeping up a steady flow of talk while Alex's eyes kept roving the room in an expectant aggressive way. She managed to reclaim his interest only at intervals. A woman is always somewhere in her deeps afraid that she is unattractive or old, wrinkled and saggy breasted, and Alex was beginning to present something of a challenge. She hated to solicit attention continually and to grub for conversation like candy. She knew she was bright in a social way. She had learned early that she would have to be. Peter had said, dandling her on his knee, "A girl who isn't pretty, better be witty." Dear Father never realized how cruel his little couplet was.

Alex was staring off to where young Bryan Destin, of the Destin shipbuilding clan, was approaching the bar.

Holding her empty champagne goblet, Barbara said, "I'd like to go home now, Alex."

"Aren't you having a good time?"

"If anyone askes me that again, I'll probably scream."

"I'll get your coat," Alex said promptly.

In the limousine, with Alex driving, she sat by the dark side window and tried consciously not to think about Karl. She was never able to fully withdraw from thoughts of him into something else. There was always a quality of him alive in her mind.

Alex said, "Do you know Patricia Layle?"

"I saw you talking to her at the party. What was that all about?" She asked the question, not because she particularly wanted to hear the answer, but because Alex would now take over and there would be a long period of semi-listening in which she could be occupied with her own thoughts.

Alex continued talking through the languor, the numbness that his words imposed. She was brooding on Karl. She was an obsessed Hindu watcher of her inward consciousness, a secret and painful meditator.

The car whirred softly through the night toward Manhattan.

After a few minutes she heard Alex again. He was still talking about Patricia Layle. There was some danger that Patricia Layle would trivial to death one day but Alex gave her the unconscious deference of those who worship money—the unspoken feeling that if they're that rich, they can't possibly be dumb.

Alex parked his car halfway down the block in a tight space between a battered Chevrolet sedan and a wrecked Mustang from which tires, upholstery, and everything movable had been stolen. The Mustang was starting to rust and there were still pools of water on the seats from the morning's rain.

"Some neighborhood," Alex said. "I never could figure out why you want to live in a place like this. Aren't you afraid to come home at night?"

"I play the law of averages."

"Why don't you move into a prison?" Alex suggested. "The law of averages is even better."

He leaned toward her.

She murmured, "Alex, please don't."

"What's the matter?" he asked, slightly aggrieved. "Are you angry about something?"

The thick bush of his eyebrows was close to her face, the tight skin of his forehead, and the black concentration of his gaze—all inverted, magnified by closeness like a face seen under a microscope.

Without warning he moved away. There was a sharpness in his features, a straightness to the line of his mouth. A memory occurred to her with such incongruity that she smiled; she had seen that same

134

expression in the face of a monk—the severity, the asceticism, and the lurking impure sensuality.

"You don't have to explain."

She owed him this much. "It isn't you, Alex. I like you. But I'm in love with someone else."

"Hell," he answered bitterly. "Why didn't you say so?"

"I didn't realize."

"Okay. At least we know where we stand."

She waited, gauging the anger and the dismay and suddenly deciding that the dismay was close to the surface, she was about to speak when strains of music reached into the car. She recognized the tune: *O Little Town of Bethlehem*. A young man in a black leather jacket and tight trousers passed on the sidewalk, holding a transistor radio with a three-foot antenna at his ear with a black-gloved hand.

"A Merry Christmas to you," Alex said.

"Thank you, Alex."

At the entrance to the building she found the long dangling iron key, inserted it in the lock and the door opened with a grating sound. She turned and inside the dimly lit interior of the car saw Alex shake his head before he shifted into gear and drove rapidly away.

*

In the living room she mixed herself a scotch and soda, undressed and put on short red pajamas. She sat with her feet drawn up onto a chair, her knees showing. It was only eleven o'clock.

She hardly moved but her body felt charged with an undelivered message that kept trilling through nerves and tiny blood vessels. It was ridiculous. How long could she keep going like this? What a painful and futile business!

There was nothing to do but wait for the morning. She lit a cigarette and picked up *Harper's* magazine and leafed sightless through it until her attention fell back exhausted.

Unwelcome awareness returned of the intolerable hours ahead. She picked up the scotch and soda. The ice had melted and she drank lukewarm liquid with distaste. Rapidly she began turning pages of the magazine. Useless, useless.

His shirt clung in places to his back when he bent over the drafting table. She could see the ripple of muscles as he moved. A few damp strands clung to the temple of his high forehead. His lips looked thin but . . . she *must* stop. A physical yearning, sharp as an ache, was beginning. She imagined the touch of Karl's hands, the rough hardness, and the nerves in her skin came alive. Deliberate self-incitement. She had not been so foolish since she was a girl. She was no longer a human being, merely a condition.

She stubbed out the cigarette, but smoke hung motionless in the air. The first had gone into advertising and become an account executive for a hosiery firm. He had been so determined to become an important writer. They had talked for hours about the meaning and importance of Art. Nervous, with his endless talk about guilt and inadequacy, numbing doglike devotion, until finally out of pity she let him. She did not solve his guilt or inadequacy, both of which were connected somehow with his father, but at least he got her over a very important hurdle.

Dedicated young George was her first real affair. He worked with her in the JFK campaign. He was interested in her As A Person, encouraged her early attempts at painting, even approved of the endless experiments that kept her from having to face the fact that when she put paint on canvas nothing good happened. Handsome, idealistic, intelligent George was Definitely It, until she discovered he was maneuvering to get the Druse fortune to further his political ambitions. When she did not marry him he ended up in an undistinguished legal capacity with Internal Revenue.

Then Henry. She met Henry at a cocktail party to raise funds for *Partisan Review*—he was a journalist who conscientiously wrote books that did not sell. Not good-looking, but she was wary of good-looking men after George and she thought his gnome-like features pleasant when he smiled. His wife had killed herself for unexplained reasons. The first time he took her to bed she learned the meaning of physical passion and even after all the books, after the boy who went to Korea and after George, it was a revelation. Her body responded without a directive from her mind. She married Henry, lived with him in Paris for a year while he worked on a book about the student riots of April 1968. She learned to shop, to outbargain hard-fisted Parisian shopkeepers, to cook and keep house. She wore cotton dirndls and sandals. She gave up painting and took up sculpting, paid five francs a week for lessons, haunted the galleries, and finally made and sold a few portrait busts.

One afternoon Henry came home, packed everything he owned into a battered and chipped trunk and said he was going off to live with another woman. She helped him to gather his things, and the rest of the night stayed up to finish a sheer white cone that was imitation Brancusi. A week later she was back in New York talking to lawyers, looking for a new apartment and a new life.

That was everyone, so far, and a poor record to show for a girl just barely on the sunny side of thirty. She had never had a chance to practice wiles and so she did not know how to go about winning Karl.

She visited his studio often, a bare third-floor large room with north light where he was turning out descriptions of the building's final shape and form. As the working drawings took shape he had to answer many questions of design and he seemed to struggle hardest with the smallest points. She was amazed by his powers of invention. It was a stunning experience to be present while he brooded over and finally arrived at an idea. The essence of most attractive men was their work; that was why it was impossible to separate Karl Schiller from what he was creating. She was convinced it would be one of the most powerful monuments of modern times. Most modern architecture, trying to express the life around it, only succeeded in calling attention to its rigidities—to the sterilized, regimented, dehumanized world in which the machine is God. Karl's building showed in every detail, in the proportion hinging on a hairsbreadth, his personal mastery of all the plastic forces involved in the construction. In any age there could not have been more than a few who might have envisioned anything so modern and so ancient, discovering in smooth finishes and right angles the massive poetry of the stone pillars of Karnak and the mighty monasteries of the Middle Ages.

In order to keep going to his studio she had to make herself useful.

137

She had become practically an errand girl to Samuel Whitefield Associates, where Karl's ideas and detailed drawings were being translated into working drawings. Alex Johns had hired Whitefield's organization to do the immense amount of work needed to fulfill Karl Schiller's ideas because no one man could possibly do the labor involved in supplementing and completing the drawings by means of plans, elevations, sections, scale details—hundreds and hundreds of drawings showing the kind, form, size, location of the materials and decorations needed. These drawings were supplemented in turn by others showing the structural system and the mechanical, electrical, heating, ventilating, sanitary, and other installations. Then there were the specifications describing the types, qualities, finish, and placing of all the components. Into the making of a building there went a tremendous amount of detail that she had never suspected. Behind the actual edifice of steel or concrete there stood a shadow structure, made up of detailed drawings as exacting as the corresponding piece that laborers would finally place in the visible structure.

She was an unobtrusive obedient assistant. Without thinking about it Karl began to delegate work to her. She spent hours in the studio on the telephone, obtaining accurate estimates of costs, securing the lowest fair market price, getting information he wanted. He only spoke to her when absolutely necessary, for he grudged any minute from his work. When he was not actually at his drawing board he was inspecting materials, equipment, finishes in the shop drawings prepared by fabricators. In spare moments he supervised the actual construction at the site, and two or three times weekly went to the draftsmen's room at Whitefield Associates where he corrected misunderstandings, arbitrated disputes, apprehended errors, making certain that the most minute mistakes were set right.

He hardly seemed to notice her presence in the studio. She appeared to have no reality for him except as she contributed to his work. Her own desires, sharpened by the absence of physical contact, reached out and found no response. Huddled in a corner of her mind, she could only yearn to break through his denial.

Ah, Karl. Karl.

*

Evening again. She was on the cot in his studio, on the side wall between opaque, diamond-spotted glass windows. The room was cool but she had a blanket wrapped around her. Karl was at his drafting board. At nine o'clock she had gone out to get him a real dinner from a nearby restaurant. A smoke-brown barbecued chicken, hearts of artichoke, a cold bottle of Pouilly Fuisse. He usually ate delicatessen sandwiches and Coca-Cola and drank cup after cup of black coffee. He was sipping coffee now and she realized she must have been asleep; she had not made coffee.

She stretched and yawned. He glanced at her, removed his eye-glasses, and let them dangle from his hand.

"If you're tired, you ought to go home."

She lifted an edge of the brown blanket. "You put this over me."

He nodded. "You've been asleep for hours."

"Well, thank you. Thank you very much."

He turned back to his work. "You will have to deliver these specifications to Whitefield's office first thing in the morning. I promised them at eight o'clock."

"All right."

He did not reply. He was crouching over his work, impatient of conversation. Behind him was a huge bulletin board with sketches, photographs, a map of the island of Manhattan, pen-scribbled memoranda and a typewritten schedule of preliminary construction from Alexander Johns. On the wall opposite her was a seven-foot-long narrow wooden table covered with a jumble of papers, magazines, brochures advertising construction materials, and blueprints. There were standing vertical rolls of blueprints propped against the table. Everything was in carefully controlled disorder. She knew every item so well that she could recall the look of this room exactly when away from it. In that open notebook on the table, with a pencil in the clasp binding to keep it open, she had inserted a clip from a magazine with a quotation of Abraham Lincoln's: "I like to see a man proud of the place in which he lives. I like to see a man live so that his place will be proud of him." She didn't know whether Karl had seen it—he never mentioned it. The notebook lay beside a large gray looseleaf book, *The City of New York Zoning Resolution*, and was surrounded by papers, staplers, Scotch tape dispensers, stamp and ink pads and large pink colored rubber erasers.

She went to a shelf in the corner of the room where a coffeepot stood, and plugged the socket into the wall. Then she noticed she was in stockinged feet. He must have taken off her shoes, also. That excited and pleased her.

When she came back with a cup of coffee, he was finishing the specifications. On the drafting table to his left was a detail drawing for a wall in the lobby. Once again the disciplined beauty of his pencilwork held her.

She began to write him a letter in her head. Dear Mr. Schiller. Dear Karl . . . Dear, dear Karl. Will you please look over at me and notice that I am actually present in the same room? That would be a beginning. Without real intimacy the intimacy of being together was degrading, but her need for him, like an unwanted embryo, continued to grow in spite of her pathetic and useless attempts to abort it.

While he finished his cup of coffee, Karl checked the specifications she had brought earlier from Whitefield's office. There was a terrible disadvantage to being a nice girl. A whore tempts whom she pleases, but nice girls are powerless in the grip of good manners. I would like to ask you if you have any interest in making love to me. What would you reply? Would I receive nothing but a puzzled stare and some quizzical evasion? I wish I could be a whore. I'm not really attractive enough to be a good one. Perhaps I could be a horrid queen in a red wig and command: *Come here, Essex*. But in the end even the hag at Windsor was cheated because she could not command love. The courtiers who dissembled so well could not give that to her. Not quite everything is purchasable. Almost everything, but not quite. You are not, Karl.

"I like that," she said, indicating the detail drawing for the lobby wall. She got back a small, barely audible grunt.

He turned the last page of the specifications and laid them down on the drafting table. "It's late. You ought to go home."

140

"It hardly pays. I have to deliver those specifications to White-field's office in the morning."

He considered this is silence. Then: "All right. You can sleep here until then. I have work to do, anyhow."

"Aren't you going to sleep at all?"

"I'm not tired. Go. You can lie down on my cot."

"It's all right. I've napped already—and coffee will keep me awake."

He turned to her. "But what will you do? You don't even have anything to read."

"I'll manage."

"More than five hours? You can't just sit here with nothing to do."

"I've done it before."

He was clearly astonished to hear it. "Why?"

"I think you're doing important, beautiful work. And I love to watch beautiful things being created."

"Very flattering, Miss Druse." He held his pencil thoughtfully near his mouth like a long forefinger. "You're a sculptor yourself, aren't you?"

"I've worked at it."

"My Eva was an artist. She did ceramics."

There was such a malignant surprise in the last few words that Barbara was momentarily at a loss.

"Your wife?" she ventured at last.

He turned back to his drafting board. "No, we never married."

His pencil moved into a bright cone of fluorescent light and stopped there, half in shadow and half out.

"Do you have any photographs of her?"

"They were all . . . destroyed. Sometimes, I try to bring back her face . . . but the memory plays tricks."

The pencil began to move again as though powered by a source other than his hand. His voice continued: "I think of her often. There is an old Latin saying. *Absentes adsunt.* The absent are present."

"Hasn't there been anyone else?"

It was a risky question but they were on new ground and she did not wish to turn back. This was their first conversation that was not stripped bare of personal content.

"No one important." He stared at the sheet of paper before him as though mentally drawing faces on it. "There is always work. Eventually, that replaces everything."

"I don't believe it," she said.

"What do you believe?"

"Love is important too. Work doesn't have to shut that out."

In his slightly widened eyes there appeared an awareness of her as a separate person.

"You seem to be an authority."

He continued to look at her, smiling gently. Suddenly she realized this moment would never return and could not afford to be lost. She had to take off the uniform of her gentility, her breeding.

All the strength seemed to have drained from her voice until it was only a whisper. "I know what it means to be in love. To have it all there in your head and heart and not be able to say it to the one you love."

His smile slowly disappeared. "I imagine that can be a problem."

"Yes, it can."

His expression became quite serious. "It's cold in here. You ought to have gone home hours ago."

"I'd rather be here with you."

What had happened to the nice girl? A mask fallen. She was being more forward than she had thought it possible for her to be, no longer trying to hold to the very fine cautiously controlled line that balanced what she said with what she was.

He was turned inward upon some incredible thought—she saw it lurking in the corners of his eyes. He spoke as though words were somehow precious and fragile and had to be carried with the most extreme possible care: "Is there any more coffee?"

"I'm afraid not."

The moment was tense with a peculiar electricity, a force feeding on sensations rather than conscious will. In a moment he would speak and everything would end. The tenuous link that she had managed at such pains to establish would snap. She waited, her heart frozen.

"Miss Druse, you are a most . . . exceptional woman. I have always . . . admired you . . . very much."

He might have found a more redeeming phrase, some more warming description, but she sensed that he was expressing a genuine feeling. There was not what she had feared, the unmistakable note of rejection. A woman can go so hungry that she will feed on any crumb offered.

"I don't suppose that you could call me Barbara."

In this bare studio room, where she had finally embarked upon self-disclosure, in this poorly lit space with a bright fluorescent at one end, and a dim shaded lamp above the sofa, she had the most inexplicable feeling that they were coming closer.

"Amazing," he said.

Everything came to inevitable standstill. She felt the moment endlessly repeating without advancing.

"Yes," she said.

She no longer wished to do anything, only wished to feel something. She had made a beginning but the process would have to continue without her aid. She was uncomfortable and weary, but not afraid. There was such strength in him that she knew there would be tenderness.

At last he said, very gently, "Perhaps you should make some more coffee, Barbara. We must talk . . ."

*

Alex Johns came out of the private bathroom to his office to find Louise standing at his desk.

"Your mother is on the phone."

"Collect?"

"Naturally."

"One day she'll pay for a call. Then I'll worry that it's really bad news."

He joked about his mother because he disliked having to talk to her so often. He had left home when he was sixteen, shortly after his father died, but he had not escaped any more than his brother Frank had. He paid a maternal tax every day of his life—a tax payable in the currency of guilt: interminable weekly phone calls, frequent letters and visits home, presents, and above all a constant willingness to do whatever Mother wanted. In little ways and big ones she was still collecting for having delivered him onto the planet. Now he listened to her monotonous accents on the telephone as other men might listen to a dripping faucet. He was annoyed but could not rouse himself to turn her off. She had an untranquilizing effect on his spirit.

She was telling him about her kidney complaint and about his brother Frank and it was not clear which she considered the malady. Frank was a bachelor and lived with her but Mother had no respect for him because he had gotten a law degree only to come back to practice in a small town.

"Frank hasn't got your get up and go," Mother said. "He takes after your father."

"I'm glad he's around to look after you."

"I wish he'd made more of himself. You were such different boys even as children."

She began telling him a familiar anecdote about how, as a boy, he had set up a watch for tourists near the monument that blocked traffic in the town's center to honor the Union dead. When tourists driving through on their way to the lakes in summer or the ski resorts in winter stopped to look at the monument, Alex handed out cards advertising their rooming house and gave a little sales spiel about how his great-grandfather had fought and died at Gettysburg. There was a Malcolm Johns immortalized on the base of the monument but he was no relation.

Alex did not try to interrupt or correct her to point out that she had made him set up the watch at the monument. He always let her talk as long as she wanted to, although afterward he often could not remember what she had said.

Louise opened the door to his office.

"Someone's waiting in the anteroom to see you," she said.

Alex covered the mouthpiece of the telephone. "Who is it?"

"He wouldn't give his name. He said you'd know him from this." Louise came in and handed him a small square white card on which in a fine scroll were two words, *The Baron*.

"I'll see him," Alex said. He uncovered the mouthpiece and said,

"I'm sorry, Mom. An important business matter has just come up. I'll call you tomorrow."

The visitor who entered had a dark face with liquid mournful eyes and he wore a sharp glen plaid suit with notched lapels.

"It's good to see you again, Mr. Johns."

"Good to see you. Any special reason?"

"We were looking over the account. You skipped payments three weeks in December."

"I told your man I needed a little more time."

"Last week you didn't see him at all. You sent word that you were in some kind of a meeting." The visitor touched the knot of a tie too small to fit the space between the wings of his high starched collar. "That's why I decided to come in person. We like all our accounts straightened out for the New Year."

"I can only tell you the same thing I told him. I need a little more time."

"In the old country," the visitor said sadly, "when men shook hands on a deal it was better than putting their names on it. *Mano morte*, they called it. The dead hand. Once you shook a man's hand you could count on him going through with a deal even if it ruined him. Even if it meant selling his wife and kids."

"You'll be paid," Alex said. "You don't have to worry about that."

The large brown eyes were mildly accusing. "We make a lot of loans to people in your line of business, but we don't have the kind of trouble we're having with you."

"How much do I owe?"

The man took out a small looseleaf notebook. He turned the pages slowly with thumb and forefinger until he found the entry he was looking for.

"Two hundred and sixty," he said.

"That can't be."

"That's what it says."

"I only borrowed two hundred."

"You haven't been making regular payments. The vig adds up."

Vigorish, Alex thought, not showing the exasperation he felt. The Mafia's word for interest. It was really extortion. Ten percent a week.

Week after week after week. You had to be crazy or desperate to get involved with people like this.

"I've got a big payment due from Zenith Oil as soon as steel is delivered."

"How long do we have to wait, Mr. Johns?" the soft voice asked.

"A few more weeks. It's the best I can do. Believe me, there's nobody ahead of you on my creditors' list."

"We don't like long-term loans. We like to keep our money turning over."

"I'm paying interest—so you've got nothing to lose."

"You're behind on the interest too."

"I'll pay off the whole loan when I get the money from Zenith Oil. Meanwhile, if you're worried, maybe I can scrape up collateral . . ."

"We don't use collateral, Mr. Johns. We do private business. No courts, no law."

"I understand."

"Okay. Here's the deal. As of now, the loan is three hundred G's. The vigorish is thirty grand a week. There won't be any more stalling on the vig, Mr. Johns. No postponements. Nothing of that kind. In return, we extend the loan."

"All I need is a few weeks."

"You're not making terms. We are. Keep in mind, Mr. Johns, that *you're* our collateral. And we'd sure hate to collect out of you."

The man got up and walked to the door with slow deliberate precise steps, as though treading an imaginary straight line.

A minute after the visitor left, Alex pushed down the button of his intercom.

"Vinnie Haleson. Get him right away."

"Yes, Mr. Johns."

When the buzzer alerted him, he picked up the telephone.

"I've got a problem, Vinnie. I was wondering if Zenith Oil would stretch a point for me."

"What exactly are you referring to, Alex?"

"I know the contract doesn't call for me to be paid until steel comes in. But I need money now."

The answer was cool: "It's our policy not to make payments without an equivalent fulfillment of contract."

146

"That's everybody's policy. But there are exceptions."

"Big companies don't make exceptions. What's your hurry?"

"I'm in a bind. I'm not blaming anyone, but this has been a jinx job for me."

"A jinx job?"

"Look at the weather. Freezing cold, then rain. The pit is four to five foot deep in water and even the pumps can't clear it out. Then there was that problem with the foundation."

"You adopted a highly unorthodox procedure."

"You had your experts in. They told you there was no loss of resiliency in the concrete."

"You were lucky. Going ahead like that without consulting us isn't a very good way to establish faith."

"I took a chance. If I lost, it'd have been on my head." Alex didn't want to argue around the fringes. "Vinnie, I've honestly gotten to the point where I can't see my way clear into the New Year without some cash in the till. I'm not talking about meeting bills." He hunched forward in his chair, pausing to form each word carefully, as though this were a transatlantic call and he did not want anything misunderstood. "I'm talking about bankruptcy." Some quality in his tone, some urgency of the phrasing communicated his real need.

"Bankruptcy!"

"If I go down, Vinnie, the whole thing goes down with me. Your Zenith Oil building too. You'll be stuck to pay off because there isn't any surety bond."

Vinnie sounded very annoyed. "I told Peter we should have one. He thought a surety bond would be a waste of money."

Alex sat quietly, stretching his knee against a throbbing pain. "All I need, Vinnie, is enough to see me through. I've never had to beg for money like this. But I can't help myself."

A full half minute ticked by, and that was promising because silence meant Vinnie was thinking it over. If he intended to say no it wouldn't take this long.

"How much do you need?"

"Half a million. There's a lot more due me when steel comes in."

"I'll put your case before Peter," Vinnie said finally.

"I need an answer quickly. When will you talk to him?"

"Tonight."

"Can I call you later?"

"If I have anything to report, I'll let you know."

The phone clicked.

Alex reached to the desktop to pick up a green bottle. He shook three aspirin tablets into his hand, and poured half a glass of water from a pitcher. A damn irony, that a man with so many important deals pending should be brought to a pass where simple survival depended on getting a single payment on one building.

He experienced a little jolt, a shock wakened by the single word. Survival. The telephone was too uncertain a line of communication; Alex had more confidence in his ability to influence a situation when he was personally in contact with developments. The dice were rolling and he couldn't wait. He had to get an answer tonight, by parking on Vinnie's doorstep.

He swallowed the aspirin tablets with the half glass of water. His bad leg was giving him hell.

*

As the limousine entered the driveway of the Queens Point mansion, it was a quarter to nine. The dark gables of the house stood out as limned black shapes against gray night clouds. Gravel crunched beneath the car wheels as it made the circle and stopped before the house.

"Come back for me in an hour," Alex told his chauffeur.

A light was glowing within a Gothic window on the left. He went up broad shallow steps toward the front door. He couldn't understand why Vinnie Haleson chose to live in a house like this, antique, ugly, weathered by seasons. It was like an island of old time within the present day. Maybe Vinnie liked it because clearly this house said: the Halesons have always lived on the hill.

When he telephoned an hour ago, Vinnie Haleson was not at home. Ann, however, insisted that he drive out to the house and wait for Vinnie to return.

"I expect him by the time you get here," she said. "He just drove over to Dad's place for a talk."

"They're discussing my problem—I'd like to be there when he gets back with the verdict."

"Well, I'll try to keep you entertained until he comes home."

"That will be fine, Mrs. Haleson."

At the front door he raised a dull bronze antique clapper and let it fall.

The door opened. Ann Haleson wore a short yellow brunch coat and blue and yellow flowered satin pants with flaring cuffs.

She stepped aside and allowed him to enter. "Vinnie called a few minutes ago. I'm afraid you'll be disappointed."

"What's the trouble?"

"He'll be another two hours."

"Perhaps you'd prefer if I came back later."

"Not at all. I'm sure you'll be more comfortable here. That is, if you don't mind talking to me."

He was struck by a sense of no one else present in the house. There is a kind of stillness a big house gives off that clearly reveals when it is empty.

"The library is the most comfortable room," she said. She began leading the way, moving ahead of him with a slight undulant movement of her hips. Her ash blond hair was tied behind with a broad blue ribbon.

While he was mixing drinks at the bar in the library, she perched on the arm of a leather chair. She seemed amused at something.

"Why are you smiling?" he asked.

"You didn't ask me what my drink was."

"Scotch sour."

"How nice of you to remember." She brushed back her hair with one hand.

"I try to please, ma'am."

"Only women, I imagine."

"Why do you say that?"

"What is Vinnie's drink?"

He poured his Jack Daniel's. "You've got me there."

"See?"

On a table in the library there was a silver framed portrait of a small boy about five years old. He had blond curly hair, wide eyes and a very sober expression.

Alex indicated the portrait. "Yours?"

She nodded. "His name is Richard. He's eleven now."

"He looks like you."

"Yes."

"Is he away at school?"

"He's at a private boarding school owned and operated by a woman who's trained to work with retarded children."

"Oh. I'm sorry."

"He's been there since he was four years old. I go to see him every Sunday. Vinnie never goes to see him at all."

"Sometimes they can do a lot for kids like that."

"They've been trying ever since he was two. Before we sent him away we took him to psychiatrists, brain specialists, X-ray laboratories."

"It must be hard on you."

"There's no cure or treatment and no hope he will outgrow it."

"You go every Sunday?"

"Vinnie says I shouldn't go on torturing myself. He says it's silly to go on trying to be a mother to a boy who doesn't even know who I am."

"I guess you can't help it."

"He doesn't care about his own child. God, what a cold-blooded fish! He doesn't have any human feeling."

"That may be just his way of trying to deal with it."

"You couldn't be that way."

"I've never had a kid of my own."

"I can tell. You'd be a good father. Not like Vinnie."

"At the rate I'm going I'll never find out."

"Not married?"

"Divorced."

"You'll get married again. Some woman will get you."

"Not if I can help it."

"You're a damned attractive man."

"Well, thanks."

"I mean that."

"Thanks again."

He dropped an ice cube out of the tongs as he was transferring it; the ice skittered off the bar onto the tufted rug.

"Sorry." He came around to retrieve it and when he bent she was there before him. Their shoulders touched.

He straightened up. "Are we alone here?"

"Why do you ask?"

"When I came in, it occurred to me the place was empty."

"Martin and Jane—our couple—have gone off for the holidays. We're alone."

He started to take another ice cube out of the bucket with his tongs. Then he put it back.

"I'd better come back later."

"Why?"

"This is silly," he said.

"What is?"

"You know."

She touched his fingers. "Hello, there."

"Hello yourself."

"They're cold. From picking up the ice." Still holding his hand, she put her other hand over his and rubbed slightly. "I'll make them warm again."

"We don't have time," he said.

False eyelashes fluttered down against her cheeks. "I told you, he won't be home for two hours."

"You really want to?"

"I've wanted to from the first minute. You didn't pay attention to me."

"You were married. You are married."

"That doesn't mean he owns me. My body is my own and I can do what I like with it."

She removed her hands from his, and slowly began to undo the looped soft big buttons on her brunch coat.

He stilled her hands, then kissed her and finished unbuttoning her brunch coat. She was wearing a blouse of blue Chinese silk underneath and within the soft tight silk he saw the shape of her breasts.

"You excite me," he said.

"I can see that. I can feel it."

He touched her breasts, sliding his fingers carefully along the slopes. She watched him do it before she slowly raised her eyes.

"I don't believe you," he said. "I just don't believe you."

"Let's go upstairs."

She was not any part of his reason for being here, but the moment was too delicious not to savor. He had spent most of his life taking any opportunity without waiting because if you did wait nothing better might ever come along.

The cube of ice slipped farther along the bar, and fell with a soft soundless plop onto the carpet.

*

Vinnie Haleson opened the gate and went through into the front garden. There he paused a moment. This was the high point—returning to where so many Halesons waited to welcome him, kinsmen linked through time by the indissolvable ties of blood.

Far in the distance he heard the hoot of a train; the 9:27 on its way to neighboring Dobbs Ferry. On time, as usual. Even the trains, somewhat antiquated, running on schedule were a symbol of a way of life that preserved old standards in the face of the steady encroachment of progress.

He put the attaché case down on a side table in the living room. Peter had wanted to take time to study the various figures with accompanying graphs and charts that Vinnie had brought with him in his attaché case. At that point, Vinnie had thought it would be a long evening but after some hemming and hawing Peter agreed to let Vinnie handle it as he thought best. That had saved a good deal of discussion. It was perfectly clear that they had to keep Alex Johns afloat until the building was complete and the subcontractors paid, or sustain a loss running into the millions.

He went into the library to make himself a solitary drink. For someone who had spent so much of his youth alone he really disliked solitude. A tumbler was on the bar, overflowing. A scotch sour.

Ann must have mixed it and forgotten. The melting ice now overflowed the glass.

He poured a Dewar's for himself, dropped in an ice cube and remembered suddenly the weekend on Dick Peabody's yacht when he first met Ann. Two days and a night on the *Menemsha*. A wonderful party. Dick Peabody was an excellent sportsman and a fine fellow.

It was clear from the first that Ann was interested in him but he wasn't quite sure whether he wanted to do anything about it. She was much younger than he, fourteen years, and obviously sure that she could get whatever she wanted. She seemed callow, an unformed personality, and she had a tendency to laugh too much.

When he kept avoiding her overtures it increased her determination. At first he was amused, then flattered by her rather shameless courtship. Finally he became intrigued because, after all, she *was* the youngest Druse daughter and while the Druse name was not entirely a social asset—Elihu had been a thorough scoundrel and his father before him a provincial bank manager—there was no question that wealth gave them entry to the best circles. Ann's coming out party had been the social event of the season.

After their marriage he had been rather pleasantly surprised to discover Ann was not as superficial as she seemed. She had an affectionate nature, a good if somewhat cynical mind, and the poise and confidence of one on whom privilege has conferred a sense of personal merit.

On the whole, their marriage might have worked except for Richard. He would like to have produced an heir who might one day succeed to ownership of the house on the hill. It wasn't likely now; the generations of Halesons would come to a full stop. It seemed unfair that so much that was venerable and true depended for its survival on sex: a spasm of muscles ending in a vague feeling of depression and dissatisfaction. Someone should have provided a wiser guardian method for the preservation of such important values.

He sat in the armchair by the fireplace and wondered if his marriage would have turned out differently if Richard had been a normal boy. Ann suited him well in most ways. She was a good hostess when she had a mind to be. There had been some fine parties in the early days.

That was before the inroads of the *arrivistes* from Manhattan, before the Beechers and Semples moved to Europe, the Pattersons divorced, old Marion Cheshire died, and Dick Peabody was killed in that senseless plane crash. Those gaps could not be filled, certainly not by the likes of the Garsons who were Ann's current favorites. In times past, when the Halesons were at the zenith, there would have been no possibility of a Garson carrying social mobility even so far as to curry friendship. There were frequent and probably documented stories about Tony Garson's escapades, and sometimes, if one could believe the rumors, liaisons with women of a distinctly lower sort. The fact that such rumors were extant was in itself proof of the wide social gulf between a Garson and a Haleson. There had been situations in his own family, heaven knew, but always handled with discretion, always worked through to a perfectly sensible solution. Chambermaids bought off, showgirls recompensed, and misalliances ended by sending an objectionable partner abroad. There had been narrow places but the Halesons always behaved with tact and discretion. There had never been a stain on the family escutcheon.

He noted a yellow piece of material partly hidden by the open door to the library. He got up and went over. Ann's brunch coat, dropped here. That was really carrying laziness too far. She was a neglectful child.

Standing in the doorway, he heard a faint noise from upstairs. He lifted his head, and identified a creaking floorboard, the one beside Ann's bed that he meant to have fixed. He had not realized the creaking was audible downstairs.

Then he heard Ann's loose untidy, open throated laugh.

A door closed and varying footsteps entered the corridor upstairs, one pair light, one pair heavy. The feet made no sounds on the deep pile carpet but the impact of weight traveled ahead to the stairway.

When they appeared at the head of the stairs neither noticed him at the foot.

They started down, their hands linked, and when Alex saw him, his grip must have tightened reflexively because Ann gave him a quizzical protesting glance. Something in his face caused her to look down the stairs.

Vinnie was sure he passed their scrutiny with a special grace. On the other hand, Alex's nervousness showed up in a sudden lack of coordination. His left hand reached for the stair banister, missed it by a fraction of an inch, finally clutched it, and quickly pulled away leaving rounded moisture on the smoothly polished wood. His right hand did not seem to know whether to let go of Ann or to slowly grind her hand into a pulp.

She finally pulled away. "Vinnie, you're home early."

Alex appeared stricken. The play of emotion on his face was ridiculously uncontrolled.

"I just stopped by to find out . . ." he began and then faltered, watching him hopelessly. "I got here a couple of minutes ago."

"I heard you upstairs," Vinnie corrected him.

"Ann—Mrs. Haleson—was showing me around . . ." His voice wavered.

Ann touched her damp disordered hair. As she looked down at him her lips had a slightly blurred look as though she had smudged her lipstick. She was wearing the white crepe dress he had always liked. Her legs were bare.

"Are we just going to stand on the staircase for the rest of the evening? I don't know about anyone else, but I could use a drink."

"There was one on the bar. You apparently left it there. And you dropped this."

He held out the yellow brunch coat. Ann ignored him and brushed past, with Alex following a step behind. Vinnie stood aside. All through his adolescence he had engaged in gallant unvictorious efforts against stronger faster boys. In track at Harvard he was the most graceful runner—arms, legs, knees, all worked in perfect rhythm with his head held high—a moving picture film of high stepping grace. But Danny Cumberland, barrel chested, graceless, all aspraddle, usually went by him in the stretch. Some people accused Vinnie of not trying because his stride appeared so effortless, because nothing interrupted its flowing movement, but he was trying until his heart felt close to bursting.

As he entered the study, Ann took her drink from the bar. She poured off a little into the ice bucket and took it with her to the armchair.

155

Alex stayed near the bar.

Ann said, "Don't be nervous, Alex. It's all right."

"I think we ought to clear this up so there'll be no misunderstanding."

"There's no misunderstanding," Ann said, sipping her drink.

Alex slowly moved the palm of one hand against the other. "I wouldn't want you to get the wrong idea, Vinnie. Ann was just showing me around. I drove out here to get the verdict from you on that advance payment . . ."

"And you arrived a few minutes ago," Vinnie said, working his lips into a smile. "You told me."

Ann slowly circled the glass in her hands, causing the ice to clink. "You're beginning to enjoy this, Vinnie. Whenever you begin to enjoy anything I begin to hate it."

"Can't we be reasonable?" Alex asked. He met Vinnie's gaze uneasily, defiantly. "There's really nothing to explain. I drove out and your wife said you'd be home in a little while, so I decided to wait."

Vinnie was contemplating overt physical action for the first time since, as an officer during the war, he had intervened in a brawl between two soldiers, and the one who was drunk took a swing at him. Vinnie had knocked him down. It had made him slightly queasy, the hard impact of his fist on a yielding face, but he was sure he would not be queasy when he did the same thing to Alex.

Ann said, "If you try to bash him, he'll probably break you in half."

His fingers had begun to clench, and she had noticed.

Ann sipped her drink, watching him amusedly over the rim of her glass. "I know he looks small but you ought to see his muscles, darling."

He had looked forward to releasing part of his anger in a single violent act, but there were other, better means of coming off effectively in the situation. As his anger began to cool, he felt relief at having avoided a violent scene.

He answered with an air of mild remonstrance, "I didn't think you'd stoop this low, Ann. You might as well have slept with a stable boy."

"I don't go in for breeding like you do, darling." Ann tilted her glass and with a sudden outward movement threw its contents over his trouser leg. "And don't get insulting, you bastard!"

Alex said, "Now look here!"

Vinnie removed the handkerchief from his breast pocket and slowly wiped his trouser leg. "If you act like a whore," he told Ann, "you can hardly be expected to be treated as a lady."

"This is stupid," Alex said. "If you'd just take my word that nothing happened . . ."

"I wouldn't take your word for anything," Vinnie said coolly. "Peter Druse and I agreed about that less than an hour ago."

Alex's black almond-shaped eyes remained steady but the pupils seemed to expand as though to catch every nuance of Vinnie's meaning.

"What are you trying to tell me?" he asked with assumed belligerence.

"Simply that Peter and I decided against making an advance to you at the present time." He felt no more compunction than he would have in swatting an insect.

"You'll be cutting your own throat."

"We've met our obligations to you and we'll continue to do so."

"You know what I'm talking about."

"We can't protect you from the consequences of your own stupidity."

"You're the ones who are being stupid."

They all heard the sound of car tires on the driveway and headlights swept the room.

"I believe that's your car, Mr. Johns," Vinnie said.

Alex did not answer. He seemed to be searching for words to throw. How much more satisfactory this way is, Vinnie thought.

Ann said, "Alex darling, will you take me as far as the station? There's still time to catch the 10:37 to town. The fucking trains always run on time around here."

"Don't be silly. I'll take you in to the city with me."

Vinnie managed to sustain an air of contemptuous amusement. "Don't you think you're acting hastily?"

"I can't see myself going into another new year with you. In the morning I'll talk to my lawyer about a divorce."

157

"Suppose I'm not willing to give you a divorce?" Vinnie asked with a mirthless smile.

"Oh, you won't contest it, darling. Think of all the distasteful publicity. The Haleson name in all those tabloids."

He knew from experience that she could be vindictive.

Ann turned to Alex. "How about it? Can you wait a few minutes for me to pack a bag?"

"Glad to," Alex said. At last he seemed to find the words he had been searching for. "You won't need to stay at a hotel tonight, honey. You can stay at my place."

*

At the long wooden table in the front room of the field office, Jim Otis was writing a work progress report.

"Anything happen while I was away?" Tom MacLaren asked as he came in. He was wearing a pinstriped suit, white shirt and tie.

"Nothing important, Mr. MacLaren."

Tom sat down and put his feet up on either side of the wooden horses that supported the work table. Sooner or later he would have to tell Otis what had happened before the commission today but he didn't mind putting it off as long as possible.

Otis filled him in on the events of the morning.

The initial contingent of Mohawks had arrived. The Indians were a legend among construction workers because of their fantastic, scientifically unexplained ability to work at great heights without the least sign of fear or giddiness. The tribe had first learned their dangerous trade when the Dominion Bridge was being put up eighty years ago for the Canadian Pacific Railroad across the St. Lawrence River near Montreal. The Dominion Company hired the Indians for menial tasks at first, but the steelworkers, clinging to dizzying heights, soon discovered Mohawks standing to look curiously over their shoulders; so the Indians were taught steelworking and the Dominion Bridge later became known in jest as the Indian Ironworking College.

The Indians were now helping to install steel anchor bolts and billet plates in the foundation. These usually arrived a week before the steel for the building's framework. Most of the billet plates were already in, and grouting was underway.

Otis told him that grouting would probably be complete by the end of the week.

"Okay," Tom said with satisfaction, "the job is moving along."

They went on to discuss an insurance company request for information about a street crane being used on the job. This rig, mounted on a truck and based on the street outside the construction site, was similar to a ten-ton, two-hundred-foot boom that had recently been involved in an accident on another construction site. That boom had buckled and smashed down into the roof of a car, injuring three passengers, and the Buildings Commissioner had convened a board of inquiry to look into safety factors involved in construction cranes operating in city streets. The insurance company wanted to know the design of the crane in use on this job, the type and strength of the metal used and the stresses built in, as well as the skill of the operator and where the crane would be placed and used on the job.

"They're getting a little edgy," Otis said. "It always happens when the steel for the framework is about to be delivered. All the new trades start moving in then and they get a lot more to worry about."

In common with most general contractors, Alex Johns insisted on wrap-up insurance, in which all subcontractors were insured by the same company. This cut red tape and confusion when a claim originated out of an accident on the job, but also escalated the risk for the insurance company.

"Tell them what they want to know," Tom said.

"There's another problem involving the insurance company. I was talking with Don Macey—the foreman of the Mohawks. There's a man he wants to put on but he's not sure whether he can."

"A steelworker?"

Otis nodded. "Name is Joe Labache. Age fifty-four, married, father of three children. A full-blooded Mohawk Indian and a member in good standing of Local 40 of the Bridge, Structural, and Ironworker's Union."

"What's the problem?"

"Joe Labache has been retired a few years. He'd been bothered by dizzy spells after an accident when a cable line lashed back and gave him a bad concussion."

"Why's he want to work again?"

"A couple of months ago he lost his oldest son, Danny, when a freak thing happened in a downtown office building. One of those million to one shots. On the thirtieth floor concrete burst out of the forms and flowed right into the open shaft. Eight yards of concrete—11,000 pounds—in a free fall all the way from the thirtieth to the nineteenth floor before it hit the stairway."

"Christ," Tom said, imagining the force of that impact.

"It carried down all the staircases from the nineteenth to the first floor and piled up three stories high in the bottom of the shaft. Danny was somewhere in that pile." Otis looked down at his tabletop. "Joe Labache has to go back to work to support his son's family."

"What have we got to do with that?"

"Don Macey would put him on, but he doesn't want the contractor or the insurance company to make a fuss about Joe's dizzy spells."

"Did Labache see a doctor?"

"Yeah. He checked out okay."

"So what do you think?"

"I told Don Macey I'd ask you. After all, you're the boss, Mr. MacLaren."

Tom had the clear feeling that Otis was mocking him. No particular inflection, nothing you could hear on a tape recorder, but a quiet insolence that made his skin prickle. Otis never used his first name, but the formality was not a mark of respect. Not the way Otis said it.

"I'm asking your opinion," Tom said.

"It's risky. Labache is with the bolting gang. You can't afford dizzy spells up there."

Tom slowly removed his feet from the wooden horses of the work table. "If Don Macey says he's ready to work, then he is. I trust these Indians. Put him to work."

"Yes, Mr. MacLaren."

There was silence for a moment while Tom went to the locker in the office to change out of his street clothes.

Otis looked over at him. "How did it go, Mr. MacLaren?"

Tom pulled on his work trousers. "I only had to testify for about two minutes."

"Did you tell the commission the collapse of the building was caused by that powershovel?"

The actual words were inoffensive enough; it was the damn attitude.

Tom nodded curtly.

"I don't think Mr. Johns will be pleased," Otis said.

"He knew what I was going to say."

Otis regarded him speculatively. "That doesn't sound like the Alex Johns I know."

Tom lifted one foot off the cement floor while he put on a rubber-soled shoe.

"Maybe you don't know him as well as you think."

"What is the commission going to do now?"

"I can't tell."

Otis pushed away the sheets on which he had been working. "They can't ignore your testimony."

"I don't know if they put that much weight on it. After all, there was a lot of other testimony that didn't agree with me." Tom pulled on his other shoe. "A lot of experts thought the accident was caused by bad subsurface conditions."

Otis answered in an affected ungrammatical drawl, "Experts ain't hard to find when you need them, Mr. MacLaren."

There was a basic chemical antagonism between them, the sort of deep inbred hostility that not even politeness could mask.

"They were giving their honest opinion. Just as I was."

"Did you tell them about the worker who wouldn't go up on the hotel building because it was shaking so?"

Again—the insolence, growing more apparent every minute. It was hard to deal with this sort of thing firmly but it was also clear that he would have to.

"There wasn't any point in that. I don't know where Al Webb is any more. He lost an arm in that accident. I think he's living in California someplace. I wouldn't even know where to get in touch with him."

"If you mentioned him, I imagine the commission could have issued a subpoena—or had somebody take his testimony out there."

"It isn't my business to round up witnesses," Tom answered sharply.

Otis drew the sheets of his work progress report slowly back toward him as though they contained testimony he wanted to examine. When he did not speak, Tom's annoyance increased.

"You're supposed to be an engineer," he said. "You couldn't get up before a commission and swear *you* know what caused that accident."

"I wasn't there, Mr. MacLaren."

"It's up to the commissioners to decide now. We can rely on them to make a fair decision."

"All they need is the facts, Mr. MacLaren."

"Well, they've got all the facts now."

"Sure, Mr. MacLaren. And I don't think Mr. Johns is going to be upset."

This was too much. It was the nearest Jim Otis had come to saying that there had been some sort of secret agreement between himself and Alex Johns about what he was going to say to the commission.

"Tell me something, Jim."

"Yes, Mr. MacLaren?"

"What makes you so unhappy? Your job? There are plenty of college graduates who don't have any better job than you've got."

"I haven't complained."

"Personally, I was always a strong believer in college. But I'm not now."

Otis smiled with his lips. "I'm sorry to hear that, Mr. MacLaren."

"You've got a pretty good opinion of yourself. But you don't know as much as you think. That business about the foundation. You were so damn sure that the whole thing wouldn't work."

Otis ran his hand over his sweater slowly. "I was only giving my opinion."

Tom buttoned his work shirt. On the outside of his locker door he kept his mother's picture hanging from a chain loop on a hook. *—Don't you know no one matters but my baby? I don't have any-*

162

one in the world but you. Her family was old Virginia. Unfortunately, the family had undergone financial reverses and she had
suffered in adolescence from a nervous condition that made it impossible for her to endure steady schooling, so she never attained the
position in life she was fitted for. Nevertheless, she tried to instill
in Tom some of her attitudes: the "redneck illiterates" who con-
stituted many of their neighbors were no better than darkies; in
fact, darkies were rather nice provided they did not forget their
proper station in life and were deferential and obliging. There were
two kinds of Negroes, the good ones and the uppity ones, and he
grew up believing that so firmly that nothing prepared him for the
likes of Sergeant Jonas or Otis.

Tom closed the locker door and turned to Otis. "You just keep
in mind who you're working for."

"I know who that is, Mr. MacLaren."

"You got any complaints, you learn to keep them to yourself."

"No backtalk, Mr. MacLaren?"

"That's about the size of it."

Wearing his work jacket and trousers, Tom went to the area of the
office that was his private domain, behind two desks placed at right
angles. On the wall behind his chair hung diagrams from the architect
and a calendar with a beautiful view of the bay at Naples. The
calendar was a present from the concrete contractor and the setting
was Italy because most concrete workers were Italian.

A few minutes later Otis brought him the weekly report to sign.
This summary of progress on the construction would be forwarded
to Alex Johns, to Zenith Oil Corporation, and to the architect Karl
Schiller. Tom read it over carefully. Otis had done his usual thorough
job.

Nevertheless, Tom made a few additions in penwriting just to let
Otis know there was someone over him in authority.

"I'll hold this for a while. There are some things I still want to
change."

"Yes, Mr. MacLaren." Again, no particular inflection.

When Jim Otis was out of the office, Tom scribbled his name
quickly on the report and put it into the outbasket for duplicates to
be made and mailed.

*

The winter sun was descending toward the distant city skyline when Alex stepped out of his limousine in front of a brownstone house on a quiet street in Brooklyn Heights. A fiery explosion was turning the city across the river into one-dimensional black silhouette, with details blotted out and nothing left but the jutting achievement.

"Don't wait."

"Very well, Mr. Johns."

Edward, the chauffeur, did not betray by the smallest inflection that he received exactly this instruction every time he dropped Alex off at this particular address. But the meeting with Ginger was not for pleasure this time. It was business. Damn important business.

At the foot of the short flight of steps, Alex paused to admire the view across the river. Some of those buildings had his bones and blood in them, were built over him as surely as the churches of Rome were built on relics of the martyrs.

He mounted the steps to the front door of the brownstone and pushed the doorbell. From within, he heard the familiar excited footsteps.

Ginger opened the door. "Alex, dear," she said.

She wore a vanilla-colored blouse and a soft flaring wool skirt that flattered her somewhat ample hips. Her erect carriage gave a fine display to a magnificent bosom.

She took off his hat and coat and hung them in the closet. She adjusted his coat on the hanger, smoothing the shoulders to the proper slope without wrinkling.

"Can I get you anything to drink?" she asked.

"I'll get myself one."

She kept the Jack Daniel's bottle on the second shelf in the kitchen. There was also a gallon bottle of Almaden burgundy on the floor shelf of the cabinet where she kept floor wax, cleaning fluid, household cement, light bulbs, and assorted hardware sundries.

He went back into the living room with his drink and they talked for a while about his mother and her kidney complaint, about his younger brother Frank who had stayed on in the house with Mother in the small New Hampshire town, about the difference between living in a small town and a big city.

"If I'd lived in a small town I might have avoided a lot of problems," Ginger said.

Her problems included two unfortunate long-term romances, one with a small-time crook and another with a roaring bully and drunkard.

"You'd have had different kinds of problems," Alex said. "You'd have married a dentist and had four kids and be a chairlady of the PTA."

"You make it sound terrible. It isn't so terrible."

He noticed with surprise that Ginger was close to tears. Arranging the knitting in her lap, she seemed suddenly disoriented.

"What's the matter?"

"Oh, Alex, I feel so useless. I don't *do* anything. I don't even have any kind of a job."

"If you had a job, you wouldn't be here when I wanted you."

"I don't feel like a person in my own right. All you have to do is walk out the door and I couldn't do a thing about it. How can I have any self-respect in that kind of situation?"

They had gotten near a treacherous subject.

"Honey, I'm just not in a mood to talk. This has been a rough day." Alex crossed his legs with a feeling that he was x-ing out this line of conversation. "You remember those bonds I gave you to put away in the safe deposit box?"

"I still have them."

"Well, I may have to borrow them for a few days. Collateral for a bank loan."

Ginger sighed, and arranged her knitting silently on her lap. "They're yours anyway, Alex. They don't belong to me."

"They're ours, baby." Her submissiveness warmed him. He was really very fond of her and he liked to give her things because she was so appreciative. He had given her this house on their first Christmas together. At the time it seemed an extravagant gesture but Alex had carefully calculated its cost—an outlay of thirty-six thousand dollars amortized by the fact he would otherwise have kept her in an expensive Manhattan apartment.

Ginger went on placidly with her knitting. "Why won't the bank lend you money without the bonds? They always lent you money before, didn't they?"

"This is a different situation."

At the recollection of how different this situation was, fear put a cold hand on the nape of his neck. There was no bank involved, no ordinary considerations of risk and default, or foreclosure. If he did not meet the next payment on this loan, the foreclosure would be on him.

What annoyed him most was that he could blame no one for his predicament but himself. If he had not yielded to momentary lust with Ann Haleson, he would have been able to draw the money he needed from Zenith Oil. He hadn't seen Ann since. When he drove her to Manhattan that evening she had gone straight to the Carlyle and in the morning when he called to suggest a drink she was cool and said she was otherwise engaged. He called again the next day and this time she made it unmistakably plain that what had happened would never happen again. She had been one hell of an expensive lay.

"You remember what you said when you gave me the bonds, Alex?"

"No."

"You said they were our security. Even if everything else went, you weren't going to touch them."

He had put the bonds in Ginger's name because there was no one else he could trust—certainly not Mother. Giving half a million dollars to Mother would be like feeding raw meat to a piranha. But the money wasn't doing him any good where it was and he needed it; half a million dollars would enable him to pay off the entire Mafia loan with enough left over to placate a few other creditors. Julius Scobie feared a concerted move by the most important creditors at any time and thought a few judicious payments might forestall it.

"You don't understand, honey. This is an emergency."

Her fingers flicked swiftly in and out of the knitting.

"You said that someday you might come and ask for them and when you did I was to say no."

He didn't like the turn the conversation had taken. He sat uneasily, his slender body tense. During the years he had watched how stubborn she could become when she wanted to. She would decide never to touch a favorite food, and she would do it. Once she even decided to cut off sexual intercourse; that was soon after their affair had begun and he had come to her paralyzed drunk after a riotous day and night with another woman. It was nearly four weeks before she opened her bedroom door to him again.

"Ginger, this is different. It's too complicated to explain but, believe me, the bonds will come back to you with interest."

"You said you'd thank me for saying no, in the long run."

His hand tightened on his kneecap. Small firm hand, well manicured. His father's hands had been rough, with broken nails, scars, and high ridges along the backs from working in the lumber mill.

"Those bonds were bought with my money. I only gave them to you for safekeeping. You'll get them back."

She let the knitting slip through her fingers. "How can I believe you?"

"What?"

"What reason have you given me to believe you?"

"That isn't fair!"

Words broke from her: "You stand there and talk about being fair! I've given you everything a woman can, my whole life, and what do I have to show for it? Sitting alone night after night waiting for the telephone to ring. I could be a streetwalker for all I mean to you! You could throw me out tomorrow!"

He was taken aback by the force of her tirade. "Don't say that. For God's sake, honey, *you're in my will!*"

"I want something from you while you're still alive. I don't need a Cadillac limousine to visit your tombstone!"

The mention of tombstones revived in him the urgency of his problem. He knew of one man who hadn't paid the Mafia; they found him with his tongue torn out and a bullet in the back of his neck.

"You can have anything I've got," he said.

167

"Words! Words and sweet talk." A tiny grimace pulled down a corner of her mouth. "If you really mean it, let's get married."

"Married!" He didn't intend to repeat the word with such astonishment.

"What's wrong with it? Most of the world is married."

His fingers quirked nervously. "Listen, baby, you're all upset. Why don't we talk about this some other time?"

"I didn't bring up the subject. You started with those bonds." She grinned with absolutely no humor. "Half a million dollars"—she extended her hand with a finger rigidly apart from the others—"for a five-dollar wedding band on that finger."

"You're not serious!"

"Why not? Everything has a price."

He had never had very good luck with women; they always took advantage of him.

"It's blackmail."

"Call it what you like."

Silently he vowed never again to be put into a situation like this. "You'll ruin our relationship. It'll never be the same."

"I don't want it to be the same."

He stood up to give physical expression to the anger that towered in him. "You can't get away with it?" he said loudly.

He couldn't believe she would do this. Along with his incredulity came a flare of violent images. He imagined his hands shaping themselves around her soft neck, pressing down until she was forced to give way, to kneel, to be suppliant before him.

"I've been waiting for you to do the right thing, Alex. I kept thinking you would, someday. Lately I've begun to wonder."

"Have I ever done you any harm?"

"You've made me feel cheap. I've never told you that before but it's true."

His hands tightened, squeezing naked skin. The thumbs fixed on the jugular and his fingers slid under her ear beneath the hair and her eyes began to protrude like doll's eyes.

"I won't stand for it!" he shouted.

Here voice became scaly with coldness. "It's the only way you'll get the bonds, Alex. You know me well enough to know I mean that."

He knew her well enough. Damnable intuition had guided her to stake everything on this issue. She could not know how desperately, crucially important it was to him.

"You listen," he began, but his voice, loud and challenging, sounded as though he were wringing his hands.

"All you have to do is say yes, Alex—and you get the bonds."

"I'll never forgive you!"

"Yes, you will. I'll be a good wife and I'll make you happy. You'll never have any reason to regret it."

It was the sort of statement recognizable not as a waystation along the road but as a terminal point.

He answered in a way that merged defiance and acceptance: "If the circumstances were different, I might have asked you. But this way . . ."

"I wouldn't have picked this way, Alex," she said. "But I have to take you any way I can get you."

He looked at her as if she were a great beaked bird that had its claws into him. His tense clenched hands unclasped and his head bowed a little.

*

A cold wet east wind was blowing down the street as Barbara waited shivering for Karl to finish talking with the building superintendent at the site. The building superintendent was a tall, slightly heavy, rather good-looking young man whose last name was Mac-Something. He listened attentively to Karl. Karl was always finding some little thing that needed changing.

His work was such a part of him and therefore so intimately connected with her feeling for him that she could not feel jealousy toward it. He would not be what he was without being what he did.

He had stopped talking to the superintendent. Now he was coming toward her. A blond woman in a short black coat passed directly in front of him and she saw Karl look after her.

It is dangerous to care too much, not to keep your emotions well in hand.

Karl continued to watch the blond woman teeter off down the street, rocking slightly on small feet in high-heeled shoes.

She went toward him, smiling uncertainly. "Someone you know?"

"Who?"

"The blonde."

She hated herself; he would guess the acute uncertainty that prompted the question.

"I was thinking something foolish."

"Foolish?" She drew her coat tighter against a prying east wind.

"I was thinking how preposterous in scale her body is to its distant extremities. Like that statue of Saint Peter in Rome with its giant-size big toe. Why are you smiling?"

She put her arm through his. "How is everything at the building? All right?"

"Seems to be. They're expecting steel any minute. Then they'll be starting on the framework. But the weather may become a problem."

"Why?"

"When the temperature drops below freezing it's harder to keep things moving along. Especially when they begin working with steel. It can get so cold up there that a worker's glove will stick to the metal. And steel itself has to be fireproofed with concrete and concrete doesn't flow when it's too cold."

Karl's thoughts moved ahead to grapple with the problems of winter protection. They would put canvas around the floor below where they kept the coke heaters—barrels filled with burning coke. That would maintain a steady flow of rising heat to where it was needed. There would also have to be people on watch constantly against the danger of fire. It wasn't simple to get fire out once the construction got above the sixth floor. That was as high as the street hydrants could carry water and the Fire Department trucks had to hook large pumps to six-inch water pipes—called Siamese because there were usually two of them—to pump water up to higher floors when needed.

Meanwhile on the site they had assembled the first derrick, and the hundred-and-fifty-foot mechanized monster would soon be working to put the framework of the building into place. The derrick had to be assembled on the site because it was too big to be carried through city streets by a truck.

"What are you thinking about?" Barbara asked.

He looked at her with surprise. "I apologize."

"What for?"

"Such a narrow range my thoughts cover. Always my work. I don't blame you for being bored with me."

She wondered what Karl would say if she told him how she really felt. She wanted a permanent arrangement—marriage. The words of the tribe were not meaningless, even though the real commitment between a man and a woman is never contractual. But after that night in the studio when they sat together for the first time to watch the sky brighten with dawn she had known she wanted to spend all her mornings with Karl. She loved him with every particle of her deepest feeling and wanted to give herself completely and let her inmost privacy be violated. Part of the reason was that she hoped he would reciprocate and at last she would learn what troubled him in depths below confiding. She sensed how much combustible material there was in his emotions. But something had locked him in to a private suffering and now he preserved a wall between himself and what he allowed himself to feel.

Until she could break through that wall, she was with him only half; she could not see the future simple and straight before them. There was a nucleus of fear: a part of his life she did not know might destroy her happiness. He never wanted to talk about his past in Germany, so that must be where the pain was hiding. Some other woman? He had mentioned Eva—but there might be another. Those times he seemed most preoccupied he might be thinking about the other woman.

He saw her shiver and put his arm about her. She had not been wrong about one quality in him—gentleness. There were dead, vacant unknowable places, but there were living places too, more of them all the time.

They started down the street and before they reached the corner he turned to stare back at the excavation.

"What's wrong?" she asked.

He was a little abstracted. "I'm not satisfied with the roof."

171

"They haven't put up the first floor. Isn't it a little early to worry about the roof?"

"I haven't solved the problem."

"What problem?"

"A flat roof leaves no room for the water tanks and lift shafts necessary in a modern building. But the roof must be flat to allow flexibility in planning."

"Every modern skyscraper has that problem. It doesn't seem hard to solve. You indicated how it would be done in your first sketches."

"I solved it on too simple a level. That's worse than no solution at all."

In the continual search for what he thought was right he pushed out of consciousness everything he had seen before. When he found what he wanted it was always his individual solution.

"Everyone liked it."

He shook his head. "There has to be something better. Something to fit in with the whole design."

They started on, and suddenly at the avenue crossing he stopped again.

"Here they come," he said.

Rumbling down the street came the first of a caravan of huge trucks with high-piled loads of steel.

The great trucks were carrying the structural members of the building, two-story-high H shapes equipped with holes and connection pieces for splicing, horizontal beams and trusses to support the floors and tie the columns together into a rigid frame, steel cut and shaped from precise specifications in the plant, cooled and marked and loaded onto trucks and carried from the fabricating works to a storage yard. In the storage yard the steel was sorted out and loaded again into trucks and sent off on an intricately charted journey through the crowded maze of midtown streets.

"I'd like to watch," she said.

"Would you?" Karl grinned like a young boy. "So would I."

They returned to the site and watched as the first truck backed in, edging up onto the ramp. The driver of the truck was muscular, swarthy, confident. He glinted with concentration. As his hands turned the big wheel the truck grunted onto the ramp of the timbered roadway that had been built into the open plaza area to eliminate the need for unloading in the street.

This was the end, Karl thought, of all the preparatory work, the job which encompassed general earth excavation, bank sheeting along the rock excavation, rock pier holes and the deep wet pier holes in the earth, the underpinning of adjoining buildings. The foundation, like a sturdy pack horse, was ready for the huge steel load to be put on it. The concrete walls, once a mere paste of cement, water, sand and crushed stone, gravel and inert material, had undergone a chemical reaction to a hardness ready to support the burden.

Another great truck moved onto the timbered roadway. As the first load of steel columns was hoisted, the shapes were made lucent, their dimensions and solidity deepened.

Other great trucks moved in to the side street, waiting their turn to deliver the bones of the building clearly marked to take their proper place in the steel skeleton.

It had all begun with an idea in the head of the man standing beside her, Barbara thought. In the beginning the building had been nowhere, beyond imagination, completely out of mind. Now it was coming into existence and would somehow change the lives of everyone associated with it. In the beginning, nothing; at the end, a building. She wished it were possible to let Karl know how proud she was. She was like a deaf mute who had learned to speak only by feeling the movement of other people's lips and tongue, but could not pronounce words exactly because there was no guide. She could only form her heart into meaning.

"It's too cold to watch any more," Karl said.

"I don't mind. It's all so beautiful."

"I'm taking you home," he said firmly.

As they were passing the shoe repair store near the corner there occurred one of those unpredictable chances. The door opened and a dark young man and a small plump woman in a bulky red plaid coat emerged pushing a baby carriage. Karl paused for a moment to bend over the carriage, smiling and waggling his finger at the cooing well-wrapped bundle. She had not been aware that he loved children. She liked any sign that he welcomed domesticity. What a sentimental creature she really was, and how much she envied other

173

women the simple taken-for-granted blessings of home, husband, family. She was quite a disappointment to herself, really. Barbara Druse, artist. Humbug! Appearances can be deceiving; art had been a surrogate for her real need.

The young people went off down the street with their baby carriage, having played the unguessable role of accident as a creative force in human affairs: Barbara wondered what it would be like to have a child with Karl.

When they arrived at the apartment house and began to climb the five flights of stairs, she was thinking: If I become pregnant we will have to move. No one could possibly trundle a baby carriage up and down these stairs every day. And this is no neighborhood to raise a baby in.

After the first week Barbara had persuaded Karl to leave the studio and live in her apartment. He had not been easy to convince. Really quite old-fashioned. She had put up a partition in the huge apartment so Karl could work in the closed-off area, and tried not to smile when he insisted on paying rent for it.

While she was cooking dinner, she was pondering such problems as precooked baby food, formulas, and Pablum. She was interrupted by a phone call from her father. For the first time, Peter seemed to be nosing around for information. He had never been quite so interested in the loneliness of her apartment or the impropriety of living in such a neighborhood. What would he say if he knew about Karl? Decide that he was some sort of fortune hunter, probably. The idea was ridiculous but her father was capable of it.

She got off the phone to serve dinner (*coq au vin*, the way she had learned to make it in Paris). While they were dining, she went back to her original obsession. It would be a shabby deceit. Granted Karl's reverence for the proprieties, it was inevitable that if she became pregnant he would ask her to marry him.

Was that wrong if she loved him so much?

She prided herself on being modern and emancipated. Certainly the equal of any man. But since she had known Karl she had been shedding personas at such a rapid rate that she was a little dizzied at her loss of identity. Or at the discovery of a new one. Distressingly like other women in love, she would do anything to get her man.

Well, it's better not to have illusions. Even if I finally decide not to, which I will, never again will I be able to look down on women who use low cunning to achieve their ends.

After dinner, while she was making a cheerful clatter in the kitchen, Karl came in to watch. She was rinsing dishes and her lean sinewy arms were buried in soap suds.

He said, "Have I told you that I like your face in fluorescent light. You have such strong exact bones."

"You didn't pick my most glamorous moment."

"You're beautiful."

Watching her, Karl could still hardly believe that she was busily doing dishes in this kitchen. How could she give up the glamour, the shimmer, her life had before? Other men knew better how to keep her amused, give her the things she was used to as a rich man's daughter. He could not compete. He had never established a foundation on which to build a proper kind of life and his past was a swamp into which no pilings could be sunk to erect a future. It was inconceivable that she would stay with him. To think of her in terms of marriage, a family, was simply ridiculous. If he dared to mention such ideas he would only frighten her into leaving sooner.

She withdrew her hands from the water, shaking them free of soap which slid off streamingly and floated in tiny bubbles.

"Well, that's done."

"I don't think I will work tonight," he said.

"Why not?"

He smiled. "I would rather talk to you."

She touched a hand to her cheek. It was altogether unfair of her. But she was an overwhelming ache and he was the only remedy.

She received the heated emanation from his body, the sweet presence of physical readiness. Their emotions were filtering together in a blaze of created light. With something akin to the extra awareness of a blind person she turned toward him, allowing her hands to drift across his chest. His face suddenly clouded with desire. She ran her lips over his mouth until their tongues joined in delicate provocation.

Soon they would lie body to body. She would use no more defenses. She would be wholly penetrable.

175

His breathing was deep and slow.
Her slender arms encircled his neck.

*

Workers were attaching guide ropes, or taglines, to a package of steel girders. A steelworker standing on the truck finished tying down the bulky package of steel with a cable. He gave a quick motion, the derrick operator pulled back on his gears and the hook lifted the steel package, balanced neatly at midpoint by the cable, twenty feet into the air.

Everything was in clear view of each other, the hoist engine, the derrick, the truck from which the steel was being lifted and the steel itself. So there was no need to send instructions over the signal box.

Don Macey, standing near the derrick, used a bullhorn to yell: "Okay . . . easy does it . . . *Up!*"

The hook lifted the steel package a few feet further into the air and swung it away from the truck. Two workers held to the taglines to keep the steel from rotating or swinging in transit.

In the midst of stationary things, the derrick was an active force, moving against gray foundation walls. The steel girders being moved were the color of old dried blood because they had been given a prime coat of fire-retarding, rust-retarding paint in the shop. The steel that was grayish black was destined to be eventually encased in concrete and so did not have to be given a prime coating.

"Slack down . . . level it up . . . *Go ahead!*"

As Tom MacLaren walked back with Jim Otis toward the field office, he said, "Last night, I saw someone waiting for you in a nice Buick Riviera."

"That's right."

"Friend of yours?"

"A very good friend," Otis said.

"What's her name?"

Otis smiled. "Are you interested in her name, Mr. MacLaren, or her color?"

Behind everything was that troublesome question.

"I didn't say anything about that, did I?"

"I thought you might be going to."

"Well, I wasn't. What you do outside is your own business. But she looked like a nice respectable woman."

"She is."

"I guess you must have gone out with a lot of white girls when you were in college."

"I had a lot of opportunities," Otis said. "I was one of those school athletes. Star player on the basketball team."

That recalled a painful past to Tom. He had spent two years in a boy's home run by the Optimist Club; that was after his mother was sent away and he had no place to live. He had tried to make the basketball team because his height was an advantage on the court and his strength helped in the close quarters struggle for rebounds. But his slight awkwardness was magnified by the swift darting movements of boys whose reflexes were faster. He ended up on the bench, watching the rapid ebb and flow of play and the large round tan ball that drew all eyes after it like a magnet.

The thought of Jim Otis moving swift and lithe around a court started a new resentment.

As they entered the outside office, Tom said in a loud voice, "I guess you think you're pretty good at all kinds of sports. One of those all-around athletes."

Two construction men who were standing in the office and the office workers at their desks turned to watch.

"I didn't say that, Mr. MacLaren."

"You keep in pretty good condition. How do you think you'd do in an armwrestle?"

"I've only tried it a few times. Just fooling around."

"But you won, right?"

"I guess I did." Jim Otis returned Tom's stare.

They had finally come to the confrontation. He had to humiliate Otis here and now in front of everyone.

"How'd you like to take me on?" Tom asked.

When Otis answered there was a quality in his voice that sounded as though he were silently laughing. "Just for fun, Mr. MacLaren?"

Tom looked at the small group that gathered around to watch. He took off his work jacket and Otis stripped down to his undershirt.

177

Otis's arms were black and surprisingly muscular and on one shoulder there was a tan vaccination mark.

They took up positions across a corner of the work table. Their hands gripped firmly, biceps swelling.

Otis made the first serious move. Deliberate steady pressure increased against Tom's close-wrapped hand and wrist. Tom met the challenge, holding firm.

When the pressure finally began to ease, Tom risked a brief smile at the others standing around to watch. Otis saw the smile and that seemed to goad him to a fresh attack.

Forty seconds passed . . . fifty. Otis's attack never wavered. Tom's gaze centered on their locked hands. His white hand locked in struggle with the black one. The knuckle curve and the humped flesh on the side of his palm. His skin wrinkled and white, the black flesh merged with it turning slightly pink and blotchy pale.

A determination, ugly and perverse, inflamed Tom. He would smash that black hand down.

Now.

He willed all his strength into his arm, sent power flowing down into his wrist and hand.

Otis's brown eyes went blank. His lips thinned to an almost invisible white line. Ridges of muscle stood out on his biceps. Tom turned on more pressure. Tiny vanishing bubbles seemed to be forcing their way to the surface of his skin. The pressure threatened to crack the bones of his forearm.

Otis's hand was still standing rigidly before him. It seemed to perch oddly atop the table, to dwindle and become another organ, shrinking before his eyes only to come back magnified, pulsing large, then small.

Why didn't Otis yield? Impossible. Incredible. That black arm trembled with a million tiny vibrations but not one signaled surrender.

The upper part of his body became rigid while apathy invaded the lower portion. On his wrist a drop of sweat sprang out and traced a path down the corded muscular arm until it sank into arm hairs like a tiny stream into a white desert. His stomach seemed displaced, sinking. His throat filled with nausea.

His hand was twined in the grip of that black hand—could he move a finger? He tried and was not sure. His temples ached, sweat trickled into his hair and down around the curve of his ear. Something crawled over his face like a living protoplasm. It was the twitching nerves in his face.

His arm stiffly erect before him. All his vital energy centered there. Endure. That is the main thing. *Endure.*

Serious black face opposite with eyes tight lidded, smoldering. Unwavering gaze.

His strength seemed to flow out of him like a milky serum. My God, my veins are bursting! He was a basin of flesh being emptied. He was drawn up into a great roaring. Everything contracted to a bitter instant.

A shout.

He opened his eyes. The face of Jim Otis swam jerkily into focus.

The door to the office flew open. A workman was standing there.

"You'd better come quick!"

"What's wrong?"

"We found someone at the bottom of the elevator pit. I think he's dead!"

A surge of bystanders away from the work table. Tom met Otis's eyes and slowly pulled his arm free. That cost a sharp wrench of pain from locked muscles.

"Some other time," Tom said.

Otis flexed his fingers. He stood up with slouching slowness. "Sure," he said, "Mr. MacLaren."

Tom still felt the twisting gripe in his biceps as he stood above the elevator pit, looking down to the bottom where in a rectangle of dark rainwater, slush and ooze a man lay face down.

"Anybody know who he is?"

"We just found him a couple of minutes ago. He must've sneaked in during the night."

A broken bottle was lying in the water beside the body. The dead man was dressed in a tweed coat that had seen better days, and a scarf was untwisted about his neck. His hat had rolled off and was lying on its rim a foot away. His shoes were partly off the heels, and he was not wearing socks.

"A bum," Tom said. "Where the hell was the watchman?"

He knew. On a cold night like last night the watchman was in the office looking at his portable TV. There was a chain at the truck entrance, and a fence around the site to keep people out, and if anyone did sneak in the watchman counted on finding them during the four A.M. check. This was a derelict who tried to sneak in to sleep off a drunk where the surrounding fences and the excavation provided some protection from the freezing night air. He was not the troublesome kind, one of the thieves who try to get away with petty loot during the night—a few pieces of lumber or pipe or chain fall. There were scavengers of this type who made a meager living by stealing and selling junk.

This man had merely been looking for a place out of the wind and weather, to finish his bottle and sleep off his drunkenness. Blundering in the darkness, trying to avoid disturbing the watchman, he found his way to the elevator pit.

The fall would not have killed him, but there was six inches of rainwater in the bottom of the pit. Lying there, stunned from his fall and the drink, he had drowned.

Later that evening, Tom watched Sophy on the sofa reading *Vogue*. She turned a glossy page and a stylized girl in riding breeches flicked over. He had told her about the man in the pit, and her eyes had teared slightly and she murmured "the poor fellow," but her sadness did not last long. Sadness never did last long with Sophy.

There was no way he could tell her about Otis and the terrible moment when he thought Otis was going to beat him. She wouldn't understand.

"Sophy?"

"Yes?"

"Remember the White Antler?"

"Of course."

Even the mention of the name evoked erotic memories for him.

"I was thinking we might take a weekend and go back."

"I'd rather go someplace new. How about Florida?"

"Florida? That isn't for a weekend."

"I don't see any sense in going away where it'll be cold. There was snow on the ground at the White Antler."

Snow hadn't bothered him. It added to the feeling of being alone in the old-fashioned high-ceilinged room with its real woodburning fireplace. Thick quilt covers were on the fourposter bed.

"It costs a lot of money to get anywhere it's warm. Just the air fare."

"If we went to a warm climate I could get some of the lovely resort things they're advertising."

She loved to buy clothes and not a week went by without bills for new dresses, new shoes, lingerie. She took such a delight in pretty new things. But it was time they began economizing. Every married couple ought to have savings.

Last week he had bought his second hundred shares of Alexander Johns Enterprises stock. Every week from now on he intended to save a substantial portion of his paycheck to buy shares. He had already figured out what to do with his profits. When the stock tripled, or quadrupled, he would sell and invest the money in building one of those automated garages, surrounded in glass and illuminated. When that paid off, he would put the money back into building a dozen more scattered all over the city. Real showplaces.

"I still think we ought to go to Miami if we go anywhere."

"It's out of the question, Sophy. We can't afford it. You just don't seem to understand."

She looked up with annoyance. "Why pick on me? Because I want to go to Florida and you don't have the money?"

"We'd be a lot better off spending it on a bigger apartment."

It had been a mistake to continue living in her place. It was really no more than a large living room, with a small space scalloped out at one end for a kitchen and at the other for a bedroom. Through the thin walls of the bedroom alcove at night they could hear the neighbors talking. Even during the heart-pounding, suffocating times he was afraid of making too much noise.

Looking at her now across the room, he was baffled by her irritation; it was like a little distance between them.

"I don't want to quarrel, Sophy."

"All right, then."

"How'd you like to go to a movie?"

Her mood changed swiftly. "Could we go to Radio City?"

The Radio City Music Hall was her favorite; she liked to enter that glamorous immense world with its glittering chandeliers and immaculately uniformed ushers.

"Sure. Why not?"

She jumped off the sofa. "I'll hurry and get ready."

An hour later while waiting outside Radio City Music Hall, Tom saw Mike Collyer going to the end of the line with a pretty blonde. He called to him, and Mike and the girl ducked under the rope to join them.

Mike's date for the evening was a waitress from a restaurant near where he was working downtown. She was one of the "followers," women who trail construction workers from one job to the next, usually taking jobs in the vicinity so they can be nearby when the men quit for the day. At three-thirty the "followers" make any excuse to get out and down to the site so they can be available for an invitation to a drink, or dinner, or whatever may follow.

On the way in to the lobby, Sophy and the blonde, whose name was Joan, moved ahead of them toward the elevators that took patrons up to the smoking section.

Mike made a circle with thumb and forefinger. "Zero. A big nothing."

"Her?"

"She doesn't know how to talk to a guy," Mike said. "Great between the sheets but afterward not ten words to say. I wish I could meet a girl like Sophy and give up the bachelor life."

"Maybe you'll get lucky," Tom said.

No one could cry at a movie like Sophy. She was so emotionally stirred on this occasion that, even after ice-cream sodas in Howard Johnson's with Mike and his girl, she was quiet and misty eyed. When they returned to the apartment, he hung up her coat in the closet, holding it a moment because he liked the feel of her clothing in his hands. When he turned to her, her eyes were still glistening.

"You're not still teary about the movie?"

"I guess so."

"Why?"

"I get this way when it reminds me of something in my own life."

"You? You don't have anything in common with that girl in the movie."

"Oh, yes I do."

"What, for instance?"

"Oh, I don't know," Sophy said, suddenly restless. "I just felt sorry for her."

She sat on the sofa, pulled her legs up beneath her, and he recognized she was having one of her moods in which he didn't dare to question her.

"I'm a little surprised at the Radio City," he said. "That was a pretty raw scene. You know, the one where her parents find her with that old guy. The one who seduced her."

"You're silly. They show much worse than that in movies these days."

"But I mean—at Radio City?"

"I'm tired," Sophy said abruptly. "I'm going to bed."

She went into the bedroom alcove, and then into the bathroom where he heard water running. She had begun her nightly beauty routine—cleansing lotion, soap and water scrubbing, then astringent, and finally night cream.

Tom poured himself a drink and sat in the living room. He was sorry now they had met Mike and that girl. If they had not spent the time afterward at Howard Johnson's there would have been a different ending to the evening. Sophy wouldn't have been so tired. He sipped his drink unhappily, thinking about the movie, the simple story of a young girl who had gone wrong after being seduced by an older man. He could not see any similarity to Sophy's life.

Against his will, out of the web of this day's tangled emotions he began to think once more of Jim Otis and the dead man in the bottom of the elevator pit.

*

A plump overspectacled young man with a rumpled shirt and wrinkled jacket rose from a seat in the fourth row of the lecture hall. In the rear of the hall, Alex Johns stirred restlessly.

"Professor Schiller?"

"Yes?" Karl Schiller, standing stiffly at the lectern, looked uncomfortable in a neatly pressed gray suit. A moment before, he had finished a lecture on Ernst Maier for the benefit of the Architectural Society and had invited questions from the floor.

"You say that Ernst Maier excelled in the engineering sciences. Do you think he was equally effective with the theory of design?"

"Ernst Maier was like Pier Nervi today—an engineer with genius. He knew that architecture is more than engineering. He understood the esthetics of building."

About eighty people were present in the auditorium. They had come to hear Karl Schiller, whose design for the Zenith Oil building was being discussed in all the leading architectural journals. A publisher was bringing out a sketchbook of Karl Schiller's drawings. The book was priced at twenty-five dollars and the first printing was already sold out.

It was unfair, Alex thought. Nobody was publishing a book about the kind of problems a general contractor dealt with. A lot of his problems required more ingenuity to solve than anything an architect came up against. He could write a whole book just on the trouble he was having trying to arrange for the transfer of a police station in the West Sixties which was located on a parcel of land he needed to complete assembling a site for a new apartment house.

Alex waited impatiently through more questions, all involved, innocuous, boring, prolix, until finally Karl Schiller held up a restraining hand.

"I believe that is all the questions I have time for. Thank you. I have enjoyed talking to you very much."

There was scattered but vigorous applause as he stepped down from the lectern.

When the crowd thinned out, Alex went to the private cloakroom. As he entered Schiller was trying to find his overshoes and Barbara Druse was helping him look. A small bald fat man was also in the room.

Barbara saw Alex in the doorway.

"Alex! Were you at the lecture?"

He nodded. "Tucked away in a rear seat."

Alex glanced at the short fat man whose skin seemed to be bristling with perspiration.

Barbara said, "Dr. Moser, this is Alex Johns, general contractor for the Zenith Oil building that Karl designed."

Alex shook hands.

"Dr. Moser is head of the Institute of Technology where Karl was a teacher."

Karl Schiller said, "Damn! What ever happened to those overshoes?"

"Here they are." Barbara found the overshoes on top of an umbrella rack and handed them to Karl. "Why didn't you let us know you were coming?" she asked Alex.

"I didn't know it myself until a while ago."

"I saw an item in a column the other day. Something about your getting married soon."

"It's true," Alex said.

She kissed his cheek impulsively. "Congratulations!"

"Thanks."

She was looking at him intently. "Did you come about anything important?"

"I think so."

Karl Schiller was pulling on an overshoe. Dr. Moser examined his handkerchief as though to find out whether he had collected a sufficient quantity of perspiration.

"Well, I should be running along. I thought your lecture was inspiring, Karl. Absolutely inspiring. Very glad indeed that I came."

With a polite dip of a glistening bald head, and a wide and friendly smile, Dr. Moser disappeared through the cloakroom door.

Alex waited while Barbara helped Karl Schiller pull on his other overshoe.

"What did you want to talk about?" Schiller asked.

"I'd like a few minutes alone with you, Professor."

Barbara wrapped a muffler around Karl's throat.

"Miss Druse is a very good friend."

"This concerns you personally."

"You may say anything in her presence."

Alex glanced briefly at Barbara, then at Karl, wondering how he could have missed the clear signals that passed between these two and spelled out their new relationship.

Alex nodded. "All right, then. A few hours ago I had a phone call from a man I know, an Undersecretary in the State Department. It was about you, Professor."

"What about me?" Schiller asked.

"He said that the government had come into possession of certain facts about you. He said it was quite possible that proceedings would be brought to deport you."

"You're joking! On what possible grounds could they do a thing like that?"

"He wasn't too clear about it."

"Why would he call you, of all people?"

"That's another mystery. He isn't that much of a friend. He was in real estate once and we did a lot of business together."

"He must have given you a reason," Barbara said.

"Oh, sure. He said he hoped I wasn't planning to get involved with Professor Schiller in any future projects. Because there was a chance that he wouldn't be around long enough to complete them."

"What did you say?"

"I told him I wasn't involved and I was going to tell the Professor about this phone call. He didn't seem to object to that. In fact, he thought it might be a good idea if I suggested to the Professor that he should leave the country voluntarily and save the government the trouble of having to deport him."

Barbara asked, "Does he have anything against Karl?"

"So far as I knew, he's never met him. And he isn't too smart. Even if he did have anything against the Professor he wouldn't be able to invent a scheme like this."

Barbara turned to Karl. "Do you have any explanation?"

Karl Schiller had a puzzled, thoughtful air, as if he were turning over possible answers in his mind. "No," he said.

"How about you, Alex?"

"I only have a hunch."

"What's that?"

"I think he's trying to keep it strictly unofficial. That's why he didn't go through ordinary channels. My hunch is that there's someone else who has a reason for wanting the Professor out."

"It seems a devious way to go about it. Did he tell you anything else—any reason the government might want to deport Karl?"

"He did mention it had something to do with his past in Germany. You weren't a Nazi or anything like that, were you, Professor?"

When Karl Schiller spoke, he seemed afraid and at the same time weary of being afraid.

"No, I was not."

"Well, it isn't any of my business anyway."

"Thank you for coming to tell me. I appreciate it."

Barbara was watching Karl with an odd expression.

Alex said, "I don't really think it's anything serious but I did want you to know about it."

"You're not really worried, are you, Karl?" Barbara asked.

"I am too tired to think now. I am very tired."

"It's just some silly misunderstanding. Don't you agree, Alex?"

"That's probably what it is."

"I would like to go home now," Karl Schiller said.

"Good night," Barbara said to Alex.

"Good night." On an impulse Alex added, "I really wouldn't worry too much about it, Professor."

Karl Schiller heard but continued on to the door. With Barbara guiding him almost as though he had impaired vision, he moved slowly through the doorway.

Alex was curious about what seemed to be an emotional fissure in a monolith of a man, but in a moment his curiosity disappeared to be replaced by a more personal emotion. Barbara with Karl Schiller? Alone in the large room with its empty standing racks and coat hangers, he thought a little sadly about missed opportunities.

The door opened and a man in a tan shirt and trousers looked in.

"We're closing now."

"I was just leaving."

He opened the door, went down a short foyer that led to the street, and emerged into darkness and cold. Barbara and Karl were nowhere in sight. A light snow was falling and crystal granules softly crackled beneath his shoes.

He took a breath of clear cold air.

*

While Karl was typing the letter, in his partitioned studio at one end of the huge apartment, he heard the groan and whine of the industrial vacuum cleaner that Barbara used on the floors.

The noise of the vacuum cleaner stopped as the doorbell rang, then there was the clicking of the police lock on the front door, the high semi-illiterate complaining tones of the delivery boy with an order of groceries, and some shuffling as packages were moved toward the kitchen.

He tore the page out of the typewriter, ripped it and threw it into the wastebasket. Thoughtfully he put a new page in. He was not fluent in English and he included more than he wished to. In German there were cumbersome portmanteau words that nevertheless expressed several meanings within a short compass. When he wrote in English he tried to get all those same meanings but needed too many words to say what he meant.

He did not look up when Barbara came in carrying a wicker basket piled with newly washed undershirts, shorts, and socks. She put the basket down on a long work table near him.

"Can I do that for you? I type much faster than you."

"I have to think this through."

She began to fold the rumpled garments.

"Is it a letter?" she asked, after a few minutes.

He said haltingly, "It's to a friend of mine in England. He offered me a teaching position. I'm going to accept."

She was startled. "You're not serious."

"I think I am finished with building. I can't work up any interest in it any more."

"That's not true."

It had been a transparent evasion. She had observed his infatuation with lumber yards and their high-piled masses of fresh shingles, boards and timbers, with the rock ledges of a stone quarry, stratified with history, where he had sat almost an entire afternoon *feeling* the stone in its unmoving grandeur, and with the smothered incandescence of the kiln where in fabulous heat and the subdued roar of great ovens all the shapes of his imagination were put forth.

"There never would have been trouble if I had not designed the Zenith Oil building," he said. "I should have remained a teacher. I need to live quietly, with no one caring who or what I am."

A long moment passed.

"Are you going to tell me?" she asked. "I want to know what disturbs you so, Karl."

"There isn't anything to tell." He added almost angrily, "I have a right to live my own life and make my own decisions."

"Don't you trust me?"

"Of course I do."

"Then tell me, Karl. Don't you see? This is the right time."

This astonishing woman was demanding a revelation that might destroy him.

"It isn't as—easy—as you think."

"It's easier than living in fear the rest of your life."

He would have to condemn himself, to fall upon his own past like an avenger. Did she imagine a man who had undergone a hellish experience? Her sympathy was ready to accept that. But the truth was far more desperate.

"Please," she said gently.

"I don't want to remember." He was safer behind exclusionary locks. He had managed to confine the past to his dreams—a recurring dream in which he was running running from he knew not what.

"Karl, I want to share everything with you. Including the bad things."

"I wouldn't know where to begin."

"Anywhere. Just start talking and the words will come." As she saw his struggle she added softly, "Because I love you."

There was no appeal she could have made that would have so moved him. In the absence of other gods, her love was all he had to believe in.

His lips felt painful. "I don't ask," he said, "for forgiveness." He had already passed sentence on himself, without hope of pardon. "But perhaps you are right. It is time for you to know."

He was about to end a terrible exile in the world of the self-condemned, a world in which all warm hues of feeling had been filtered out. Indeed, he was already beginning to relive the old horror, and the words therefore would not be long in coming. The enormity of what he had done! He had drowned in the shallows of his own soul.

*

A long time ago, in Germany
(Karl Schiller said, sitting ramrod-straight in the chair by the typewriter)
we were all a little mad in those days . . .

Down Kaiserdamm Street they had marched in the torchlight procession to the stroke of a drum major's baton. Stiffly on parade, thousands of slow-marching feet. Somber red and black flags in the glare light of flickering torches. Crowds watching from the sidewalks. The twisted cross on thousands of armbands and massed voices singing: "For the flag we are ready to die." Above the tattoo of the drums an occasional *Sieg Heil!*

Karl watched from the window of Ernst Maier's office as the marchers passed below in the street. Some were his neighbors. Then appeared a face he knew too well, round faced and red complexioned, gray hairs showing beneath a visored cap, eyes fixed forward. *Sieg Heil!* His father's short plump legs rose and fell in regular rhythm.

Kurfürstendamm was filled with rustling and murmurs as he sat in the cafe with Ernst later that night.

"I can't live at home any more, Ernst. Not with him."

"Where will you go?"

The stony pavements whispered.

"I don't know. But I'm going to pack and leave in the morning."

Ernst touched his arm. "You are welcome in my home, but it would not be safe."

"Why don't you leave Germany?"

"I am an old man and I want to live out my time in the land

where I was born. Go, Karl, there is still time for a young man like you."

"We have a duty to resist."

"You also have a duty to yourself. You are an artist."

"I would like to stay with you, in your house, if you will let me."

He kept a room in Ernst Maier's house for five months. After the first few weeks there were no more insulting letters from his father. He saw no one but the people at Ernst's studio, and Eva. Eva had a job in a studio in the same building as Ernst Maier, where she worked at ceramics, vases, ornamental plates, and objets d'art which were sold to exclusive shops. Eva was a shy, dark-haired girl with lustrous huge eyes. He began to time his leaving the studio so they could take the same bus. She got off a mile before Ernst Maier's house, but there was time to talk and they talked about their work, about architecture, and the new ceramic designs. She, too, was an admirer of Ernst Maier. One day he got off the bus with her, and at her invitation went to her two-room furnished flat. She was the first girl he had ever known in that way and he could not get out of memory her head turning, her mouth open, tiny pearly teeth showing, the sudden tearing gasps. It was a kind of love totally free from emotions of shame and guilt. When he was with her and their bodies linked, the entire significance of his life acquired a new meaning.

Eva did not have much interest in politics but he would discuss with her the necessity for defying and resisting the Nazis. She never had much to say. He could move her to tears by a simple tale of cruelty—a Jewish professor forced to scrub the sidewalks, a young boy assaulted by a youth gang. But when the issue surpassed the simplest human scale she became lost: her reference point was people and she could not identify with the great political movements.

Ernst Maier was spared longer than most Jews because he had a reputation and admirers both in Germany and in the rest of the world. Then one morning a yellow star bloomed on the door of the office: A Jew Works Here. In itself, the yellow star was nothing, a mere symbol, but clients were no longer willing to enter through that door.

Soon afterward Ernst Maier's best-known building, a department store, was denounced as a butcher's design. A new architect was

191

commissioned to make changes in the completed structure. The name of the building was also changed and Ernst Maier's name was razed from the cornerstone block.

There was no way to meet the payroll. First Wilhelm left, then Rudy, then the last two draftsmen, and finally Hilda the secretary. Ernst Maier sat and stared out the window and twiddled a pencil in his capable fingers. His fat sad face grew haggard and heavy pouches appeared beneath his eyes.

When a commission finally came it was for a small private residence. The client was a merchant for whom Ernst Maier had once designed a store; nevertheless, the client was cautious. These were troubled times, and the client insisted the work appear to be done by someone other than Ernst Maier himself.

Ernst told Karl Schiller to become the architect of record. Karl refused—he would feel guilty, as though deserting a post under fire.

"It is the only way the house will be built," Ernst said. "The name that goes on it is not important. What matters is that the building will exist."

Their debate continued after the working day, under the lamps, with strong cups of coffee. It was the only argument Karl ever had with the man he admired most in the world.

In the end, the debate proved meaningless. Two days later Ernst Maier suffered a heart attack, and the doctor would not allow him to leave his bed or do any work. Ernst asked Karl to design the house because they could not afford to lose the commission.

He went to Eva that night, heavy hearted, through streets where brownshirted men walked wearing ostentatious swastika armbands. Talking to Eva, he determined that he would make the new house something worthy, something fit to sustain human life, something that would not add to the ugliness in the streets . . .

He created a design by strictly following Ernst Maier's principles. He began by shattering the stupid box with its bad conception of inner space, roughly dividing the main building form and adding details which belonged to the main trunk like branches to a tree. Mentally he combined different building materials into the final design, changing amorphous masses of wood, brick and iron into a new entity, a home. It was good. Ernst Maier said he could not have done better, and the client was pleased.

That private house was the last piece of work done from Ernst Maier's studio. An overdue rent notice was sent. The next day, under the provisions of a new Aryan law, the landlord sent Ernst a letter of eviction.

Karl read the letter to Ernst at his home that evening. There was no way to keep the news from him. Ernst began to dictate a letter of reference to a well-known architect in Düsseldorf.

Karl shook his head before he finished transcribing it. "I'm not leaving you, Ernst."

"They will close the office and keep the furniture as payment for the rent. You can bring the papers to me from the files. Only the important papers—the drawings, the plans. Burn the contracts. They might be used against those who have done business with me."

"You mustn't worry about those things, Ernst. You must get well. When you are strong enough to work, there will be work to do."

Ernst said gently, "You do not yet realize what you are up against, Karl. There is nothing more to keep you in Germany. You must go now, while there is time."

Karl did not believe him. He worked up a sketch in a competition. When he was interviewed before the selection committee, they questioned him about his method of composition. They could not believe that anyone so young could have done such superior work.

"I make demands of a building," he told them. "I ask it to be practical and solidly built, and to look well in twenty or even thirty years. Then I ask the house to convey to me some idea of how it is meant to be lived in. Will life in it be gay or quiet, active or restful? Will the people in it be good neighbors and will their house live at ease with the building next door, with the street and trees outside, with the passing traffic and the sky. I make the house reply to these demands honestly in the way my master taught me."

"Who is your master?"

"Ernst Maier," he answered boldly.

He heard no more from the committee.

They arrested Ernst at his home one August afternoon. Karl was not there when it happened. He arrived at an empty house and the woman who lived next door finally answered his knock with frightened wide eyes in a partly opened door.

"I am a friend of Ernst Maier. I just went in and there's no one home. He was too sick to leave by himself."

"I know nothing."

"You must have seen something."

"I saw nothing."

"Do you know if he was taken to the hospital?"

"I know nothing about him. Go away!"

From the superintendent of a nearby apartment house he learned that two SS officers had come for Ernst Maier a few hours before.

"He's a sick man. He couldn't be taken like that."

The thin face leered with contempt. "You'd be surprised how far a man can walk when he has to. It's better for everyone to be rid of him. Jews make nothing but trouble."

In the house the closets were empty of clothes and bureau drawers gaped. Karl's clothes, too, were no longer hanging in the closet in his room. Rumpled sheets were on Ernst's bed and beneath a pillow he found a notebook in which Ernst had been making entries. He must have been working at it and stuffed it out of sight as the SS troopers arrived at his door. In the notebook was a concept, developed in several different plans, for a prefabricated house that could be bought in pieces at a factory, a growing building which could start with a small nucleus and continue to be built over a generation. In a note beneath this final sketch Ernst wrote that the government could put up the frame and people would add their own labor to complete the home. "Even people who cannot afford cash to buy a home can afford to work."

Up to the last Ernst Maier was struggling with the problem that concerned him all his life: how to serve his fellow man.

Karl's father came to see him later that afternoon in the empty house. Father wore his uniform with the twisted cross armband and black boots, and his stomach bulged to part the buttons of his brown shirt.

"I have a letter for you, Karl. Eva asked me to give it to you in person."

She wrote that she did not wish to see him again, that it would be wrong to love him because he was not loyal to his country and therefore not worthy of a true German woman's love. She said that she was going to burn books he had given to her because she did not wish to give evidence that would incriminate him as an enemy of the state.

"I can't believe she would write such a letter," Karl said.

"I was there when she wrote it. One reason she wished me to deliver it was to convince you that she means what she says."

"You forced her to write it!"

"She heard of your behavior before the selection committee. She was ashamed. Why do you want to link yourself with a Jew? You can have a great future if you act sensibly. Are you trying to ruin yourself?"

"Ernst Maier is the finest man I know."

"You will end up getting yourself arrested. I came to warn you. This is your last chance to save yourself."

"Why bother?"

"You are my son. You must not drag the name of Schiller in the dirt."

"You are the one doing that, Father."

His father struck him.

"You are beyond hope." His father put on his eyeglasses to glare at him with authority. "I have done everything I can for you, but I will do nothing more. I had hoped that with the Jew out of the way you might come to your senses."

A terrible suspicion—a suspicion that made him almost whimper.

"Father, did you have anything to do with Ernst Maier's arrest?"

Eyeglasses glittered. "The arrest was made at my order."

He had the curious intoxicating feeling of being removed from all human contact with his father, the fatalism that ended concern about what was going to happen next. He did not remember exactly how the argument developed, how it progressed. The rage in him was like a broken electric line wildly spewing its power. They went from shouting to insults to that moment his father took out the gun.

He remembered only fragments of the struggle. A table crashing, his father's face red with exertion and anger. There must have been

195

blows rained on him; his father was a powerful man, stronger than himself. But he had the strength that comes from madness.

Only in the aftermath did reason return and all his false strength drain from him. In the quiet room the face staring up at him from the floor was unrecognizable. He looked at it with primitive selfishness, ancient antagonism. He threw away the gun. Now all he possessed were the clothes on his body and the thoughts in his brain. Something had been violently taken away—something he both owned and belonged to.

Father!

He stepped back and eyeglasses crushed beneath his heel. With the breaking of that symbol of authority, he felt a tremendous release immediately followed by such overwhelming horror that his knees unjointed. He fell and tried to rise and could not. He did not have the strength.

He left that charnel room like a child, crawling on hands and knees. . . .

*

When he finished speaking he leaned back against the typewriter chair. He needed support behind him.

"What happened afterward? How did you escape?" she asked.

He was unable to look at her. "I left on the train and was across the border in the morning."

"Didn't anyone try to bring you back?"

"No."

"How can you be sure it happened the way you say?"

"I don't understand."

"You might not have killed him."

Somehow he had transferred a part of his guilt to her. Her questions proved that. He stood up and turned his back to prevent her from guessing how much he regretted having told her. He had been unable to purify his present of the past. All he had succeeded in doing was involving her.

"Barbara, when I left him, he was dead."

"How about the newspapers? Didn't they report what happened?"

"The next day the Fuehrer marched into the Sudetenland. News-papers were too full of that to bother with an ordinary murder."

"And the police?"

"After a time they lost interest. With talk of war in the air, what was one more life?" Despite a desire to be fair and reasonable, he was really in no mood to talk any more. The business of the con-fessional was finished.

"Who else knows?"

"No one. I have told no one."

She came toward him. "Poor Karl . . ."

He reached up with one hand as if to guard himself. As a child there had been a plaque on the door of his house: *No Beggars.*

"I do not want pity."

There was an aura about pity that froze his heart. He had a chill knowledge of its unconscious power.

She put her head against his shoulder. "I love you, Karl."

"If I leave the country, there will be no further investigation. I must go somewhere that I am unknown."

"Karl, don't you understand what you're doing?" She drew back her head to look at him.

"What do you mean?"

"Condemning your own life. Your life as an artist."

From outside the window came street sounds, people strolling on their lunch hour, cars, a distant fire siren. The day seemed misted over with a kind of illness, the blemish of some still uncured disease.

"You want to build a prison for yourself," she said.

"It isn't enough. What I did deserves a worse punishment."

"You've been punished more than most because you have more capacity for suffering. It's time you stopped, Karl. You've done your penance."

He examined her strained, anxious face as though to determine if she meant what she said.

"You don't understand. I killed him."

"Ernst Maier was your real father, Karl. That man you killed was Ernst's murderer."

"No man has the right to take justice in his own hands . . ."

"In that time and place, where could you have found justice? The

197

Nazi courts would have agreed that Ernst Maier was an enemy of the state."

Different pressures produce different results, as molds create different things from hot molten steel. But the tensile strength of steel does not change. He had hardened a certain image of himself. Had he been wrong? Had he fashioned himself from the wrong mold?

He stared at her. "What do you think I should do?"

"Stay here. Keep doing the sort of things only you can do."

"And forget what happened in Germany?"

"Try to forget. I'll help you. I want to help."

Nothing had changed between them. It was amazing how a revelation like this could take place without changing anything.

He removed his eyeglasses and rubbed them with a small square of cloth and held them loosely in one hand, not looking directly at her. A thought pierced the armor of his incredulity. He had told her the worst of himself, and she still loved him.

That was the miracle.

*

In former times Joe Labache was a member of a four-man Mohawk riveting gang; one man, the heater, bent over a coal-burning forge in which there were a dozen five-inch rivets, while the other three hung a rope and wood sling from the girder to be worked. Then the heater plucked two white hot rivets with tongs and tossed them on the sling to the sticker-in who caught them in a funnel-shaped bucket, fished them out with his tongs and jammed them into lined-up holes between girder and column. Then Joe Labache and another riveter brought their pneumatic hammers into action and in a few seconds of unbearable ear-shattering sound the rivets would be set, capped and the workers would move on to continue setting four to six hundred rivets a day.

Today the rivet had given way to the high tensile bolt and only two men were needed to secure the girders and columns with a wrench. The clatter of the riveting gun was gone but Joe Labache was still on the job and doing it as swiftly and expertly as in the old days.

When not on the job, Joe Labache spent most of his time at home with his wife, Irene, watching TV. He was a baseball fan, and rooted for the New York Yankees. He also liked to visit the bar in Brooklyn where his Mohawk friends, all steelworkers, gathered beneath a huge color painting of General Custer's massacre and drank Canadian beer and traded stories of exploits on the high iron.

Only last week he bought a color TV set for the widow of his son Danny and her three small kids.

*

Music was Sophy's therapy. She put an Aretha Franklin record on the hi-fi and curled up on the sofa. Jasmine came out from beneath a chair, stretched sinuously and leapt to join her. Sophy read *Vogue* while she stroked the cat's neck.

"What are you reading?" Tom asked.

"An interesting article. About how old people really are and how old they think they are." Forced to look up from the page she was reading, Sophy's hand continued to rub and stroke Jasmine's neck. "Only there's one part I don't understand."

"What's that?" Tom was glad to have gained her attention.

"It says if you live to be seventy-two that comes to six years for every month in a single year. It says that can help you decide what season of life you're in—spring, summer, or fall."

"Seems clear enough."

"What would I be in?"

"Well, you're twenty-three."

"You know I'm terrible at figuring."

He made a quick calculation. "Around May first."

Her mouth formed an O. "I couldn't be!"

Aretha Franklin wailed to a halt. He got up and turned off the hi-fi. When he returned, she seemed to be struggling against shock.

"What's the matter?"

She bit her lip. "Before I know it I'll be old!"

"You've got quite a way to go." He stood, watching her with a teasing smile.

"I remember Walter telling me once that everyone thinks he's a special person who will never get old. That's exactly how I feel."

"Who?"

She gave him a puzzled frown.

"Who's Walter?" he asked.

"Oh. A friend of my parents."

"I don't think you've ever mentioned him."

"Didn't I?"

"Who is he?"

"He's a lawyer."

The offhand manner of her reply stirred his curiosity. Somewhere Sophy had acquired strange little bits of information. She hardly ever read a newspaper but she knew about such things as the coddling of criminals by the Supreme Court and the difficulty of proving libel in a courtroom.

"How well did you know him?"

"Oh, we dated for a while."

"Dated? When was that?"

"Some time ago. Before I met you."

"How long did you go out with him?"

A slight tightening of her mouth. "What's the difference?"

"I'd just like to know."

"A couple of years."

Years! He felt a slight lurch inside him. Suddenly he recalled the movie, the young girl and the older man who was her seducer, and the angry return of the girl's parents to the compromising bedroom.

"Just how important was he to you?"

She closed her magazine with a sound like a slap. "I don't know why you keep going on like this."

He had to force his voice through tightening throat muscles. "Was he your lover?"

"I never said anything like that. Besides, I don't want to talk about it. It's over. It happened before I met you."

He wanted to seize the magazine she was holding and fling it against the wall.

"Why didn't you marry him if you were so crazy about him?"

She became still, her lips slightly parted. "Walter *is* married."

"*Married!* You were dating a married man?"

There were scowling lines between her eyes. "What's so terrible? I never said I was a nun before I met you."

He was trying to control his temper. That side of his nature was terrifying, even to him.

"Did your father find you with Walter?"

He saw her surprise.

"You said that movie reminded you of your own life."

"Please, Tom." She turned away and her shoulders seemed to hunch together.

Anger mounted in giddy circles to his brain. "What kind of a girl are you? Good Christ almighty!"

"If I could change anything, I would." She was crying.

Violence shuddered in his shoulders, his arms. "You'd better tell me about it. I want to know everything."

She lifted Jasmine from her lap. "I don't know what to tell you. It was a long time ago." Her voice was unsteady. "He used to come to visit my parents' house. I was only sixteen so I didn't pay much attention to him. Not at first. Then my friends began to say he liked me and I . . . noticed . . . things."

"What things?" The shock had not fully penetrated. Only sixteen!

"He always wanted to talk to me. He would pat my hand when we talked. Then he began kissing me on the cheek when he came to visit. And he always brought me something. A box of candy, flowers, a present for my birthday or Christmas. Things like that."

He realized she was about to tell everything and he was afraid. He did not want her to say it. That impulse was quickly followed by another: let it come out, all the unburied filth.

"Once—he made it look like an accident—he kissed me right on the lips. I didn't say anything."

"And then?"

"One night he arrived when my parents were away. We started talking . . . and then fooling around. Then he got excited and he wanted to so much . . . and I . . ."

She could not go on. She was really sobbing.

He tried not to think about that scene because it was like keeping

201

a negative in a developing tank—the image came too sharply into focus.

"Was that when your parents came home and found you?"

She shook her head without looking up. "That was a different time. Later."

She lay back in tears with her dark hair spread against the sofa pillow, and her face changed with pain.

"Tom, will you get me my medicine?"

She had been having stomach upsets for several days. He got the bottle from the bathroom medicine cabinet and watched her spoon out the white liquid.

Her bare feet were curled beneath her on the sofa. Her feet were dainty and small, with a high arch, and her toes were round and pink right to the silver-painted nails. They were like little pink grapes of flesh.

"Tom?"

"Yes."

"Something else. You're probably not going to be too happy about it."

He stared at large knuckled fists with a kind of wonder. How much was he supposed to take? When would it be over?

"I'm three weeks overdue."

"What?" At first he did not understand.

"I think I ought to go see the doctor tomorrow."

His mood changed slowly. "You're pregnant?"

A baby! She was carrying his child.

"You said I wasn't going to like it?" he asked incredulously.

"Where will we live? How can we pay for a baby?"

Happy images began swirling in his mind.

"Don't you worry about it."

"I could get an abortion. I'm not afraid. I know what I'd be letting myself in for."

"Don't be crazy."

There were such wonderful possibilities opening up for them. He had forgotten—almost—about Walter. He couldn't be angry with her now. Her image shifted, began to shiver like a reflection in water. He saw her with a big belly. Twice as beautiful.

There was a light giddy feeling in his chest. Every man who is any sort of man wants to have a child. It proves something. A man who can create life is really a man.

"It's easier than having a baby. It's even less dangerous," Sophy said.

"Naturally, you're upset. It's all new to you."

He knelt beside her to cradle her. Little Sophy. He loved her more than ever.

"Darling, I think it's great. I really do."

After a moment he turned up her salt-stained face and kissed her tenderly.

*

The quiet environs of the Knickerbocker Club awoke in Vincent Haleson a faint distaste.

Vinnie belonged to the Revere Club, a more ancient and hallowed institution. All the Halesons had belonged to the Revere Club since its founding in 1801, and his grandfather had been a major combatant in the embittered social struggle which culminated in the withdrawal from the Revere of twenty-six members who formed the Knickerbocker.

Vinnie still experienced a faint uneasiness whenever visiting the Knickerbocker—a feeling as if he were trafficking with the enemy.

The gentleman at the desk greeted him with appraising you-are-not-a-member eyes.

"I beg your pardon, sir. Are you expected?"

Vinnie resented the smugness of Knickerbocker people, the impression they tried to give of everyone being an intruder into this special demesne of wealth and privilege.

"Mr. Haleson. I'm to meet Peter Druse at two."

"Oh, yes. Mr. Druse is in the library, sir, and expecting you."

Shrewd appraising eyes veiled with approval of his new status. If not a member, at least an invited guest. There is nothing in the world, Vinnie thought, quite so dignified as the dignity of upstarts.

The library was hushed with the ponderous authority of leatherbound books, and with the ponderous quiet of members reading or gazing out at Central Park from profound windowed privacy.

Peter Druse rose from a dark club chair in a corner and came forward. They shook hands.

"Glad to see you, Vinnie. Would you care for a drink?"

"Not now. Thanks."

Peter led the way to a corner window in which two club chairs faced each other in the apex of a triangle.

"I thought we could talk more privately here than in the office. Of course, it's strictly against club tradition for any business to be discussed here."

Vinnie's reply was muted. "I believe that rule was carried over from the Revere."

"Oh, yes," Peter said, "that's your Club, isn't it?"

"Yes."

"I prefer it here. Less stuffy."

The echoes of the old rebellion had not entirely disappeared, were still fading into heavy oaken walls and deep carpeting. The Revere stuffy? Everything at the Revere was assigned to its proper place. Even dissidence.

Vinnie sat down. "Well, I suppose there are some things about which we will never agree, Peter."

Peter nodded, and for a time they talked of peripheral matters such as the recent appointment of an Undersecretary of State who was a member of the Knickerbocker. The man in question was the oldest son of a prominent real estate man. He had been given a chance in the family business, but when he began to spend all his time on a huge downtown airport project that would have required over five billion dollars in federal, state, and city money, his father decided that such boldly imaginative thinking belonged more in government than private enterprise. Peter conceded that the Undersecretary was incompetent; he even seemed to take pride in the man's inferior talents. Vinnie understood the implication: the Undersecretary had attained his high position only because he belonged to the right Club.

Vinnie sat back in his deep leather armchair, looking as unruffled at five o'clock in the afternoon as he had at ten o'clock that morning.

His shirt with its thin horizontal stripings was fresh and starched and his thinning hair was perfectly groomed. He stared at cloud shadows moving across the avenue while he listened to Peter's stumbling, slow discourse and wondered when the man would ever come to the point.

Peter was saying now, "I've been a good father—at least I've tried to be. I found out she's living with him in her apartment. Why would Barbara do a thing like that?"

"She's old enough to look after her own affairs, Peter."

"I don't understand it. Twenty years older—and a foreigner. And I could tell you other things about him that would shock you. He isn't right for her at all."

"She isn't necessarily going to marry him, Peter."

"I asked her on the phone last night if she was considering marriage. Do you know what she said? 'I would in a minute—if he'd have me!' If he'd have *her!*" Peter struggled in silence a moment with this indignity. "Wait until she finds out what sort he is. I've had his background looked into."

Vinnie coughed defensively. The gesture of coughing allowed him to cover up another reaction. He did not want Peter to guess what he was thinking because he was thinking that Peter was an ass.

Peter stared at him, then turned away and looked out the window for a moment.

"Emily and I had dinner at the Yacht Club last night," he said. "With Ann."

This new turn in the conversation was clearly the reason he had been asked here at the close of the day.

"Did you have a good time?" he asked politely.

Peter turned to confront him. "Ann isn't very happy these days, you know. It's been almost a month and I'm beginning to wonder when the two of you will come to your senses. Don't you want a reconciliation?"

"Ann told me the other day she's talked to a lawyer about a divorce."

"She doesn't know what she wants. She's confused. It's up to you, Vinnie, to take matters in your own hands and do something about it. That is, if you care about her at all."

"She has a right to make up her own mind."

"Ann's a wonderful girl, and I know she cares about you, but there's always been that big tragedy in your lives. That sort of thing is hard for a woman. She needs understanding and help."

"That happened eleven years ago, Peter."

"It's still going on for her. She's living that tragedy. You have to make allowances."

It must be reassuring, Vinnie thought, to be Peter Druse and to dwell in the simplest of all possible worlds.

"I tried to, Peter. Apparently things didn't work out. I don't think either Ann or I can be blamed for that, because we did try our best."

"I'm not so sure of that, Vinnie."

"You don't know all the circumstances."

"I don't want to. All I want is a straightforward answer. Vinnie, are you going to make an effort to reconcile with Ann—or will you let the whole marriage go down the drain just because you're too stiff-necked to do anything to save it?"

The whole tone of the question wakened Vinnie's anxieties. Peter held the whip hand and would not mind bloodying it. Vinnie had made an enviable record in charge of Zenith Oil's International Division, pushing up sales twenty percent and increasing the net nearly seven percent, and as executive vice-president he was clearly next in line for the presidency, but all this would mean nothing if Peter turned squarely against him.

"I don't believe that's a fair way of putting the question, Peter," he said.

"I'm not interested in fairness. Or in wishy-washy answers either. I'm interested in my daughter's happiness. Are you going to be a man and go to Ann and make up whatever it is that's come between you two?"

"Have you talked about this to Ann? A reconciliation requires two people, Peter. Even if I were willing to make another attempt, are you sure Ann would be?"

"Of course she would."

"That isn't my impression. I've talked to her, and I haven't had the least indication of it."

206

Peter plaited the right side of his trouser leg with one hand. "Does Ann have some particular reason for wanting to divorce you?"

"A particular reason?"

"I mean, is it some other woman?"

"Nothing like that."

"That would be unforgivable. Especially for someone as loyal and loving as Ann."

"I know how you feel about her."

"I'll be frank, Vinnie. There's been scuttlebutt about you and that secretary of yours. What's her name?"

"Norma?"

"I never paid attention to it before, and I still hope it isn't true. But do you think Ann heard? Is that the reason?"

"There was never any grounds for that scuttlebutt, as you call it."

Vinnie came very close to adding that there had been considerable rumor-mongering a few years ago about Peter Druse and the very elegant wife of Paul Collins, a member of Zenith Oil Corporation's Board. In fact, Vinnie was certain there had been a shallow physical affair up to the time Diane Collins died suddenly of complications after an attack of influenza. He had never been sure if Paul Collins knew of the liaison but one thing was certain—Collins was one of three directors on the Board who always voted against Peter.

Peter said, "I suppose it's going to go on to a divorce if you're not willing to do anything to stop it. In that case, I hope it will be an amicable one."

"I have nothing but the friendliest feelings toward Ann."

"There won't be a demand for alimony or anything like that." With obtrusive artlessness, Peter added, "There will have to be a property settlement, of course."

"We don't own a good deal of property."

"You're living in the house at Queens Point."

"That belongs to me."

"Part of it belongs to your wife. And it's worth a couple of hundred thousand dollars."

"You hold a mortgage for a hundred and twenty-five thousand."

"I'm coming to that. I have a suggestion to make. In case there is a divorce, Vinnie, you ought to pay that off, and I'll turn the money over to Ann as her share of the settlement. Fair enough?"

"Except for one thing."

"What's that?"

"I don't have the money."

Peter nodded. "I know. But there's your pension fund—that amounts to over a hundred thousand by now . . ."

"I can't borrow against it. And I won't get the principal until I retire."

"That's another problem I want to discuss with you."

"What is?"

"Damn it, Vinnie, don't make things harder than they are. If you've done something to Ann bad enough to make her divorce you, you can't expect me to be completely impartial."

"We can keep our business and personal relations entirely separate."

"It doesn't work that way. I'm still pulling for you and Ann to effect some sort of reconciliation. But if you don't, well, I'm going to ask for your resignation, Vinnie."

"I have to refuse."

"We'll make it look good. There'll be a handsome severance . . ."

"I won't resign, Peter. That's final."

"Don't get me angry, Vinnie, or I'll say things I shouldn't. I've been covering up for you just about long enough."

"Covering up?"

Peter grumbled something. Then: "Like I did on this matter of a loan to Alex Johns. The last I heard you said we'd have to advance half a million dollars to save him from going bankrupt. Well, we didn't and I notice he's still around doing business."

Vinnie said, looking in the other's face, "I decided not to give him money after studying the situation further."

"And he went and raised the money somewhere else. Sounds to me as though he hoodwinked you, Vinnie."

"It might be fairer to say he tried to."

"Then there was that business earlier about the building foundation. He used a pretty risky procedure to fix that. He went ahead and did it without any authorization from you. That's the sort of carelessness I mean. You should have been on top of that whole situation. There'll be no more covering up when you make blunders like that."

Vinnie replied with polite weary patience, "We never took a risk. If Alex's gamble hadn't worked, we would have made him take down the wall."

"A lot of things like that have been sliding by," Peter said, testily. "From now on I want you to clear all decisions with me. As president of the company, I don't intend to abdicate my responsibilities to you."

"There's never been a question of that."

"I want everything in writing from now on. Don't come to me to talk over any problems. Put your thoughts down in writing, and I'll get back to you."

Meanwhile, the memos in Peter's file would pile up until somewhere in the growing mass Peter would find an excuse to compel him to resign. Given sufficient documentation, and the will, anything can be proved against anyone. It was typical of Peter's devious approach. He always took the circuitous route.

"Is that all?" Vinnie asked coldly.

"Not quite. You know that deal you were contemplating with the Hayden Bank? Well, I've broken off negotiations." Peter clasped pudgy hands on his left knee. "I've made a better deal with Allied Continental."

"Babcock?"

John Babcock was president of Allied Continental Bank, a member of the Knickerbocker Club and a golf-playing crony of Peter's. Vinnie, whose entire attention had been riveted on his own problem, and the various ramifications of it, felt as though he had been crawling through a narrow dark tunnel and saw ahead a chink of daylight.

"Yes—a very sound man," Peter said.

"It's hard to say that people at Hayden Bank are less sound. I understood our deal was practically set."

"I'm not saying anything against the people at Hayden—but my deal with Babcock is a better one. I got the best value for our company out of that particular piece of property."

There were consequences of this unlooked for decision Vinnie was quite sure Peter had not explored.

He said mildly, "Of course, Alex Johns will be very upset."

"What's he got to do with it?"

"He suggested Hayden Bank as a tenant in the first place and went to a lot of trouble to line them up for us."

"I'll explain it to him if it becomes necessary. I'll assure him that this was a pure and simple business decision."

Peter did not fully understand the problem. He did not know, for example, that Alex Johns was in a financial situation in which the continuing support of the Hayden Bank was absolutely crucial. There was a two million dollar line of credit from the Hayden Bank. Vinnie had taken the trouble to uncover the existence of this credit when Alex Johns first began pushing the Hayden Bank as a tenant, but there was no question of the Hayden Bank's desirability and they were offering to pay a fair price so there seemed no reason to pursue the matter. Nevertheless he was sure that if the Hayden Bank lost this space they might, in turn, put further pressure on Alex. At this point, further pressure was something Alex Johns might not be able to withstand.

In the room behind him Vinnie vaguely heard moving around. Then there was the clinking of glasses as drinks were served. He looked into the uncomprehending eyes of the older man opposite him.

"Perhaps Alex won't think that you made a pure and simple business decision, Peter."

"What are you trying to imply?"

There is a moment in every contest in which one of the contestants clearly confronts the prospect of final defeat and then he must make a choice either to surrender at once or to redouble his efforts to avoid his fate. Vinnie had little sympathy for Alex Johns. Not too long ago, for personal reasons, he would have been willing to let Alex go over the brink, but at least he was aware this would have been counter to Zenith Oil's corporate interests. Peter was not aware. Within this new situation, in which he was entirely on the defensive, Vinnie felt it wise to reserve the high ground.

"I think we have a certain responsibility to Alex. I can't help feeling sorry if he should become the innocent victim."

"Victim?"

"It's clear enough that the Hayden Bank isn't being passed over for business reasons. John Babcock is getting the space because he's a personal friend of yours."

Peter jerkily rubbed one cheek as though he had been slapped.

"Obviously, we've reached a point, Vinnie, where I have no choice. If you won't resign after this, I'll make you go."

All of Vinnie Haleson's vital powers, psychological and physical, the secretion of such fluids as adrenalin and courage, poured into his veins.

"You have the power to discharge me as vice-president, Peter. But I still retain my job as a director until the Board decides to relieve me of it."

"You can't fight me."

"Yes, I can. I have a few friends there."

Peter's chin quivered. "I know you've been playing up to Fred Feist. But Feist only controls three places on the Board. In a showdown, I've got the votes to kick you out."

Waning rays of sunlight came through the window to strike athwart the chair in which Peter was seated. In the gloom he appeared as a gray shadow.

Vinnie said, "I'm going to send you a memo, Peter, on why I disagree with your decision for Babcock against the Hayden Bank. With duplicate copies to all members of the Board."

"Vinnie, from this moment, I don't even consider you a part of management."

Vinnie turned casually in his chair to look for a waiter. "I will have a drink before I go. Provided one can get any service in this confounded Club."

*

Thursday was payday. At seven-thirty this blustery March morning men were lined up outside the shanties waiting for the armored cars to deliver their checks. In former times armored cars had brought cash but there had been too many robberies so now the workers were paid only by check.

On the job, the framework was going up at a rate of two stories a week. After the raising gang got steel up to the top and put the members into place, lining up bolt holes with drift pins and putting in fitting bolts to secure the joints properly, the bolting gang installed permanent high strength bolts impacted to the proper tightness with airpowered wrenches. The bolting gangs worked swiftly so the concrete workers and cement finishers due to follow them would not be held up. The nature of the job was changing rapidly. Other trades were coming in: carpenters to form out steel for the concrete, and strippers to take the wood forms off after the concrete hardened, steamfitters and plumbers and painters, bricklayers, and electricians. As more trades joined the work, the problems increased.

*

In the superintendent's office, with its plaster block walls and cement floor, Jim Otis was alone at his desk. The work day had not begun. He had been fingering a key in his trouser pocket for several minutes, thinking of Margaret and the curious little smile that seemed to be saying she knew something about him he didn't know. Her soft cajoling voice wanted to be helpful, to do something for his pride, never sensing that even as they were making love the only way his pride could be saved was to hate her. When he was in bedwarmed ease with her she could not guess the huge wrath in his thoughts. And when he took her his hate was penetrating her as much as his love. She meant nothing to him. An ofay. A honkie.

Margaret had given him the key that morning when he was leaving her apartment. "So you can come and go as you please," she said, smiling. She assumed that he would be coming and going from now on. He didn't know how to answer. If he refused the key, it would be a rejection and he didn't want to reject her. But if he accepted the key he would be involved, and he didn't mean to become involved. He had to be on guard against Margaret.

She was a schoolteacher; she taught at a school for the deaf someplace. He had met her at a party two weeks ago and she had become interested in him. She was one of those conscious progressives who are always getting information about people. They talked about civil rights, discrimination in the building trade, Martin Luther King, and Bobby Kennedy. She held strong views about what was happening in the world. But all the while he knew that what was happening in the world related to the two of them. The possibilities were slowly overcoming them. Her talk gave him a chance to appraise her and decide whether he wanted to or not. She wore a pale voile shirtdress that showed the beginning softness of her breasts at the low neckline. Why not? A keen desire to sleep with her took possession of him as he imagined her all naked as though clothed in white fur. When he lay beside her, later that night, he saw her white face thrust to him. She put her hand on him and the heat of her touch stroked upward through his whole body.

"I know you've taken other girls like me to bed. You're not just working off race hatred, are you?"

He said, "You look good to me."

And she did. She was interesting in a way that only New York girls of a certain type were. She was educated and liberal, knew how to dress and talk and had a personality that was clear and self-aware and neurotic in an interested way. She had style, unlike the girl Tom MacLaren had married. Sophy had visited the office once. MacLaren was obviously proud of her and showing her off. She was pretty enough but too carefully made up, too deliberately husky voiced, her miniskirt a bit too short and her earrings a bit too flashy, and when she laughed it was oddly jarring and shrill. Margaret was the same age as Sophy but years older in poise and in some indefinable quality known as class.

He gave a small grunt and sat lower. Margaret was just another honkie, and there was no future. The key in his pocket was an illusion. His resentful mind turned itself into a canker of self-loathing. Ought to know better than to start feeling that way about a honkie.

Office workers entered, nodding and speaking to him. He nodded back. There would be a number of people missing today. The Long Island Railroad was on strike. That was one of those problems you could not foresee when laying out a schedule. Last night Bernie Seligson, one of the assistants, had said there was a good chance he wouldn't report for duty tonight. He lived in Port Jefferson an hour and a half away on the railroad even when trains were running. That wasn't a problem because they could handle his job, but there was no way to replace absent steelworkers or concrete workers. Union halls had no one. There was so much construction work in New York right now that you couldn't keep a regular crew unless you guaranteed them overtime.

Tom MacLaren entered the office.

"Good morning, Mr. MacLaren," Otis said.

"Good morning. What's this I hear about trouble with the mason tenders?"

Jim Otis filled him in on the dispute. It was one of the omnipresent jurisdictional problems. A contract to do work on the building was given by the builder, Alex Johns, but the unions had the final say on who was to do what. The mason tenders were now claiming that unloading and loading of lumber onto the hoist was their job, even though the material in question was part of the carpenters' contract. The lumber was needed to close off an open shaftway and protect the workers below. Each union was trying to reserve as much work for its own men as possible, and each was aware that any decision might set a precedent. On the next construction, whether or not jobs were defined in the books or by the union regulations, someone would be sure to say: well, we did it that way on the Zenith Oil job.

"What do you think we should do?" Tom MacLaren asked.

"Let them fight it out between themselves, Mr. MacLaren."

"Okay. Tell them so." MacLaren went to his desk to check his diary about what progress was supposed to have been made by today, what meetings were scheduled, and what new work was about to start.

This super's office was the control point; toward it came problems, and from it flowed solutions. Otis was better fit for the job than MacLaren, but there was nothing to do about that. It was a simple matter of black and white. It was the same reason his father still worked as a hall porter and his mother worked in a steam laundry. They thought the reason was their lack of education so together they had somehow scraped up enough money for him to go to college. A

partial scholarship for playing basketball and hard work during sum-
mers at various construction jobs helped support him but when he
came out with an engineering degree he found that it was easy
enough to get a job but next to impossible to get the kind of job
that meant putting him in charge of white men.

When Tom MacLaren finished with the diary, and with his preliminary phone calls, Otis accompanied him on the tour of the building. They started at the top and walked down through each floor to
see if what was planned had been accomplished, and if not, why
not. There were eight floors erected so far, but there was always
something. Planks hadn't been tied down securely enough to the
beams to make sure a wind would not blow them off, a valve was
left open on the temporary water line used by the cement workers
and plasterers, the labor foreman and his crew had not cleared the
sixth floor for the cement finishers to do their work. By ten o'clock
when they reached the ground floor again, Jim Otis had a notebook
full of things to do. As they entered the office the timekeeper told
them how many of the men checked in for the day. Twenty percent
were missing.

At ten-thirty there was a new complaint from the Highway Department. An inspector read Jim Otis the law: no piece of equipment
can occupy more than one third of the street. Their street crane
extended ten feet from the curb and the side street where it was
parked was only twenty-four feet wide. Otis asked to see his badge.
There were a certain number of fake inspectors in the early stages
of a construction. Only yesterday one man had come up about the
signs posted on the fences when the law said there could be no signs.
It happened that was true about the law but when Otis asked for the
man's identification, his credentials were from the Department of
Water Supply and Electricity. He had no authority at all to order
signs removed from street fences. He had been hoping to create a
nuisance value for himself.

The Highway Department inspector, however, was legitimate, and
didn't seem interested in a bribe. They had to promise to have the
crane moved off the side street no later than noon, and the inspector
gave them a violation anyway.

Later that afternoon there was a demonstration at the building site. A group of Negro demonstrators showed up with signs protesting the discriminatory hiring practice of the unions. Their signs called for more Negro apprentices in the better paid mechanical trades. A tall Negro with a Fu Manchu moustache kept chanting that eighty percent of the New York plumber's local were sons or nephews of members.

Tom MacLaren put through a call to Alex Johns' office and after a minute handed the phone to Otis.

"I understand there's trouble from colored people down there," Alex Johns said.

"That's right, Mr. Johns."

"Are they causing damage?"

Negro children were crawling under halted trucks and pickets had formed human chains to prevent deliveries from being made to the site. Two youths had stormed the crane, in its new location, climbed to the hook and clung there. Police had chased them down.

"No real damage, Mr. Johns."

"You ought to be able to handle this," Alex Johns said. "Get out there and show them that we've got their people on the job."

"They've seen me, Mr. Johns."

Several of the demonstrators had hurled insults. A Negro woman spat at him while two cops were holding her.

Uncle Tom!

You look like a black man but you a whitey!

I smell black pig!

Alex Johns said, "You get out and tell them that before we can give jobs to Negroes there's got to be skilled Negro workers. One good way is to ask them for a list of Negro building trade workers. Nobody's got a list because there aren't any. Tell 'em if there are, we'll hire 'em."

Otis knew it wasn't the contractor's fault, nor the client's. The unions didn't allow Negroes to be trained for high-paying construction jobs.

"They're in no mood to be talked to that way, Mr. Johns."

"Every minute they're holding up deliveries costs us money."

"They won't stay long."

"You get down there and talk to them. They'll listen to you."

"I'm not sure they will."

"Why not? You're one of them."

"That's just the reason they won't. I'm on the other side of the fence."

"You're working for me, Jim, so do what I say. Talk reasonably, but talk to them. And if they start real trouble get the police to clear 'em the hell out of there."

Swift words, habitual words, came to him, and they seemed a frail defense against the anger rising in him.

"I'll do what I can, Mr. Johns."

As he was leaving the office he met Tom MacLaren's gaze and felt his face flush, but one advantage of being black is that it's harder to tell. He wished he knew what he was going to say. It would be easier if he knew that.

On his way down from the office to the scene of the demonstration, he put his hand in his pocket and found the key Margaret had given him. He took the key and flung it into one of the rubbish containers as he passed by.

*

Less than half an hour before the ceremony Alex Johns was sure he could not go through with it. He didn't understand how the thing had grown so quickly. Ginger had agreed to a small wedding, just his mother and brother Frank and a few close friends, then somehow the list grew to include a few of Ginger's relatives and some of her girl friends and suddenly invitations were being mailed out to business associates and mere acquaintances and there were decisions to be made about everything. Who the ushers and bridesmaids were going to be. The minister and the church. The wedding gown. The flowers. The refreshments for the reception. Alex helped Ginger choose what presents to give to the ushers and bridesmaids, and some of her ideas were so extravagant that he rebelled.

"A ruby clip for each of the bridesmaids. What's the point of that?"

"I like the color ruby. The bridesmaids' dresses are all going to be that color."

"I don't give a damn what color dresses they wear. We're not going to spend a couple hundred bucks apiece on bridesmaids. Screw the bridesmaids."

When the wedding was first discussed it seemed comfortably far in the future, not a real threat. But now the day was here, the very hour, he was overwhelmed by the imminence of everything.

"How do I look?" he asked.

"You look fine," Frank said.

Frank, his best man, looked like a dressed-up monkey in his cutaway suit and striped trousers. He was taller, heavier, softer than Alex but they resembled each other more closely than most brothers.

"I'll bet," Alex answered mournfully. Beneath his starched dress shirt his skin was oozing and when he lit a cigarette his stiff cuffs abraded his wrists.

"Will you stop worrying?" Frank asked. "This isn't the first time you've been married."

Mention of his previous marriage brought back unwelcome memories. Laura had seemed shy and feminine and sweet, even willing to give up her career for him (a career that consisted of TV commercials and a few guest shots on nighttime TV) but it hadn't taken long for her to change. You couldn't let a woman get in control or the next thing you knew you were getting weekly enemas for constipation. His mother had given him enemas until he was almost fifteen.

"Put a smile on your face," Frank said. "This isn't an execution. It's a wedding."

"Easy for you to talk. You're a bachelor." Alex chuckled painfully. "How's Mom?"

"Out front in the chapel."

"I mean, how is she taking it?"

"Don't worry."

"What is that supposed to mean?"

There had always been rivalry. Frank resented the fact Alex was in a position to do more for her and possibly he suspected that Alex was her favorite. Mother had a well-developed regard for success.

"She cried most of the night," Frank said.

"That's a hell of a thing to say."

"I had a terrible time getting her to sleep. Do you want me to lie to you?"

"Why is she so upset?"

"The way you did it, I guess."

"You mean getting married? I told her weeks ago."

"I told her not to worry. *I'll* always be around." Frank crossed to the door of the room. "I'd better go out now. I wasn't sure she'd even get here for the ceremony."

"It's ridiculous," Alex said without conviction. The door opened and closed behind Frank. "I'm getting married. I'm not passing out of the picture."

Nevertheless he was worried. He had a perfectly fine affair with Ginger for five years. Why must it degenerate into marriage? Even at best, a wife was a trespasser and he resented anything that trespassed on either his possessions or his privacy.

A warning prickle of heat told him that his cigarette was burning too close to the finger joint. He snuffed it in an ashtray as the door opened. Julius Scobie entered.

"Alex, can I have a word with you?"

Alex adjusted his cutaway tails before an oval mirror and touched the fresh white boutonniere in his jacket lapel.

"How do I look?"

"Okay."

"Is that the best you can say?"

"Alex, this is important . . ."

"If it's business, Julius, this is my wedding day."

The door swung open and a crowd of tuxedos surged in. The small room filled with men who wanted to shake Alex's hand.

"I never thought any woman would do it . . . What'd she give you, Alex, a love potion? . . . Why'd any woman wanna marry a bandy-legged wreck like you?"

"You're all invited to come see us in Westport," Alex said.

A few days before he had agreed to purchase a Westport estate with twenty-two acres of woodland, an immense garden, two swimming pools and a fourteen-room house in Georgian style.

"Never thought you'd go for a big church wedding, Alex. Thought you'd just scoot off to City Hall and . . ."

He glimpsed Julius skulking on the edge of the crowd.

Julius's scanty hair lay flat across his narrow forehead and his jowls hung like a bulldog's. Something about that forlorn expression began to communicate anxiety to Alex.

Laughing, ushering well-wishers to the door, he said, "After I told her yes, everything went black. Clear out of here, will you, guys? I've only got a couple of minutes."

Turmoil and hilarity flowed out through the door. Alex closed it, turned the lock, and faced about.

"All right, what is it?"

Julius Scobie looked like sorrowful flotsam tossed up on the beach. "I had a special delivery from Vinnie Haleson this morning. Peter Druse has decided not to make the deal with the Hayden Bank."

"*What?*"

Alex had only experienced a shock like this when a mortar shell tore through a roof to make a shambles of the commissary and leave him with a leg dotted with pieces of shrapnel.

"What?" he said again.

"He's signing with Babcock at Allied Continental."

"He can't!" Alex's leg began sharply paining him. "He *okayed* Hayden! So did Vinnie."

"They didn't sign anything."

"What's that got to do with it? Zenith Oil is a responsible corporation. I have the word of the president and the executive vice-president. What else do I need?"

"They had a legal right to close with any tenant they chose. Peter Druse decided to change his mind."

"That's irresponsible!"

"Vinnie Haleson sent a memo to everyone on the Board of Directors disagreeing with the decision. But he told me there isn't a chance of changing it."

"Hayden Bank only extended my line of credit because I got them that space."

"I know."

"Our loan is callable in forty-eight hours. They could close me out. They could put me in bankruptcy."

"That's why I came to tell you right away."

"Peter Druse *can't* change his mind! What's wrong with Hayden?"

"John Babcock is a good friend of his."

"That's no reason." Sudden fury seized Alex. "Why am I standing here talking to you? I have to get hold of Peter Druse. Where's a phone?"

"There's one in the hall."

Emerging from the room into the corridor Alex was surrounded by late-arriving guests. He went to the telephone.

"Who you calling, Alex? A girl friend?"

Raucous laughter moved chapelward.

Alex finished dialing. "Zenith Oil," a pleasant female voice answered.

"Mr. Druse, please."

In a moment another female voice: "Mr. Druse's office."

"This is Alex Johns. I've got to talk to him."

"I'm sorry. Mr. Druse is out of town today, sir."

"Where can I reach him?"

"I'm afraid you can't. He may call at five o'clock and I can give him a message then."

"That's too late."

"I'm sorry, Mr. Johns."

"Look, this is an emergency. I've only got a couple of minutes." He hesitated, weighing alternatives, and there was nothing else: "Switch this call to Vinnie Haleson."

"Hold on a minute, please."

In a few seconds another aloof female voice: "Mr. Haleson's office."

"I've got to talk to Mr. Haleson."

"Mr. Haleson isn't in the office today, sir. Who's calling?"

"Alex Johns. It's a crisis. I've got to talk to him."

"He's working at home today, Mr. Johns, and left explicit orders that he did not wish to be disturbed."

"It's an emergency. Look, I've got his unlisted phone number, but I don't have it with me." He didn't have anything in the pockets of his damned striped trousers. He searched vainly with one hand for what he knew was not there. "What is it?"

"I'm sorry, Mr. Johns. I can't give that number."

"I tell you, this is important!"

"Perhaps if you give me the message I can . . ."

"I have no time!"

"I'll try to reach Mr. Haleson. Is there a number where he can call you back?"

"If Mr. Haleson doesn't get this call he's going to be angry."

"I'm sorry, Mr. Johns. He left quite explicit orders."

"What's your name?"

"Norma Brown." There was hostile emphasis as she added, "Mr. Haleson's private secretary."

"Now you listen to me, Norma . . ."

"Alex. What are you doing?" Frank had returned with the faintly exasperated air of someone dealing with a recalcitrant child.

"What does it look like I'm doing? I'm making a phone call. Leave me alone! . . . Now, Norma, I want Mr. Haleson's home phone number. I want it now."

Through the walls came the faint opening strains of the organ.

"They're ready to start," Frank said.

"Let 'em start without me! *Norma* . . ."

The phone was dead.

Alex made pawing motions at his other trouser pocket. "*Damn!* Julius has the number."

He started back into the waiting room. Frank intercepted him. "They're waiting!"

"They'll have to wait."

Julius Scobie found the number in his small thick carefully indexed memorandum book. Alex returned to the hall telephone. Frank was pacing up and down the corridor.

"You can't stay here," Frank said. "She'll be coming through in a minute."

"Who?" Alex asked, moving Frank away from the telephone.

"Ginger. The woman you're going to marry."

"I can't worry about that. This is important." He began to dial Vinnie Haleson's home telephone number.

"More important than your own wedding?"

"Don't bother me!" He finished dialing the number.

"A bride and groom can't even see each other before the wedding!"

Ringing began.

"Don't give me superstition at a time like this!"

Twice. Three times.

"Be sensible, Alex."

"Why don't you go back and look after your goddamned mother?"

Frank waited, shocked speechless.

"Hello. *Hello!*" Alex had to raise his voice above the noise of the organ.

"Mr. Haleson's residence."

"Let me talk to Mr. Haleson."

"Who's calling, please?"

"Alex Johns. Tell him it's urgent."

There was a silence and then after a minute: "I'm sorry, sir. He isn't in."

"I know he's there. If he doesn't talk to me, he'll be sorry!"

"He's gone for a drive, sir. I don't expect him back for an hour."

"I'll call him back in an hour. Tell him to wait."

Frank plucked at his sleeve.

"Alex, come on!"

Alex shook off the restraining touch. He dialed the number of Henry Tratner at the Hayden Bank.

"Henry—Alex. Alex Johns. I just got word of what happened at Zenith Oil."

"So did we."

Alex could have sworn the telephone was a gun against his head.

"They must be crazy. They had no reason. I don't know why the hell they did it. But don't worry. I'll handle it."

"Naturally, Alex, this changes everything. Our whole deal."

The blue muzzle was pressing tightly against his temple. "Don't panic. It's going to be all right."

"I'm pointing out that if there's no deal on the building there is no deal on extending your credit. We'll call in the entire two million dollars."

A red black roar of annihilation went through his brain.

"Don't do anything," Alex pleaded. "I've already got a call in to

223

Vinnie Haleson. I'm going to get Peter Druse, too. If necessary I'll go over their heads to the Board."

"Alex, I had one devil of a time selling your proposition to our people in the first place. I won't be able to hold them in line when this news breaks. There's going to be tremendous pressure on me."

"Don't sell me down the river."

"It's a rotten situation, Alex. But my hands are tied."

"Don't reach any decision until I get back to you." The chill air in the high-ceilinged corridor seemed to draw closer about Alex's shoulders. "I know it sounds like I need a miracle, but you know me. When I need a miracle I *make* a miracle."

"You're insolvent right this minute."

"I've been insolvent for years. That's why I'm a rich man today."

"It's no joking matter, Alex." Henry Tratner did not consider anything having to do with money a fit subject for humor. "But because we're old friends, here is what I'm prepared to do . . ."

The noise of the organ filled the corridor with resonant sound. "What? What's that?" Alex demanded.

Trying to concentrate on hearing, deep grooves appeared in Alex's forehead and his dark brows quizzically hunched together.

"I said . . ."

The organ drowned out the words again.

"Speak up," Alex pleaded. "I can't hear you, Henry. I'm in a goddamned *church!*"

Accompanied by her maid of honor, Ginger came out of a room farther down the corridor, wearing her eight hundred and ninety-five dollar wedding gown. Her maid of honor, Sybil Carlson, was a homely girl with eyeglasses.

Both women saw and heard Alex's last words.

Alex slowly replaced the receiver. He had heard Henry Tratner: "I'll stall them as long as I can, Alex. But when Zenith Oil signs with Babcock, there's nothing further I can do." He stared at the telephone resentfully. No deadlier weapon has ever been invented.

Ginger gave him a faltering smile. "Hello, darling."

"You're looking beautiful," Alex said. "See you at the preacher's."

He joined Frank to walk down the corridor. Frank refused to look at him. The organ had been playing for several minutes.

"I hope you're satisfied," Frank said. "It was disgraceful."

"It'll be all over soon," Alex replied. A husked thrilling came in his chest when he tried to imagine what the future would bring.

Suddenly he chuckled. "Did you see the look on the maid of honor's face?"

"I don't see what's so funny," Frank said crossly.

Alex's eyes were bright with pain. "I'm in so deep they probably can't pull me out with grappling hooks. It's going to be some laugh when I say 'with all my worldly goods I thee endow.'"

Frank shook his head in bewilderment. They proceeded to the place from which they would make their entrance into the chapel. The organ swelled profoundly in the music of the Wedding March.

*

On the way to work that morning Tom MacLaren had to restrain himself from suddenly breaking into a run. He wanted to shout with joy. Huddling into his heavy leather work jacket and keeping his gloved hands in the side vent pockets, he was flowing over with good spirits that he wanted everyone to share with him.

Some distance from the structure he made his usual mental check of floors down from the derrick on top. The derrick wasn't moving.

It was probably too windy today for steelworkers. There were rips in the canvas shield around the perimeter of a floor below. Violent March gusts had blown most of the night.

He was a block away from the building when he finally saw two police cars and a fire rescue truck parked on a side street near the construction. There were police at barricades and traffic was being diverted.

Tom's first thought was that there had been an accident. He hurried his steps and at the nearest barricade was stopped by a patrolman.

"Do you work here?" the patrolman asked.

"I'm Tom MacLaren, the superintendent."

"The captain wants to talk to you. He's in the trailer."

When he entered the field office, Jim Otis was conferring with a police sergeant. The captain, who was talking on the telephone, hung up.

"Hear what happened, MacLaren?"

"No."

"Well, there's trouble. Wind blew some steel off your building. It was piled too near the edge and wasn't secured properly."

"Off the building? That'd have to be a pretty big blow. You sure it was steel? Maybe it was timber."

"It was steel, Mr. MacLaren," Otis said. "Small stuff, clamps and angles. Started about five o'clock this morning and cops came and blocked off the streets. Wouldn't let any cars or people through."

"You're lucky no one got hurt," the sergeant said.

Only a few days before, the city Highway Department had called Tom to complain that flying concrete had broken a street traffic light and while he was calling the insurance company to report it the Department of Air Pollution also called to complain about the flying dust. Tom had flung his helmet against the wall in anger and no one had been able to talk to him for an hour.

Now he said mildly, "I'm sorry, Captain. I'll get after the steel contractor and find out why that stuff wasn't secured. I guess he didn't expect the wind to blow that strong."

"You're going to get a violation," the captain said. "I'm just trying to figure a way I can arrest somebody."

"We'll make sure it doesn't happen again." Tom turned to Otis. "Call the insurance people."

"I already did, Mr. MacLaren."

"That steel could've made one hell of a mess on the ground," the captain said. "Especially if there were people around. It was early in the morning, that's all that saved you." The captain added bitterly, "They called me at five-thirty in the morning to come down to the precinct. I'd like to arrest somebody."

When the police captain left, Tom saw that Otis was watching him with baffled interest.

"Anything the matter?"

"I'm surprised, Mr. MacLaren. You don't seem upset."

"Why should I be? No one got hurt."

"That isn't how you felt the day we got the calls from the Highway Department and Air Pollution."

"Maybe I'm not in a mood to get angry at anybody today."

He felt cool and watchful, fully capable of mastering those sudden tempers over which he usually had such precarious control. Everything that happened was part of a process, every incident was a link in a chain that ended in happiness.

"That's a good mood to be in, Mr. MacLaren."

"You know what? You ought to get married, Jim. You ought to settle down and have a family."

"Thanks for the advice."

"I mean it."

"I haven't met anyone I want to get married to."

"Keep looking. Maybe you'll get lucky."

"I'm satisfied the way things are, Mr. MacLaren."

Tom felt a little sorry for Otis. No man could really be satisfied until he was married to the right girl and she was having his child. That was what life was all about.

Otis brought a requisition to sign. They were ordering a half-dozen new rubbish disposal cans. Twenty of the giant red cans were now scattered through the building to collect the tremendous amount of firewood, paper, wrappings, and discarded building materials that had to be disgorged out of the foundation. The cans were rented from a rubbish removal contractor and were designed so they could be attached to garbage trucks and dumped automatically after the hoist brought them down to the ground floor.

"Is that all for now?" Tom asked.

"Yes, Mr. MacLaren."

"Then I guess I'd better begin the tour. I won't need you with me, Jim. You handle things here in the office."

When Tom emerged from the office a few late workers were drifting into dressing shanties on the ground floor. Each contractor on the construction had a shanty or street trailer where workers changed into work clothes, and changed back to street clothes when leaving the job. They were checked in and out by a timekeeper who had their names and tag numbers on his payroll sheet. Not until a worker actually checked in and began the ascent to his work did his working day begin.

Tom got on a hoist that went up through the main elevator shaft. This installation took the place of the usual exterior hoist that had to be taken down when a building was complete. Alex Johns had put a temporary machine room across the main elevator shaft at the twelfth floor within the core of the building. This room was waterproofed and power had been brought in to lift a simple plywood cab installed on the permanent platform. The advantage was that there was no temporary installation to be torn down and all the work went toward the completion of the main building.

This kind of attention to detail had made Alex Johns a big success and Tom was glad that he had put every cent he saved into the stock of Alex Johns' company. He had even taken out a personal bank loan to buy stock. It was risky but he liked the idea of linking his fortunes with a man like Alex Johns. That way he was sure to get ahead. Sunday morning he had passed a church that had a framed black sign in white letters in front—ARE YOU USING GOD TO MAKE YOU A SUCCESS IN LIFE? Well, some people used God and other people used the brains God gave them; he put his faith in Alex Johns.

The hoist rushed upward past floors where the cement was set in and the area marred with wooden forms. They were forming steel on the eighteenth floor now. Tom got off on the twelfth floor, which was as high as the hoist went, and climbed to the top. On these exposed upper floors the wind cut like a razor. Even the Indians who usually ran across the eight-inch beams were not running today. On windy days it was too risky. You had to balance against the wind and if the wind suddenly stopped even an Indian could lose his balance and never get straightened out. He nodded to several of the Mohawk ironworkers: Joe Labache and Pete Miller and Johnny Tontour.

Don Macey came over to him. The foreman's bulky body was made even bulkier by the two warm jackets he was wearing one on top of the other. He rubbed his gloves briskly together.

"A mean day to be up here," Tom said. "How's it going?"

Don seemed pleased at this unexpected sympathy. "We can't do much. Just tighten a few bolts and things."

"You get in all those A series high tension bolts?"

"Right over there," Don Macey nodded.

Tom checked the planking to be sure there was enough deck to protect those working below from falling objects.

Over the rattling of a nearby air wrench, he heard a whoop of joy.

Pete Miller was standing on a cross beam, holding a pocket mirror carefully in his hands and angling it at the sun.

"She got it! She sees me!"

A week ago, working on the sixteenth floor, Pete Miller, the youngest Mohawk in the bolting gang, had developed a romantic attachment for a girl secretary who worked two floors higher up in a nearby building. Everyone knew about it. She was a very pretty girl with dark hair who worked near an office window partly obscured with flowers and books.

Now the tower had risen to a level with the office in which the girl was working and Pete had his first chance to make contact.

Tom MacLaren followed the clear angle of dazzling light from Pete's pocket mirror to the window of the building across the way. Standing near the window, with one hand raised to shield her eyes, the dark-haired girl was looking out.

Pete Miller waved happily.

"She's waving back! She likes me!" he shouted.

The girl was not returning a friendly greeting. She was trying to signal Pete to stop blinding her with the light.

"Hey, beautiful!" Pete yelled.

The girl gave an annoyed signal. Pete blew her a kiss. She turned away from the window without a word and in a moment a venetian blind came down to intercept the light with sharp obliterating corners.

"Boy, she's sure crazy about you!" Tom called.

Pete grinned and gestured for him to go away.

Tom MacLaren felt good. While he gossiped with Don Macey about the Yankees' chances in the new baseball season, he was thinking with a part of his mind about Sophy and the baby.

He saw Johnny Tontour come out of the temporary john two floors down, a plywood shed with a rude toilet bowl connected to permanent piping. The plumber's contractor installed the temporary facility, one bowl for every fifty people on a job, and at least one toilet for every six floors, but on a cold day like this many workers preferred to hold in nature until they could go downstairs to a restaurant.

Johnny Tontour climbed to the floor Tom and Don Macey were on.

"You must have a frozen ass," Tom said.

Johnny Tontour gave him a surprised grin. "I got the runs. All that corn bread and steak yesterday."

"Just make sure it doesn't get you when you're out there on a beam."

"If it does I'll let it happen."

"Somebody'll get a surprise down below if you do," Tom said.

Johnny Tontour went over to the salamander to warm himself near the fire burning in the fifty-gallon drum. "That's okay. When I'm out there I don't let nothin' upset me. You can go up a thousand feet in the air every day, but you go down once—and you're six feet under."

"That's the truth." Tom looked down through the open steel framework to where two workmen several floors below were preparing a mechanical equipment floor, laying down a coat of tar and unrolling waterproofing material over the slab. "Well, I guess I'd better be getting back to work."

He descended past carpenters putting in forms for the concrete to be poured, glaziers filling window frames with glass, and steamfitters and electricians and plumbers installing within eight-inch-thick floors of foamed concrete the one-inch-thick electrical ducts for power, telephone, low voltage intercom, and the cables for closed-circuit television. The building was in a different stage of construction on every floor.

Downstairs on the ground floor Jim Otis greeted him with problems. There was a dispute about scheduling deliveries to the job. Everything that went into the construction, except steel, was delivered on the materials hoist, called the "hod hoist," which was an elevator shaft walled with chicken wire and set on the exterior of the building. It was called a hod hoist, or hoddie, because at one time bricklayers had carried their materials on a hod up to the job. Now the hoist had taken over as the chief means of transporting building supplies, but it was still called the hod hoist. There were three working on this job—the east, west and bucket hoists. Time was closely scheduled on the hoddies, which were the heartbeat of the construction job.

The current dispute, which Otis explained as they walked to the office together, was between plumbers who wanted a hoist to deliver piping they needed, and bricklayers who wanted the hoist to deliver bricks and mortar. The plumbers had been scheduled but missed their time by a few minutes when the pipes didn't arrive. Now bricks were being sent up instead. In his office Tom tried to mediate the dispute between the angry foremen. Finally he worked out a compromise where the time for the next hour would be shared between them with alternate loads going up. Not once during the dispute did Tom raise his voice or begin to lose his temper. This was the kind of day on which trouble could not reach him.

"That was a pretty good show, Mr. MacLaren," Otis said when the foremen left the office.

"No sweat, Jim. No sweat at all."

It was even possible that he would learn how to handle Otis. He could afford to be sympathetic to a black man who was his subordinate even though a qualified engineer. There was really nothing to fear from Otis, the poor bastard, and in time they might work out a relationship.

When he came out of the office with Otis walking beside him, an ironworker was in the back of a truck tying cable around steel piled in the back. When the ironworker finished he signaled for the load to be hoisted away by the derrick. The package of two-ton steel beams started up and the next truck started in.

The driver of the new truck had to follow instructions while he was backing up and the ironworker kept signaling him on. Suddenly there was a terrible cracking noise. The truck stopped. In backing up too far, the truck had torn down a part of the sidewalk bridge.

The driver began shouting and the ironworker yelled back.

Otis headed toward them on the run.

"What's the matter?" Otis called angrily to the ironworker who had been giving the signals. "You drunk or something?"

Tom smiled. There was always something going wrong on a construction job. It was hard to be angry about it.

*

"There's a letter for you," Barbara said. "The delivery boy brought it up."

Karl Schiller swiveled around in his chair and took the brown envelope with a Chicago postmark. They were in the partitioned area which Karl used as his studio.

He opened the letter and read carefully an invitation to become professor of Advanced Design at Chicago's most progressive architectural school, a school that turned out men usually in the forefront of such issues as housing and regional planning, the battle against the entrenched conservatism of vested interests, the struggle against the restrictions of dollar-pinching legislation that sought to preserve land value without any awareness of the many social ills that are attributable to the lack of planning, foresight, and purpose in building. There was no doubt that the offer was proof of his new status in his profession.

He gave the letter to Barbara.

"I'll write them a nice letter and explain why you can't accept," she said.

"I should consider it. I enjoy teaching. And I don't seem able to do anything else."

"Didn't it go well today?"

"It didn't go at all."

"Maybe you're trying too hard," Barbara suggested.

The toll of effort was clear in the fatigue-blunted softness of his features. "Only when I drive myself do I get anything at all."

The floor around him was littered with sketches he had thrown away. He was finished with the Zenith Oil building—it was no longer a part of him—but there were times when he wondered if he had not said all that he wanted to say in one design.

He had no idea why his ability to make visible expressions of some changing harmony within himself had suddenly deserted him. Only his technical skills remained—the sort of thing on display in the sketches now littering the floor. He needed to experience again that exhilarating self-discovery in which ideas flowed from him that he scarcely recognized as his own.

"What you need is some new challenge," Barbara said.

"I've had plenty of things offered to me."

Zenith Oil Corporation had taken out a full-page advertisement which ran in the *Architectural Forum, The Wall Street Journal, Life,* and *The New York Times.* "Great Architecture," said the ad, "Is the Result of a Great Architect Working With a Great Client." There was a reproduction of the Zenith Oil tower, and then: "Each Stays With the Other's Requirements and Gets a Building of Which He Can Be Proud. We Are Very, Very Proud of This Building."

After the ads appeared there had been many offers to design other office buildings. But in trying to work up ideas he had only succeeded in losing contact with his creative imagination. He began relying on acquired skills to perform in the most mechanical way, concerning himself more with technology than with the art of building. Like a musician he had to know his scales but knowing his scales could not make him a musician.

"You're emptied out, Karl. I suppose you have to allow time before you can start again."

Neither of them mentioned that it had been an emotionally exhausting time. That also might have affected his work. There had been the fear of deportation, the risk of further exposure, and the painful process of self-revelation. But he had finally passed beyond a frontier he believed he could not pass and pursued to the end what he feared would destroy him.

"It's time you got out of this place," Barbara said. "We'll go for a walk. Let's see how work is coming on the Zenith Oil building."

"I'd like that."

When they reached the building site it was almost two o'clock. Looking up, Karl caught a glimpse of the angled derrick and boom on the eighteenth floor. Its webbed steel frame radiated guy lines and below it steel beams were piled near the edge. He saw an ironworker straddling a beam, placing drift pins in the new columns. Another man was "plumbing" or straightening beams. Across a precarious connecting girder still another worker carried a heavy keg of

233

bolts to a new location, and a fourth man was descending along a two-story-high column to the connecting beam below.

Where a bird won't fly a Mohawk will climb, said the adage. Karl Schiller was as fascinated as any bystander at the casual daring of men working without safety belts or nets—with only their nonskid shoe soles and agility between them and death. He had ridden to the top on days when clouds and winter haze obscured the very beams on which the Indians did their giddy work and men seemed to hang suspended in a milky emptiness.

Usually he walked through the construction to take notes. There was always some little change or amendment or addition to be made, some instruction not being followed from the diagram. Today he merely stood and watched from the sidewalk. He dictated a few desultory comments to Barbara who wrote them in a notebook. It seemed a long time to him since he had had even the smallest sort of really creative idea. The last time had been when he finally hit upon a solution to the problem of the roof design. Since then there had been only suggestions on how to handle the mechanical problems. It would be months before the building was ready for occupancy but the notes he dictated now were concerned with the water supply and air conditioning. Three massive pieces of air conditioning, with a combined weight of eighty tons, would have to be moved from street level to the mechanical equipment room in the basement and put permenently to rest on huge concrete bases. The water tank would be erected on top of the building because the city water system could not force water to the top floors. Water would be pumped up to the tank and flow down to the upper floors by gravity.

As he finished dictating the last of his notes to Barbara, a load of steel rode up on a derrick hook to where, high above, fitting gangs waited to take it in, pivot and hammer the beams.

Eventually his Zenith Oil tower would join other proud silhouettes on the skyline and everyone who had worked on it, from the iron-worker's apprentice to the structural engineer, from the lather to himself, would say: I built that one. Each would be telling the truth. They were all the builders.

But he did not wish to continue building solemn temples of commerce. What could he do next?

Looking at the tower, he began to sense a rivalry with his own creation. He did not know how to equal or surpass it. There it would stand, beyond the conflicts that troubled him, forever performing at its best.

Barbara watched him uneasily. At first she had told herself that his inability to create would pass and he would find again that strange country where he saw forms that grew and developed from a rhythmical movement patterned in space. Gradually she became aware of how deeply rooted his problem was. At his drafting table he had a look of concentration on his face as he struck out a sketch with a soft pencil and finally flung it away with an impatient, "No, this won't do." He would begin again, the expression on his face calm, then increasingly troubled, making small changes, working in spurts, hurriedly and unevenly. Barbara was an involuntary witness to the agony of his inner world, was seeing something no one ever has the right to see—the struggle involved in the act of creation. She knew he had to rediscover his talent or die. He was one of those artists who work for his own survival.

As they left the site the A and B derricks were being jumped to the eighteenth floor. Each derrick was raised by disconnecting the mast from the boom and then each separate member raised the other one by means of the hoisting engines.

Karl walked slowly up the avenue with Barbara at his side. Visiting the Zenith Oil tower had not helped his depression. In a mood of nostalgia he recalled the high-ceilinged classroom walled in different shades of gray, where the afternoon sun descended through high narrow windows onto drafting tables in rows in a cheerfully littered room. Advanced Architectural Design. A small pond of worshipful young faces staring up at him, clinging to his every word as an infant clings to the teat. Suddenly he longed to see students at work again, to hear the muted creaking of stools, and watch the T squares and triangles softly gliding over the tracing paper on their boards. Creative work demands too much sacrifice. All the best works are paid for in human tragedy. For those few blissful hours in which an artist is in command, doing work he knows to be right, there are many days and weeks that are like nails driven into the skin. A man who wishes to create mounts the hill daily ready to die for the salvation of something in which he has faith—but the Cross is not always waiting to give meaning to his sacrifice.

"Let's go to the museum," Barbara said. "I really want to see that exhibition."

"All right," he said resignedly. "If you insist."

There was an exhibition of models of his previous designs at the Contemporary Museum. The room was on the second floor, off the corridor. In addition to the models, they had blown up and photostated some of his sketches to hang on the walls.

Karl put on his glasses to study them. In two glass cases just inside the entrance to the room were two scale models of an apartment house and department store he had designed twenty years before. Karl examined them with interest, noting their faults, experiencing within himself the basic elements of the architecture, the horizontal planes, the vertical walls, the solidity and texture.

"Nodody's built any of these?" Barbara asked. "Why not?"

"Each has a different story."

"That first model. The apartment house."

"No one commissioned it. When I was finished, no one was interested in building it either."

"How about that other one, the department store?"

"An entry in a competition. It was disqualified."

"Why?"

"I didn't meet the conditions laid down in the program."

Examining some of the other models, Barbara thought of another reason Schiller's designs hadn't been built. Most people simply didn't understand what he accomplished. It looked simple, but would be impossible for anyone else to design in the same way. The problem was something like trying to imitate the Parthenon: you have to reproduce the proportions exactly or you never get the same effect.

"How do you feel about them now, Karl?"

He said indifferently, "They're all right."

A man approached. He was moderately tall, with a somewhat tough competent look, strong chin, ill shaped nose, straggly eyebrows. A white collar circled his throat.

"Miss Druse, it's a pleasure to see you again. I haven't seen you in church very often lately."

"I've been something of a sinner, Pastor Haines," Barbara said.

"Come and confess your sins. I can almost guarantee absolution."

Barbara said, "Karl, I'd like you to meet the Reverend Ramsey Haines, minister of our church. Pastor, this is Karl Schiller."

"Ah. I rather thought so. What a fortunate coincidence that we should meet here." He talked rapidly, with sharp up and down emphases in his speech. "Mr. Schiller, I've been looking at your models and I'm impressed. Very impressed. I'd like to extend you an invitation."

"An invitation?"

"To enter our competition. Our church is going to build a new cathedral in New York City. We've gotten up a pamphlet outlining the conditions of the competition and the general budget to be followed. Can I send it to you?"

Karl said firmly, "I don't think I'd be interested, Reverend."

"We want it to be the most impressive religious building in New York, maybe in America, maybe in the world." Ramsey Haines had the lecturer's habit of gesturing emphatically to make his points, and he had to stand back a little when speaking at close range. "We've asked all the leading architects to join the competition."

"I'm flattered that you would invite me."

"Then you accept?"

"No."

"What is your reason?"

"Well, Reverend, for one thing I don't believe that a competition results in anything worthwhile."

"I know, I know. The first thing a jury does is go through all the designs and throw out the best and the worst ones. What they are left with is an average and then they try to pick a winner by choosing the most average of the lot. That's not the way we intend to handle it."

"It's the final result of any competition."

"Maybe this will convince you. Albert Falkland has consented to be a consultant to our selection committee."

"You couldn't have picked a better man."

"And we intend to follow his advice."

"I hope you will."

"Then you'll reconsider?"

"I'm sorry, Reverend. I still must refuse."

"Why?"

He had been pursued to the point where he had to tell the truth. "Reverend, I am simply not a religious man."

Ramsey Haines smiled as he ran a short solid hand through thinning hair. "Proves you had the wrong kind of education. I was fortunate, born on April Fool's Day in a small town in Colorado near the top of the Rocky Mountains—started out about as near to God as I could get. I've got nothing but forgiveness to offer people who weren't born and raised as fortunate. I'm willing to overlook your lack of faith, Mr. Schiller."

"I've never even attended a church."

"Does that mean you can't build one? Every architect has one great church in him. I don't want you to preach—that's my job. I want your sermon to be in stone and brick and concrete."

Karl said, "I don't think a man without faith can possibly do justice to a cathedral."

"'Except the Lord build the house, they labor in vain that build it: except the Lord keep the city, the watchman waketh but in vain.'"

"What's that?" Barbara asked, looking at Ramsey Haines and smiling.

"Psalm one hundred twenty-seven. All you really need to have is faith in people, Mr. Schiller. That's what the Lord had. He works in strange ways. Why, in my youth I wanted to be a baseball player. Then I threw a pitch that hit a man and fractured his skull, and that decided me. I became a full-time minister. You start designing this cathedral, Mr. Schiller, and you may discover you've got more faith than you thought."

"It is a matter of conviction, Reverend."

"If you can respect what other people believe, you can build for them. There are too many people in the church who don't have faith and too many outside it who have."

"I suppose that's true," Karl conceded.

Barbara said gently, "There are even deeply religious people, Karl, who don't believe in God." She almost added what she knew: he was one.

238

"There's a difference in that kind of faith," Karl said.

Ramsey Haines said, "Perhaps only in men's eyes. Not in His."

There was no definite moment in which he decided that he might try it, but the possibility was growing in the stony soil of negative emotions.

"I appreciate your invitation, Reverend. And I won't make up my mind about it until I've given the idea serious consideration. That's all I can promise."

Ramsey Haines was smiling slightly. "That's all I can ask."

*

Alex Johns recognized that the atmosphere of anxiety on the Fernwood Country Club golf course was created by himself. There just wasn't much he could do about it.

To reduce the possibility of his inner tensions becoming discernible, he adopted a jesting tone with Fred Feist about their golf game.

Stepping up to the tee, he said, "Well, Fred, I guess I've fooled around long enough. This is where I start to lower the boom."

Fred Feist chuckled pleasantly. He was a rather tall man with a large head and a broad corpulent trunk perched upon long thin knickered legs.

Alex hooked his drive into the rough two hundred yards away. He tossed his driver to the caddy in disgust. Fred Feist moved to the tee, and after a single preliminary swing, drove his ball a short distance onto the center of the fairway.

Alex shook his head in rueful admiration. "I'm having trouble with you today."

"Patience and persistence," Feist answered complacently. "You've got to hang in there, Alex. It's the same in sport as in business. When I was in school there were cleverer fellows but they never had my staying power."

During the first seven holes, Feist had discoursed on his favorite subject: himself. Strolling over bright green fairways in the hazy light of the April afternoon, Alex uncomplainingly followed Feist through his youth to his junior year in college when he quit and went to work as a rigger "under a sun that struck like a fist." It was

239

clear that Feist intended to continue detailing his career in the business world and by the seventh hole Feist had worked his way up to become president of his own company. While Alex took three putts on the green Feist sold out to Zenith Oil in a dispute about oil properties and that transaction made him Zenith Oil Corporation's largest single shareholder.

On the way to the eighth hole, Feist temporarily abandoned his autobiography for a reflection about his personal philosophy.

"I've always believed in two rules. Don't yield easily and never act on impulse." He teed up, twisting the ball and the wooden tee into hard resisting ground.

"Those are pretty good rules," Alex said.

Feist stood up and waggled his driver experimentally. Two golfers on the green ahead were performing their putting devotionals.

"Well, when are we going to come to the point, Alex?"

"The point?"

"You want something. Or you wouldn't have asked me golfing today."

"I like playing golf," Alex answered with a light concealing laugh. He perceived that the leading stockholder of Zenith Oil was in an unpredictable mood. "But I'll admit that I do want to talk to you."

"What about?" Feist stared ahead at the distant golfers as though willing them to disappear.

Alex resolved to move carefully. "A recent decision by Zenith Oil. One I think is very bad for almost everyone concerned."

"Especially you?"

"It's bound to hurt Zenith Oil Corporation in the long run too."

"Why talk to me?"

"You're the principal stockholder."

"Peter Druse is president. He's the man you ought to talk to. What's holding up those two? I've a good mind to drive into them."

"They'll be finished in a second. It wouldn't do any good to talk to Peter. He made the decision I want to talk to you about."

"I'm not management. I'm just on the Board. How about Vinnie Haleson?"

"There are reasons why I can't expect any help from Vinnie."

"Personal?"

"Very."

"Hmm," Feist said. On the green the golfers put the flag back into the hole and started off, followed by caddies and carts.

Feist stepped up to the tee. He drove two hundred and twenty yards down the center of the fairway.

"A damn good shot," Alex said.

"Not bad. I didn't know you'd had a falling out with Vinnie."

"These things happen."

Alex teed up his ball, took a stance and after a few preliminary swings, stepped up and hit a long slicing drive deep into the rough.

"Can you tell me what's behind your problem with Vinnie?" Feist asked.

"All I can say is that right now he wouldn't give me the latest weather report."

They reached Alex's ball lying in the deep rough, and Alex tossed it out to take the stroke penalty.

Feist shook his head with hypocritical sympathy. "This is a tough round for you, Alex. Well, if the reasons aren't business they must have to do with Vinnie's domestic problems. I understand his wife is getting a divorce."

"She's a lovely woman."

"You've met her?"

Alex hit his second shot into the trees a hundred yards distant.

"I don't think, as a gentleman, I ought to go into that," he said.

Feist winked and his whole manner radiated that he got the message. As they walked along together, he chuckled. "What's this problem you wanted to talk to me about?"

"The decision to switch away from the Hayden Bank and give the new building annex to Babcock and Allied Continental. When we first changed the design and added the new building, the deal was set for Hayden to move in."

Feist gave him a suspicious stare. "What's that got to do with you?"

"I've got my biggest line of credit with Hayden. I promised them they'd get the space."

"There wasn't anything actually signed, was there?"

"No."

Feist shrugged. "Then there isn't anything anybody can do about it."

He used a three iron to hit a long ball that rolled onto the green only a few feet from the cup.

"By damn, I ought to get a birdie on this one!"

"If Hayden doesn't get that space," Alex said, "they're going to call my loan."

"You can't expect us to pull your chestnuts out of the fire."

"You could talk to Peter Druse about it. You're Zenith Oil's biggest stockholder. He'd have to listen to you."

Feist, who was expecting to be congratulated on his shot, answered irritably, "Why should I? You've got to look after your own business, Alex. You can't expect Zenith Oil to do it for you."

"I've tried everything I can think of. You're absolutely my last hope, Fred," Alex said. "If I go under, it means Zenith Oil will be left holding the bag for millions in debts to subcontractors."

"Don't we have a surety bond against a contingency like that?"

"No, you don't. I'm like Samson. When I go, the whole thing goes down with me."

"Are you sure?"

"Peter decided a surety bond would be an unnecessary expense. I guess he thought I'd stay solvent."

There was no further conversation. They parted to go in different directions, Feist going toward the green, and Alex to where his caddy had stopped by his ball. Alex used a four iron to lift to the edge of the green and then chipped close to the hole. Then he two-putted in. Feist lined up his four-footer with care, getting down on his knees to study the lie of the green. His putt circled the rim of the cup.

"Tough break," Alex said.

Feist tapped the ball in with the heel of his putter. "How close are you to the brink now, Alex?" he asked.

Alex drew in a breath to keep his voice from trembling. "It may be too late already. Once word leaks out Hayden has called in that loan, it will start a panic among my other creditors."

Feist took out a crumpled cigarette pack and shook it. "Smoke?"

"No, thanks."

"I suppose if you do go under, the blame rests with Peter."

"He's the one who made the switch to Babcock."

"And didn't have foresight enough to take out a surety bond. I've got the picture now."

"Will you help me?"

Feist said slowly, "I'm afraid I can't, Alex."

"As the largest stockholder . . ."

"There's something you don't know, Alex. Peter and I haven't seen things eye to eye for some time. We've been having an undercover battle of our own."

"But you both want what's best for Zenith Oil Corporation."

"This is no ordinary battle, Alex. It's for control. I only have three votes on the Board—four if you count Vinnie. That isn't enough to swing matters."

"Peter has to listen to anything you say."

"The Board would back Peter in any showdown—because he's the president and so far nobody's been able to prove that any of his decisions have done Zenith Oil any harm."

"I don't see what you're driving at," Alex answered faintly. But he saw pieces fitting together in a pattern.

"If Peter's decision isn't changed, and you do go bankrupt, it will cost Zenith Oil millions of dollars. You see, Alex, how you've given me ammunition."

"You'd let that happen just to win your fight with Peter?"

"At the next quarterly meeting of the Board this could make for a very interesting session."

Alex saw himself so clearly in the role of sacrificial lamb that he almost felt wool growing on his shoulders.

"You're a bastard," he said huskily.

"Aren't we all?" Feist asked, with a wide indulgent smile. "By the way, I don't feel up to playing eighteen today. Why don't we quit after nine?"

In the locker room, after they finished playing nine holes, Alex sat on a wooden bench. Feist changed into fresh undershirt and trousers. His paunch folded out in levels like a terraced hillside.

From an adjoining room Alex heard voices in a familiar litany.

"What was bid? . . . Two diamonds . . . I'll double three diamonds . . ."

In the dull green mirror of his locker door Alex saw his own face, ravaged, with haggard lines.

"Funny thing, I really thought the son of a bitch would outsmart 'em all."

"I've seen him tied down with chains, padlocked, gagged—and he always found a way to screw 'em. Two clubs."

"Is this definite?"

"Half an hour after Hayden announced, they suspended trading in the stock. Alexander Johns is all washed up."

Voices became lost in the sudden clatter of metal locker doors. In harsh unshielded overhead light Feist's brown eyes were silky with triumph in their pouches. Alex studied him a few seconds, then tucked an immaculate white linen handkerchief into the breast pocket of his dark blue blazer.

"I hope you and Peter both get it in the neck," Alex said. "That's what I hope."

*

On the ground below him Tom MacLaren saw darkly reflecting pools of water from yesterday's rain, glinting with the light of the afternoon sun. As the man-hoist continued its rushing descent a wide shaft of golden dazzling light broke through the open structure of the building above.

The hoist reached the platform in a jolting stop and he left and crossed the open cement floor to the field office. He nodded to two men standing idly at the desks there, noted their look of guilty surprise, and passed through the large outside room where other men were supposed to be busy at various jobs, some on construction engineering, some on work layout, others writing out labor instructions or engaged in the coordination of subcontracting assignments.

"Where's Otis?"

Someone replied, "I saw him a minute ago. He's around."

"What's everybody standing around for?"

No answer, only a peculiar shuffling of feet and interchange of glances.

"Back to work," Tom said. "It isn't quitting time."

He hurried past the room reserved for people working on project accounting, material purchasing and personnel hiring. No one was at a desk. He crossed the corridor into a room occupied entirely by tables, filing cabinets, and wooden racks for storage of plans, specifications, and materials samples.

Jim Otis was seated at a plans table, on the telephone.

Tom leaned over the table and put both hands down. "What the hell is going on? Nobody's working."

"You can't blame them, Mr. MacLaren."

"Since when can't I?"

Otis slowly replaced the telephone. "I just talked to the office." Otis's hand remained on the receiver. "It's pandemonium there. But I got through to confirm the report."

"What report?"

"Alex Johns is out of business. Bankrupt." Otis removed his hand from the receiver, carefully disengaging himself.

Tom MacLaren asked sharply, "What, what?" Without making a clear gesture of denial, he winced away from acceptance.

"It's true, Mr. MacLaren."

Tom heard him really for the first time, experiencing the painful aftershock.

"It isn't true," he said with angry lack of conviction. "It's a damn lie."

"It won't change anything," Otis said. "They still have to finish the building. Zenith Oil will just take over."

"How could it happen?"

"I guess Alex Johns just took one chance too many," Otis said.

"That son of a bitch!"

"We'll just keep going the way we did before until we hear something. Zenith Oil is a big company. They won't let anything happen to slow up the job."

He was wiped out. Everything he had worked for and saved was gone. It was someone's fault. The blame reached down to the lowest levels. Nobody getting the work done or giving an honest day's effort for an honest day's wages. *Nobody caring.*

"Why is everybody sitting around in the office out there?" Tom demanded. "Get off the goddamn phone and do something useful. Get them off their asses!"

Otis looked at him with bitter mirth in his eyes.

"I'll do that right away, Mr. MacLaren."

Tom left the office in a daze, not returning the glances of anyone. On the ground floor was the hoist engine that had helped to put the first beams and columns into place. The powerful cables that operated the derrick wound around drums in the gas power unit in the cab. On the topmost tier of steel above his head a bellman was standing to act as the operator's eyes, transmitting signals from a hand-held control box. The signals caused lights to flash on a panel inside the cab of the guy derrick and told the operator what series of gears to shift to direct the movements of the mast.

Tom entered the hoist in the elevator shaft. On the floors going past as the hoist rose, he had watched the steel bolted into place. Near the top workers were now adding steel pipe sections to the elevator hoists so the elevator could keep pace with the steadily increasing height of the building. Three weeks after a floor had been installed structurally the elevator service had to be underway; that was a union regulation. The union didn't want their men to walk up too many floors. There were all sorts of regulations for the workers' comfort and convenience. No wonder work didn't get done. The men were spoiled. That was an important reason for what had happened. Maybe the most important.

The man-hoist let him off at the twentieth floor where temporary flooring was being laid and stairways put into place. A steady warm breeze blew through the steel frame of the building. Tom climbed to the top where the ironworkers were swinging H-shaped columns to splice them at the holes with connection pieces. They were holding ropes to help position the steel. Cable bound girders swung in slow motion.

It was not his job to speak directly to a worker when he saw anything wrong but he had screwed up his emotions into a ball of hostility that he was ready to shove at anyone.

"You bastard, what do you think you're doing?"

Don Macey, the foreman, hurried over.

"Anything wrong, Tom?"

246

"Goofing off. Look at him over there!"

He pointed to Pete Miller who had stopped his work of sorting out steel members according to their markings. Pete was looking alertly at the west side of the building.

"Hey! Hey, fellas," Pete yelled. "*Look!*"

Pete ran toward the open framework on the west side.

"Hey, *look!*"

Light danced crazily off the side of a steel column, vanished, re-appeared, skittered off the red side of a beam.

"It's her!" Pete Miller halted at the edge, took off his hard hat and waved it wildly.

Other ironworkers stopped moving their package of steel girders into position as they watched Pete Miller. The girders swung slowly around.

"She's signaling back!" Pete Miller turned, grinning boyishly, put his metal hat back on his head at a rakish angle. "I told you she liked me. Didn't I tell you?"

Tom muttered something in a muffled, hoarse, unintelligible voice. Then he shouted, "Hey, you damn lazy Indian! Get to work!"

"What's the matter, Tom?" Don Macey demanded.

"Keep them off their lazy butts!"

"They're doing a job," Don answered. "Why don't you calm down?"

"Sitting Bull! You sons of bitches are licking your fingers."

Don's eyes turned to slits in his mahogany face. "You got no reason to talk like that."

"I'll talk any way I damn please!"

Don Macey turned quickly away to call an order to an ironworker in Caughnawaga dialect. The worker shinnied up a column to help steady the girders.

Other Mohawks maneuvered a girder until one end was near a bracket in the center of an erected column. Johnny Tontour made the first connection with a long tapering pin he took from a loop in his belt and another worker took a short thick bolt from a bag attached to his belt, unscrewed the nut, and pushed the bolt through a pair of matching holes in the column and girder. Then he threaded the nut back on the bolt. Tom turned irritably to Pete Miller who was sorting out steel members.

"Don't take half an hour to read markings! You want everything in Mohawk?"

Pete looked up. "We read just as good as anybody."

"You bite off beer bottle caps with your teeth. What kind of civilized is that?"

Pete rose slowly, brushing off his hands on his shirt. "Looking for trouble?"

"I'm not running away from it."

Pete's cement-soled boots made definite clocking sounds across the wooden flooring.

"Hey, Pete," Don Macey called. "He's just got a big mouth."

"He better not use it around me."

"You keep a civil tongue in your own mouth, tomahawk head," Tom said.

He saw Pete about to swing and a joyous surge poured into his arm muscles. This was what he needed—some release.

"Hey, Pete! Over here!" Don Macey called.

Pete hesitated, held irresolute. Come on, Tom urged him. Come on.

"Pete, *for Chrissakes!*"

Don Macey prevailed. Pete Miller, with a sullen glance at Tom, crossed over to where Don was keeping an eye on a worker standing on a beam and with a tagline keeping a package of girders from rotating or swinging as they came abreast of the floor.

"Move back! You'll get it fouled up," Don yelled.

The worker with the tagline was new and he became momentarily confused. He grabbed hard at the tagline trying to keep the twisting red load of steel moving smoothly through the air. It began to swing dangerously.

"Hey, Joe! Give a hand here!" Don called.

Joe Labache, working nearby, methodically driving in high strength malleable bolts, tying columns together with the rolled beams that had been fabricated to fit into place easily, put down his hammer and hurried over.

248

"Stop that swinging! *Steady it!*"

Spinning whirling steel coiled up wires, hung knotted, began again rapidly to unroll.

Joe Labache leaned out to try to straighten the dangerously swinging load.

Pete Miller leapt over a pile of planks. He shouted: *"DUCK!"*

Joe Labache held the tagline, suddenly a little puzzled. He was a still uncertain point in the midst of gyration.

Then the swinging edge of a steel column caught him.

The blow sent him hurtling violently sideways and broke his hold on the tagline. He landed chest first on the surface of a connecting girder and skittered off into clear air.

Pete Miller gave a cry of anguish. *"He went over!"*

"God almighty," Tom MacLaren whispered.

Through open space below he caught sight of the plunging man who seemed to be trying to find a new footing in the unsupporting air. He turned over behind an obliterating floor beam, appeared for a brief instant, rapidly dwindled.

A thwacking sound came up.

A whistle shrilled. The hoist stopped. All work stopped. A thick black stream of workers began running down the stairwell.

The tagline swung to and fro like a severed noose.

A spinning vertigo rooted Tom to the spot, a vertigo composed of mixed images of whirling columns and a tumbling human figure.

After a minute he saw he was alone. He was suddenly afraid. He went over to the materials hoist and descended in the transparent wire cage holding firmly to the bar.

On the ground floor level Jim Otis and a crowd of other workmen were standing around a lumpy tarpaulin that was turning a bright shade of maroon. Where the maroon did not show through, the tarpaulin was a dirty brown color with patches of black dirt. From beneath it a slimy viscous pool was oozing, of brain and intestines. These floated like oil patches on the rivulets of crimson.

Tom was ringed about by hate. Don Macey and Pete Miller were looking at him with stony cold eyes, as though what had happened was somehow his fault.

Tom felt sick to his stomach. He stood silently above the bloody tarpaulin concealing the silent crushed pulp.

"Joe Labache," Don Macey said, "was a good man."

*

Peter Druse did not enjoy having dinner at the Yacht Club, especially on the day before a race when nothing was spoken about at any of the tables except the boats, their skippers, and their prospects. Every meter of last year's race was gone over in detail, each tack, maneuver, and mistake. Yachtsmen had omnivorous memories.

Peter would not have come to the gala party at the Yacht Club except that Ann insisted. The Garsons were going to be there and she was very close with the Garsons.

Now he sat silently with his wife Emily at a ringside table near the dance floor and half-listened to the six-piece band playing.

"Do you remember this?" Emily asked suddenly.

"What?" he asked, lifting his head. Then he realized she meant the melody the band was playing.

"It's *Careless*."

"Well, I can't remember every song that . . ."

"No, no Peter." She placed a restraining hand on his arm. "I mean *Careless* is the name of the song."

"Oh."

She hummed the melody under her breath. Then: "They played it at that club in London. The place we went to during our honeymoon. It was raining and we didn't know it was a private club. It was called the Blue Cockatoo. The cab let us out in the rain and we found out it was a private club when we met the man going downstairs . . ."

"The ad should have mentioned the club was private." He was obscurely angry at this long-forgotten grievance and at the same time he wished she would stop with this game of reminiscence. She was better at it than he was and the trivial talent had larger implications: it seemed to say she remembered a fuller, more complete life than he did.

It so happened that he had a very good memory. It was necessary for him to have a good memory to maintain the continuity of a business against manifold and unpredictable threats. His good memory was a guarantee of his security, of the integrity of his purpose. If he forgot anything, or his memory of it became vague or blurred, he would be in acute danger. If he did not keep constantly in mind, for example, the reasons for his vendetta against Vinnie Haleson, he might have drifted with whatever winds were blowing.

Only his steadfastness held him to the course which he was sure would eventually prove successful. He had allowed no abatement of the struggle to force Vinnie out. Perhaps other men in his position would have preferred a direct confrontation. He had the power to dismiss Vinnie as executive vice-president, but that would have required explanations he did not care to make. Far better to prepare the way by subtle methods which would compel Vinnie to resign. That was what he was doing. When he was finished there would be no questions raised even by Vinnie's friends on the Board of Directors. The campaign was going well. By now, other executives in the corporation had picked up the scent and like hyenas were circling in toward the place of the kill. The chief tactic was petty harassment. Vinnie had not been invited to the last several top-level conferences in Peter's office and had been posted to Washington on a minor errand at the time of the last monthly meeting. There had been constant demands for reports and data covering intricate corporate transactions, always coupled with a request for immediate delivery. Vinnie's interoffice phone calls to Peter were not being returned and when other executives learned that they too began returning Vinnie's calls late, with only hurried perfunctory apologies. The stage was set for a climax now but Peter hoped Vinnie would have the good sense to resign.

"Look who's coming to our table, dear," Emily said. "Nell Garson."

Nell Garson's features were sharp, her nose aquiline, her mouth a touch severe. Her skin was a classic pure ivory and her blond hair was pulled back so tightly that individual strands seemed about to snap.

"Hello, Druses. I'm so glad you came tonight. Mind if I sit down?"

Peter Druse got up to assist her pull out a chair at the table, then waited until she was seated before resuming his seat.

"Your daughter and my husband are having a fine time," Nell said, looking at the dance floor where Ann and Tony were dancing a samba.

"Yes, they seem to be," Peter said.

"Do you know they're planning to go away tomorrow?"

Peter was not sure he heard correctly.

"Go away? Where?"

Nell Garson's face seemed to go dead. "I believe the destination, not yet official, is the Grand Bahamas."

Emily sat absolutely erect. "I can't imagine where you heard that."

"From the best possible source," Nell said, with a harsh undertone. "My husband."

Peter decided to interpose his own presence between Nell and his wife. "There isn't a word of truth in what you say, Nell. And I can't permit you to talk about my daughter in that way."

"Why do you think Ann is getting a divorce?"

"The whole thing was Vinnie's fault."

Nell grimaced. "Everyone in this club knows that Tony is the reason Ann and Vinnie split up."

"Nothing of the kind."

"In fact, everyone knows the story about Vinnie coming home unexpectedly and catching your precious daughter and Tony en flagrante."

There was simply no limit to which a jealous woman would not go.

"I won't sit and listen to this," Emily said suddenly.

She was a woman of great delicacy of feeling. She never liked to discuss anything that pertained to sex. Peter respected her for that; even in their most intimate moments he was careful not to offend her sensibilities.

"I think you'd better leave, Nell," Peter said.

The way Nell held her head high brought into pronounced relief the clear line of chin and jawbone.

"If you don't believe me, my darlings, why don't you ask Ann?"

"I have no reason to. I know my daughter."

"You're afraid to find out the truth."

The remark startled Peter slightly. He was unable to maintain an attitude of superior disdain when the target shifted to himself.

He answered angrily, "I don't mind asking Ann anything. But I'll tell her why I'm doing it, and I'm afraid you're going to look like a fool."

"I'll risk that," Nell said. The cords of her long neck stood out. "You tell Ann this. When she does leave with Tony, I'm going straight to my lawyer. I think I can make quite a lurid story of it for the tabloids."

"There won't be any story. You'll have to apologize when you find out how wrong you are."

"Oh, for God's sake! I only talked to you because I thought you might have influence with your daughter. But you're as stupid as she is." Nell rose from the chair. "Goodbye, good people. I'll see you all in the headlines."

She moved away from the table.

Emily crossed her wrists on the table. "I never realized Nell Garson was an hysterical woman."

"Neither did I." Peter suddenly realized that the music had stopped.

"It isn't the end of the world," Ann said, as she returned to the table. "But you two look as though it were."

She laughed, a warm easy laugh, and Peter had a sudden fierce conviction that nothing Nell Garson said could possibly be true.

"Nell Garson was just here," he said.

"Oh?"

"She's worked up a fantasy in her mind. I'm afraid she might cause trouble."

Ann took a stalk of celery from a dish. "What sort of fantasy?"

Emily broke in, "Nell says that you and Tony are planning to go away tomorrow."

Ann stripped the pale green wings from the celery. "Well, that much is true. Tony and I are sailing to the Bahamas after the race tomorrow."

Emily made a slight shift of position so that her body was thrust

253

at a slight angle toward her daughter. "This isn't a joking matter, Ann."

"I'm not joking."

Peter cleared his throat. "You can't mean that there's been anything between you and Tony."

"Quite."

The band began to play a soft slow romantic ballad. The silence at the table appeared to shape itself to the rhythms of the music.

Finally, Peter said, "I absolutely forbid you to go anywhere with Tony Garson tomorrow."

Ann dropped a small remnant of celery into his plate. "Now, Dad. It's been a long time since you were able to absolutely prohibit me from doing anything."

"Don't you realize what will happen? What the newspapers will do? The scandal?"

"At least when it's over Tony and I will be free to marry."

Emily's shocked whisper, "I can't believe you're talking like this."

"How about us?" Peter asked. "Don't you care about us at all?"

Tony Garson, wearing a blue blazer with an ascot, found his way to the table. "Dance?"

Ann smiled at him brightly. "Love to, darling."

They danced away. Peter and Emily continued to sit awkwardly in a silence that had a pulse of its own.

Emily said, "What are we going to do, Peter?"

"I'll have to think about it." He was appalled at his powerlessness.

"She'll ruin her life if she goes through with this."

"If she wants to make a fool of herself, I don't see how I can stop her." He felt blood rush tingling to his cheek. "You know who's to blame for this, don't you?"

"Tony?"

"*Vinnie.* If he'd been half a husband, Ann never would have got herself into such a mess." There really was no option. At whatever cost, Vinnie would have to be forced out immediately. "Let's go," he said.

He stared directly ahead at the aisle between the tables as they left the dining room. Waiting at the hatcheck counter he pushed up into a more erect posture.

"He won't get away with this," he told Emily.

"Who?"

"Vinnie, of course."

The fifty-cent piece he gave the hatcheck girl felt rigid and cold between his fingers. When she dropped it into the plate he half-expected it to break and shatter into silver twinkling fragments.

*

On the last Sunday of every month there was a special Caughnawaga service in a Presbyterian church in Brooklyn. The minister gave Bible readings and said prayers entirely in Mohawk.

This Sunday featured a special service in memory of Joe Labache. When the minister finished with his prayers, he said a few words about what a fine family man Joe had been, and how he had helped look after his son's widow and his grandchildren after Danny was killed. Now Joe too was gone, and everyone who knew him mourned for him. He said a special prayer in which he asked God to give Joe's family strength to bear the sorrows which had come upon them and to rejoice in the fact that Joe was now with his Heavenly Father. Irene, his widow, sat in the front pew with Danny's widow, Elaine, and all the children. They rose to join in singing hymns, such standbys as "The Old Rugged Cross" and "Onward, Christian Soldiers" which had been translated into Mohawk, and were printed in the forty-page Caughnawaga Hymnal.

Of all the Mohawk men gathered for the service in the small yellow brick church, only one was not a high ironworker. He worked for a roofing contractor because the pay was steadier.

After the service four Mohawks put on their own memorial service. As they had done with Joe Labache on many previous Sundays, they donned warpaint and carrying tomahawks and tom-toms, sat on the church floor in full regalia including feathers and blankets. They sang old Mohawk songs of valor and conquest around a campfire made of sticks and a cluster of electric light bulbs.

The final number of this memorial service was *Ka-na-wa-ke te-tsi-te-we*—which meant "Let's Go Back to Caughnawaga."

*

Barbara telephoned ahead from the train station and when the taxi entered the driveway of the house in Southampton, moving around the circle in a fine but penetrating yellow mist, her mother was waiting on the front stone staircase. Emily wore a shawl over her dress. Tendrils of fog partly obscuring her made her look like a ghost.

Barbara paid the taxi driver and ran up the stairs to embrace her mother. A slight coloring told her that Emily was pleased.

"Dear," Emily said, with a wan smile, "you couldn't possibly have come at a better time."

"Why is that?"

"Your father's been so upset the past few days. We haven't gone anywhere. All we've done is stay home and watch TV. He's been waiting for you to call."

It would never occur to Father to telephone her, Barbara thought. Nevertheless she was touched by the picture of her parents sitting home before the TV set, patiently waiting for her call.

"Is something wrong?"

"Oh, everything. Ann's gone off with Tony and Nell has filed for a divorce."

"I know. I read about it in the papers."

"You know how your father hates scandal. And then there's Vinnie."

"What about Vinnie?" Barbara asked as they started up the stairs.

Emily's hands fluttered. "He's making trouble for your father in business. He had to be dismissed as a vice-president and now there's going to be some sort of Board meeting about it."

"Where is Dad now?"

"Waiting for you. In the study."

They went through the door into the large open hall. When she entered the house, with Mother at her side, Barbara felt as if she were taking steps back into her youth. Everything was cold stone and marble, unwarmed by the heavy draperies. Their footsteps echoed eerily and their voices were chilled into near whispers.

"You don't have any . . . special . . . reason for coming, do you?"

"Yes, I do, Mother."

Emily stopped as they reached the double mahogany door of the study. She seemed uncertain, confused.

"Oh, dear, it isn't more trouble, is it?"

"No, Mother. I'm the bearer of good tidings. But I want to wait to tell you and Father together." She did not wish to be cruel and add: there would be no point in telling you alone. You would not know what to think until you consulted Father.

Emily sighed, and made a wraith-like gesture toward the door. "Good news will certainly be welcome around here."

Her father was standing by the wide windows in the study. Behind him, directly outside, was the terrace with its massive stone fountain and statuary of dancing boys and girls with linked hands. Once there had been a party on that terrace for over a hundred people, lawyers, bankers, businessmen. Everyone was well fed and well cared for while they argued out the details of an infinitely complicated deal. It had all been exciting and wonderful to Barbara at the time and her father had seemed a Napoleon, small but victorious among the other captains. Later she was told that an entirely new subsidiary of Zenith Oil would rise in a distant Mideastern country.

Her father opened his arms and waited smiling for her to come. He never welcomed her in any other way. His standing motionless while she approached was a token of the submissiveness he demanded.

She kissed his cheek. "I've really missed you, Dad."

"I'm glad you're here. There's so much we have to talk about."

"I'm afraid I can't stay too long."

"You don't have to run back to New York," Peter said. "This is your home. You hardly come to see us any more."

"I can't help it this time."

"At least you can stay to dinner," Emily said. "I've already told Fred and Alice you're staying."

"All right. I'll catch the nine o'clock train."

"No. You'll fly back in with me on Monday," Peter said.

"I'm sorry, Dad. That's impossible."

Peter usually flew in on Monday mornings. The plane took thirty minutes to reach the private aircraft section of La Guardia Airport. As a young girl Barbara enjoyed the flying, but she remembered the drive in from La Guardia as depressing. All those buildings hemmed together, jammed tight around narrow roadways, plastered in identical legions against every hillside were full of people who worked like brutes all week to pay for a few hours of backyard privacy on weekends. These were the people who swelled subway crowds and platforms, hung to swaying bus straps, endured torture and monotony that would have caused oxen to rebel and then briefly fled the city that in its monolithic obliviousness caused their daily humiliation and pain. She had sensed this, but never so acutely, articulately until Karl.

Karl.

"I have something important to tell you, Dad," she said when they were seated.

"What's on your mind, dear?" Peter asked.

"I'm going to be married."

Emily uttered a startled gasp. "Karl Schiller?"

The fog was clearing. A shaft of sunlight moved across the floor with dust motes floating in it.

"I didn't think it would be much of a surprise."

"When is it going to be?" Emily asked in a curiously high-strained voice.

"This Sunday. A small ceremony. Of course you and Dad are invited."

Peter had not uttered a word. He sat with tumbler of scotch in his hand and Barbara sensed the change in him before she could define it precisely.

He said sternly, "Barbara, I won't allow you to marry that man!"

Her father favored flat declarative statements. Such declarations seemed to preclude debate and remove his authority from challenge.

Barbara asked, "Is there a particular reason?"

"I can't tolerate that man."

"I'm not asking you to marry him."

"He's all wrong for you."

"He may be all wrong for *you*, Father. But he's entirely and magnificently right for me."

"I don't understand what you find attractive about him. Too old. Not good-looking. A foreigner."

She felt her cheeks grow hot with resentment.

"I'm in love with him."

"I can't believe it," Peter said. "He certainly isn't in love with you."

She knew only too well her father's estimate of her attractiveness. When she was young he had convinced her that spinsterhood was her lot.

"If you weren't so moonstruck," Peter went on, "you'd realize he's like the others. After your money."

She spaced her words deliberately. "You're quite wrong about that."

He shook his head with exasperation. "I'm trying to keep you from making the worst mistake of your life."

"Not marrying Karl *would* be the worst mistake of my life."

She heard him breathing in the chair opposite, out of her reach, a portly sullen intransigent shape. She could guess what he was thinking. *It's sex.* That had been his explanation for Henry and he had been closer to the truth then. Henry had fascinated her in a physical way. It was quite different with Karl. Sex was not exactly a problem but it was certainly not one of their solutions. They would probably work it out in time but even if they never did she would go on loving Karl. Her design for life, striking in its simple proportions—marry, have a home, a family, live with one man until death —needed only the right man. She had found him.

Peter was looking at her in a cautious appraising way. A thin coating of uncertainty seemed to have been applied to his belligerence.

He asked finally, "Why do you have to marry him? To protect your good name?"

A discussion with Father afforded her the same delight as opening a novel from a bygone era; it put her back in touch with convictions from which the world had demonstrably moved away.

"Don't be silly, Dad," Barbara said, not unkindly.

Emily sat silent, trembling in alternations of fear and hope, really wanting nothing except for her husband and daughter to stop quarreling.

"You know what I'm asking," Peter said.

"I'm afraid I don't."

"Barbara, I want to know if you're getting married because you're in trouble."

"Pregnant?" She was tempted to tell him: yes, I am carrying Karl's child. But that would only convince him he was right. "Women don't get pregnant these days unless they really want to," she said, compromising.

Peter's lips tightened. "I don't like to be spoken to that way, Barbara."

"You ought to learn the facts of life, Dad." She was unable to check the unconsidered response.

"Barbara!" Emily's hands nervously clasping and unclasping were pleading. Without having to touch her hands, Barbara knew they would be cold as ice.

"I'm sorry, Mother."

Peter's voice grew firmer; he always took a more decided tone when he was bluffing. "If you're not pregnant, I will not permit you to marry Karl Schiller."

"You don't even know what sort of man he is."

"I could tell you a few things about him that would shock you."

She really did not want to ridicule her father's pretensions, but he provoked her to it: "What kind of thing do you think would shock me, Dad? Is he a Communist?"

"I don't know anything about his political opinions."

"I don't think you would approve of them."

"I'm sure of that."

The stiffly moral tone evoked whole buried attitudes of disdain.

Barbara was sufficiently annoyed to say, "If he painted a hammer and sickle on the bedsheets I'd sleep with him under them every night."

"Barbara," Emily said faintly. A stain appeared on the pale dank cheeks.

"I'm sorry if I shock you, Mother. But it can't be helped. Sex is a fact in the world—and so is Karl Marx."

"But my dear . . ."

"Stay out of this, Emily," Peter said sternly.

Emily lapsed into silence, resting her sad face on her hands. A clock struck. Barbara counted the chimes as she had counted them in her youth. How long had it taken to transform her mother into this almost invertebrate woman? She knew a little of Emily's early life: at nineteen she had been in love with a young man who had the proper social qualifications but was considered "reckless" because he drank a bit too much, drove a bit too fast, and held irregular convictions such as an admiration for Franklin Delano Roosevelt. When that young man died, prosaically, of jaundice and subsequent pneumonia, Emily ceased to believe in life's possibilities and settled eventually for simply believing in Peter Druse. By then she was a post-deb, with her best chances clearly behind her, and she had to believe in something.

Peter was silent, considering what to say next; he was like an accountant who had to carefully check each emotional entry before proceeding to a clearly defined statement.

"Barbara, that man arrived in this country under false pretenses. He said he was fleeing Hitler. But he was actually fleeing from the police."

"Who told you that?"

"I have my own methods of finding out things."

"What else did you find out?"

Peter, blinking, answered, "That he's a wanted criminal."

The crushing in her chest felt as though a wheel had rolled over her.

"That's a pretty serious thing to say, Dad—unless you have proof."

Peter fixed her with a harsh level stare.

"I have a deposition from police files in Germany. Signed by a woman named Eva Klauber. It accuses Karl Schiller of having murdered his own father."

"Then why wasn't he arrested?"

"The woman died. If she was still alive and could bear witness against him, they might have brought him back for trial. He'd have been extradited from this country."

Barbara squinted. It was difficult to clear a line of vision to her father. "I should have realized."

"What?"

"That idiotic investigation. That imbecile at the State Department."

Peter paused, irresolute; he did not know how to cope with her new attitude. "I don't know what you mean."

The air seemed suddenly too rarefied to breathe.

"You were trying to get something on Karl. When you saw there wasn't enough evidence to get him deported, you wanted to frighten him into leaving. You got your friend at the State Department to help."

"The people in our government are entitled to the facts."

Her tone was low but carried its full charge of hostility: "Didn't you know I'd resent it?"

"I was doing it for your own good." The need to be peremptory urged him: "I couldn't let Karl Schiller make a complete fool of you. I had to take a risk—for your sake."

"What an evil man you are."

"Evil?" Peter nearly choked. He reached down to unbutton his vest.

Emily said, "Dear, you mustn't say that to your father. You know how he cares for you."

In the ever shifting balance that constitutes a human relationship Barbara recalled for an instant a little girl in a tomboy skirt and sweater, with streaked dirty face and mouth pressed tight against the pain of some injury, running to him to find comfort for her young anguish. That remnant of feeling passed. It had been years since she had known any comfort or affection from her father. The realization was a blend of pain and joy, the same feeling one has when a match flame burns too close to a finger and is allowed deliberately to burn out against tender skin.

She said evenly, "I can't change the fact that he's my father. If I could, I would."

"Barbara!" Emily raised trembling hands.

"I won't allow you to speak to me in this way," Peter said.

There was ferocity in her calmness: "You're not merely evil—you're stupid."

Emily's hands, pleading not to say the irretrievable, slowly lowered.

262

Peter said stiffly, "When you apologize you will be welcome again in this house, Barbara. Not until then."

"What makes you think I'd ever want to come back?"

Emily's wide forehead glimmered with chill perspiration. "Peter, dear, I don't think you ought to . . ."

His look of anger must have penetrated into the marrow of Emily's soul. She subsided.

"It's all right, Mom," Barbara said. "I understand."

She got up to leave and as she threw her coat over her shoulder, Emily began to cry. Peter glanced at Emily and with a quick shake of his head turned away.

"Goodbye, Mom."

Emily seemed to be pulling against an invisible chain. The chain snapped. She got up and went to her daughter. "Darling, I do hope you'll be happy."

Barbara hugged her. She was aware of what strangers they were: that evidence had been accumulating for years. But she could not help being moved by this rare act of courage.

"Thank you, Mom. I'll be in touch—if you want me to."

"Of course I want you to, dear."

Barbara went to the door of the study, opened and closed it behind her . . .

In the quiet room the closing door sounded uncomfortably loud. When Emily began to sob, Peter felt everything seizing him. The demands on him had grown enormous.

"I wish you wouldn't carry on, Emily."

"There's no one left."

He had no sympathy with pointless sentimentality. Barbara had been defiant, rude, insulting. That was the crux of it. He could not yet guess the strength of what had happened, estimate its duration, inspect the inner damage done, but of one thing he was sure. He had behaved as temperately as anyone could who was unquestionably in the right.

"Sooner or later she'll come to her senses," he said. "She'll realize how unfair she's been to me."

Emily's face seemed a wide accusing domain of damp white skin.

"Both our children. You've driven them away, and they won't come back."

Having Emily talk to him in this fashion was unsettling. In her tear-blank eyes he saw a dim question forming, and the question was about him.

*

Alex had lunch with Julius Scobie at Phil Gluckstern's restaurant on West Forty-eighth Street. It was Julius's favorite restaurant. Alex buried light crisp brown blintzes with heavy dollops of rich sour cream. Julius picked at a whitefish salad.

"You never should have got ambitious," Julius said. "That was your big mistake."

"I made more than one."

"We had a good business as general contractors." Julius stabbed at the fish, carrying a small forkful to his mouth. "You never would listen to me, Alex. I tried to warn you against branching out."

"I had to gamble big to make it big, Julius."

"You just never learned to be satisfied."

Alex was anxious to avoid controversy. This lunchtime he wanted to sit and relax, mourning gently with his old friend and business comrade. He had spent a sleepless night and this morning his hand was so unsteady he cut himself twice while shaving. He could still feel a slight pucker of pain from the healing cut near his chin.

"I don't see any reason to hold post-mortems," he said. "What good does that do?"

"You don't realize what you've done to a lot of people. People who worked for you, put their trust in you."

Alex watched with irritation as Julius continued to search among lettuce leaves for itinerant bits of whitefish. "It's not like I'm getting off scot free."

"At least you don't have to go through it alone."

"What?"

"A wife can be a big help at a time like this. It's harder for someone like me who has nobody."

"Oh, come on, Julius." Alex sawed off with his fork half an inch of blintz. "Stop feeling sorry for yourself. You've still got the first nickel you ever came into this business with."

"That shows what you know."

"Don't try to tell me you haven't got it socked away."

Julius ate in moderate-priced restaurants, wore the same suit to work for a week, and paid a modest rent for a one-bedroom West Side apartment where night after night he sat alone with stains on his underwear. Julius must be sixty, maybe more, and he lived on a fifth of the money he earned.

Julius said, "It's all with my older brother."

"Your older brother?"

"You know him. You met him once. A skinny fella. Bald, with a little moustache."

Alex didn't even know that Julius had a brother. But after a minute he remembered some years ago meeting a bald, skinny man with a moustache at a small gathering in an apartment Julius lived in at the time, an East Side apartment in the Eighties. It had been some sort of cocktail and housewarming party. A Negro bartender was hired for the occasion. There was a terrace.

"Oh, yeah," Alex said. "He tried to sell me mutual funds."

"That was his business," Julius said, defending his brother. "Of course it was before it all happened."

Alex nodded a little sadly in response to the tone of Julius's voice. He hadn't any idea what Julius was referring to.

"It's a pretty terrible thing. ALS."

"ALS?"

"Amyotrophic lateral sclerosis. One of those diseases there's no cure for." Julius's head was down and he wagged it. "A pitiful thing. A truly pitiful thing."

"How long has he had it?" Alex asked.

"Can I forget? September 1964. That's when the hospital in Danbury performed the tests. They told him he had two years. Imagine. A man with five children told a thing like that! Since then I've paid for everything, wife and kids, all the medical. Neurologists from the Mayo Clinic to the Harkness Pavilion. Whole batteries of doctors. But the final answer is always the same."

"It's been longer than two years, though."

265

"Those doctors keep him alive but the disease keeps spreading. Nerve by nerve, muscle by muscle. First one leg, then the other, then both his arms. Nothing stops it. Now his mouth overflows with saliva. No muscles in the cheek. Tongue muscles going. It's a terrible, pitiful thing."

"It certainly is, Julius."

Their intimacy was confined solely to business. Alex knew nothing of Julius outside the office.

"That's why I worry about the future," Julius said. "It's cost everything, even the mutual funds I bought from my brother. When the last of those are gone, I don't know what to do."

"You'll get a good job. Everybody knows what you did for me."

"I've already accepted one," Julius said, bending his head to sip a scalding cup of hot tea.

"Where?"

"The Lone Star Contracting Company. They needed a treasurer."

"That's fine. A good reliable firm. You'll be happy there."

"I won't earn half as much. I don't know what I'm going to do about my brother and his family."

"You've done everything a man can be asked to do."

"He's my brother," Julius said sternly. Then he apparently picked up a morsel of whitefish with too much lemon for his expression turned sour. "If you'd only listened to me. You had to go ahead and do everything your own way. Wouldn't even look at the figures."

"Don't be bitter, Julius."

"Why shouldn't I be? I spent a lot of my life working, slaving, to help you build a big company. Now I'm old, and I have to take a rotten job at less than half what I was making. I have nothing to show for all those years. Who should I blame for that?"

"You got some good years out of it, Julius. It wasn't all bad." He didn't want to quarrel, but he couldn't listen to preposterous accusations. He had paid Julius well for services rendered.

Julius said, "You were always so sure of yourself. I could show you hard facts and you'd say to me those aren't facts. You'd try to twist it around to be the way you wanted it. Well, now look."

"I nearly pulled it off, Julius. If they hadn't yanked the rug from under me with that Hayden Bank switchover . . ."

Julius's lips drew back over surprisingly fanglike teeth. "I wish to God I'd never met you!"

Alex tried to smile, not knowing what to say. They had almost nothing in common but had spent so much time in each other's company that Julius was closer to him than a relative. This enmity was uncalled for, a fresh betrayal from an entirely unexpected source. He had often disagreed with Julius because he believed in the probability of failure while Alex put his faith in the possibility of success. But he had never attacked Julius personally. Julius was a mirror image of himself, his burden and his accusing conscience. Strange dear old man.

"That's not how I feel about you, Julius."

"Don't give me soft talk," Julius said. "I know you with your soft talk. If I'd never listened to you, I'd be a happier man today."

"Don't make things worse than they are."

"How can I?"

They sat in silence, lunch finished, and other people waiting for their table. This is the last time, Alex thought. This is the sweet end.

Finally Julius said, "I'll never forgive you. I want you to remember that."

Alex lifted his teacup in which a small amount of tan liquid remained with the scattered moist tea leaves. Some people thought a fortune could be read in tea leaves but the future had never assumed identifiable, predictable form to him.

"Julius," he said, "we had a lot of fun while it lasted."

*

Tom MacLaren didn't feel like going to work any more. He had suffered an overwhelming personal defeat in the bankruptcy of Alex Johns and nothing that happened on the building really interested him now. But he kept showing up for work because he could not think of anything better to do.

This morning he accompanied a Fire Department inspector on a tour of the building while the inspector checked the water supply mechanism to be sure that everything indicated in the building plans

267

had been done. The inspector said he was satisfied. Tom's feeling was: What's the difference? What did anything matter?

When the long day ended Tom stopped at a bar to have a few drinks to fortify him against the evening to come. He had to put on a cheerful face. Sophy hated him to come home and "glum around," as she called it.

Finally, at almost six o'clock, he arrived at the apartment. The drinks hadn't made him feel any better. He was in a vaguely belligerent mood. When he opened the door the light was on in the tiny kitchen. A bag of refuse tilted limply against the range, spilling a waxed paper carton of milk, crumpled tinfoil, and one half an eaten grapefruit from its overflowing top. Dishes were piled in the sink from this morning's breakfast. He opened the refrigerator door; the shelves were bare except for a fresh container of milk and a bowl of limes.

As he closed the refrigerator, Sophy called out from the bedroom: "Is that you?"

"It's me."

For three days now Sophy had hardly left her bed. He brought her breakfast each morning and she did not even get up to wash the dishes. Taking advantage of her pregnancy, he thought sullenly.

He went into the bedroom alcove where Sophy lay propped against pillows. Several magazines were lying on the blanket and the floor beside the bed was strewn with newspapers, a pair of long floppy boots, and a few torn and discarded envelopes. On the window sill, as they had been for the past three days, were Sophy's scarf, gloves, a bottle of fingernail polish and mascara. Keeping things tidy was always beyond Sophy's powers, but this was ridiculous. At least before she got pregnant she had occasionally gone on a cleaning binge for a day or two before the slow accumulation of neglect began again.

"What's the matter? Still sick?" he asked.

"Yes."

"You ought to call the doctor."

"I don't need him. I'll be all right."

"You can't be all right if you stay in bed all day."

"I can't help it if I don't feel well." Her eyes widened slightly with self-pity.

He sat on the bed, a bit dizzy from the steady drinking of the last two hours, in need of encouragement.

"Anything in the house for dinner?"

"I thought you were going to bring home steak."

He had forgotten.

"I had a few drinks." He looked vaguely about the room. "I'm hungry."

"There isn't anything. You'll have to go to the supermarket."

"God, this place is a mess!"

"What do you expect me to do?"

"You could try to clean up a little. You're not dying. All you're doing is having a baby."

"There may be something in the freezer," she said.

"There isn't. I looked."

"We can order Chinese in."

"I don't want Chinese."

She said, "I wish you wouldn't drink. You promised you wouldn't after the last time."

"I've got to do something!"

"It doesn't do any good. You just feel worse afterward."

"I could go crazy thinking about it if I didn't. You don't understand what a thing like that does to a man. I worked damn hard to save that money. It all went in a single day."

"You've still got your health. And a job."

"It'll take years to get back on my feet. I owe everybody."

"It won't help to cry about it."

He should have known he couldn't expect comfort from Sophy.

"What do you say we go out for dinner?"

"I can't. I'm not dressed."

"It won't take long."

"My hair isn't done and my face isn't made up."

"Honey, I can't stay in tonight."

"I'm not in a mood to get up. If you're not going shopping, then let's order something."

She didn't care about anything but herself and what she wanted.

269

He didn't expect that anything he said or did would change that but that was no reason to keep giving in.

He moved closer. "Come on, honey. I'll help you get ready." In playful fashion he tried to slip down the shoulder straps of her negligee.

"Stop that! *Stop messing me!*"

Her eyes glinted sharply.

He hadn't done anything to make her so angry. Instead of withdrawing, he held her tighter with one hand and plunged the other inside the filmy protection of negligee.

"Tom!" She struggled with a fierceness that startled him.

Still with his hand on her breast, he slipped his arm farther around her, between her shoulder and the pillow, and drew her toward him. She tried to turn her face but his lips found hers. She began writhing against him.

She broke free, gasping for air. "Damn you!"

"What's the matter?"

She pulled up the straps of her negligee. "I don't like you pawing me. I want to be left alone."

There was no mistaking the antagonism in her tone. He could not let it stop there. From the first touch there had unfolded in his imagination quick scenes of passion—and these remained as vivid as his feeling of rejection.

"Maybe I can get you in the mood," he answered huskily.

She hardly had time to draw back before he was on top of her with only bedclothes between them. She beat a fist against his shoulder and fought with silent desperation as he pulled the negligee down to her waist. Once her flailing hand struck the night table nearby and sent her earrings flying—the new gold dangling pair that were her favorites.

Her mouth was close to his ear. She said savagely, "I won't be any fun."

"I don't give a damn!"

He was feeling his power. The last time he tried to make love to her had been a humiliating failure. He could do it now.

He held her with one powerful arm while he pulled the negligee farther across her navel. Roughly he pulled the negligee still farther

270

down, to her knees. A square white accusing patch nestled in her crotch.

"What's this?" he asked.

She lay back on the bed, breathing heavily, hands holding her slender bruised arms. "What does it look like?" she asked harshly.

"You don't need that thing."

She lay in almost total nakedness. "You're impossible! You really, really are!"

"Why are you wearing *that*?"

"I was going to tell you. You had to find out this way."

He was stricken. "Are you bleeding? Is that why you're in bed? Did the doctor tell you . . ."

"I never wanted the baby in the first place."

This was not a logical answer. For a moment he couldn't understand why it was not.

"Then what is it for?"

Her temper flared. "I got rid of it, that's what!"

Something stirred like hot lava in the depths of his subconscious. He pushed back and stood. His feet crushed one of her shoes beneath the bed.

"You had an abortion?"

"Yes!"

The individual parts of her face had no relation to each other—the lips and teeth, the nose, the separated eyes. He could not seem to put the parts together into any recognizable pattern.

"When?"

"Three days ago."

"Three days!"

She had stayed home from the office. She had told him she was feeling sick to her stomach because of the baby. She had deceived him. The baby was already dead; she had killed it.

A flaw in her story. "How did you know where to go?"

"My friend Gloria."

"Where did you get the money?"

"I borrowed it."

"From Gloria? She hasn't any."

She bent her head. "I try to tell you but it doesn't do any good. You don't believe me."

"Don't lie to me, Sophy."

Something dangerous was established between them, a powerful emotion as jolting to his stomach as raw liquor.

"You're awful! I hate you!" She was struggling not to cry.

"Sophy, it won't work."

"You can't order me. I know I'm a child in some ways but not in that way."

"Damn it! I want to know."

"You lost everything. We didn't have enough to raise a baby or get a bigger apartment."

He yanked at a shirt collar that seemed to have him in a tight grip, squeezing him. Other men—except for Alex Johns their names were unknown—had taken advantage of him. He felt a sharp twisting pain in his genitals.

"Never mind about that," he answered in a thick muffled tone. "Tell me where you got the money!"

Her mouth was open and quirking. "This is some kind of torture. You enjoy torturing me!"

Silly, stupid child!

"Was it from a man?"

He saw fear enter her eyes. "You never cared how I felt. I didn't want a baby. You knew that! You didn't have any feeling for me at all."

"Who is he?"

She became almost incoherent, babbling. "The night before I did it you were asleep. I was up most of the night. Four o'clock! I was so unhappy. I had to go through with it. It would have been too late in a little while."

"*Who is he?*"

She drew a deep shuddering sobbing breath. "I was all alone. I didn't have anyone to turn to."

Anger erupted out of the depths. He leapt on the bed to reach for her. His hands were at the base of her slender shoulders when she expelled words in a single breath:

"Walter says you'll go to jail if you hurt me!"

Surprise caused him to slacken his hold.

"Walter?"

He was dangling in space at the end of a rope. Then he began plunging through a vast fearful emptiness.

"Have you been seeing him?" Certain suspicions, latent in his memory, rushed into being. A cocktail party at the office until all hours, a matchbook in her purse with the name of an expensive restaurant, a whispered telephone call which he interrupted when he entered sooner than expected. "*Sleeping* with him!"

Some instinct warned her. "It isn't like that at all. The other night, the night you were playing poker with your friends, he called. He asked me to have dinner with him. I didn't see any harm."

"And afterward?"

"I don't understand."

"What happened after dinner?"

"Tom, you've got it all wrong!"

Words choked in his throat. "Where'd he take you? To a motel?"

"Tom, stop it!"

He held her in the same grip he had once held a captive bird, feeling the fragility of her light bones.

"That's when he agreed to give you the money, isn't it? What does he get out of it? More chances to sleep with you?"

"You're hurting me."

"How were you going to tell me?"

Her voice slowed. "I thought when I was feeling better, when I had a chance to talk things over with you . . ."

"You're lying!"

"Tom, please . . ." Tears stained her cheeks. "I can't talk to you when you're like this. Nobody can."

"You crazy little cheap little whore!"

"You're frightening me!"

He was frightening himself. His control was slipping. What did he see in the room? The bed, the view from the window, plasterwork. Kicked off party shoes in a corner.

"Did you have a good time in bed with him? *Did you?*"

He flung her half across the bed. She lay there crumpled, breathing with deep hoarse sibilance.

273

She raised her head very slowly. "I hate you!"

He struck her face with the back of his hand. A demon had taken possession of him. Leave her, you simple-minded cuckold. Leave her! How could he make sense of the chaos inside his head? Everything was jumbled. She had betrayed him. He could kill her! No one would blame him.

The room seemed to have become enormous and illuminated with a pitiless electric light that cast no shadows.

"Sophy?"

No answer. Waxen, artificial, a life-size puppet, she lay naked on her stomach. A terrible dread seized him.

He touched her bare foot. Metallic, without warmth.

"Get out!" she suddenly screeched.

Quickly he drew back his hand.

"Don't worry. I'm going!"

She was crying and trying to talk. The words were faint, broken, fluttered.

"Dirty . . . bastard! . . . It wasn't . . . your kid anyhow!"

A chilly ripple moved across his chest. What kind of world was this? He could sense things, feel emotions, but nothing reached his mind. There was blood on her face. His hands tingled with the ache of still undelivered blows.

He went back into the living room and methodically began to empty drawers into his gray suitcase. None of this was his fault. He picked up the valise, fingers clutching the sweaty handle. She had done it all.

"Goodbye, Sophy," he called.

He expected no reply.

As he closed the apartment door, his reflexes quickened to the point of pain. Awareness flooded into him under enormous pressure. What had happened didn't change the fact that he wanted her. One thing never cancels out another. It was painful for him to move, to stand at the elevator. Behind him the apartment door seemed silently accusing.

The elevator arrived and as he entered: Damn her! He stepped into a well-lit empty cubicle. The door slid into place. Sinking descent began. Someone had to pay for what he had gone through.

If there was any justice! A solid mass of anger and hurt formed in his chest. His throat choked with tears. Jesus. Jesus Christ. Jesus. Jesus. Jesus.

*

In the good times Alex Johns had arrived at his office each morning with the expectation of a deal to be closed, a new and involved transaction to be moved toward final unraveling, a bold fresh concept to be initiated, a goal to be reached. The telephones were always ringing.

Now, inside the sanctuary of his office, an unnatural silence spoke more for what had happened than any words.

Ginger asked, "How about the paintings? Do they belong to you?"

"I don't know. I guess some do."

Large rectangular paintings dominated three walls of his office. The one facing him on the far wall was the Synon Building, his first skyscraper. Until the Synon he had built only a few smaller things: a cooperative garden apartment complex, a small factory, a suburban supermarket. To undertake a contracting job the size of the Synon Building could easily have sunk his business without a trace, but he believed that when a large opportunity came along, a big challenge, a man had to forsake security. There was a double element of risk with the Synon because it went up a few months after the completion of 99 Park Avenue, the first office building to be enclosed in a glass and aluminum curtain wall. The Synon also was designed for a curtain wall and the necessary factory methods and machinery had not really been tested. There were alarming reports that the curtain walls leaked or that seams opened in a strong wind. But Alex gambled that the new method of enclosing a steel framework, replacing the brick and pre-cut stone façades of previous buildings, would be quicker and cheaper. He entered a bid so low there was a real possibility of losing money. To make sure the building was completed on time, he put crews on a twenty-four hour schedule during the final month of erecting the curtain wall. The Synon Building was finished eight weeks ahead of schedule, and he made a modest profit. Most important, his future as a big-time contractor was assured. The Synon was still standing and much admired as architectural art; there was particular admiration for the dramatic turning of the north corner façade. That sort of detail Alex happily left to students of the inconsequential. What mattered was that the Synon Building had turned a corner in his own career.

On the side wall an oil painting depicted the frenzied activity on the floor of the stock exchange, with brokers milling around, gesticulating. It was the work of a left-wing painter who intended it as a satire, but the sense of movement had caught Alex's eye.

When the shares of his stock were selling for eighteen dollars, his staff had given him the bold slashing red and yellow abstract now on the other side wall. It had been a Christmas present and they gave it to him because for some indecipherable reason the painting was labeled: *Tycoon.*

Alex indicated this painting. "You can have that one if you want it. It was a present."

Ginger regarded it critically. "It looks awful."

"You don't have to take it."

Everything was being claimed by creditors. He was under the strictest compulsion to take nothing that might conceivably be an asset of the defunct corporation now being reorganized under the Bankruptcy Act.

Ginger made a mark in a small leather notebook. "We may be able to sell it. How about the furniture?"

"Belongs to the corporation."

"Even the liquor cabinet?"

Alex nodded. "When can we get out of here? This depresses me."

"It won't take much longer."

Alex settled back into his chair behind the desk, playing with an ivory-handled letter opener. A horde of photographers and reporters were waiting outside the office. There was no place for him to go.

Ginger began to take an inventory of items on his desk; gold-plated ashtray, Atmos clock, silver photo frame, hand-rubbed mahogany cigar humidor.

"How about that?" She indicated the ivory-handled letter opener he was playing with.

"How do I know?"

"I'll ask Louise. Maybe she knows."

Alex tossed the letter opener onto the desk blotter. "Nickels and dimes. A lot of junk!"

"If they belong to you, you ought to have them. Why should creditors get everything?"

"The whole thing can't be worth more than a few hundred. I've tipped people more than that."

"It's still money. You can't afford to throw money around like confetti any more."

Everything around him grew small and menacing.

"It isn't going to stay like this."

"I know, Alex darling. All I'm saying is we have to be a little more cautious about money."

The spindle on the desk before him was crammed with messages that would never be answered, calls from subcontractors who hadn't been paid, from superintendents complaining they weren't getting approval on shop drawings, with notations about schedules being fouled up. Ginger didn't appreciate what a stand he had made. Hours on the telephone putting off delivery on materials that could not be paid for, prodigies of postponement, delay, evasion. He had retreated only to hold the line elsewhere. The spindle was a visible record of the ingenuity and effort he had put into temporizing with the inevitable.

"I don't believe in thinking small," Alex said. "It gets to be a habit."

Ginger smiled. "It's dangerous to think things are always going to turn out your way."

The remark slid like a dagger between his ribs. "Is that supposed to be a crack?"

"I'm sorry, darling."

"I don't appreciate that remark." His black eyes switched nervously to the desk with its spindleful of unanswered messages, to the paintings on the walls. Tycoon! "I built this whole business from nothing. I made and lost but I never worried. Every time I was down I knew I'd get back on top."

"It's different this time, Alex."

He began to feel like a defeated general who has suddenly discovered treason in his own ranks. He answered angrily, "You don't realize! Nobody knows the kind of odds I was up against."

"But we have to face facts. There isn't going to be much of anything left."

"If that bastard Peter Druse . . ." His throat filled with resentment. "Him and his goddamned building!"

Unexpectedly, shamefully, his voice broke. The betrayal was too fresh. The myth of his invulnerability had always sustained him but now with a baffled curious rage, as though the idea itself were a lethal weapon, he considered the possibility that he might not come back.

Ginger put down the notebook and came to him. She put her arms around him.

"Alex, darling. I'm so sorry. I didn't mean to upset you."

"Leave me alone!" he said. "I'm all right."

*

Tom MacLaren shuffled through the main office of Alexander Johns Enterprises. A few people seated at green metal desks were talking to each other, some having swiveled around in chairs to talk to the occupant of the desk behind. Others were gathered in small talkative clusters in the aisles and at the water cooler.

No one bothered to ask him where he was going. A private elevator delivered him to the top floor where Alex Johns had his private office.

In the outside room Louise, the secretary, was trying to placate a crowd of men milling around, some with cameras. Her light brown hair was falling over her ears and her complexion was pink. The door to Alex Johns' office was closed.

"Isn't he ever gonna come out?" one man asked.

"Mr. Johns has no further statement to make. I gave you the press release. That's all he's got to say."

"Is he in, Louise?" Tom asked.

Several men turned with surprised stares. They saw a tall man wearing a slightly shapeless suit and several days' growth of beard.

"Who do you think you are, mister?"

"I worked for Mr. Johns," Tom said.

"He's not seeing anyone," Louise said. "He left strict orders."

"Oh, he'll see me," Tom told her.

He pushed through the crowd toward the door of the private office. Louise hesitated, then shrugged and pushed the switch down on the intercom.

Tom was closely followed to the door. He turned, with his hand on the knob to survey the men hovering near.

"Nobody else," he said.

A young man, bolder than the rest, pushed forward. He wore his hat tilted back from his forehead.

"If he sees you, he sees the press."

Tom's hand moved horizontally swift. The flat of the palm caught the young man in the pit of the stomach and he bent in several directions simultaneously, legs buckling, knees going forward, center caving in, chest going forward and neck bobbing. Two men caught him as his knee touched the floor.

"Just me," Tom said.

He put his shoulder against the door, but before he could apply pressure the door opened.

Alex Johns quickly closed the door behind Tom and threw the lock.

"What are you doing here? What do you want?"

Tom swayed like a huge rock teetering on the edge of a precipice.

"I've got no time to talk to you," Alex said.

Tom brought his hand up to brush something from his face. "You took every cent. All my savings. Everything. My wife . . ."

Ginger said with an odd flat note, "My husband has enough trouble without your coming here crying to him."

She did not realize the emotional depths in which Tom was laboring.

"Double-cross," Tom said. "I'm gonna fix you." His big hand closed suddenly on Alex's collar. "Son of a bitch!"

"Let go, you big ape," Alex said.

Tom began to shake him. Alex was strong for his size and he put up surprising resistance. Dread lay as heavy as poured concrete in Tom's brain. When he began to lose his temper he was unsure where it would stop.

Ginger said loudly, "Take your hands off him, you goon!"

Alex struggled like a squirming mass of billowing canvas. He almost freed himself from Tom's convulsive grip. Tom's fist made a clublike pawing motion. Blood appeared on Alex's face.

Ginger screamed. A strange shrillness in Tom's ear canal, exploding along his nerves.

He seized Alex tighter, shaking him with one hand, using the other like a sledgehammer. Alex's eyes filled with shock and he tried to hit back. Pressure mounted in Tom's brain like a prolonged roll of drums. He brought his fist down heavily again and again. The livid bleeding face before him appeared dazed, as though listening for some sign, something to explain the incredible thing that was happening.

Ginger hurled a marble ashtray. It struck Tom on the shoulder. He never felt it. Ginger came at him with her fists until finally he pushed her away. She staggered and fell over the edge of a chair.

She kept screaming. Bright aching sounds.

Someone battered at the locked door.

Tom held Alex against the desktop, pummeling him and watching his head bounce against shattering glass. He braced himself to lift Alex's slipping limp body into place; it hung unresisting in his hands. After a while Tom stopped pounding with his heavy fist and let Alex slip soddenly.

Someone shrieked something that made no sense: "You've killed him!"

He turned to silence her, to deny, then the door burst open and people began flooding into the room. Intermittent glare of many blinding lights. My God, taking pictures! He started out. When someone tried to stop him he swung his arm mightily. There was no further resistance. He left the office as though descending from a great height, sick, his heart pounding. No one tried to stop him. There was excitement all around. He was calm. A few people were gathered near the elevator door. He shouldered past them into the elevator and the door closed. As he pushed the down button he noticed badly scraped knuckles. His hand was trembling.

At the ground floor he stepped out of the elevator and went away, wrapping a handkerchief slowly around his bleeding knuckles and staring ahead of him at nothing in particular.

FAÇADE

LUNCH whistle echoes dwindled shrilly. Men scrambled down the high iron like sailors going down a ship's rigging. They lined up at hoists to wait to be delivered to the ground. There they would disappear into bars and grills along the avenue, or eat stand-up lunches at small sidewalk stands where orange drinks and frankfurters were for sale beneath striped umbrellas.

On the fifty-sixth floor a half-dozen cement workers sat on an outside beam with their legs dangling nine hundred feet above the ground. They opened their lunch boxes.

"Jeez! A banana and some kinda meat. Cat meat, I bet."

"Did'ja have a fight with your wife?"

"What is this stuff? Smells like fried gut!"

"I heard about a guy once, his wife put sleeping pills into his coffee. She wanted he should fall off and break his neck."

"What happened?"

"Dozed off on the catwalk. Super found him and canned him."

"Serves her right. I hope she hadda go on relief."

The completion of the building wasn't far away. While crews continued to sheathe the structure, the finishing trades had moved into the construction timetable. Inside, the last floor slabs had been poured and all the cellular floors carrying telephone and power services were in. The finish white coat of plaster was being applied in some areas and almost three thousand lighting fixtures were being installed on the second and third floors. Marble work was underway and electricians were all over the building, installing power lines and a master control panel that would govern motors throughout the building with an electronic scanning and switching device.

On the fifty-sixth floor the cement workers dumped empty beer cans and soda bottles into the concrete being poured around the

285

steel pillars. Then they returned to sit on the beam high above the street. From this extreme height the landscape below resembled a contour map.

"Ain't no good for scenery watchin' this far up. Can't see what they got."

Loud laughter.

"I seen an ad for this buildin' in one of them magazines. While I was havin' my hair cut."

"What'd it say?"

"I dunno. I think it's suppose to be somethin' special."

"Who says?"

"Yeah. Looks like all the rest. You seen one you seen 'em all."

"Hey, I was wondering. Whatever happened to that super who was here before Otis? Tom MacLaren."

"He nearly killed that guy."

"Yeah. That one."

"I dunno. Haven't heard a word."

*

Looking down the shaftway of the hoist, Jim Otis seemed to be staring down the steadily narrowing walls of a bottomless pit. On the floors below a battalion of steam fitters, electricians, and plumbers were swarming to dump loads of brick, lumber, wire, concrete, lighting fixtures, pipes, and plumbing supplies.

Curtain wall panels were being fitted into place, bolted to outer horizontal beams with a slotted angle iron, and then vertical metal supports fastened to the angle irons and finally the panel bolted to the vertical supports. The panel had a ready made window frame so glaziers could begin to install windows as soon as the panel was in place. The glass seemed to float between wall and wall, imponderable and sparkling as air.

Otis moved toward the building edge, dodging nimbly out of the path of a motorized buggy on its way to the main hopper to take on a load of concrete. The buggy drivers were the most notoriously reckless workers on a construction—they acted like racing drivers zooming across to the main hopper where the operator pulled a lever to dump a load of concrete into the small hopper in front of the buggy, then racing away to brake sharply at almost the very edge of the building corner and pinpoint drop the load.

Standing by the edge of a steel girder, Otis watched the boss of the raising gang signaling—arms out and palms down—for the crane operator to lower the hook and bring up another load. This might be the last load of steel to make the climb to the very top. Far below he could see the miniature dashes that were cars and the dots that were pedestrians.

Nearby, a man jumped down onto a scaffold instead of crawling out on it.

"Never mind saving seconds," Otis said mildly. "Save your own neck."

Pete Miller's teeth flashed in a rust-colored face. "I never fell down yet, Jamey."

The Mohawks called him Jamey. They considered his color a bond between them, and liked him.

"We lost one good man up here," he told Pete Miller. "I don't want to lose another."

"You don't have to worry."

"I worry whenever I see somebody try a fool trick like jumping onto a scaffold."

"Okay, Jamey."

He was doing a good job as the superintendent. He knew how to lay on authority without using a heavy hand. When Tom MacLaren did not return, the job had been open and Otis got it because Zenith Oil, not Alex Johns, made the decision, and the giant corporation lived in a world full of colored people with whom it did business and could not worry about a handful of intransigent bigots.

Otis moved along to where other workers were putting up scaffolding on the wheelbarrows and motorized buggies could be trundled within reach of the crane.

Don Macey came over to him. "We're topping out today. That last beam's going to come our way an hour after lunch."

Otis said, "When that flag is in place they're breaking out champagne."

"You kidding?"

"Straight from the bosses. Imported champagne."

"Tell the truth, Jamey, I like hard liquor better."

"Don, I'll give three bottles of good scotch to the man who brings me the flag."

"Three bottles?"

"For whoever brings it to my office in a plain paper bag. I'll have the liquor ready."

"I'll tell the others," Don promised.

The flag, which was attached to the final, gold-painted beam, never stayed in place more than a few hours. Some adventurous climber always went after it as a souvenir. On this job, because it was his first as a super, Otis wanted the flag for himself.

Don's square serious face assumed a sheepish expression. "You ever come to Brooklyn, Jamey?"

"Not often."

"Mrs. Labache—Joe's wife—she cooks every Saturday night in a diner. Real Mohawk. A lot of us go there on Saturday night. Helps to show she brings business in. This Saturday is a little special."

"Why?"

"Pete Miller's girl. You know, the one in the building across the way."

"I remember."

"They're getting engaged. We're having a little dinner for them. How'd you like to come?"

"Saturday?"

"My wife hears me talk about you and she'd like to meet you," Don Macey said.

"I've got a date," Otis said. "Can I bring her?"

Don Macey smiled broadly. "Sure."

At a little past two o'clock that June afternoon, balloons were released on the ground level and began a jogging ascent toward the height of the building. A twenty-foot gold-painted beam was moved into position for the guy derrick to pick up and was fitted out with a hundred helium-filled balloons and a ribboned fir tree.

At a signal the balloons, beam, fir tree, and a flapping American flag began their nine-hundred-foot skyward journey.

This topping-out ceremony, celebrating the last piece of steel put into place on the building, was a rite that went back almost three thousand years, and began with a desire to protect a new structure from demons. Over the centuries the rite had lost its religious, mystical overtones. The worker who leaned out to pour a few drops of chicken blood from a plastic bag on the symbolic golden beam did not know he was continuing a tradition in which Romans sometimes made a human sacrifice to dedicate a new building to the gods.

Eager hands reached out now to the golden beam as it swung opposite the top floor. As they brought it in, Don Macey waved a long rope made up of all the handkerchiefs of men working on the job. This was to signal that the steelwork was now complete. Pete Miller scrambled up to fix the final beam in place sixty stories above the ground.

At that moment, on ground level, representatives of the Zenith Oil Corporation watched President Peter Druse make the first slice into an eight-foot-tall cake. A film and sound crew from a television network was on hand to record the event.

"Mr. Druse, will the new building be named after Zenith Oil?"

"I have decided to honor the former president and founder of this company, Elihu Druse, by calling it the Druse Building."

Four cases of champagne were loaded into an outside hoist to begin a happy journey to the ironworkers waiting at the top.

*

Alex Johns sat beside the shallow edge of the pool dangling his legs in the water. Warm water was soothing, warm sun was penetrating to do its healing work.

Ginger sat on a chaise longue near the cabana, combing out her copper red locks, keeping a wary eye on him.

"Darling, you ought to move in the shade. You're getting too much sun."

"I'm fine where I am," Alex said.

Ginger came over with white ointment to rub on his chest and shoulders. She had become obsessive about his health. In earlier stages of his recuperation this worried him because he was sure the doctor had told her some truth about his injuries not shared with him. Now he accepted that her concern was motivated by affection.

She adjusted the visored suncap on his head.

"You're not getting a headache, are you?"

"No."

"Too much sun can give you a headache, you know."

"I don't have a headache."

"At three o'clock," Ginger said, "we'll go upstairs and you'll lie down and take a nice nap."

They had been living in a two-room suite in a hotel apartment in North Hollywood Beach, Florida, while he slowly regained his physical strength. He was also recuperating from the shock of his bankruptcy. Other contractors had taken over some of his incomplete projects and the mountain of debts he had accumulated was being whittled down by settlement, cancellation, or by others becoming responsible. Zenith Oil Corporation had paid the multitude of subcontractors engaged in work on their building.

The telephone rang in the cabana. That was Mother with her daily telephone call, and it would be a lengthy conversation. Ginger always gave his mother exhaustive detail on how they had spent their day.

Alex slipped into the pool and floated, resting his head on an inflated rubber cushion.

The low voice droning from the cabana was soothing and restful. He dreamt on chlorinated water. The time had come to make a comeback. Actually he had never stopped scheming, even in the most difficult times. As he began to feel more confident of his physical condition he had begun writing letters. He reserved an hour a day of the public stenographer's time at the apartment hotel where they were staying. When friends and business associates visited Miami he always had lunch or dinner with them, working up schemes to help him get what he wanted. What he wanted was simple: a new corporation with sufficient financial backing to let him pursue his goals without the distractions that had harassed the last months of Alexander Johns Enterprises. He had learned something. He would not again be guilty of the dissipations, extravagances, and follies that had contributed to his ruin.

Floating in the warm pool, soothed by these thoughts, he began eavesdropping once again on Ginger's conversation. She was telling his mother his temperature for the past twenty-four hours, including variations of a fraction of a degree. There was satisfaction in listening to this. He became even more interested when the talk shifted to the tiny (and by himself unnoticed) variations in his mood that had taken place. This continued up to the episode of the pool, in which he had refused to come into the shade and had seemed a bit cranky when she applied the sunburn lotion.

Alex smiled to himself. The telephone call from Mother appeared to be ending so he climbed out of the pool and moved into the shade of the cabana. Ginger glanced at him, mutely inquiring if he wanted to talk to Mother. Alex shook his head. Ginger got off the phone a moment later and prepared a comfortable place for him on the chaise longue beside her own, propping his head on a pillow. It was time for his good news hour.

She began by telling about the Portuguese jellyfish that had invaded the beach at Fort Lauderdale but were inexplicably not showing up on their beach and the lifeguard had told her that if the jellyfish had not shown up by now they probably wouldn't show up at all. The new refrigerator freezer that the hotel had installed in their suite was working well, the steaks which she had put into the freezer had frozen in less than fifteen minutes, and there was three times as much storage as in their old one. Fat Roy, the obnoxious elevator starter who talked too much, had finally been discharged and the new man, a Cuban exile, was much nicer and quieter.

Then she paused, ribboning up her hair, and regarding him in the bright anticipatory way which indicated it was time for the day's best tidbit.

"There was a phone call for you at noon after you went down to the pool. From Leslie Schwarz."

"Who's Leslie Schwarz?"

"We met him last week at that party. You remember. He's the Mayor's right-hand man."

"Oh, yeah."

"He wanted to talk to you about the Mayor's wonderful new plan for rehabilitating the north section. The Mayor knows the things you've done in other cities. That's why he wants you to take a new job."

"What new job."

Ginger's bare knees peeked out of her beach coat as she leaned forward. "He wants you to become chairman of a new planning commission that will handle the rehabilitation of the north section."

"You tell Mr. Leslie Schwarz that I won't do it."

"He was speaking for the Mayor."

"You tell the Mayor I won't do it."

She rested elbows on her knees and appraised him. "Why?"

"Honey, I've got something cooking that beats hell out of any city planning board."

"What is it?"

"A deal with Elliot Francis of the Mortgage and Finance Bank."

"Darling, you're not well enough to . . ."

"Listen, he's buying up a lot of West Side slums in Manhattan to build new apartments and business properties. His bank puts up most of the financing, and he wants me to handle the general contracting."

"I don't think you can work that hard any more. The doctor said . . ."

"Stop acting like a goddamn nurse!"

His loud voice penetrated the nearby cabanas. Sun-oiled heads turned in displeasure.

The pounding began slowly, a long swing with a mallet against the inside of his head. He sat back gently, hoping that the tempo would not increase. He lay with his face turned away from her but she guessed at once.

"I knew it," she said. "I'll get your pills."

His whole body shook with vibrations as if he were a gong being struck. She brought a cool cloth and a glass of water with a large round bisected white pill. He swallowed the pill with water and lay back absolutely motionless while she put the cool washcloth over his eyes. She sat beside him and held his hand.

In a few minutes he was sure the pounding would not get worse.

"These headaches don't mean anything."

"You have to learn to take it easy, Alex."

"I'm not going to be chairman of any planning board."

"You do what you please, dear."

Through the washcloth bright daylight penetrated. He felt the cloth warming. In a tropical climate all a man can do is lie around and simmer.

"Next week I'm going up to New York and meet with Elliot Francis. We'll probably close the deal then."

She patted the back of his hand. "Try to be quiet, dear. It's better not to talk."

He was convinced that if he let this slip by he would somehow have made an important concession.

"I mean it, Ginger. We're going back to New York."

"I know you mean it, dear."

"This damn cloth is too hot."

She removed it immediately, and came back with a fresh cool one. Folding the cloth across his eyes, she said, "I don't know what to tell Mother about that acreage in Palm Beach. She was so delighted with the idea of our buying land and all of us settling down here to live."

"When did you talk to her about it?"

"Yesterday."

"You had no right to do that. We only looked at it. It wasn't anything definite."

"She needs something to look forward to, Alex. She's an old lady. It would be so wonderful. She could sell the old house she's living in . . ."

"I'll make so much money with Elliot Francis that she won't have anything to worry about."

She stroked the back of his hand. "I don't want to put pressure on you, dear. But sometimes with old people it doesn't work out the way we want it to. Something happens and we never get another chance."

"Why, is she dropping dead all of a sudden?"

"I didn't mean that. I just hate to think of how disappointed she'll be. I wouldn't have the courage to tell her, she's got her heart so set on it."

The headache was coming back, stronger, in huge mounting pulsing waves. He lay still with his eyes closed and after a minute he heard running water in the cabana. She was getting him a fresh cool cloth. Then there was a metallic clink—probably she dropped something—like the clink of a closing trap.

Goddamn Zenith Oil and their lousy building, he thought irrelevantly.

*

If all the windy words in Peter Druse were laid end to end, Vinnie thought, they would stretch beyond the horizons of endurance. He tried to stay awake in the windowless room while Peter droned through his report to the Board on the future prospects of the company, emphasizing the declining income from motor fuels, the menacing trend toward electric cars, and the soaring income from petrochemicals such as plastic and solvents.

The report also touched on other points, ranging from a discussion of the decline in profits for the quarter (three percent), to the cost squeeze resulting from increased labor costs and the adjustment on the pension plan, from a current court dispute in which Zenith Oil Corporation was being asked by the government to divest itself of some profitable parts, to the repercussions of the bankruptcy of Alexander Johns.

Vinnie stared sightlessly at walls washed with light of uniform intensity. The background lighting was diffuse and indirect from warm fluorescent tubes.

Good Lord, would Peter never come to the end?

Peter put down the thick sheaf of pages on a table. "That's all," he announced. "The meeting is open for questions."

Ron Hurstwood, one of the two banking directors and the vice-chairman, wanted to know why a surety bond had not been taken to guard against the loss of more than seven million dollars caused by Alexander Johns' bankruptcy. Finding the question hard to answer, Peter became peevish and curt. He sulked openly while Paul Collins read to the Board a letter written by Vinnie recommending the purchase of such a surety bond. When Paul Collins attempted to have Peter explain why he had not accepted the recommendation, Peter's temper got the better of him.

"That was my best judgment at the time, Mr. Collins, and I am not prepared to be examined by you or anyone else on this subject." A slight stutter made this reply, otherwise impressive for its arbitrariness, slow and halting.

Fred Feist broke in: "You can't run the company as though it were your personal possession. Seven million dollars is a lot of money to lose simply because you didn't have sense enough to take out a surety bond."

"I haven't recognized you, Mr. Feist."

"How about now?"

"I'll recognize you when you have something worthwhile to contribute to the discussion. At this point, if there are no objections, we will move on to the next item on the agenda. It has to do with a change in the Board of Directors."

This was Peter at his worst, peremptory, discourteous, quarrelsome. A whisper passed over the Board room like a shiver of cold. Vinnie toyed with a pencil in his hand without looking up.

"I recommend that Mr. Haleson be relieved of further responsibilities as a member of this Board. We all know that Mr. Haleson has been dismissed from his position as an executive vice-president of the corporation." Peter's doughy complexion appeared a translucent veil behind which anyone could discern the dark arterial currents of anger. "Therefore, I see no particular reason why he should remain as a member of the Board."

This was the moment toward which all the intricate, behind-the-scenes maneuvering of the past weeks and months had been building. Since the first shock of his dismissal (he had not believed Peter would have courage to act so directly), Vinnie had been trying to line up support for himself among the directors. Now he would discover how successful he had been.

The first questioner was Harvey Sloan. "Mr. Chairman, there are rumors that the dispute between you and Mr. Haleson is entirely personal and has nothing to do with the affairs of this corporation. Would you care to comment?"

"I don't wish to go into details. Those who know me know that I would never let personal sentiment influence me in a business decision."

Other hands immediately shot up. Peter ignored them.

"I don't see why we should not move promptly to a vote. The question is whether Mr. Haleson should be relieved of his duties. Does anyone second the motion?"

Frederick Feist said, "If a dispute can't be settled behind closed doors, it's a sign of something wrong with the administration."

"You are out of order, Mr. Feist."

"You've refused to recognize me."

Peter recognized Ed Bailey.

Ed Bailey said, "I think a thorough discussion of the pros and cons should precede any final decision by the Board."

Dan Gilroy added, "It might be easier if both principals to the dispute were absent while we discuss the question."

Peter's tone became chill, imperious. "Are you suggesting that I should leave?"

Ron Hurstwood said distinctly and slowly, "Peter, it isn't a bad idea. It will make for a freer, more open discussion."

Peter looked with vehement bewilderment at all these familiar faces registering unfamiliar hostility. His fingers curled up on the table as though squeezing a tennis ball.

"All those in favor?" he asked.

A majority of hands rose. Vinnie could guess the thoughts running through Peter's mind at that moment because he had heard Peter on other occasions when his stewardship was questioned. Peter resented the diffusion of power and the close scrutiny a corporation president was subject to from his associates. He was fond of saying that Zenith Oil was earning ten times what it earned in Elihu's heyday and was worth twenty times more in assets all over the world, and that all this growth had taken place under his leadership, and this proved that he knew how to run the corporate business without any harassment.

"Will both the Chairman and Mr. Haleson be good enough to withdraw?" Hurstwood inquired.

Peter sat unmoving. Vinnie pushed back his chair, rose, and without a glance at Peter left the Board room.

Peter still waited, expecting someone to say it would not be necessary for him to leave. No one spoke. The situation was without precedent.

Finally, in a tone made heavy by its burden of rebuke, he said, "I'll be in my office when you want me."

With all eyes on him, he made his way out of the Board room.

*

Paul Collins said, "Vinnie was always the heir apparent. I couldn't have been more shocked than when I first heard Peter had fired him. What happened?

"I'll tell you the answer," Feist said. "Vinnie went ahead and divorced his daughter. Vindictiveness, that's all it is."

Hurstwood said mildly, "None of us knows enough to say that."

"What other explanation is there?" Feist asked.

Ed Bailey said, "We have to give Peter the benefit of the doubt. It's hard to quarrel with management as long as the company keeps growing."

Dan Gilroy said, "Our profits are off this year—and all other companies are up. Peter was too slow getting over into petrochemicals."

Other voices spoke in quick overlapping succession:

"He's too conservative."

"He won't take advantage of the next opportunity. It'll be the petrochemicals story all over again."

"How about his failure to take out a surety bond? A seven-million-dollar blunder."

"There's never been any question," Paul Collins said firmly, "that Vinnie is the better businessman."

"Hear, hear," Jack Kragen said.

Hurstwood's stern mouth was framed at the corners by vertical frowning lines. "Many of us harbor doubts as to our president's capacities. But that isn't the question before us."

Feist said, "The question is whether Peter can have a free hand to dump Vinnie simply because he's no longer a relative by marriage. And that certainly goes back to Peter's competence."

"Unscrupulous about getting what he wants."

"I'm inclined not to give in to him this time."

297

Hurstwood asked, "Shall we put it to a vote, gentlemen?"

As the voting was about to begin, Feist took out a letter and spread it on the green square of cloth before him. "I have with me a letter from Barbara Schiller. As you know, Barbara is a member of this Board, representing the considerable block of shares left in trust to her by Elihu Druse. This letter empowers me to cast her vote as I see fit."

"Everything in due course," Hurstwood murmured. "You will cast your vote—and Mrs. Schiller's—when called upon."

Nevertheless, the reaction traveled around the oval table. Peter's own daughter was in opposition to him.

Appraising the mood of his fellow directors, Feist decided the time had come.

"I'd like to put everyone on notice," he said. "If this vote goes against Peter, I want to propose that he be kicked upstairs to an honorary chairmanship—and let someone else take over as our chief executive officer."

Silence followed. "One thing at a time," Ron Hurstwood cautioned. He understood that Feist had been awaiting the opportune time to put forward his motion, and that the letter from Barbara granting her proxy had been calculated to carry the waverers. Feist had been determined for some time to find an issue to move him further along the road to a seizure of power.

Ron Hurstwood did not wholly approve of Feist because the man appeared to have dim and unresolved goals—the only program he seemed to favor was more profits. Hurstwood's experience taught him to beware of men who were able to keep totally separate a desire for power and the understanding of what to do with it.

But as he passed out voting slips to each of the directors at the table, an odd thought struck him: Feist's suggestion was bold, unexpected, in a sense impertinent to the issue which they were supposed to weigh and consider, and not a single voice in the room had been raised against it.

*

Just inside the door of Peter Druse's office was a dark statue of a woman by Nadelmann, copper smooth and graceful. Elihu had done a good deal of collecting and much of what he collected was now in museums. Peter did not pretend to be a patron of art but he had kept this particular statue because its smoothness and symmetry pleased him. Those qualities should inhere in business as well as in art. The Board of Directors would simply have to understand and accept that. It was his duty as president to smooth out rough spots in the company's operation, and Vinnie was a rough spot. Doubtless Vinnie had sympathizers among the directors, men with whom he had worked so long, but Peter made up his mind to accept nothing less than what he asked for.

What was happening was indefensible. He should never have been asked to leave the Board room, thereby putting him on an equal basis with Vinnie. If the Board offered a compromise, he would simply not accept it. He had to be firm, show the iron hand of his authority. If there was quibbling or spineless backtracking from the Board, he, Peter Druse, would let them know that without a clear mandate he would not carry on. A threat like that would bring them into line quickly.

It was astonishing that he should even be forced to consider such drastic measures, a guide to how much Vinnie's smooth duplicity deceived otherwise sober businessmen. Oh, Vinnie was a cool customer, all right, entirely without human warmth or feeling—he had betrayed himself in his dealings with Ann.

Peter stared out the window, across town, at the mammoth tower of the Druse Building outtopping its neighbors. In a few minutes Hurstwood was announced.

Peter met him at the doorway.

"Well, is it over, Ron? Have you finished?"

"Yes, it's over."

"Then perhaps we'd better go back and get the voting over with."

"That won't be necessary, Peter."

A cleansing wave of triumph swept over Peter; they had knuckled under. At the same time he felt a warmth of gratitude that reached out to envelop his colleague. He was restrained from showing it by the rather solemn manner in which Hurstwood communicated the news to him.

"I know how you feel," he said generously. "You're fond of Vinnie. But when a man becomes arrogant, when he can no longer make proper judgments, he isn't fit to remain in the top level of management."

Ron Hurstwood had a rather queer expression when he answered. "Yes, that's true, Peter."

"I'll help Vinnie find some face-saving way of ending his association with Zenith Oil Corporation."

"That isn't how it has worked out, Peter."

Peter's jaw muscles tightened. "Ron, I will not accept a compromise . . ."

"I regret having to be the one to tell you, Peter, but the others are waiting for you now and they thought if I had a few words with you first, to prepare you . . ."

"Prepare me for what?"

"We realize that fundamentally it had to be a choice between Vinnie and you." He began to speak faster as though wishing to have it over with: "We made that choice, Peter. It wasn't easy for us but we hope you'll realize that we think it in the best interests of the company."

"I don't understand."

"We've elected Vinnie Haleson as president. He's going to take your place, Peter."

His heart began to beat rapidly. On every ground of logic, of reason, what he was hearing was monstrous. His voice faltered. "You can't mean that you've all turned against me."

"There were ten votes in favor and five abstentions. We agreed to make it unanimous for the record."

"Impossible!"

Not even Vinnie Haleson could have beguiled them so completely out of their senses. The only explanation was conspiracy. Vinnie, and Fred Feist and . . . Hurstwood said *ten* votes in favor! Ten Judases! Little men with private spites, petty hatreds.

"It couldn't have been unanimous. How about Barbara?"

"She gave her proxy to Fred Feist."

"To Feist? I don't believe it!"

His own daughter! That business about Barbara's marriage. He had only been trying to do what any decent father would have done. How could she have done a thing like this to him?

Peter shook his head, and his erect posture broke at the shoulders. "There were no votes against? None?"

Hurstwood shook his head regretfully.

They would be sorry, sooner than they expected. Everything would go to rack and ruin. Did they think a corporation so huge, so powerful, so complex, could continue to grow without a powerful leader at its head?

He said, "They've made a terrible, terrible mistake."

He was approaching a gradual stunned realization of what had occurred.

"Do you know what you've done?" he asked.

He clung to the hope that the full meaning of their action had somehow escaped them.

Hurstwood said compassionately, "We all agreed to offer you the honorary chairmanship."

He felt betrayed, shamefully, shamefully betrayed.

"I won't accept!"

"Don't make up your mind now, Peter."

"I'm forced to sever all connections with Zenith Oil Corporation." He had trusted people, put his faith in those who did not deserve it. "I must say, I'm surprised at you, Ron. I never thought you would betray me."

"I'm sorry you feel that way, Peter."

"How do you expect me to feel? I've worked with you all these years. Then you turn against me like this! What have I done to deserve it?"

He stopped, appalled at his own angry echoes.

"Good Lord," he said in a whisper. "I can't believe it's really happening."

Peter slowly returned to the window and was not aware when Ron Hurstwood left the office. From his window the tower of the new Zenith Oil office building was visible in fading daylight. That bold new profile on the skyline would always be a tribute to him. Violet hues of twilight were swallowing the top of the tower and filtering in around the steel beams on the upper floors. Soon, the lights would be switched on as they had been for the past few days and the mighty structure would become a candelabra, a mighty beacon in the sky.

There was something that rose beyond challenge or betrayal. Little, spiteful men in Board rooms could do their worst. They would never remove a single stone from the mighty edifice of his accomplishment. He felt one with the proud new building that bore his name, compact of the same enduring materials. What a gift to leave behind to coming generations, what a testament to his vision!

It was fitting that this architectural landmark would be known forever as the Druse Building.

*

That night Vinnie Haleson entered the drafty mansion at Queens Point, and went directly to the room he used to store so much that was familiar and dear. He paused at a cabinet to look at the Bible saved from Ambrose Haleson's wanderings, at the faded oval portrait of Ambrose's wife, dead at twenty-three, for whom Ambrose had celibately mourned fifty-one years. Ambrose was one of the very few chaste Halesons.

Here was a tiny wooden desk, with scarred wooden top and empty black hole of inkwell, that belonged to Jeremy Haleson of Civil War fame when he was a boy of seven. It had been saved by order of the government in gratitude for services rendered and kept for a long while at the town museum until they could no longer find room for it.

Deward Haleson, his wig: a foppish gentleman whose bald head beneath that peruke had housed a surprisingly formidable intellect. A chair in philosophy was named for him at Harvard. In a display case at the window were glass objects—from the Sandwich factory Uncle Samuel had owned. Delicate shimmering colors, graceful carving. At sunset, the light from the arched window behind the glass illumined it beyond description.

All these mementos spoke to him in this quiet room; they were his witnesses; he stood among them waiting for some signal, exactly what he did not know, perhaps only the sound of ghostly applause.

*

Early the next afternoon, as Tom MacLaren was returning to his rooming house near the ferry slip on Staten Island, he saw a police car double parked with the turret light revolving. His blood seemed to turn hot, and his fingers twitched; his whole body turned into one intense question. Casually, to avoid attracting attention, he walked back past a boarded-up Laundromat to a typewriter store and pretended to look in the window at an Olivetti.

Two police officers were descending the stoop from the rooming house. Unhurriedly he walked a block and turned south to a public telephone booth on a corner.

As he waited for his number to ring, the police car raced past on the street.

Mr. Rublowsky's heavily accented voice answered.

"Hello."

"Mr. Rublowsky?"

"Yes."

"This is Mitchell. George Mitchell."

"Oh . . . yes." Hesitation in the guarded tone.

"I was calling to see if there were any messages for me today." A pause.

"No messages, Mr. Mitchell. Where are you?"

He enjoyed playing cat and mouse with the ridiculous man. "Where am I?"

"I mean . . . is there any place I can reach you . . . in case I get any messages."

"I'm calling from a public phone booth in Brooklyn. There's no way you can reach me."

"Oh. What time do you think you'll be coming home then, Mr. . . . Mitchell?"

"The usual time, Mr. Rublowsky."

303

The poor stupid old man, cooperating with the police. He would never go back to that rooming house.

In a nearby diner he drank coffee that was hot and black and ate a doughnut that was mealy and sweet. He couldn't afford more—he had worked only a few weeks of the last months, as a common laborer, always moving on to a new job in order to escape detection.

No one had to tell him what a crazy thing he had done. He had nearly killed Alex Johns. The injuries listed in the newspaper account included a fractured skull, a concussion, and several fractured ribs. The whole episode seemed unreal, something that had happened but which had no connection with him in any way except that he was now a fugitive from the police.

When he left the diner he walked to the ferry slip and took the ferry across to Manhattan. He had to get money somewhere and leave the city. A sudden vision came to him of silver sand beaches and blue water, fishing boats and tanned girls on water skis. Escape!

The architect of the bus terminal in Manhattan had not attempted to make the edifice beautiful; a huge gray bulk rose in midtown streets amid crawling traffic. On the west the terminal was flanked by grimy shops and dim unalluring small hotels and tenements.

He entered the stone archway of the terminal through a glass door that opened before him. A circular newsstand was ahead in the high-ceilinged interior, gaudily arrayed with magazines and tiers of candy shelves, and beyond that was a smaller circle with a sign: INFORMATION.

He strolled about the terminal for almost an hour until he found what he wanted. Three people were waiting on line at a ticket window, and he saw one man reach into his breast pocket for a wallet bulging with banknotes. The line shortened to two people, and the man with the wallet was holding it ready in one hand as he reached down with his free hand to slide a tan suitcase further along the marbleized floor.

Tom moved purposefully toward the grilled window with the imprisoned ticket seller. Only one person was ahead of his chosen victim, a plump woman in a wide curving hat and a print dress. Tom drew near enough to hear her ask for a ticket to Memphis.

The man with the wallet was holding it loosely. It would be easy to reach out, snatch it, and . . .

Someone watching.

Suddenly the great open space echoing with the noise of voices, tramping feet and metallic squawks of arrival and departure announcements became a tight confined area of white lights and nausea.

Tom looked across the paper strewn lobby to a policeman standing beside a pillar. There were lines of people waiting at other ticket windows and idlers who seemed to have nothing to do but stand around reading free colored brochures for vacation resorts, and other people staring into the display windows of the terminal shops. The policeman wasn't looking at any of them; his gaze was leveled at Tom.

Tom saw the woman get her ticket, then his man stepped up to the ticket window, resting the precious wallet on the marble ledge now while he extracted the price of a ticket from it.

Tom turned swiftly and hurried away. He didn't look around to see if the policeman was still watching. A vision came to him, darkly —an escorted trip through the terminal with curious crowds watching, the steel bite of handcuffs on his wrist, the final grim destination.

"Mister?"

A voice somewhere behind and to his left. He stared wildly at his questioner, a big man wearing a dark blue jacket open over a vest in which two cigars protruded from a pocket. The face was gross, big nosed, with small shrewd eyes.

"Can you tell me the way to the men's room?"

Inside the jacket the tip of his black billfold showed. When the man returned his cigar to his thick lips the end was wet and shining with specks of spittle.

"Sure. I was just headed there myself."

They moved in and out of an endless stream of people in the main lobby rotunda.

"Where you from, mister?" the fat man asked. "I'm from Chica . . ."

The question ended in a surprised *hahhh* of explosive exhaled breath as Tom sank an elbow into his stomach. The cigar dropped

305

from fat lips, and as the fat man started to sag, pain and puzzlement on his gross features, Tom reached into his jacket and seized his billfold. Then he ran.

"Just a minute. Hey you—*you!*" someone yelled.

Tom raced out through swinging doors.

The fat man slipped to the marbleized floor and sat there grunting with pain.

"What happened? I saw him poke you!"

The fat man ran an aggrieved hand over his stomach.

"Son of a bitch," he said, "stole my billfold!"

Other men began hurrying out in self-righteous pursuit.

"Stop that man! Stop, thief!"

The fat man was helped to his feet where he stood, winded and angry.

"I came to meet my wife," he said. "She's arriving from Chicago. A thing like this happens, nobody's safe any more!"

The group of bystanders nodded sympathetically.

"Did he get much?" someone asked.

The fat man reached into his pocket and took out a wad of bills. "Not a damn thing. I keep my cash here. Billfold only had American Express checks. He can't use them nohow!"

Several people laughed. The fat man grinned triumphantly.

*

An ordinary man, Karl Schiller was thinking, might be dwarfed by the dimensions of the huge apartment but Albert Falkland enlarged himself in the liberating atmosphere and his manner became more grandiloquent as though to fill up the surrounding space.

"Yours was the only design worthy of the name," Falkland said in that voice which seemed to have within it a low rumble of thunder. "The others were clichés—buildings that only made sense in terms of technology. You did something entirely different. A building based on entirely new ideas and emotions."

"Thank you." Karl was seated beside Barbara across from Falkland's white-maned figure in the black swivel chair.

"You saw what had to be done," Falkland went on. "This is a

cathedral. It had to be a clear new entity, something no one had thought of before."

Karl was pleased by Falkland's appreciation of the sketch. It was only a single facet of what he intended the final product to be, only a beginning. If he accepted the commission, he would drive nearer and nearer, as a lapidary would, until he revealed the whole diamond hidden behind coarse layers. But he was not going to accept. In the weeks of waiting for the decision he had made up his mind to do something else.

"Well," Falkland said, "when can you start?"

"I'm flattered by the offer," Karl said. "But I'm afraid I can't design the cathedral."

"What?"

There was a queer air of expectancy in Falkland, as if he had completed preparations for a ceremony and the guest of honor had just announced he would not be present.

"I've had time to think about it and I'm convinced I'm not the right man."

Falkland's slow voice rose in theatrical anger, "You've no right to refuse!"

"I'm sure you'll find someone else."

"I've chosen you. It's your design that must be built."

"You may keep my design."

"Keep it? You mean you'd give it away?" Incredulous, Falkland rubbed the pink scalp beneath his high white bush of hair. "Only a damn fool would do that!"

Karl smiled faintly. "I do my work in the public domain."

"Nonsense!" Falkland clearly found it annoying to talk to someone who expressed such feelings. He turned to Barbara. "Speak to him, Mrs. Schiller. Tell him what a dreadful mistake he's making."

"I'm sorry, Mr. Falkland, I can't do that."

"Don't *you* care?"

"Very much. But it's his decision."

"You've seen his sketch. Aren't you excited by it?"

She answered, with a slightly hesitant glance at Karl, "I think it's beautiful."

"Perhaps I should explain," Karl said. "When I finished the sketch and submitted it to the committee, I wanted very much to be chosen to continue the work. I was excited by my ability to . . . create something I liked . . ."

Unbidden, the vision had come to him. Blind dumb searching Man, reaching out toward a mysterious Thing. A vaulted roof soaring upward. Coarse stone, materials of earth, unrefined, because those materials are put there for man and should properly be used by him to express thankfulness. A nave open to blessed sun and air, gifts from Him that made life on earth.

"What happened?" Falkland inquired, with the air of a doctor inquiring into the origins of a nervous breakdown.

"I have an opportunity to build something else," Karl said. "Something that interests me more."

"What could that possibly be?"

"You probably won't approve. I've accepted the job of designing Monument City."

"A housing project!"

Karl shrugged. "I suppose you might call it that."

Monument City was the name given to the proposal for the world's largest housing community, the largest low-income apartment development in the world. It was to be built on Staten Island by a non-profit foundation, an entirely new city of 100,000 people in 30,000 apartments on almost 650 acres—an instant new city.

Falkland exclaimed, "Damn it, man, you'll spend most of your time worrying over problems such as plumbing, heating, electricity, building codes. Building codes! You can waste months, even years, just in mapping and zoning changes. And you'll *never* get what you want!"

Karl wondered if the thought ever occurred to Falkland that what he wanted was not necessarily the best of all possible solutions. There was no doubt of Falkland's faith in the omnipotence of the artist. He had forced an entire city to change its building code to accommodate one of his buildings.

"I don't expect too much trouble," Karl said. "I've talked with the financiers and they approved my preliminary ideas."

"It's absurd. They won't let you try any innovations because innovations drive up costs." Falkland's large blue-veined hands clasped impatiently. "They don't want it better. They just want it cheaper."

"I think I can build in a way that won't cost more and will still create a more livable community."

"You're creating a work of art. You can't afford to compromise with the city's experts and consultant site planners and landscape architects."

"They all may have something to offer."

"You can't listen to them! If you do, you'll end up satisfying only the most superficial needs."

He did not hope to persuade Falkland of his belief that the highest goal of anyone who lives in a world of men is to contribute to human happiness.

"I don't think that the needs of a hundred thousand people can be superficial," he said politely.

"What will you create for them? More closet space? Better-functioning toilets?"

"There's nothing wrong with that."

"It's no job for an artist."

"Perhaps I'm only an architect."

Falkland's granitic features scowled. "An architect signs his name to the building, doesn't he? He's responsible. If it falls down, he's the one who gets sued. If it stands up and looks beautiful, he gets the credit. In medieval times when a cathedral was finished the master builder had to stand underneath the stone roof until the last of the wooden supports were knocked away. If the roof fell, it fell on him. *That's* being an artist."

"Times have changed."

"Not that much. Nobody can put up a building of mine except the way I design it. If something goes up wrong, no matter how many tons of steel or concrete are involved, I make 'em tear it down. *That's* being an artist."

"It's a cooperative art, Mr. Falkland. There are a lot of other people involved—the client, the contractor, the subcontractors, the union officials, the building inspectors. Above all, the workers. Men who sometimes give their lives so your building can go up."

"Architects fall off buildings. Back in the thirties there was a whole rash of 'em. Even the architect of the Canterbury Cathedral fell from a basket that was being lifted on a rope. It's a violent trade. Violence is built right into the process. That's got nothing to do with it. *This* cathedral is your chance to create a really spectacular thing."

"That isn't what I'd like to do."

"It's what every architect would like to do."

"For me, the beauty of the boulevards of Paris is not due to the fact that they are lined by very beautiful individual buildings. The beauty is *in* their conformity—because Haussmann laid out the boulevards and imposed restraints on the architects who built there."

"That's another thing. Other people will come along and build in and around Monument City. You can't stop it from happening. And what they build will change the character of what you do."

"Not at all. The cafes of the Champs Elysées never appeared on Haussmann's drawing board. The Parisians themselves made them. But they fit into Haussmann's larger order because the order was there in the first place."

Falkland's piercing eyes glared from the sides of his promontory of a nose. "This cathedral will be part of the spiritual evolution of this century. You can't pass up a chance to make your name remembered along with Sir Christopher Wren's—and mine."

When historians of the future, Karl thought, look for the missing link between the most primitive communal buildings and the splendid architecture of their own civilization, they will probably find it is Falkland. But Karl wanted more than to conquer the world of architecture with a personal style. He wanted to match his designs to the demands of the world, those demands an artist must sense before they become coherent. He did not want ego to intervene between his work and the need for it.

"I can only design what I believe in," he said mildly.

"Practicality—or worse! That's what you'll be settling for!" Falkland rose and grasped his cane. "You should be creating masterpieces—the way I did." His stentorian tone gave the command an almost Biblical authority. "Build the cathedral!"

Karl answered simply, "I can't."

*

Leaving the apartment building, Falkland heard the pulsing roar of a plane overhead. The sky, almost gray with moonlight, was the perfect canvas for the plane that moved across it as though the steady hand of a master painter were drawing a line across the horizon. What a miracle! He never ceased to marvel at this flying house that could defy both the power of gravity and the wrath of weather. A human habitation that could move safely through the eye of a hurricane. That was architecture at its most imaginative, using all the dimensions. Houses like these would soon move across the mind-chilling distances of outer space, encapsulating pioneers. What a pity he would not be alive to see it.

As he thought about his interview with Karl Schiller he felt within himself a remoteness that might have been the approach of weariness. He was so loaded with honors that he was in danger of becoming fashionable. Any day he might get an official commission from the government to design an embassy or a consulate, or God forbid, a military academy. Younger men were now coming along, with their extravagant notions that seemed as crazy to him as his ideas had once seemed to others. To create beauty an artist must follow a personal vision of what is beautiful—and by being faithful to his vision he had served himself as well as others. Now he had fame, power, money. These new men probably regarded him as an impractical individualist interested mainly in experiment. But he believed in his genius. What did they believe in? If he asked, they would probably give only the dwarf's answer in the fairy tale: something human is worth more than all the wealth in the universe.

But there was a reason for that answer being in a fairy tale. It did not belong in the real world. An artist worthy of his labor wanted more than to be absorbed into the progress of mankind; he wanted to be a page in the history of his time.

A damn shame. Schiller's sketch had been done with such power and imagination. The bold, clear-cut forms, the rhythmic alternation of concave and convex forms produced an effect of order and harmony. That was how the Roman ruins looked—the great main frames, the noble wall masses with their vaults, columns and niches. Schiller's cathedral would have had that same simplicity and poetry, that same splendor, but no one else could take his sketch and make it as great a building.

Falkland sighed as he walked slowly along the streets of the Lower East Side. Eight o'clock in the evening and nowhere to go. At Karl Schiller's age he had been up until all hours of the morning. He had worked and played hard. Those were the great times, the wonderful times, and no honors that had come to him since could make up for what he had lost with the wild strength of his youth. Nothing, even now, held as high a place in his affections as those who had loved him. Women, especially. Ah, a woman's love was the true accolade. He was fond of all the companions of his lovetime. There was no one woman for him, as there obviously was for Karl Schiller, but each was important in her way and he would not have been the man he was without them. They all made their contribution and passed on. He mourned them with flaccid organs. To be a true creator a man must have blood in his veins. He must also care deeply for his work and fight hard to impose his vision on others. Art was an entirely personal matter—to be yourself was a necessary part of greatness . . . He knew that in the course of time even the most fundamental values undergo a sort of sea change, but he could not understand why Schiller did not want to create a thing that would make his name remembered.

He had been walking uptown along a nearly deserted avenue—an avenue which seemed not to belong to the real city. His eyes lit suddenly on an inscription at the base of a building: *This was erected in the year 1947 as a monument to the victory of the imagination of man over obstacles. This is an address to that future time in which all things will have a new name.*

He looked up at the familiar curving shape free of superficial embellishment and pretentiousness. This was the last building he had ever designed in the city. He read the inscription again and smiled. That future time was here but nothing had changed. Years had gone by and nothing had been given a new name. Not one single thing.

Night had closed upon the city. Albert Falkland stopped in the darkness between two street lamps, hesitating, like a departing guest searching for an acceptable way to say goodbye. He did not wish to be abrupt.

*

Tom MacLaren rode uptown on the subway and emerged into a familiar neighborhood. He imagined the terror on Sophy's face when she answered the door to his ring. Anger brooded over bits and pieces of treachery recalled. God knows she owed him plenty. Through all the complex interwoven strands of his misfortunes there ran the single colored thread of Sophy.

In the darkness, he turned up his coat collar and walked farther uptown. The weather was turning cold again. Soon he reached the apartment building. He waited across the street. A few cars passed, partially blocking out the lighted entranceway of the building.

He crossed the street, projecting ahead to people he might encounter on his way in. There was no doorman, and the elevators were self-service. The tall Negro superintendent, Arthur, at this hour would be locked away in his first-floor apartment with his petite French Canadian wife and their two light-skinned children.

In the self-service elevator, he pushed the sixth-floor button. On the way up the elevator stopped at the third floor, and two people got on. The man was in shirtsleeves and the woman wore a simple gray wool dress.

"Going down?" Tom asked.

"Going up," the man said.

The man pushed the button for eight, which meant they would ride with him all the rest of the way. He stared ahead at the seam in the door.

"Listen, when I say it's time to go, then it's time to go," the man said.

"Why is it up to me?" the woman asked in a voice rising higher with complaint.

"Let's have some kind of a signal. When I light up and say something, then you'll know it's time."

313

"If they're so damn boring, why do we play cards in the first place?" the woman asked.

The elevator stopped at the sixth floor and Tom got out.

He wasn't sure his key to the apartment would still fit the lock but Sophy was careless about matters like changing a lock. He eased the door open, half expecting Sophy to be huddled on the sofa. The room was in darkness. On the loveseat near the door a skirt was lying, half over the edge, giving the illusion, in the light from the hall, of the slow grace of twisting hips.

He turned on the light, finding the switch without hesitating. Familiar outlines became familiar realities.

He began a thorough search, looking for money or any valuable that might be changed into money. In the large combination bookcase and desk he found several envelopes, from Con Edison, the telephone company, Bloomingdale's, a mutual fund to which Sophy was supposed to send twenty-five dollars a month, and Cay's Drugstore. The envelopes were still unopened. Nearby was a diary. Scribbled notation: *Walter—6:30.* With sullen hatred he thought: that's where she is.

In a compartment of the desk he found the brown manila envelope of her checking account at the bank and discovered that she had a balance of one hundred eighteen dollars. Then he looked in the blue ceramic pencil cup in which she often kept pin money; there was nothing. He looked under the round faced wooden clock where she sometimes hid cash. Again, nothing.

He opened a drawer, found a small box with earrings in it. While he was going through the box, a grayish white blur appeared at a corner of the door leading to the sleeping alcove, became a well-muscled slinky body with long narrow head, ears set wide apart and tapered to sharp points, and short slightly kinked tail held high.

Tom ignored the cat went on with his search. Jasmine regarded him with cool hostility from blue slanted eyes. As Tom was taking Sophy's undergarments from a dresser drawer, a pair of white panties drifted silkily to the carpet. Jasmine bounded forward, struck at them with its forepaw.

"Get away!"

His voice sounded unnaturally loud in the deserted apartment, alien, a forgotten noise recurring in stillness. Jasmine recoiled slightly, then attracted again to the filmy white on the carpet, made a lightning fast spring, leapt, and with unsheathed claws tossed and batted the panties. The sudden move startled Tom, his mouth winced.

He aimed a kick at Jasmine, but the cat sprang clear with an agile sidewise leap. Its back arched. Pointed teeth bared. The long tail swished slowly back and forth.

Rage began growing in him as he continued to search. He reached above the closet and flung down a tangled array of hats and scarves, an old umbrella, a rolled group photograph (he knew what it was— Sophy in high school with her graduating class), a dusty old black empty imitation leather handbag, two or three empty boxes from stores which might once have contained handkerchiefs or gloves. He had never been able to teach her order. Her nature was scattered, lying in useless fragments without connective tissue—all worthless traits in search of a character.

He reached up to feel the back of the shelf hidden from view. A rustling warned him—too late. Claws raked his hand. A blurred shape moved along the top of the closet shelf. He made a quick lunge. Then his vision disintegrated in swift white exploding.

He seized Jasmine with one powerful hand and flung the cat belly up, struggling and writhing. A warm furry sack flying through the air while its haunches propelled claws uselessly. Spitting snarling clawing hatred.

The cat hit the wall and lay stunned beneath the window ledge, in the breath from a partly opened window. Green tendrils of philodendron drooped over it like a fragrant mourner.

A few minutes later Tom left the apartment, carefully locking the door. He had not found anything. He was close to a convulsion of rage and frustration.

A cruising patrol car slowed down while its occupants looked him over, then the car sped away. Tom turned at the next block and walked swiftly. What was he going to do?

Then he remembered where money was to be had. Several hundred dollars, and not in useless American Express checks either.

He went into the subway again and rode downtown. When he came out of the kiosk he was in midtown and walked a few blocks

315

farther along the avenue, staying close to building walls and avoiding street lamps. Finally he stopped and looked up. Asymmetrical, leading the eye on from the dynamism of thrusting corners and beams to the purity of its rising profile, the Druse Building became a momentary stabilizing of lines and mass, then irresistibly rolled upward, tier after tier of metal imposing a coherence on itself, a mystery ending in satisfaction. Standing in the presence of a structure which had wrung so much order out of chaos, he absorbed its meaning in no conscious way. He lifted his hand involuntarily, as though in salute to a well remembered antagonist.

Fifteen months ago he had begun work here on the wrecking gang, and had been in charge when there was nothing but a huge hole with cranes and a small army of steel riggers, welders with spewing orange torches and laborers dumping loads of wet cement. Now the great skeletal torso was almost enclosed. In recent weeks he had searched the newspapers for any item about the building. There had only been one, a week ago, when a curtain wall panel plunged forty-six floors from the building near a busy corner. The curtain wall panel was being lifted into place when it slipped through a cable loop, fell, and ramming a hole in the blacktop street, bounced once and toppled over to crack a manhole cover and send chips of concrete flying up from the sidewalk.

Tom found the very spot. An imprint remained—the outline in blacktop of the edge of the panel. He measured the distances and whistled soundlessly.

A light on the second floor drew him like a night flying moth. He climbed the short flight of steps and hesitated a moment before turning the knob of the superintendent's office.

Jim Otis was working at a long bare wooden table strewn with papers. He glanced up, blinked, and his expression turned gradually to surprise.

"Mr. MacLaren!"

"Anybody else here?"

Tom glanced through to the adjoining room.

"I'm working alone. Had some stuff to catch up on. I didn't expect to see you again, Mr. MacLaren."

316

"I'm leaving town, Otis. I need everything you've got in the cash-box."

Otis rested a hand on papers neatly stacked beside him. "What's this about?"

"There's cnough in the cashbox. I know it's in the safe in the next room."

"You're not thinking straight, Mr. MacLaren. You couldn't open that safe. There's a new combination."

He had forgotten. Of course they would change the combination to the safe. Everything suddenly stabilized and he was very cold and very sure. He went to the table where Otis was seated and leaned both hands on it and stared at him.

"Sometimes I believe in luck. Maybe it's luck that arranged for you to be here when I came."

Otis paused, then stood up. "I'm locking up for the night."

"You hear what I said?"

"I heard."

"Then listen good, you goddamn nigger!"

Otis raised one shoulder in a shrug. "Mr. MacLaren, you've been a long time getting that said."

Otis turned out a fluorescent light above the table. Tom gripped the blue collar of his work shirt. Otis brought his forearm up in a swift cutting stroke to break the hold. His chair fell backward and made a wooden clatter in the small room. Papers on the table rose and slowly settled.

Tom went around the table and closed with him. As they staggered back to the wall he chopped his hand down hard on the back of Otis's neck. Otis slipped to all fours and Tom's knee caught him under the chin and flung him like a tarpaulin on the floor. Otis lay sprawled on his back with his knees uplifted.

Tom went over and slammed a foot into Otis's ribs. "What's the combination?"

Otis looked up out of a pain-wrenched face. "Go to hell!"

"Okay, nigger boy. I'll break every goddamned bone in your body."

Tom reached down to haul Otis up. Otis's foot hooked behind Tom and sent him toppling backward. In a second Otis was desper-ately scrambling on him. They rolled over, struggling. An elbow locked into place against his throat. The naked overhead light swam and blurred.

He made a great heaving effort and broke the pressure on his windpipe. Fingernails raked his cheek. A thumb gouged his eye.

"You . . . spade . . . bastard!"

He got to his feet, catching his breath in great sucking sobs. Something grabbed him from behind. His arm wrenched and agony tore at his shoulder.

"You be good now, you hear?" Otis said.

His head was yanked back. He brought his foot down heavily on Otis's instep, then whirled quickly so the sweaty weight of his body pressed close and his arm couldn't be torn out of its socket. Like two clumsy wrestlers they reeled across the room.

He got free first, picked up a chair and swung with all his might. The heavy chair leg caught Otis in the face and battered him down to the floor. The chair leg broke off, and Tom snatched it up to use as a club. He battered Otis again and again until the man lay still.

Inside, Tom was crying. *Now, look what you've done.*

Otis lay on his side with his legs drawn up and one hand extended. Part of his head was caved in. His lips had parted over bloodstained teeth.

Tom threw the chair leg away. *How did I get into a mess like this?*

He went out into the cold night air. Lights shone like specks of diamonds amid dark posts and beams of the building.

A lantern winked.

"Why, it's Mr. MacLaren!"

The lantern swung higher. In the pool of light he recognized the night watchman, Ed Fregoni.

"Hullo, Ed."

"You all right? Your face is marked up."

"I had a bit of trouble."

Ed's gaze swung toward the open door of the superintendent's office. "Jim Otis in there?"

"Yeah."

As Ed hurried toward the office, Tom walked slowly to the hoist, stepped in and threw the switch. He began to ride upward to the stars.

318

At the very top he stopped the hoist. Over the newly poured plaster floor there were board planks. The night wind blew. He had often been frightened up here but had never let anyone know. At the worst times, when he was sick to his stomach, he returned for a cup of coffee and fought down his panic before going out again.

In buildings all around there were squares of light. What a city. Never sleeps. Always someone around to see what you do.

A glaring light bulb suspended from a girder illumined him out of darkness. He moved out of its radiant center.

Yesterday, Sunday, he had been in a little park on a bench beneath a stone monument and through closed white doors of a church heard the organ and massed voices. When the church doors opened he could make out the dim interior and the corridor leading to an overwhelming altar.

Oh, my God, I am heartily sorry.

Far below he picked out a police car that raced up the street making orange and blue pinwheel reflections from its revolving turret. A carnival show with light and shadow and color. The police car stopped near the building. Two silhouette figures emerged and raced across the wide plaza. Directly below, the dark figures became topped with ovals of white—faces looking up. Then the two figures began racing toward the hoist.

They'll be here in a minute.

He stared down with no sensation of dizziness.

Go on.

He had seen an ironworker freeze to a girder, clinging so tightly that the steel made deep incision marks on his arms and legs. Fear attacked everyone at times.

Is everybody watching?

Feet clattered on the floor planks. How quiet it was. He remembered ironworkers' sledges hammering, ratatatat of a welder's gun driving rivets, all the noise of the making of a great steel building.

He had always been afraid to be afraid.

Hello, down there!

HELLOOOO!

In lit windows, in all the buildings, no one to summon him back. Currents of air washed over him as gently softly he fell. Sounds of

319

rushing air accompanied him on the long plunge. Here are the lights swinging up. Under the interrogating light, no questions, no answers. What's your name? How old? Now, why in hell did you . . . ? Darkness and diminishing fading sounds.

How bright! bright.

He dwelt in a swift cone, a mote in brilliant candlepower before one great whiteness spread over him in a coruscating blaze.

*

Minutes later, leaving the Comedie Humaine Restaurant, a couple raced for a taxicab. The woman wore a three-quarter length silver blue mink coat, a beaded black dress and tripped along on high heels, laughing breathlessly. The man who held her hand, urging her along, was tall and thin and looked graceful in his black form fitting coat and gray homburg.

They ran beneath the covered sidewalk bridge of the Zenith Oil building.

"Oh, *Harry!*"

"Come on, honey. There's a cab!"

"My coat. Look!"

A bright red fleck on the long soft fur.

"I got *paint* on it!"

Between the crevices of the wooden sidewalk bridge, crimson oozed, gathered, hung pendulous, fell.

"Somebody spilled paint up there. Damn careless!"

"What can we do? Oh, I'm miserable. My lovely coat!"

"I'll take down the number of the contractor. It's on that sign."

"What good will that do?"

"We can't stop now or we'll miss the theater. I'll write a letter in the morning. Come on!"

He jotted down the number. The woman moved aside as another drop splattered down to spread widely in jagged starlike pattern on the sidewalk.

He grabbed her hand again. They began to run.

"Taxi!"

Through the crevice crimson liquid gathered, became a drop that lengthened, lengthened . . .

And fell.

August 22, 5:08 p.m.

Leaving the offices of Duncan, Deerham and Brazo, Ernest Parkey hesitated, slightly bewildered, until he saw an arrowed sign to the central lobby. He waited for the elevator, admiring the space that seemed to eddy and flow toward these thick elevator shafts and the compact efficiency of the building's utility core. The man who designed this was an exceptional custodian of his talent; the marks of compromise were not easy to find. After the Druse Building the future of architecture in the cities might never be quite the same.

The elevator arrived, silent, luxurious, and as he was about to step in he saw the indicator light glowing. He had pushed the UP button. He got in anyhow, and rode up to the roof garden. It was really this roof garden, more than anything else, that set the Druse Building apart for him from all other buildings in New York.

The garden was bordered by a high parapet of trees and filled with flowers and shrubbery, with benches and fountains and with great funnels through which air breathed out of the building and which in turn formed elements of the design. In the middle was the huge vaulted structure where people could sit to hear music in a small auditorium, and on the other side a planetarium projector showed films and a lecturer told about the mysteries of the night sky. This garden in the sky reminded Ernest Parkey somehow of the pure serenity of a Bach fugue.

He sat down on a chair on a viewing platform, and after a minute a girl came to sit down too. She was about twenty-five with a long, serious, pretty face.

"Do you have a cigarette?"

"Sure." He gave her a Winston. "You come here often?"

"Not often."

"I do. I like it."

"What do you do?" she asked.

321

"I'm a musician." Then, noting her surprise, "A composer."

"Oh. What brought you to the Druse Building?"

"A big advertising agency offered me a job. Duncan, Deerham and Brazo. Ever hear of them?"

"I work for Zenith Oil. In fact, I'm secretary to Mr. Haleson, the president."

"Sounds like a big job."

"There's a lot of money in it. For a girl."

"The agency wants me to compose tunes for advertising jingles. I've never done that kind of work."

"No harm in it if they pay enough."

He was silent, staring out at the wide surrounding plaza that was like a park set into the midst of a stone and concrete jungle. There was in every living man such a quiet place—a place that was truly his own—amid the jangle and noise and pollution of the world.

"I suppose not. But money isn't really what interests me." Suddenly sure, he added: "I'm going to keep writing the kind of music I enjoy. Someday people will listen. Just the way they come to see this building."

"I just work here," she said.

6:03 p.m.

The avenue filled with cars, taxis, and limousines headed to the bright expensive pleasures of the midtown district. In a taxi, hurrying to the restaurant, Sophy was impatient. She glanced out the window to find where she was. For an instant her lovely face sobered and she smoothed her black gloves. She was opposite the Druse Building, near the very spot where Tom MacLaren had died.

"Can't you get me out of here?" she asked the driver irritably.

"I'm doing the best I can. This traffic is murder, miss."

She stared straight ahead until the taxi began to move and the Druse Building slipped behind, out of sight, into the sad past.

Sophy looked forward to her date for cocktails with Walter. She discarded painful memories almost as quickly as the shadow of the building fell behind on the glittering avenue.

7:28 *p.m.*

At the far end of the plaza Karl Schiller and Barbara watched the sun setting in a mighty burst of yellow and orange behind dark buildings. A soft breeze blew across the ponds and stirred the evergreen trees.

Above them loomed the tall profile of the tower. To reduce the problem of sky glare the windows of the Druse Building were tinted, and Karl had used the fact that no glazier has ever succeeded in setting two panes of glass exactly adjacent to each other. The windows were tinted slightly different shades—gray, blue gray, blue and bronze in a pattern that constantly changed with the color and intensity of light. Now in the glow of the setting sun, the whole curtain wall seemed alive and shimmering in response to the changing sky.

Solving any new problem, Karl Schiller thought, became all consuming. He had to find an architectural style that would create a community way of life, a special kind of shared environment. This would be total town planning to surpass even the famous Scandinavian experiments, Vallingby and Farsta in Sweden, and Tapiola in Finland. Despite its monumental size and scale it would have to please the knowing eye. There is such difference between true beauty and the conventional forms we associate with it.

He had made a hundred false starts, directing his imagination against old modes of thought, trying to break with the comforting power of tradition. He had succeeded, at least a little. But then new problems arose, even more awesome.

Now, as he looked up at the tower of the Druse Building, he had the anxious feeling of something he had overlooked or left undone. The steep rise toward the heights seemed to be yearning toward something more.

Barbara said, "Would you like to have dinner out tonight? You've been working too hard. It might do you good."

The tower was complete but there was an interplay taking place between the finished work and his critical intelligence. With fresh eyes, cleansed of fatigue, of self-indulgence, he was able to look at what he had created.

All that was needed was the right use of essential principles. Forget old battle cries: form must follow function, less is more, beauty is utility. The new battleground is elsewhere. The place to look for it is where one feels the lack of something.

The sky lost the sun and the wide plaza darkened. Now the walls of the building glowed with light from illuminated ceiling panels that extended inward from each window. From this vantage point the rise of the tower appeared to be almost an impressionistic mural, the details obscured and the subtle shadings of light and dark emphasizing the enormous impact of a tall many-leveled structure sweeping upward from the plaza.

There came a quickening within himself, a symptom Karl recognized, a hint that zestful ideas might be about to break in.

"Well?" Barbara asked. "How about it? Dinner and a movie tonight?" She looked familiar and dear, less formidable somehow with her protruding belly and waddling walk.

He took a breath before daring to say, "Would you mind? I'd prefer to work." With queer apologetic shyness he added, "I want to try some new ideas I have for the town center and the recreation hall."

Her smile was wonderful. "I've got steak in the freezer."

She slipped her arm through his and they turned up the street. He did not look back. A man's creation can sometimes acquire a life of its own and show him his way.

324